DARKLINGS

DARKLINGS

RAY GARTON

OPEN ROAD
INTEGRATED MEDIA
NEW YORK

ISBN 978-1-4976-4261-4

This edition published in 2014 by Open Road Integrated Media, Inc.
345 Hudson Street
New York, NY 10014
www.openroadmedia.com

This one is for
Dr. Edward Bigliari
and the delightfully distorted group of
people at Ward 18 (including those who
have since moved on).

After all those years of
tests, drugs, and needles,
I've finally come up with
something that bites back!

ACKNOWLEDGMENTS

There are several people who made invaluable contributions to this book, without which it would probably not be in your hands right now. I'd like to thank them all for their generous help.

My agent, Ashley Grayson, my editor, Michael Bradley, and my friends Scott Sandin, Derek Sandin and Dori Ostermiller, for carefully reading the manuscript and making all kinds of keen suggestions that kept the book from being stupid.

Richard Swinney, Wayne Kleinsteiber, Lynda Longhofer, Alyssa Ford, Marylynn Malone, Tom Bland, and, once again, Derek and Scott, for their technical assistance, which kept me from *looking* stupid.

Mr. Coffee.

And, of course, all of my Seventh-day Adventist "friends."

BOOK ONE

It's *gonna* come now.
　　—Jeffery Collinson

1 - ER

THE SOUND BEGAN as a muffled gurgle, rising slowly to the surface of his sleep until it finally broke through, ringing shrilly, jarring him awake.

Dr. Martin Hunt sat upright on the bed, the covers of which he had not pulled back, opened his eyes wide, blinked a few times, then reached around and picked up the phone.

"Hunt," he said. He swung his legs over the side of the bed as he listened, scratching his reddish-brown beard with his free hand. "Okay, be right there." He hung up the phone, stood, grabbed his white coat, which he'd tossed onto the foot of the bed earlier, and slipped it on over the wrinkled, comfortable surgical greens he always wore while on duty. He grabbed his cigarettes from the nightstand, lit one, then slipped them into his coat pocket as he glanced at his reflection in the full-length mirror by the door. His eyes twinkled in the dark, the tiny lines around them seeming to smile even though he didn't. He smoothed his hair and beard with one hand, then went out the door of the little yellow house that served as quarters for the ER doctor working on call. Glancing at his watch, he saw by its luminous dial that it was just a few minutes past three in the morning.

A chilling fog had settled over the valley and a soft glow rose from the lampposts in the parking lot on the other side of the hospital building. Hunt hurried down the short walkway from the house, his shoulders hunched against the cold air, then clanked down the metal staircase that led to the side door of the emergency room. As he went inside, the sudden alertness that always overcame him when he was awakened by the ringing of the telephone began to wear off. Weariness began to ache in his knees and elbows.

Julie Calahan sat at the small, semicircular desk sipping a cup of coffee; she looked up and smiled warmly at Hunt as he walked in. Along with sunsets and nice views of the ocean, Julie's smile was one of Hunt's favorite sights. It was not conventionally attractive, perhaps; it was a bit crooked, and her teeth were not the straight, perfectly shaped teeth one might expect to see in toothpaste commercials. But it was so like a pair of open arms waiting for a hug, so filled with genuine warmth, that it always made him smile, too.

"Good morning," she said.

He stepped around behind her, bent down, and kissed her gently on the neck, taking in the fresh smell of her short, honey-colored hair. "Hi," he said quietly. "What's happening?"

Julie backed her chair away from the desk a bit, its little wheels squeaking, then turned to face Hunt. "Couple guys in an accident over by Pope Creek. One who got hit by a car, and the drunk who was driving it."

"How bad?" He took one more long drag on his cigarette, then put it out in a small ashtray on the edge of the desk.

"The driver has some minor lacerations, probably a broken leg, but the other guy is worse. Broken arm, lacerations, possible head injuries."

Hunt sighed and scrubbed his face with his palms. "Is there any more of that coffee?"

"Sure," Julie replied, standing. She walked over to a little table in the corner and poured some coffee into a Styrofoam cup, then handed it to Hunt. "You look tired."

"I feel like I'm a hundred years old."

"Don't be silly. You don't look a day over forty."

"I'm thirty-eight, for Christ's sake!" He sipped his coffee.

"Forty is a very distinguished age, though."

"Not if you're thirty-eight. Where's Carl?"

"He's in back getting ready for the patient. It's been a slow night."

Pushing himself away from the desk, Hunt leaned over, kissed her on the lips, and said, "Thanks, Julie." Then he left the office and walked into the dimly lighted emergency room, where he could hear Carl preparing for the incoming patient: metallic objects clanging together and a curtain partition hissing as it was pulled back.

As he ran his fingers through his thick, dark, rust-colored hair, Hunt realized that it *had* been a very slow night, a pleasant rest after the previous night's horrendous three-car accident on Howell Mountain Road, quickly followed by a coronary and a little boy who had swallowed some Drano. Hunt had gotten little sleep, which was why he'd so warmly welcomed the little bit he'd been able to sneak in tonight. He wondered if the patient being brought in by the ambulance was going to be the beginning of another rush. He hoped not. He hoped this one would be easily taken care of with no complications. He was stiff and tired and didn't want to have to deal with anything out of the ordinary.

Of course, Hunt thought, *we don't always get what we want, do we?*

"Dr. Hunt?"

Hunt looked up to see Officer Birney crossing the emergency room toward him from the direction of the entrance. He was holding a piece of creased paper in his right hand.

"Hi, Birney."

"Show you something?"

"Sure." Hunt sipped his coffee.

Hooking one thumb into his pants pocket and leaning to his right a little, Birney gestured with the piece of paper as he said, "You got a guy coming in from Pope Creek. Got hit by a car."

"Uh-huh."

"Name is Jeffery Collinson."

Hunt nodded, wishing the balding policeman before him would not ignore the first word of each sentence as he so often did. Hunt had worked with him before and the man's habit annoyed him.

"Found this on him." He handed the letter to Hunt.

Hunt quickly read over it, the tip of his tongue running back and forth along the lower lip. "Holy God," he sighed.

"Cops all over California have been getting letters like that for the last two and half years or so. And there's always a murder to go with each one." He shifted his weight from right to left. "This guy may be the killer of twenty-two people. Maybe more."

The emergency room was silent as Hunt stared at the letter. Then they heard the ambulance arrive outside the entrance.

"'Morning, Tom."

Tom Conrad, slumped on the sofa in the laboratory's lounge, a Ken Follet paperback laying open on his lap, started from his light sleep at the sound of his name. The book slid down his legs and dropped to the floor. "Huh?" he blurted, sitting up. He panicked for a moment and checked his watch; he was supposed to get a patient's blood sugar at four o'clock. Seeing it was only a little after three, he relaxed. Smacking his lips, he looked over at the short, stocky man who was sweeping the floor. "Hi, Sherman. How goes it?"

"Slow, Thomas. Same as always. How's your wife and kids?"

"Just fine," Tom answered mechanically, bending over to pick up his book, then standing and stretching his arms out before him. Tom was rather tall, anyway, but when his lanky frame stood next to Sherman, he looked even taller than usual. Darker, too. He walked over to the "kitchen" (a small sink, a counter, and a few cupboards in the corner of the lounge) and took a Coke from the small green fridge. Slipping his paperback into the fat pocket of his lab coat, he snapped the Coke open and drank some, then went back to the sofa and plopped down onto it again.

"You oughta get a normal job," Sherman muttered. He kept pushing the broom ahead of him, making his fleshy jowls jiggle, as he made his way back over to the door. "'Specially with a family at home like you got."

"Oh, it's not so bad," Tom said with a soft smirk. This was the same conversation—almost word for word—that they had twice a week when Sherman swept his way through the lab. "I get paid for reading and watching TV or sleeping, and most of the patients I draw are too sleepy to complain when I miss their veins, I don't mind."

"Whatever. Now, *me* ... If *I* had two fine boys and a wife—a pregnant wife, yet—at home, I wouldn't be working no crazy hours like this. Oh, well. Not my place to tell you." He swept his way out the door. "Have a good one, Tom."

"'Bye, Sherman." Tom took another drink of Coke, then looked around him for the television control. He picked it up off the end table and turned on the television that rested on a card table a few feet away.

"You can't come in," Shirley Jones was saying on the screen. "I've taken a tranquilizer."

Tom changed the channels until he came across a giant spider crawling down a desert highway. He chuckled. It was even a slow night for TV. Yawning, he thought to himself that at least there was Mrs. Plitkin's blood sugar at four. That was *something* to look forward to.

* * *

They heard him before they saw him.

"*Giui cahisa lusada oreri od*—Second Key, the Second Key—it's gonna come—*lape noanu torafe*—gonna come, gonna happen!"

The ragged, frantic cries grew louder as the paramedics pulled the patient from the ambulance.

"Sounds like the guests have arrived," Hunt muttered to himself as he crossed the emergency room with long, smooth strides, sniffing once.

The gurney was pushed in by a large man wearing a yellow jumpsuit with red and white ambulance patches on the shoulders. He tossed a glance at Hunt and said, "Gonna need some help moving him. Guy's wild."

They removed the restraints and Hunt helped move the patient from the gurney to the neatly prepared bed as a second paramedic brought in the other accident victim. As Hunt helped restrain the first patient on the bed, the young man kicked and thrashed, his shouts occasionally breaking into high-pitched cackling, then low, throaty sobs.

"C'mon, c'mon," Hunt urged firmly, "*stop* it, now, you're only hurting yourself, fella."

Carl stepped over and tried to help soothe the young man, but without success.

Julie, in the meantime, tried to settle the other patient—a short, potbellied Mexican man in his fifties who reeked of alcohol—who was much less violent, but almost just as loud.

"I didn't meana hit him!" the man shouted. "I *didn't*. Miss ... really, I swear! I was—"

"Just calm down now," Julie said softly, patting the man's hand gently as she glanced over at the paramedic on the other side of the bed. "You wanna cut his clothes off while I get his vitals?" Swiping a nearby IVAC thermometer up in her hand, she said to the patient, "Can you slip this under your tongue, please?"

"Is he gonna be awright?"

"Let's not worry about him right now, okay? We'll just—are you in pain? Where do you hurt?"

"I wanna know if he's okay! Am I gonna go t' jail?"

"He's gonna be fine. Let's just work on *you* now, *okay?*"

While Julie struggled to avert the older man's attention from the other patient, Hunt leaned over the young man, Jeffery Collinson. Carl was trying to cut off his clothes—a grimy plaid shirt with one sleeve already torn off for the splint that held his broken arm rigid, dirty blue jeans with a little blood splashed on them, and heavy old hiking boots—while the paramedic tried to hold Collinson still.

His face was puffy and his head was swollen, looking as though it didn't belong on his scrawny neck. His bulging eyes floated disjointedly in his sockets and a thick, clear substance seeped around the edges. His red hair was greasy and matted; it clung together in spikes that flared from his head and added to his crazed look. He reeked of sweat and a clinging, bloody odor. His clothes, moving stiffly as Carl tried to cut them away, had obviously not been washed, or even taken off, in weeks. Perhaps months. His thin lips, chapped and cracking, pulled back often, revealing yellow teeth that had gone unbrushed far too long.

"It's gonna come, now," he hissed at Hunt. "It's gonna come and dying won't matter, won't make a difference." A laugh like sandpaper tore from his throat.

Placing his fingers on Collinson's restrained wrist for a pulse, Hunt said, "Can you move your toes, Mr. Collinson?"

"It's gonna come, now," he rasped again.

"Carl, get his vitals when you're done there."

"Yeah."

"Julie?" Hunt called.

"Busy!"

As if he hadn't heard her, he went on. "I want someone from respiratory therapy down here *yesterday,* and someone from X ray for a C-spine. I want a CBC, a chem panel with blood sugar and electrolytes run and reported *stat—*"

"Am I gonna go t' jail?" the other patient whined, craning his head around to look over at Collinson. "I ain't had much to drink, really, and I got a wife—"

Hunt reached up, wrapped his fingers around the hem of the beige curtain between the two beds, and pulled it across so the older man wouldn't be quite so distracted. "Quiet him down if you can. I want PSCE, comprehensive drug screen, BAL, ABG, U/A, type and cross, four units. And osmo. Stat. And Carl, two peripheral lines running lactated Ringer's, hundred and fifty cc's per hour."

"Right away."

"Whatta you want me to do with *him?*" Julie snapped, sticking her head around the edge of the curtain, sticking a stiff thumb over her shoulder.

Hunt was at the older man's side in two quick steps.

"What's your name, friend?"

"Huh-Hernandez."

Hunt took the chart from Julie and scanned her assessment of the patient's condition. "Okay, let's get a lactated Ringer's going, hundred cc's per hour, C-spine, BAL, ABG, CBC, BL, and an X ray of the affected leg."

Julie turned immediately to go to the phone in the office.

Hunt looked over at the paramedic. "Keep an eye on him. I'm gonna be busy with this guy over here." He returned to Collinson, removing his stethoscope from his coat pocket.

"It's all starting," Collinson croaked. "This ... this is just the beginning." His breath made Hunt think of something dead and bloated.

"You wanna hold still so I can take a look at you, here?" Hunt asked. "What were you doing in the road, anyway?"

Carl came over and hung the IV bottle above the bed, then prepared to inject the needle.

Hanging the scope around his neck, Hunt picked up the chart on Collinson and glanced over it. "Huh?" he asked again. "What were you doing in the road, fella?"

"*I am the Dark Christ!* Holder of the Second Key!" He began to jerk and writhe on the bed, pulling against the straps again, clenching his teeth and jutting his chin, making the muscles in his neck stand out like steel cables. "'O you, the great spawn of the worms of the Earth, whom the Hell fire frames in the depths of my jaw, whom I have prepared as cups for a wedding—' "

Hunt gently probed Collinson's ribs, then placed the end of the stethoscope over his heart and listened.

"'—for you are become as a building such as is not, save in the mind of all the All-Powerful manifestation of Satan! Arise! saith the first. Move, therefore—'"

Hunt jerked the stethoscope away and winced when Collinson's string of words disappeared in a sudden spasm of wracking coughs. He lifted his oversized head and his whole body convulsed with each cough. Red-black blood sprayed from his mouth, speckling his lips and stubbly chin. He suddenly dropped his head back and seemed to relax a little, his chest rising and falling with each wheezy breath. He moaned quietly and the tip of his tongue slipped out to lick his lips; it was red with blood. He turned his head and looked up into Hunt's eyes, his own bulbous brown eyes cloudy and unsteady. And he smiled. Chuckled slowly. He said, "I. Am. The. Dark. Christ."

Tom wrapped his long fingers around the empty Coke can and crunched it together in his hand. In his other hand he held his book open, reading it leisurely, checking the time now and then.

The phone in the office bleeped and Tom stood, tossed his crushed can into a wastebasket, and went out to the phone, putting his book down on the desk. It was always a temptation, at such a deserted hour of the morning, to answer the phone with something like, "Ajax Umbrella Factory and Opium Den, may I help you?" But he never did.

"Laboratory, Tom speaking."

"This is Julie, Tom." Her words came through the phone rapidly, frantically.

"Hi, there." He smiled and sat back in the chair, happy to hear his friend's voice, however harried it sounded. "So how are things in ER?" He had a pretty good idea what the answer would be, judging from the voices in the background.

"Well, it *was* fine, five minutes ago. Now all hell's breaking loose. We've got a car accident. A couple—"

Julie stopped talking and Tom could hear Dr. Hunt's voice in the background, shouting at her, mixed with loud shrieks and coughs.

"Okay, okay," Julie said. Then she repeated the list of tests Hunt had ordered and Tom jotted them down on the pad by the phone as he listened.

"Sounds like you're having fun," Tom muttered as he wrote.

"This one guy's a wild man."

"Okay, I'll be there in just a sec, Julie. Chin up." He replaced the receiver and rubbed his palms together rapidly as he stood. He went to the back of the lab with a little spring in his step. "Whatta you know? Something to do."

Collinson was screaming now, not words, just long, tattered screams, tensing his whole body.

"Jesus Christ on a pogo stick, Julie, where the *hell* is respiratory and X ray?" Hunt snapped, ripping the curtain back and looking across the room at Julie.

She was just coming out of the office, but immediately spun around on her heel. "I just called 'em, but I'll call 'em again," she sang out.

Hunt grumbled quietly as he turned around, reached up, and switched off the light that was shining over the bed, taking his penlight out of his pocket with his other hand, flicking it on with his thumb. He held the little light over Collinson's face, pointing it into his right eye.

"Could you hold *still*, please?" Hunt asked, leaning forward to see the eye's reaction to the light.

Collinson was beginning to shiver uncontrollably; his jaw jerked up and down and his teeth clacked together loudly.

"Carl, you wanna get this guy a blanket?"

"Sure." Carl stepped away from the bed.

Hernandez began to shout in the next bed and the paramedic who was with him called, "Can somebody give me a hand with this guy?"

Hunt looked up at the yellow-suited man beside him. "I'm okay here. Go take care of Hernandez." Then he turned back to the patient and shined the light in his eye again as Collinson let out a long, heavy moan from deep inside. And then Hunt saw it. It was long and thin and black, like the earthworms he used to collect before going fishing with his grandfather. It squirmed its way smoothly out of the man's left nostril, a total of about one foot long, then slid over his cheek and onto the bed.

"What the hell?" Hunt breathed heavily as he leaned away from the tiling, almost dropping his penlight. His jaw fell open and his eyes widened.

The thing dropped from the bed to the floor with a soft *splat!* by Hunt's foot, then disappeared under the bed. Hunt swallowed hard and his throat clicked dryly as he looked around his feet. "God ... *damn.*"

He squatted down and looked under the bed. He could see it, a small black mass on the floor. It had flattened out and was no longer thin and long. His mouth still open, he reached his left hand under the bed to grasp the thing and heard a quick but soft *whissshhh* sound and felt an icy sting before he could jerk his hand back protectively. A cut had been slashed across the back of his hand and was starting to bleed moderately. Hunt massaged the wrist with the fingers of his other hand as he swore again quietly, the penlight clicking to the floor. Clenching his teeth, he got on his knees and swiped a hand under the bed quickly but cautiously, making a little grunting sound as he did so.

The black thing shot like lightning from under the bed, fluttering across the hard, cold floor, Hunt trying to follow it with his eyes through the foot or so of space between the bottom of the curtains and the floor, just as the door leading to the hospital corridor opened and two feet appeared. Its speed making it little more than a blur, the thing darted between the feet and disappeared out the door.

Hunt gut on his hands and knees at the foot of the bed, his mouth gaping, and he reached up to jerk the curtain all the way back. Tom Conrad was standing in the doorway, his phlebotomist's tray at his side.

"Did you see that?" the doctor hissed.

Tom looked down at the floor, looked behind him, then back down at Hunt, shrugging his shoulders.

"Goddammit! Did you *see* that?" Hunt repeated, louder this time.

Tom began to shake his head. "I ... no, I ... uh ... no."

Hunt stumbled to his feet, snapping, "Look out in the corridor!"

Tom stuck his head out the door and Hunt was immediately beside him, his eyes scanning the long floor that led to the main lobby, the snack bar, and the main bank of elevators. One of the elevators opened and an X-ray tech noisily wheeled the portable X-ray machine into the corridor.

Hunt stepped back into the emergency room, sweeping his right hand back over his hair, holding his other hand out before him to look at the cut on the back of it. It wasn't bleeding badly, but it stung like hell. He looked over at Carl, who was standing beside Collinson's bed. The curtain was pulled all the way back and Hunt noticed for the first time that the patient was now still and silent.

He noticed it just before Carl snapped, "Dr. Hunt! He's fibrillating!"

Thirty-five minutes later, Jeffery Collinson was dead.

2 - HUNT

HUNT LOWERED HIMSELF with a sigh into the vinyl-covered chair in front of Rudy Pazulo's desk. The chair's cushion hissed quietly beneath Hunt's weight and the vinyl made soft crinkling sounds.

Pazulo, the hospital administrator, was on the phone. When Hunt walked in, Pazulo had looked up at him, held up one finger, and mouthed, "Be right with you." Then he turned his attention back to the telephone conversation, nodding and saying things like "Sure" and "Oh, of course" as he quickly jotted down notes.

Hunt reached into his coat pocket and pulled out a cigarette, lit it, then leaned forward wearily, pulling the ashtray on Pazulo's desk closer to him. It wasn't even eight o'clock yet and Pazulo was already in his office and had asked to see Hunt. He hadn't said why, but Hunt knew the reason for the little meeting, for Pazulo's earlier-than-usual presence at the hospital. He took a long drag on the cigarette, his eyes closing to little slits as he did so, enjoying the feeling of the smoke. Nearly every part of his body ached and he wanted badly to sleep. His cut hand still stung, but not as sharply as before. A small white bandage covered the laceration.

"Okay," Pazulo was saying into the phone, "that sounds fine to me. Right, three-thirty. See you then." He hung up, turned back to his pad, and continued writing something, his concentration looking a bit too intense for Hunt's tastes. Hunt thought that the little shows Pazulo put on for those around him—trying to act and look busier than he really was—were laughable. He'd probably just been talking to his wife or his sister-in-law (with whom, word had it, he was having an affair), but would rather have Hunt think he was talking to someone very important, like the goddamned governor. Pazulo continued writing for a few seconds, then looked up and smiled, reaching up to brush back a few strands of his salt-and-pepper hair that had fallen down onto his forehead. He had a thin face with sharp cheekbones and a hawklike nose with a pronounced bump near the top of the bridge. He clicked his tongue pitifully and shook his head. "Still smoking," he said. "You're a doctor. You should know better."

"Filthy habit," Hunt said, putting on a disgusted expression. He held the cigarette up between the first two fingers of his bandaged hand. "This is my last."

Pazulo leaned back in his chair and crossed his legs. "Heard you had a rough night in ER."

"I'm sure you did," Hunt said quietly, nodding.

"This place is swarming with reporters. You really made the news."

"*I* didn't make the news. Jeffery Collinson did."

"Yes, but he was in *your* care. You were the last one to see him alive."

"Look, we busted our butts trying to revive him—"

"Oh, I'm sure you did everything you could," Pazulo said sincerely, leaning forward and folding his hands on his desk. "Even if you hadn't, I don't think anyone would mind. The guy was a mass murderer."

"Death sentences aren't my line of work, Rudy." Hunt reached forward and tapped his cigarette over the ashtray.

"Have you talked to any of the press people yet?"

"I've avoided them like the syph."

"You going to talk to them?"

"Oh, I suppose I'll have to eventually."

"What are you going to tell them?"

Hunt chuckled darkly, breathing smoke. "Isn't that why I'm here, Rudy? So you can tell me what to tell them?"

Pazulo sighed, fidgeting in his chair. He twisted his thin, immaculately manicured hands and his knuckles cracked loudly. Hunt winced at the sound and shook his head, annoyed. Pazulo smirked. "You smoke, I crack my knuckles."

"Smoking's a lot quieter."

Pazulo stood and stepped out from behind the desk, perching himself on its corner. "Tell me about what you saw in ER last night,

Martin—when you were treating Collinson." He positioned his hands comfortably in his lap, absently fingering his wedding ring. "I'm sure you've heard the whole story by now, haven't you?"

"You know how things get twisted. I'd like to hear it from you."

Hunt sighed, putting his elbow on the armrest of the chair and leaning his head on his palm. "Well, I was standing over him and this ... *thing*, about a foot long, black, thin, crawled ... no, it *squirmed* out of Collinson's left nostril. It dropped to the floor and went under the bed. I tried to get it and it cut my hand." He held up his bandaged hand. "I don't know *how*, but it did. Then it shot across the room, out the door, and disappeared."

"Did anyone else see it?"

"Well, it went right between Tom Conrad's legs, but it was moving so fast that he didn't really see it. No, I guess I'm the only one."

Pazulo reached up and tugged on his earlobe, pursing his lips and breathing in deeply through his nose. "Are you planning on telling the press that story?"

"That thing is loose in the hospital, Rudy. It could—"

"But you don't need to tell the world about it, do you?" His words were spoken calmly and levelly.

"Okay, so I don't need to tell the press. But it cut my hand. It might hurt some—"

"You might've cut it on the bed, a jagged piece of metal sticking down from—"

"Dammit, Rudy!" Hunt exclaimed, shooting to his feet and circling the chair. "I *heard* it! It made a ... a *whipping* sound. And I *saw* it there under the bed."

"Martin, there's already been quite a stir over Collinson. I'd rather not make things any worse."

"You'd *rather not*," Hunt repeated icily.

"Look, if there was some kind of bug on Collinson's body—"

Hunt sighed and dropped back into the chair, rubbing a palm over his face.

"—in his hair, or something, I'm sure it's gotten outside by now, out of the building. I'm sure it's nothing to worry about."

"Rudy. It wasn't a *bug*." Hunt spat the word disdainfully. He held up one hand, his fingers splayed. "The damned thing was as big as my hand once it hit the floor and spread out. And it wasn't in his *hair*, either. It came out of his *nose*."

Pazulo stood and walked around behind the desk again, sitting down. "You have to admit, Martin, that *is* a bit hard to swallow."

Hunt nodded slightly. "I know, I know, it sounds crazy. But that makes it all the more disturbing."

Pazulo's hand flattened out on the desktop and his slender fingers drummed quietly. "Look at it from my position. If you tell this story to the press, not only will it look bad for you, but it'll play havoc with the hospital's reputation, which has suffered enough in the last year, I'd say. And I don't need to remind you that you were rather outspoken during the last ... scandal, if you will."

"C'mon, Rudy, that's old news."

"We learn from our mistakes."

"It wasn't a mistake," Hunt replied quickly, leaning forward in his chair. "I don't regret standing up for Sam Porter. It wouldn't have hurt any if you'd done the same."

"There was nothing I could do about that."

"Bullshit! You just didn't *try.*"

"Martin, when a doctor is accused of molesting a patient—"

"*Accused* is exactly right!"

Pazulo held up a quieting palm. "The evidence was irrefutable. There was too much going against him. It would've been better for everyone concerned if you and Porter had been quiet about it. Especially *you.*"

"Sam was my best friend. I *know* he was innocent. He was set up."

"Unfortunately for Dr. Porter, friendship does not stand up in court. But that's not what we're here to discuss right now, is it." It wasn't a question. Pazulo leaned back in, his chair and tugged on his earlobe again, silent for a few seconds. "You're long overdue for a vacation, Martin. You've been working very hard, long hours. I think you should take some time off. Go someplace. Take a nice long trip somewhere. Enjoy yourself. Forget about all this for a while. While you're gone, I'll keep my eyes and ears open, and if anything comes of the ... the thing you saw, I'll do what I can."

Hunt took one last drag on his cigarette and punched it out in the ashtray. He leaned forward with his elbows on the armrests and said quietly, "Come on, Rudy, show some sense." He started to continue, but Rudy interrupted.

"No, no, Martin. You're the one not showing any sense. Because if you don't leave this alone ..." He shifted his position in his chair, curled his fingers over, and examined his nails, avoiding Hunt's eyes. "Well, I don't want to sound threatening, but if you don't leave this alone, you're going to find yourself in a rather uncomfortable position." He looked across the desk at Hunt again and coughed softly. "I've tolerated your outspokenness for some time now, Martin. Bitching about hospital conditions, crusading for the nurses, the techs. Jumping on nearly every conceivable bandwagon concerning hospital policy. Stirring things up in general. That business with Sam Porter was the last straw. You're a doctor of emergency medicine, not Martin Luther King, Junior. Don't get yourself into any unnecessary trouble."

Hunt looked over Pazulo's shoulder and out the window behind him. Steel-gray fog shrouded the view of the valley usually afforded by the window. Hunt clenched his teeth a few times, flexing his jaw. *Why couldn't this have happened to someone else?* he wondered. *Someone who hasn't already had more than his share of trouble with this pencil-pushing prick and his envelope-licking, ass-kissing friends.*

Hunt began to nod slowly, then turned his gaze back to Pazulo. "Okay, Rudy. I don't like it, but, okay."

Pazulo smiled thinly with obvious relief. "Good," he said. "Take Julie on a cruise, or something. Maybe Greece."

Hunt blinked. There was something very discomforting hearing his relationship with Julie spoken of by Rudy Pazulo. Sort of like Julio Iglesias singing an Elton John song.

"*If* she can get some time off," Hunt said pointedly. "This place is so incredibly understaffed now ..."

Pazulo's lids closed slowly, heavily, over his eyes and his lips tightened together slightly. "You're doing it again, Martin," he said quietly.

There were a few seconds of stony silence between them. Words were unnecessary to confirm their dislike of one another; the silence did nicely.

Pazulo opened his eyes again and a smile twitched over his mouth. "God, do something relaxing. You deserve it."

"Sure, Rudy. I just might do that. I can rest easy knowing this place is in your competent, concerned hands." Hunt stood and walked to the door; Pazulo stood up behind his desk. With one hand on the doorknob, Hunt turned to him again. "But," he said just a bit coldly, "be careful those hands don't get bitten." He held up his bandaged hand, a warning disguised as a wave, and left, closing the door softly behind him.

Hunt passed through the empty outer office and stepped out into the corridor. "Christ," he muttered, stopping.

He was met by a wave of questioning voices coming from sharply dressed men and women with microphones, tape recorders, Hasselblad and Contax cameras around their necks, television cameras mounted on their shoulders. They all stepped forward and spoke at once.

"Please," Hunt said, his eyes crinkling with annoyance, holding up one hand. "I don't have time to talk with you right now, but I promise that, when it's available, the coroner's report will be passed on to you." He turned and shouldered his way through a few of the reporters and started down the corridor. Most of them followed him.

"Did he confess before he died?"

"What were his last words?"

"Did he show any remorse?"

"How did you feel when you found out who he was, Dr. Hunt?"

Hunt's strides became longer as he walked, slowing to a stop only when he came to the door with the word STAIRS on it. As he stepped through the doorway, he realized that they were going to follow him, so he turned to them and smiled slightly, just enough to give his bearded face a warm but weary look. They were suddenly quiet.

"Look," Hunt said to them, "I've had a very long night and I'm very tired right now. So tired, in fact, that I don't think I would be able to answer your questions the way they should be answered. I'd be happy to talk with you later, though. Maybe this afternoon."

Some of the reporters smiled at him, and a few even took a step back away from the door.

Hunt nodded pleasantly at them, then went into the stairwell, letting the door swing slowly shut on its own. His feet made little *chitch* sounds on each step as he went down to the basement. *Goddamned reporters,* he thought. *They use the First Amendment as an excuse to gather like vultures and circle their prey—*

He sighed and shook his head as he neared the cafeteria, thinking, *Calm down, Hunt, they're just doing their job. Like you.*

From the kitchen in back of the cafeteria came the sounds of clattering dishes and clanging pots and pans. The usual early morning mixed crowd was seated at the tables and standing at the vending machines: doctors and nurses, white and fresh, all ready for another day of work; other doctors and nurses looking tired and haggard, ready to end another night of work; friends and relatives of patients, their clothes wrinkled and then eyes sagging, hoping for the best, but expecting the worst.

Julie was seated at a table by the door, sipping a cup of coffee. Hunt noticed that she wasn't wearing her red sweater; she didn't look ready to go home. She'd taken out her contacts, as she usually did after a night of work to give her tired eyes a rest, and her large tortoiseshell glasses were perched on her pixie nose. She smiled when she saw him, and her smile, though weary, made him feel better.

Hunt sat down and they joined hands on the table. "Ready to take off?" he asked.

"Can't. Shirley Hogan called in sick, so I'm working a double."

"But you're exhausted," he protested quietly.

She shrugged. "Oh, it won't kill me. But I was looking forward to catching up on my sleep with you."

The two of them had been able to spend very little time together outside of ER, and they'd planned to spend the day together. Ever since they'd met and started seeing one another, they'd tried to arrange their schedules so they could be together. More often than not, however, they were unsuccessful.

"What did Rudy want?" she asked him, a bit apprehensively.

Hunt chuckled and picked up her coffee, taking a drink. "He wanted me to come in so he could give me a vacation"—he replaced the cup—"whether I wanted one or not."

"I was afraid of that."

"He wants me quiet and out of the way until this business about Collinson is over."

"Did you tell him about what you saw?"

"That's why he wants to get rid of me. So I won't start spreading stories about—"

"Mind if I join you?"

Hunt and Julie turned to see Tom standing by their table, bending toward them a bit. His lab coat was gone and he wore a rust-colored sport coat over a maroon sweater. He looked like a writer, not a lab tech.

"Please do," Hunt said, with a bit more enthusiasm than he wanted to show. He'd been thinking a lot about Tom just before

going in to see Pazulo. Tom was the only other person to have
seen the black thing dart out of the emergency room, however
vague his glimpse of the creature might have been. He'd had
only a few seconds to speak with Tom in all the confusion; Hunt
thought the man might be able to give him a little support.

Tom pulled a chair over from the closest empty table and sat
down with them. He primped his hair and jutted his jaw—a
parody of a star—as he said, "I'm going to be on the news tonight.
Channel 50. I figure it'll only be a matter of days before I start
hearing from major Hollywood agents and movie producers."

Julie giggled and Hunt grinned tiredly.

"Sorry I wasn't able to stick around a little longer this morning,"
he said, a little more seriously. He turned to Hunt. "I understand
Lord Rudy called you on the carpet."

Hunt ran a hand over his beard. "Word travels fast."

"Faster than wildfire in this place."

Hunt gave Tom a brief synopsis of his meeting with Pazulo. "I
think you might be able to help me, Tom—if you would."

Tom sniffed, reached around, and scratched the back of his
neck. "Yeah?"

"You saw it. It went right between your feet and out the door."

Tom inhaled deeply and glanced at Julie. His face was uncertain,
a little timid. "Look, Dr. Hunt, what I saw ... it could've been a
shadow. I ... I just don't know."

Hunt had known Tom for a few years. Not really on a social
basis, although they'd talked over a few beers a time or two.
They weren't the closest of friends—not close enough for Tom to
stop calling him "Dr. Hunt," anyway—but Hunt could tell from
the expression on his face what he was afraid of. He didn't want
to make any waves. Tom didn't like Rudy Pazulo any more than
anyone else Hunt knew, he was sure, but he didn't want to rub
the administrator the wrong way. Feeling the ache in his lower
back that came with exhaustion, Hunt knew he was too tired to
lay successfully to rest any apprehension Tom might have about
lending his support.

"Tell you what," Hunt said, breaking the uncomfortable
silence that had descended over the table, "I'm too tired to hold
a coherent conversation right now. Why don't we get together
later." He waited for a reply, but Tom simply turned his eyes
down to Julie's cup of coffee, twisting his mouth nervously. "I'd
really appreciate it if we could just talk about it."

One shoulder twitched with unconvincing nonchalance as Tom said, "Sure. Just ... give me a call, I guess."

Half of Hunt's mouth turned up in a smile and he nodded. "Good. What I'm going to do now is go home to bed." He stood, pushing his chair back. He gave Julie a kiss on the forehead, told her not to work too hard, and whispered in her ear that he loved her. Then he patted Tom on the shoulder. "I'll talk to you later, Tom." Then he turned and left.

As he walked down the corridors of the hospital, three nurses—all young and very attractive—smiled brightly at him. One winked and one said, "Good morning, Dr. Hunt," in a voice coated with honey. He smiled and nodded at each of them as he continued walking.

"You know," his old friend Sam Porter used to say, "most nurses hold doctors in disdain, but they all love you. What the hell do you have that we don't?"

Hunt usually replied, "A pretty face." He always said it jokingly, but, without conceit, he supposed there was some truth to that. He wasn't sure what it was, exactly, but he was frequently being told that he had a "pretty face." Maybe it was his eyes. They were sort of squinty sometimes, sad, but with a sort of purposeful look to them, a determination. Who cared, as long as it looked good, right?

It was cold outside and the wet pavement of the parking lot dully reflected the sky's mournful gray light. He lit a cigarette, and smoking it felt good in the icy morning air. When he got in the car he started it up and switched on the radio. He turned the volume up a bit so the music's heavy beat would keep him awake until he got home. He glanced at his reflection in the mirror, then looked again, longer. *Yeah,* he thought, *maybe it is the eyes.*

"You spend any more time in front of the mirror flirting with your reflection," his father had once said to him, "and you're going to get yourself pregnant."

That had been just before Hunt had left for California. He'd just started growing his beard and was styling his hair differently; he was very concerned about the image he would project.

"Your image isn't going to save anyone in the emergency room, son," his father had assured him.

Hunt backed the car out of the parking slot, then drove onto the road, smiling at the thought of his father. He expected to hear from his father sometime in the near future, probably a letter, maybe a phone call if the old man was in a good mood. He'd want to comment on hearing his son's name in the news, as he most assuredly would once the Collinson story started to get around, which it was doing even as Hunt drove home.

When, at the age of twenty-nine, after getting out of medical school, Hunt had decided to move to California and escape the torturous winters of the East Coast, his father had accepted it well. He had not protested, not like most staunch New Yorker fathers might. He'd sat on his overstuffed easy chair, silently lighting his pipe. (Whenever Hunt's father picked up his pipe and began the slow, comfortable process of filling and lighting it, it usually meant he was going to render an opinion.)

"Awfully nice in California," his father had said, puffing smoke. "Spent some time there with your mother before she died. Before you were born. It's very pretty. Friendly people, too. Of course, it's all going to fall into the ocean someday soon, so I guess all that makes very little difference, hmm?"

It was his father, also a doctor, who had brought out Hunt's interest in medicine. Wallace Hunt always spoke very candidly, and fondly, of his specialty, gynecology.

"There's nothing more intricate and mysterious than the female body," he'd once told his son, "except maybe outer space. Only real difference, I guess, is that in space the black holes are bigger." Then he'd chuckled, clamping his teeth onto his pipe.

Gynecology was not for Hunt, though. He needed something that could properly handle his level of energy, something that would allow him a certain amount of pressure. So he had taken up emergency medicine. Although he felt that gynecology would have been a far wiser decision ("Women are *always* falling apart," he'd said with a wave of his hand), Wallace had been happy that his son was at least carrying on in the field of his father, his father's father, and so on: medicine.

Hunt wondered what his father would say if he'd heard the story Julie and Tom had heard from him earlier.

"Well, now," he might say, lighting his pipe and puffing, "that's a pretty disturbing thing, I'd say. 'Course, it'll also have you stuffing burritos down at the Taco Bell within a week and paying regular visits to your local shrink if you tell anyone else. So shut your trap."

But Hunt couldn't do that. He couldn't shut up entirely, anyway. Thank god he had Julie. She might have a hard time swallowing the story, but at least she was *there* for him. As much as he hated to admit it, he sometimes needed someone he could lean on, and Julie was a pillar. She didn't really look as strong as she was. She looked rather bookish, actually, as if she might even be a bit boring. That had been his very first impression of her, at least.

He'd first seen her about three years ago when she'd begun working in ER. He worked the day shift then and they'd met for the first time during the change of shifts. They saw each other occasionally after that and would exchange greetings. It wasn't until about a year and a half ago, when he'd started working nights, that they got to know one another. And they'd clicked together like two pieces of clockwork. For a few years before he met Julie, Hunt had been very cautious with women. He'd been engaged once to a veterinarian. They'd met at some local benefit and had become too serious too fast. She'd left him, four months before they were to be married, for another doctor. A surgeon at the medical center. They'd married and left California, perhaps to freeze to death in one of those torturous East Coast winters. One could only hope.

You're vicious, Hunt, he thought.

During the ride home, the radio playing, the heater warming his legs with a whisper, it occurred to Hunt that, over the years, he'd forced himself to be open-minded, and his willingness to accept the unusual had served him well; it allowed him to treat his patients more efficiently, it afforded him more success in discovering and diagnosing ailments that were a little better hidden than others. His perspective had suddenly changed, however, and he began to think that perhaps his open-mindedness had turned on him.

Whatever it was that crawled out of Collinson's nose, Hunt thought with a frown, *was long, too long to have been hiding in his sinuses. Then it had spread out like a little pancake on the floor. At least, I thought it did.*

Aha! *A ripple of doubt disturbs the surface of what had been, a little while ago, a perfectly smooth pond of certainty. Maybe it'll all be better after a long, hard sleep.*

Maybe it's a lack of sleep that's brought all of this on in the first place.

Hunt's mind turned back to Tom. He had seen something, too, even if what he thought he'd seen was only a shadow. Glancing at his bandaged hand, Hunt chuckled softly, thinking, *Now, there's a shadow I wouldn't want to box with.*

"It's gonna come now," Collinson had spat in ER, his wrists and ankles strapped to the bed. "It's gonna come, and dying won't matter, won't make a difference."

Oh, it came, all right. Right out of his fucking nose, it came!

He pulled his silver BMW 2002 into his driveway just as a Beatles tune came on the radio. Hunt turned the ignition off and sat behind the wheel, smoking his cigarette, paying little attention to the song. Just before he switched the radio off, however, the last line of the song *Come Together* made Jeffery Collinson appear in his mind just as clearly as if Hunt were standing at his bedside again, the man's rancid breath seeping between teeth caked with old food, his liquidy brown eyes bulging so severely that they seemed ready to shoot from their sockets like bullets.

Hunt turned the radio off and got out of the car, throwing his cigarette down to the ground hard, as if to kill it.

(dying won't matter)

He walked into the house and went to bed.

3 - TOM

WHEN TOM GOT home, his oldest boy, Bobby, was seated at the breakfast table in his Chewbacca pajamas eating a Hostess Twinkie. With cream filling spotting his lips, his hair tangled and mussed from sleep, the boy looked up at his father and smiled.

"Hi, Dad," he said, his mouth smacking on the cake.

"Bobby, you shouldn't be eating that for breakfast," Tom protested, opening the refrigerator and taking out a pitcher of orange juice. "That's not breakfast food. Where's your mom?"

"Think she's in the shower." He licked his sticky fingers. "How come, Dad?"

"Huh?" Tom was pouring himself a glass of juice.

"How come Twinkies aren't breakfast food? I mean, if I can eat them the rest of the day …"

"You shouldn't eat them *then,* either. They're not good for you. Junk food. How come you're not ready for school?"

"Because Mom's in the shower. She's taking a long time."

Tom was drinking his juice, but he took the glass from his lips and put it down on the counter, a small tingle of fear—one that was becoming all too familiar these days—passing through him. "*How* long?" he asked.

Bobby shrugged, walking over to the trash can with the Twinkie wrapper. "I dunno."

Tom left the kitchen, chiding himself all the while. He was too paranoid with this one, this pregnancy. It was their third. With the other two, he'd been the picture of calm. No sit-com daddy here. No comedic prancing around to dust the furniture and wash the dishes to protect the fragile mother-to-be from the rigors of domestic labors. No stuttering or stammering or putting pants on backward when the moment finally came, no fainting in the delivery room. It had all gone as smooth as silk with both the boys. This one was different, though. This one had been different from the very beginning.

He hurried through the living room and down the hall to the bathroom. When he opened the door, he was met with heat and steam and the hissing sound of the shower running. A picture suddenly flashed into his mind, vivid, but at the same time distorted, like a negative with the lights and darks reversed: *Kimberly on the floor of the shower in a heap, hot water cascading down over her still form, a bit of blood swirling around her as a result of her sudden, unexpected*

(intentional?)

fall, her body huddled over her swollen belly like a hill of flesh.

"Kimberly!" he called, startled by the loudness of his voice.

"What?" She sounded alarmed and a little irritated.

"Are ... are you all right?" The shower suddenly turned off and only the sound of water dripping softly remained. Tom put one hand on his hip and reached around with the other to scratch the back of his neck. The shower door opened a crack and Kimberly's head peeked out, her light blond hair now wet and dark, clinging to her skull.

"*Yes,* I'm all right," she said. "Why shouldn't I be?" A drop of water shivered on the end of her nose, threatening to fall.

Tom shook his head and a little burst of air came from his nose, a sort of airy, embarrassed laugh. "Bobby said you'd been in here a long time. I just thought ..." He shrugged. It was the same shrug that Bobby had picked up from him over the years.

Kimberly's nose wrinkled a bit and her head tilted. "*Thomas*" she said, and that was all she *needed to* say. In speaking his name, she said all of the things that, after ten years of marriage, could be said in a mere gesture, expression, or word.

Tom sighed inwardly. He knew she hated his caution, his watchfulness. He didn't know, however, whether she hated it because it made her feel incapable of taking care of herself, or because he was showing signs of concern that had remained hidden during two pregnancies and were now coming out during the pregnancy that she did not want.

"Sorry, hon," he said softly.

Her arm snaked out of the shower, her hand reaching toward him. "Could you hand me that brown towel, please?"

He turned and took the towel from its rack and handed it to her. He could hear her begin to dry herself briskly with the thick towel on the other side of the frosty-glassed shower door.

"What time is it?" she asked.

Tom checked his watch. "Few minutes before eight."

"Oh, Jesus, I've got to get the boys off to school. Could you get them started? Get Bobby in here to shower and get Luke a bite to eat. I don't even know if he's out of bed yet."

You're a little slow this morning yourself, aren't you? Tom almost said. But he decided against it, knowing that it would only set Kimberly off. It didn't sound like her mood was a terribly good one, anyway. He walked silently out of the bathroom and down the hall to the boys' room. Luke, sure enough, was still curled up in his bed, a still lump under the blankets.

"Hey, tiger," Tom said quietly, reaching down and gently shaking his son. "Time to hit the deck."

The boy stirred and grumbled and tried to pull his shoulder from Tom's grip and go back to sleep.

"C'mon, kid, let's go."

"I'm tired," came the croaky reply.

"The whole world's tired, tiger, but it's time for 'em to get up, anyway."

Luke turned over on his side and looked up at Tom with sleepy, squinty eyes. "But *you're* gonna go to bed, aren't you?"

Tom chuckled. "Yeah, but I don't lead a normal life. C'mon, get ready for school so you can grow up to be an educated person."

The boy threw the covers back and hung his legs over the side of the bed, rubbing his eyes vigorously. "Are you eddicated, Dad?"

"Sometimes I wonder. Come out to the kitchen and I'll fix you something to eat. Some cereal and toast sound okay?"

Luke nodded and Tom went back out to the kitchen. He could hear the shower running again, so he assumed Bobby was in it. Tom opened the cupboard over the left side of the sink and pulled out the box of Rice Chex and put it on the counter, thinking, simultaneously, about Kimberly and Dr. Hunt. What would Kimberly say if he agreed to back up Hunt's story? *If,* mind you. He still wasn't certain of what he'd seen. But there seemed to be ... something on the floor when he opened the door to ER. Something fast and dark. Like, he thought doubtfully, a shadow.

(Or something black and glistening and gelatinous that moved with incredible speed and bit and made little whipping sounds ...)

Tom mentally slapped the thought away and poured the cereal into a bowl.

Standing up for Dr. Hunt would mean going against Rudy Pazulo, and whoever he might have behind *him,* which would also mean seriously endangering his job at the lab. Kimberly would be pleased as punch about *that.* She would probably say something sardonic, like, "Sounds like a great idea. I'll make a phone call and reserve a spot in the unemployment line for you."

Aside from the obvious complications, there was something else. Dr. Hunt was a great guy and Tom respected him a lot, but he seemed to have quite a knack for getting himself wrapped up in scandal and controversy. It was getting to the point where the fact that he was a good doctor was being overshadowed by the fact that he was a troublemaker. Tom didn't want that to happen to him, even if he were to lose his job at the medical center. He was good at what he did, he knew, and he didn't need some nasty reputation to taint that. He also knew that it would probably be better all the way around if he just kept doing what he did so well and kept his mouth shut.

Luke sauntered into the kitchen, his shiny blond hair sticking out in all directions, his pajama bottoms sagging a bit too low in the crotch. As Luke climbed into the chair, Tom put the bowl of cereal on the table before him, then got the milk from the refrigerator and poured it over the crunchy squares.

"Where's Bobby?" Luke asked.

"In the shower." Tom got out a slice of bread and slipped it into the toaster.

"Can I have a spoon, Dad?"

"Oh, yeah," Tom snapped at himself, opening the drawer and getting out a spoon. As he handed it to Luke, he said, "Sorry. I'm not used to this, I guess."

"'S'okay. Mom forgets, too." He stabbed the cereal with the spoon, holding the handle in his chubby fist, then plunged it into his mouth and chewed heartily, his little teeth clacking a bit against the metal utensil. "Did you work good, Dad?"

"Yep. I worked real good, Luke. Did you sleep good?"

"Yep." He chewed some more as Tom poured him some orange juice. "Dad?"

Tom leaned against the counter with his arms folded across his chest, waiting for the toast to pop up. "Hmm?"

"When you work at night, do you ever see any monsters?"

The question hit him like an eighteen-wheeler and he had to force his mouth not to drop open.

"Do I ever see any ..."

"Monsters. At night."

It's just a six-year-old's question, he thought. *Normal. Typical. He's asked questions like this before.*

(Did you see that?)

Besides, why should he find it disturbing? He hadn't seen any *monster*, for god's sake. He hadn't seen anything. Except maybe a a shadow. But only *maybe*.

(Goddammit! Did you see that?)

Tom stepped over to the table and sat down across from Luke. The chair made a muffled scraping sound on the tile floor as it moved and Tom's foot hit the table's leg, shaking it a bit and spilling a little milk from the cereal bowl. Neither of them noticed, though.

"Why do you ask that, Luke?"

The little boy wrapped his small fingers around his glass and tipped back some orange juice, gulping it loudly. He was in no hurry. After he'd set the glass back down, a little orange juice mustache on his upper lip, he said, "Because Andy Carmichael told me that, at night, after everybody's gone to bed, monsters come out. He says there really are monsters, and at night's when they come out. But I told him that everybody never goes to bed all at one time, 'cause there are people like you who work at night. Right?"

Tom nodded. "That's right." The toast popped up and Tom started just a little.

"He still says they're real, though," Luke continued. "Monsters, I mean. And they come out at night. So I was wondering if you saw any when you worked." He stuffed another heaping spoonful of Rice Chex into his little mouth, never averting his eyes from Tom's, waiting for a reply. When Tom didn't speak right away, though, Luke was patient. He knew his father would say something.

Tom put one elbow on the tabletop and touched the knuckle

of his index finger to his lower lip. He smiled a little and shook his head reassuringly. "No, Luke. I don't see any monsters. All I see are sick people."

"But do you think they're out there?"

Tom stood, stepped around his chair, and walked over to the toaster. He uncovered the butter dish, took a knife from the drawer, and slowly, thoughtfully, began to butter the toast.

"No. There aren't any monsters. Day or night. There are bad people who do bad things, but there are no monsters. Only in books and in the movies, like on 'Creature Feature' on Saturday nights."

"And those are just made up, right? People made up to look like monsters?"

"That's right. And you can tell Andy what's-his-name that I said so, okay? Here's your toast."

Luke reached out and took the toast with a smile. "Okay, Dad." He took a big bite of it, some of the melted butter catching on his lips and glistening.

Tom thought absently, *No adult living eats as lustily as that boy.* But as he watched his son eat breakfast, something tugged at the back of his thoughts.

Monsters.

Bad people who do bad things.

Like Jeffery Collinson. After he had found out who the commotion-causing patient in ER was—after he'd learned that this was the guy he'd read about in all the papers, the guy who'd killed so many people and who had made Tom fear for the safety of his children on the playgrounds and his wife when she drove to Safeway for groceries—he'd stepped over to the bed that held the still form of . the man who had been the object of a two-year-plus police search. Not too close, just close enough.

His fists, bound even in death by the restraints, were balled tightly. His mouth was open; at first it looked random, as if his jaw had just fallen open that way when he died, but after a closer scrutiny, it seemed that he was ready to speak or ready to grin. Just ... ready. His eyes, now glazed, were bulging out of his swollen head, and his wildly mussed hair made him look as though he had a current of electricity passing through him. The yellow, crooked teeth looked dry and Tom half expected the point of a pink tongue to slip out and slide back and forth over them, framed by that almost-grinning, almost-speaking mouth.

Tom did not look very long at Jeffery Collinson.

Perhaps, he thought, *there are monsters. Sort of.*

"How are my men?" Kimberly asked as she came into the kitchen in a furry blue robe with a towel wrapped around her head. Her belly stuck out as if she were hiding something beneath her robe.

"Just fine and dandy," Tom said, his voice beginning to sound tired.

"You almost done with breakfast, Luke?"

"Yep."

"When you are, hit the shower. Bobby's out." She turned to Tom and wrapped her arms around his neck. "How'd work go?"

"Well, we had a little excitement." He gave her a brief account of the incident in ER.

"You mean the killer they've been looking for for so long?" she asked quietly, a bit of awe curling the edges of her voice.

"Uh-huh. But they aren't looking for him *anymore.*" He told her he was going to be on the news that night and she smiled.

"My husband the celebrity. Hey," she said, moving her face a little closer to his, "sorry I kind of barked at you. I'm not feeling so good this morning. As usual."

Putting his hands on her hips, Tom said, "Well, a couple more months and that'll be over." He regretted it as soon as it was out.

Kimberly's smile crumbled and her brow wrinkled a little. "*That* part will be over, you mean," she said with more than a little bitterness. She stepped away from him and went over to the refrigerator.

"I guess," Tom sighed, "I'm going to bed, folks."

"No breakfast?" she asked flatly.

"No. Not hungry. You have a good day at school, tiger."

"Will, Dad." The boy's mouth was full.

Tom roughed the back of Luke's blond head as he walked behind his chair. Passing the bathroom, he wished a good day to Bobby, then went to his own room, took his clothes off, and climbed into the bed from which Kimberly had come a while before.

(That *part will be over, you mean*)

There had been a time when Tom thought Kimberly would come around as the time neared, change her mind about the baby. But she hadn't. If anything, her feelings had gotten worse. At first, she had been pretty restrained about it. The fact that she did not want another baby remained well hidden—outwardly, at least. But Tom sensed it. Now she seemed to want the baby even less than when she'd first learned she was pregnant again. No abortion. That was out of the question as far as she was concerned. As was adoption. She could never live with that, she claimed. And yet, Tom could not shake the nagging fear that, because she felt so negatively about the baby, she might have some sort of ... accident. An accident that wasn't *really* an accident. Like that maybe-not-so-unintentional fall he'd imagined she'd had in the shower a little earlier.

What bothered Tom even more than the fact that she was going to go ahead and have a baby she didn't really want was *why*. She seemed to feel so intensely about it that he couldn't believe it was just the idea of having another mouth to feed and another child to care for that bothered her. It had to be something more. And yet, here she was more than seven months pregnant and they'd not talked about it. Not honestly, anyway. Not the way they needed to.

Humph! And Hunt wants me to chase little black creepy crawlers with him.

Tom rolled over on his side, curled up under the covers, and tried not to think of grinning corpses with bulging eyes.

4 - JULIE

THE MORNING IN ER was fairly uneventful. A cheerleader from the high school in St. Helena came in with a badly twisted ankle and flirted with the doctor on call. An old man from Calistoga brought in his wife, who had given herself a nasty cut with a kitchen knife. The worst came from Rutherford: a little boy who had been attacked by a neighbor's pit bull.

Julie yearned to go outside, even though she knew it was cloudy and cold. Double shifts always wore her out and made her feel claustrophobic; ER had no windows, and the longer she worked, the smaller and more confining it seemed to get. Today there were long slow periods between patients during which ER was totally empty except for Julie and Tony. Christine was supposed to come in and work today, but she got the flu, too, just like Shirley. Carl had stayed over awhile to fill in for her, but they told him to go home. With Dr. Vernon there, they'd told him, they would do just fine.

During those slow, quiet times, Julie sat in the office and chatted with Tony or Dr. Vernon, or she sat by herself and read a magazine. It was at those times that Jeffery Collinson would come knocking on the door of her thoughts.

She thought of the things he'd shouted while lying on the bed under the examination light and she felt the tiniest bit of a chill dance over her scalp. His rantings made her think of her childhood. Not just *think* of it, but actually *feel*, for a moment or two, like a child again. All that screaming about being the Dark Christ had made her think of her grandparents, who had raised her after the death of her parents. They'd been very strict Seventh-day Adventists, her grandparents. They'd warned her often, as a child, of false Christs, servants of Satan posing as the Messiah, and she'd believed them, and in believing, she'd actually felt fear. They'd lived just up the hill above the valley in the little town that was then, and still was, a sort of Seventh-Day Adventist colony, so her grandparents' beliefs had all been confirmed by everyone else in the village, making them even more potent in the eyes of a little girl. Julie had been certain that, one day, someone would come to their door—

—a man, probably in his early thirties, maybe even with old, slightly grown-together holes in his palms and ugly scars on his forehead (they'd always told Julie that these false Christs would be very clever)—and say that he was Jesus Christ and he'd come back to make everything just fine.

As many times as that haunting thought had come to Julie, despite her efforts to keep it away, she'd never decided exactly what she would do in such a situation.

Julie had thought of all these things in a matter of seconds when she'd first heard Jeffery Collinson scream that he was the Dark Christ. He had made her palms break out with a thin sheen of sweat, which she'd wiped off on her white uniform.

What stood out in her mind just as vividly, perhaps even more so, as she sat at the front desk with a cup of coffee by her elbow, thumbing through the latest *Ladies' Home Journal* in the late morning and early afternoon of that Tuesday, was the look in Martin's eyes when Julie dashed out of the office after hearing him raise his voice. He hadn't just raised his voice; Martin was raising his voice all the time while he was working, so it was nothing out of the ordinary to hear him yell, especially when a badly hurt patient was at stake. No, there had been something different in his voice. There had been a touch of fear, of ... maybe it was amazement, or disbelief.

"Did you see that?" she'd heard him shout, his voice squeaking a bit. "Goddammit! Did you *see* that?"

She'd come out and found Martin and Tom standing in the doorway with their necks craning out into the corridor. Then Carl had spoken up and said that Collinson was dead. Everyone had sprung over to the bed and they'd spent several minutes trying to revive him. After they'd found there was no use, Martin had taken Julie's elbow and led her aside, saying, "Jesus Christ, Julie, something came out of him!"

Julie had actually blanched a little at his words.

"Something squirmed out of his nose," he went on breathlessly.
"Martin—"

"Did you *see* it?"

"No, but—"

"It was black, like a worm, and it came right out of his nostril! And, Julie, it..."—he'd held up his hand and there was a thin, red cut across the back of it—"... it cut my hand, it *bit* me." He'd looked at her then, his eyebrows turned downward over the top of his nose, his forehead creased, and the little wrinkles that surrounded his brown eyes looked deeper, like tiny, bloodless cuts. Julie noticed, for the first time, streaks of gray in his finely trimmed beard of rust on each side of his white, tense lips. He was at a loss, a total loss. But even more disturbing was the fact that he suddenly looked much older than he really was. Julie had never seen him that way in the year and a half she'd known him. Martin Hunt was a rock—granted, loud at times, irritable and snappy, but a rock, nonetheless—logical and confident, firm and unshakable. It made Julie very uncomfortable to see him in such a state.

She had put a little bit of disinfectant on the cut and bandaged it nicely for him, and all the while he had been shaking his head, mumbling to himself.

"What the hell *was* it? What could it have been? It came right out of his nose!"

She'd kept her thoughts to herself at that time, knowing that they would only make it worse. She'd thought that he was very tired, a little excited; he'd just lost a patient, after all. He was overworked and under-rested. Perhaps Collinson's rantings had touched something in him

(someone's knockin' at the door)

as they had in her. In any case, she didn't like seeing him that way and it occurred to her then that the best thing for him would probably be a vacation. But she'd decided to wait until he'd calmed down to suggest it to him. Maybe the next day.

Rudy Pazulo had beaten her to it, though. And it had been more than just a suggestion. She regretted not bringing it up herself when she'd first thought of it. It would have been much better coming from her. Maybe if she'd spoken up then, if she'd not worried about sounding skeptical and making Martin think that she didn't believe him, she could have helped avoid the little mess that had arisen from it all. Maybe she could have persuaded him to keep it to himself and not cause trouble.

Do I believe him? she wondered as she set aside her magazine a few minutes before her shift ended. Well, she didn't *disbelieve* him. Martin wasn't the type to see things. He'd seen *something*, even if perhaps it hadn't crawled out of Jeffery Collinson's nose.

"Whatever it was," he'd said to her after things had calmed down that morning, "it's loose in the hospital somewhere, and it could hurt somebody else. Maybe a lot worse than it did me."

As Julie put on her red sweater when it came time for her to leave, she felt the rumblings of her empty stomach and decided to stop by the cafeteria for something to hold her over until she got home. She went to the candy machine and punched the button underneath the Milky Way display after depositing her coins. The candy bar dropped into the tray below, and she bent down and got it. When she stood up again, Tracy Parker was standing at her side.

Tracy was a surgical nurse who always wore just a tad too much makeup and always smelled strongly of perfume. She was the same age as Julie, twenty-seven, and she was very pretty, yet she was unsatisfied with her looks and was therefore always striving to improve them. She and Julie had studied nursing together up the hill at the Seventh-day Adventist college, and they frequently bumped into one another at the hospital. They weren't particularly good friends, though, and if their paths never crossed, Julie would probably make no effort to stay in touch with her. When it came right down to it, Julie didn't really like Tracy Parker.

"Hey, Julie," Tracy said perkily, "what's cookin'?"

Julie smiled as she tore off the end of the candy bar wrapper. "Next to nothing. How are you?"

"Oh, next to nothing, my eye, child," Tracy replied, putting some coins into the vending machine. "I heard about all the excitement this morning." She pushed a button and a Baby Ruth fell out for her. "Don't be so modest. Let's sit down a sec. I want to hear all about it." She stepped over to a table and sat down, looking up at Julie, waiting for her to follow.

I'm too nice, Julie thought as she sat down across from Tracy.

"There's really nothing to tell," she said. "A guy got hit by a car, came into ER, and then he died."

"Oh, come *on*, kiddo, he was a killer! A mass murderer! And worse." She daintily removed the wrapper from her candy bar and took a bite of it, her glossy lips hugging the candy seductively, and, Julie decided, after all these years of *trying* to look seductive, probably quite unintentionally. "I read in the paper today that he was into all kinds of sick shit—bestiality, necro ... necro ... oh, you know, when you fuck a corpse. Stuff like that." She licked some chocolate off her lips, then leaned toward Julie over the table. "I understand," she said deliberately, "that Martin—er, Dr. Hunt—saw something."

"Oh, really?" Julie bit into her Milky Way. Hard.

"Yeah. Something ... gooey. Crawled out of this killer guy, is what I hear. I hear Dr. Hunt really went berserk trying to find the thing, too. Any truth to that?"

"Well, Tracy, you know how it is. Nobody's ever satisfied with the truth, so they have to decorate it a little."

"Yeah, but I hear he's been ... uh ... reprimanded."

Julie began chewing the candy a little harder than she needed to, secretly releasing her slowly building anger on the chocolate bar.

"I hear Rudy Pazulo has ... *asked* ... him to take some time off." Tracy tilted her head a bit and cocked one finely plucked brow. "Zat true?"

"Come on, Tracy, it's not like that. There was a lot of confusion this morning. Some misunderstanding. Martin's very tired and overworked, is all. Don't believe everything you hear."

"Hah!" Tracy snapped a hand in the air beside her face, a sort of tell-me-about-it wave. "Don't talk to me about *overworked*. At least you've got somebody who's young and clear-minded."

Here it comes, Julie thought with irritation.

For the last eight months or so, Tracy had been having an affair with Dr. Roland Hollister, old and near retirement. Given the opportunity, Tracy would complain to *anyone* about the perils of being involved with an aging surgeon. Before Hollister, she'd been sleeping with one of the radiologists, and, before that, another surgeon. Tracy seemed to feel that nurses were obligated to sleep with doctors, and she spoke to other nurses of her affairs as if they were all members of a club. Julie sometimes wished that she was not a nurse, or that Martin was not a doctor, so Tracy couldn't include Julie in the group.

"Sometimes," Tracy went on, still eating her Baby Ruth, "I think Rolly's losing it altogether."

Rolly, Julie thought. *How nauseating.*

"I mean, he's really starting to get scattered, you know? It's kind of scary, him being a surgeon and all. I mean, he forgets things, he repeats himself a lot. He's been looking really tired lately, too. Just the other day, he said to me, he says, 'You know, Tracy, sometimes you get so fed up,' he says, 'that you just want to reach inside your patient and scrape the sucker out. Just because you can.'" She looked at Julie and sort of curled her lips back into a look of disgust. "Not a pretty thought, huh?"

Julie blinked a few times at the horrible idea, taking the last piece of her candy bar from the wrapper, then crumpling up the paper in her free hand.

"I don't know, though," Tracy said. "He's sweet. He gave me these." She reached up and pulled back her full auburn hair to show Julie the tiny diamond earrings she was wearing. "Nice, huh?"

"Very." Julie's mind suddenly turned its back on Tracy and her earrings and she thought maybe she should get some take-out Chinese food and drop by Martin's with it instead of going home. She'd been thinking about him all day and wanted to be with him. She didn't really want to be alone, anyway.

"Yeah," Tracy muttered, fingering one of the diamonds, "I guess I can't complain ... too much. But *you*"—she stabbed the bitten end of the Baby Ruth toward Julie—"you've got it made. Dr. Martin Hunt is a very sharp guy, and pretty damned good-looking, too, if you don't mind my saying. In fact, if you hadn't gotten to him first," she said and giggled girlishly, "I might've taken a shot."

Ho-hum, Julie thought, nearly saying it.

"If Dr. Hunt has been working too hard," Tracy continued, "that can be taken care of. Unfortunately, you can't avoid oncoming senility with a few hours of sleep."

Julie was thinking about how nice it would be to crawl into bed with Martin, surprise him quietly. She finished off the candy bar and dropped the wrapper into the ashtray in the center of the table. "I'm going to hit the road, Tracy. I'm bushed." She pushed her chair back and stood. "I just finished a double shift. Nice talking to you."

"Well, hey, there's no need to rush off so fast like," Tracy said, turning in her chair to watch Julie go.

Oh, yes, there is, Julie replied wordlessly, thinking about eating egg rolls in bed with Martin.

"Oh, wait, Julie!" Tracy called.

Julie turned back to the young woman, trying to hide her annoyance. "Hmm?"

"Do you remember the last time we were together? You promised to give me Randy Sheckley's address, remember? You wouldn't happen to have it with you, would you?"

Randy Sheckley had been a "real piece of work" (to use Tracy's words) from their college days, and Tracy had chased him for two years. But he'd been going with a proper, upright Adventist girl named Janice to whom he'd remained faithful, despite Tracy's advances. Word had gotten out recently, however, that Randy and Janice had divorced, and suddenly Randy Sheckley was once again on Tracy's mind, as she so faithfully reminded Julie each time they were together. Julie *did* have Randy's address (they'd had several classes together and had become good friends) and she *had* promised to give it to Tracy. She decided she wouldn't forget it this time; maybe it would get Tracy off her back.

"I *swear* I'll bring it tomorrow," she promised.

"You gonna be here tomorrow afternoon?"

"Well, I may have to work another double if Shirley doesn't get better."

"Just swing on by OR, then. I'd *really* appreciate it," she said, her voice implying all that she hoped to do with Randy Sheckley once she found him. "See you tomorrow."

Julie turned again and left the cafeteria, thinking once again of those egg rolls as she walked briskly down the corridor toward the staircase. It felt good to be going home to her man.

5 - MEGAN

MEGAN CRAWFORD FOUND it next to impossible to stay awake in study hall. She failed to see the necessity of a period in which she was required to do her studying when she did all of her studying at home in the evenings, at home—where it was *possible* to study. Here it was too quiet—the silence was deadly—and the room, good old 114 with the nameplate on the door that read MRS. WASHLEY, was almost always stuffy and uncomfortable, definitely not conducive to good studying. She preferred to study in her bedroom at home with her cat, Boston, nearby so she could stroke his fur now and then, with music playing on the stereo.

"I do *not* understand," her mother was forever saying, "how you can concentrate on your studies with that music playing."

Megan, however, could not do it *without* the music.

To make study hall even more unbearable, it also happened to be her last period of the day. She spent most of it writing letters to her friend Bonnie in Canada or filling out those self-tests in *Cosmo.*

(What Kind of Lover Are You?)

Sometimes she just stared at the clock, waiting for the bell, as she was doing today. The clock in room 114 was three minutes fast, so two o'clock came around sooner than it was supposed to, making the period seem to last even longer. Only three minutes longer, of course, but study-hall minutes were *long* minutes.

When the bell did ring, Megan closed her biology book, which she'd left open before her to give the appearance of studiousness— Mrs. Washley was very observant, the old battle-axe, so you had to make sure she had reason to think you really were studying—

and stuffed it into her book bag, then left the room with the rest of the students.

"Hey, Megan!"

She'd just stepped into the corridor with her book bag hanging from her shoulder and she turned at the sound of her name. It was Winny Albertson, hurrying toward her while trying to hold a stack of books in her arms.

"Wait a sec!" Once the girl was at Megan's side, they began to walk together. "How's it going?"

"A lot better now that I'm out of there," she replied, jerking her head in the direction of room 114. "How 'bout you?"

"Oh, I'm fine." She dropped one of her books and a few papers fell from it, sliding over the floor.

"Why don't you get a book bag, Win?" Megan asked as her friend bent down to retrieve the book and papers.

"Oh, I don't know. I guess I will someday." She stood and her movement tossed back some of her long black hair. She smiled, her lips held tightly together, something she'd been doing ever since she got her braces, and started walking with Megan again, still juggling the books in her arms. "You got your hair cut."

"Yeah. Got a permanent, too." Megan tossed her head mockingly, like someone in a shampoo commercial, making her dark blond hair swing back and forth above her shoulders. "Like it?"

"Yeah, looks good. How're things going between you and Ross? I heard you guys were ... well, that you weren't talking to each other right now."

"We're not."

Winny's face tightened, her mouth curling into a little O, as if she hadn't really believed the news when she'd heard it and had expected Megan to deny the rumor. "How come?" she asked, her voice breathy with disbelief.

"Oh, lots of things. Mostly, though, because he said he thought we should date other people. You know, not be so serious."

"Gawd, how come?"

"Well, he said he thought we were too *intense*. That was his word."

"But the St. Patrick's Day dance is coming up in a few weeks!" She sounded panicky. "Who's he gonna take if he's not gonna take you?"

"Probably Pam Brewster," Megan said. "I think she's the

reason he wanted to date other people in the first place. Intense, my ass! He just wants to get his hands on those big boobs of hers."

"You think so?"

"Well, doesn't everybody! All the guys on campus have been creaming their jeans since she arrived in January."

"But doesn't this just slay you—the thought of breaking up with Ross? I mean, aren't you really depressed? You guys were so *serious!*"

"We weren't *that* serious, Winny. I mean, we weren't going to get married or anything. Well ... not right away, anyhow."

"But, you two were *the couple* around here."

"Just because he's senior class president, is all. It's no big deal, Winny. Really. *I'm* fine, anyway."

"Oh." Winny was silent for a while as they walked down the locker-lined corridor and neared the front exit. As they went out the door and down the steps to the parking lot, she said, "Hey, you wanna come with me over Margie Withers's place tonight? Her parents are gone for the evening and we're gonna watch some fuck films on the VCR." She let her lips turn upward into a mischievous smile, revealing her shiny braces.

"Ah, I really shouldn't. This is my day to work at the hospital, so I'll have to do my studying this evening. I don't think I'll have time."

"Oh, c'mon. Screw the homework. We've got *Never So Deep* and *Bucking Broncos,* a gay film."

"You mean guys? With each other?"

"Uh-huh," Winny replied with a quick, staccato nod.

Megan frowned a little, but it was an amused frown, even a little interested. "Well, I'll call you. Let me see just how much I have to do. I may just show up. Okay?"

"Sure." Winny started to walk away from her, toward the other end of the parking lot. She gave a little wave, then turned her back.

Megan got her keys out of the pocket of her brown coat and unlocked her dark green Mustang. She got in, started it up, and drove up the hill from St. Helena to the Napa Valley Hospital.

Megan had lied to Winny. Her situation with Ross *was* a big deal, and it *did* upset her. Ross had given her a heart pendant at Christmastime, with the promise that he would always love her. Hokey, maybe, but it meant a lot to her. Now this. She'd thrown the pendant in his face a few days ago when he told her he thought they should back off a little. She regretted that now, not because she wanted the pendant, but because it had made her look silly and immature.

She *wasn't* immature! She had to keep telling herself that because ... well, because Ross treated her like she was, sometimes. Sometimes her parents did, too.

It's not like he's my first love, or anything, Megan thought. *I've had boyfriends before. But Ross is different. He said he wanted to* marry *me!*

Megan found a parking place at the hospital, a small miracle, and went inside, past the information desk in the lobby, and into the office of Volunteer Services.

"Hello, Mrs. Munson," she said to the little black lady behind the desk.

Mrs. Munson looked up from the package she was wrapping and smiled, her dentures clicking quietly. "Hello, there, Megan. Good day at school?"

"There's no such thing," she replied as she removed her coat and hung it on the coatrack inside Mrs. Munson's small closet. She stepped in a bit farther and removed her candy-striper uniform from its hanger. When school was in session, the number of candy stripers dropped severely, and there were so few that Mrs. Munson let them keep their uniforms in her office closet. During the summer, however, there were so many that they had to keep them in a separate closet made expressly for that purpose. "I'm going to go freshen up a little. I'll be right back."

Mrs. Munson smiled and blinked her eyes cheerily, then went back to the package, her slightly clawed fingers working slowly but efficiently.

Megan left the office and turned left into the ladies' room. She hung her uniform on the door of the stall, then turned to the sink, looking at her reflection in the mirror on the wall above it.

Not exactly a Pam Brewster, she thought, *but I can't complain too much.*

Her hair was a sort of dirty blond, which she wasn't so crazy about. But if it didn't shine a whole lot, at least it was full and looked very soft. Her eyes were a pretty blue and were rather round. A boy in the eighth grade had once told her, with a nervously quivering voice, that he'd like to spend a whole Sunday afternoon just staring into those eyes. The memory made her laugh now, but then, just three years ago, she'd lived for weeks off of the remark. Megan thought her lips were her face's strong point. They were nicely shaped, very kissable. Sometimes people thought she was wearing some sort of lipstick when she really wasn't.

She went on to her neck, frowning a bit, wondering if it was a nice neck. She couldn't really tell. She looked at the reflection of her small breasts in the mirror

(Definitely *no Pam Brewster there, kiddo; in fact, there's hardly any Megan Crawford there*)

and wanted to spit, they made her so angry. What the hell were *breasts* but a couple of lumps of fat with little rosy hats on? What was the fascination guys had with them, and what the hell, besides big tits, did Pam Brewster have that Megan Crawford *didn't?*

(*Maybe he just doesn't like you anymore, maybe he's just bored with you and Pam-baby is a little more exciting. Did you ever think of* that, *didja, huh?*)

"He's just an asshole," she hissed at her reflection, *"that's* what his problem is." Realizing that she looked and sounded like a little girl, she turned away from the mirror and changed into her uniform.

She was standing in front of the mirror again, running a brush through her hair, when the door opened and Beth Lim came in. She was a tall, thin Oriental girl with hair that fell nearly to her waist. She was a candy striper, too, but Megan knew her mostly from school. They exchanged greetings and Beth went into the stall.

"Did you hear about what happened early this morning, Megan?" Beth asked, her words accompanied by the rustling of her movements.

"No. Where?"

"In ER." Beth told her what she'd heard on the news that morning.

"God, that's awful," Megan replied, halfheartedly, as she rummaged through her purse for her lip balm. Her lips were beginning to sting and she wanted to keep them from getting too chapped if she could.

"Not so awful. The guy *did* kill over twenty people, you know."

Megan could hear the trickling sound of the girl urinating.

"Know what else?" Beth asked. "Dr. Hunt—you know, in

ER?—everybody's saying he thinks he saw something crawl out of the guy's face. Out of his mouth or nose or something. It was a worm, long and black. Crazy, huh?"

Megan's hand, the lip balm held between her fingers, stopped halfway to her face. Her eyebrows curled together and her forehead wrinkled. She'd worked with Dr. Hunt before, delivering things to ER for him or one of the nurses. Seeing him always seemed to brighten her day; he always made her feel good.

A worm?

"What was it?" she asked.

"Nobody knows. It crawled away. Convenient, huh?" The toilet paper roll began to rattle as Beth unrolled some of it.

"What do you mean by *that?*" Megan asked defensively, turning toward the closed stall.

"Well, just that ... c'mon, Megan, you don't think he really saw something like that, do you? That's crazy." There was more rustling. Then the toilet flushed loudly.

"He must've seen something."

The stall door opened and Beth stepped out, running her hands smoothingly over her uniform. "The guy's just too fast at the mouth, that's all. Remember that thing with Dr. Porter?"

"He was just trying to help his—" Megan stopped abruptly, stepping aside so Beth could wash her hands. She really didn't know Dr. Hunt that well, she just *liked* him. He was so nice to her, and he was ... well, he *was* very good-looking, she had to admit. Very appealing.

Knock it off, she thought. *He's just a nice guy and you're trying to stand up for him, is all.* She quickly applied the lip balm.

(Of course, there was that dream a few nights ago when you licked him all over. Remember that, kiddo? Huh?)

"I guess it is pretty crazy," Megan said quietly, returning the lip balm to her purse. "I'll see you later, Beth." She left the bathroom and went back to Mrs. Munson's office.

Mrs. Munson was on the phone, but she ended the call just a few seconds after Megan came in. She told Megan that the lady in room 307, bed A, needed to be taken to X ray.

Megan caught an elevator in the lobby and punched the button for the third floor. The elevator had apparently just been cleaned because it smelled of some sort of disinfectant. Everything smelled funny in the hospital, but Megan got used to it rather quickly.

It had been her mother's idea that she do volunteer work

at the hospital. Megan had said something, just in passing, about becoming a nurse, like her mother, and the woman had immediately taken in a breath and started talking.

"Well, then, Megan, it's about time you started hanging around the hospital, because nursing isn't all 'General Hospital' and 'Medical Center,' it's real stuff, and if you really want to test your potential as a nurse, then become a candy striper, or some other kind of volunteer. *Then* we'll see what kind of nurse you'll make."

Megan hadn't been too crazy about the idea at first, but she'd found that she really did enjoy the work. The work itself wasn't always enjoyable. Sometimes it was very depressing, in fact, being around so many sick people, people who had lost their minds, who were old and dying. But the fact that she was doing it made her feel kind of good about herself. She was seriously considering nursing now.

Just as long, she often thought, *as I don't have to work with Mother.*

When the elevator stopped, she stepped out and turned right, going through the double doors that led into the geriatric ward. The smell hit her like a gust of wind. It was always there waiting on the other side of those doors. It was stale air that carried the smell of urine and disinfectant with it. And there was something else mixed in, too, something that Megan had never been able to identify. It was sweet, almost a pleasant smell. But there was also something rank about it. It was very weak and sometimes she didn't smell it at all. Whenever she had to spend any time on that ward, though, it usually hit her sooner or later.

It's almost as if you can smell the people in here wasting away, it occurred to her.

Clair wheeled by. She always seemed to be there, riding in her wheelchair up and down the corridor, her wrinkled old face determined. She would get to the double doors Megan had just come through, and then she would turn the chair around and wheel down to the window that looked out on the garden below at the other end of the corridor. Then she would turn around and do it again.

Megan stopped at the nurse's station and told the nurse that she'd come for the lady in 307-A.

"That's Mrs. Webster," the nurse said, pointing across the corridor to the room.

Megan stepped into room 307. Mrs. Rosella Webster was sitting on the edge of her bed, smacking her lips. She was a big woman, a mountain under a multicolored, short-sleeved robe. Huge folds of flesh hung down over her elbows and quivered when she moved, and her lips, moist and rubbery, never seemed to stop moving. Now and then her mouth would fall open and she'd take in a deep breath, then let it out loudly. Her gray hair looked dirty; it clung together in clumps, leaving patches of her scalp open and looking bare.

"Hello, Mrs. Webster," Megan said with a smile, introducing herself and telling the old woman why she was there. There was a wheelchair folded up against the wall by the bed and Megan pulled it out and opened it up. "You want to just sit in here, Mrs. Webster?"

"Take me out of here," the woman said, and her voice startled Megan. It was like the sound the drain in the kitchen sink made when the last of the dishwater gurgled down the pipe. "'Bout time. I hate this room, you know that?"

"Why's that?"

"See her?" Mrs. Webster lifted her massive form from the bed, turned, and lowered herself into the wheelchair, at the same time pointing one fat finger toward the other bed in the room.

A fragile-looking old woman lay in it, still except for the tiny breaths she was taking through her gaping mouth, which looked like it had sort of fallen in on itself. With each breath, she made a little mewing sound. Her wide, foggy eyes stared up at the ceiling.

"All she does," Mrs. Webster said in her rattly voice, "is lay over there and whimper. Whimper-whimper-whimper. That's all she does. Can't get a word out of her." She stopped talking for a moment, but those rubbery lips kept twitching and wiggling. She looked down at Megan, who was adjusting the footrests on the chair. The woman's eyes were reduced to small, wrinkled slits because of the puffy skin that hung down over them from below her eyebrows, and because of her great, round cheeks. The cheeks were pale and pasty, like the rest of her skin. Megan noticed that there was the shadow of a mustache above her upper lip.

"Well," Megan said reassuringly, "I'm sure she's a very sick lady."

"*I'm* a sick lady, *too*," Mrs. Webster gurgled. "Don't know why they don't take care of me."

Megan wheeled the heavy woman out the door and down the

corridor. "You're taken care of, aren't you, Mrs. Webster? They take good care of patients here."

"Not *me,* they don't. I never get enough to eat. They never feed me. Just those little snacks three times a day. I'm *hungry.* And I *never* get enough to eat around here. I get so hungry I could eat that whiner in my room. It'd shut her up, at least."

Megan had to stifle a little laugh. "You wouldn't want to do that, Mrs. Webster."

"They don't keep this place clean, either."

Megan wheeled the chair into the elevator just beyond Three-South and punched a button. She didn't reply to Mrs. Webster's remark.

"This place is just *full* of things," the old lady continued.

"Things?" Megan asked absently.

"Diseases. There are *diseases* crawling all over the place. On the floors and walls, under the beds. Black, ugly diseases."

Megan noticed that Mrs. Webster's hands were clenching and unclenching the ends of the armrests on the wheelchair, constantly moving, just like those moist, rubbery lips.

"Well, it is a hospital. There are a lot of sick people here. It's a lot of work to keep the place clean, but they try." Megan was getting used to these kinds of conversations. Patients were always complaining to her about the hospital and the workers, telling her they were being held prisoner against their will, or that they secretly owned the hospital and were just checking up on its efficiency.

(It's a nice place to visit, but ... et cetera, et cetera)

The elevator doors opened and Megan pushed Mrs. Webster out. When they got to X ray, Megan told the receptionist that Mrs. Webster had arrived. Then she stood before the woman in the wheelchair and smiled.

"I'm going to go now, Mrs. Webster," she said, "but someone will be back to get you when you're done with your X rays."

"Will you come back?" Mrs. Webster croaked.

"I might. If I can."

"Know what? I used to look like you." Those wiggly lips that seemed to have a mind of their own turned up in what seemed to be a bizarre parody of a smile, revealing long, Old teeth. "I used to be pretty, like you."

Megan wanted to say something like, *Well, you're still a handsome woman, Mrs. Webster.* But she couldn't. She simply couldn't. So she just smiled and swallowed the wet lump that was starting to grow in her throat.

(Yes, Mrs. Webster, and someday I may look like you, so I guess I shouldn't complain too much about these little boobs of mine right now, should I?)

"Maybe I'll come visit you, Mrs. Webster," Megan said through her stiff smile.

Mrs. Webster's head nodded and the sack of flesh in which her chin was buried trembled. "Yes, I'd like that. I'd like that." Her smile disappeared and her face suddenly became solemn. "Watch out for those diseases, now, you hear? They're crawling all over the place."

Megan nodded weakly.

"And," Mrs. Webster whispered, trying to lean forward a bit, "maybe you could bring me something to eat."

Megan decided not to tell her that she wasn't allowed to do that, because she wanted to be somewhere else right now. Anywhere else, it really didn't matter. She took one more look into those glistening eyes half buried in flesh, smiled, and left X ray, getting back into the elevator.

6 - HUNT

WHEN SLEEP FINALLY came to Martin Hunt on that morning, it brought with it strange dreams. One of them found Hunt in ER, alone, with the lights down low. He was smoking a cigarette, knowing full well that he wasn't supposed to smoke in the emergency room; but he was doing it anyway. He heard a sound, the sound of feet shuffling over the hard tile floor, and he suddenly noticed that Jeffery Collinson was standing beside him in the shadows. His eyes were bulging and watery, his clothes were dirty and torn, just like before, but the splint on his arm was gone. His arm was still broken, though; it was crooked and lumpy. There was blood on his clothes and he smelled dreadful. He smiled, those dirty, crooked teeth sticking out in all directions, the thumb of one hand hooked in his pants pocket, the other hand holding a cigarette. The cigarette was bent and dirty, with ... was that a ... *yes,* that was a tire track on the cigarette. It had been run over right along with Collinson.

"Hey, Doc," Collinson rasped, "you got a light? I need a smoke. Need t'clear my sinuses. Got something crawlin' around up in my sinuses. Gotta clear it up. You got a light, Doc?"

Hunt took out his Bic, flicked it, and held it up to Collinson's cigarette.

"Gotta be careful, though," Collinson mumbled with the bent cigarette in his lips, "them things bite."

And it had come then—that black, wet-looking thing had poured from Collinson's nostril and wrapped itself around Hunt's hand and wrist, and it just kept coming and coming from Collinson's nose, crawling up Hunt's arm to his shoulder until he could hold his scream in no longer and the dream stopped suddenly.

So did his sleep.

He got up and smoked a cigarette and ate half of a pastrami sandwich that was in a Baggie in the fridge. He'd just popped the last bite into his mouth when the phone rang.

"Martin Hunt," he said.

"Hello, Dr. Hunt," said a pleasant female voice. It sounded as if she was smiling into the mouthpiece of the receiver. "My name is Candice Bentley. I'm a reporter for the *San Francisco Chronicle*. I wanted to ask you a few questions about Jeffery—"

"Collinson, yes, I know," Hunt finished for her. "But there's really nothing I can tell you except that I examined him when he died."

"Did he say anything before—"

"He said nothing that I wouldn't expect from someone in a great deal of pain."

(It's gonna come now)

"Well, is there anything you can tell me about—"

"Look," Hunt interrupted gently, "I'm going to prepare a statement for the press that should answer all of your questions. I haven't even gotten the coroner's report yet. I will pass the information on to you, though, all right? And, Miss ... uh ... Bentley, I'd greatly appreciate it if you not call me at home anymore, okay? Goodbye." He hung the phone up with a sigh.

He wondered, as he went back into the kitchen for a beer, what Candice Bentley of the *San Francisco Chronicle* would have said had he told her what he'd seen, what had *really* happened. He would have if he'd had someone to back him up, someone else who had seen that thing. Someone like Tom Conrad. He'd just popped the tab on the beer can when he heard voices outside his front door.

"—just a friend of Dr. Hunt's. I really can't answer any of your questions."

The front door opened and he could hear several people all speaking at once, but he couldn't make out what they were saying; their words were all jumbled and quickly spoken. He didn't need to understand them, though, to know who they were. Putting the beer down on the counter, he hurried out of the kitchen and into the living room, where Julie was just closing the front door. She twisted the lock on the knob, then turned, her eyebrows bouncing up a little when she saw Hunt. She held a white bag in one arm.

"You're up," she said simply, a little disappointed.

"Are those reporters out there?" he asked her, walking toward the door.

"You didn't know? Good god, it's like a convention in your front yard."

"Jesus! Don't they ever give up?" He turned the knob, found it was locked, and started to fumble with the lock button.

"Uh … Martin."

He looked over his shoulder at her.

She looked him over with a smirk. "It wouldn't look very good for you to face the press looking like that."

He looked down at himself; he was wearing a T-shirt with a faded picture of Beethoven on it and an old pair of gym shorts. He chuckled, dropping his hand from the doorknob. "Yeah. Guess you're right." He walked over to her and took the white bag from her, peeking into it. "This smells suspiciously like food," he said, sniffing theatrically. "Chinese, no less."

"Thought I'd come crawl into bed with you and we could munch out between the sheets." She took off her sweater and tossed it onto the sofa. "I'm not sure I have enough energy *left* to crawl into bed. I'm exhausted."

He stepped over to her and kissed her with a smile. "Then crawl into bed you must. I'll be right in. I'm going to call Tom." He curled the top of the bag over and handed it to her, then turned and went back into the kitchen.

"You mean about this morning?" she asked, following him.

"Uh-huh." Hunt sat down at a little table covered with pads and pens, scraps of paper, some loose change, and a phonebook. The telephone was on the wall beside a little magnetized bulletin board.

"You really think you should push it, Martin?"

He put one elbow up on the table and shrugged. "You know him better than I do. What do you think?"

Julie leaned on the doorjamb and sucked her upper lip between her teeth thoughtfully. "I don't know. He's afraid of rocking the boat. Tom's always been that way about nearly everything. But I suspect he'll have especially strong feelings about this because it involves his job."

Hunt reached up and slowly whispered his fingers through his beard, staring at the phone silently. He wished he'd become better friends with Tom Conrad earlier. They'd certainly been working together long enough to have developed some sort of after-work relationship. It was too late for that now, though. He would have to work with what he had. He reached up and removed the receiver, opening the phonebook with his other hand.

"I'm going to give it a shot," he said decisively. "If he doesn't want to speak up, that'll be fine." He thumbed through the directory. "Well, it won't be fine, really, but I'll have to settle for it. If there's a chance I can get his support, though, I don't want to pass it up."

Julie walked over to the counter, tripping on the rectangular plastic floormat below the sink, almost dropping the bag. "Goddammit! Martin, get *rid* of that thing!" She put the bag down on the counter, moved over behind Hunt, squatting down to his level and putting her arms around his neck. "Can I say something?" she asked quietly.

Hunt turned his head around as far as it would go to look at her. Her voice had a very serious thread running through it. He replaced the receiver and scooted the chair around a bit so he could face her. He patted his thighs and she perched herself on his lap. "What is it?"

Julie looked up at the ceiling for a moment, choosing her words, then back down at Hunt. She put a hand on his neck as she said, "I really think that you should drop the whole thing, Martin."

"You don't believe I saw anything?"

"I think you saw *something*. I just don't think it was exactly ... what you thought it was. Please don't feel insulted by that," she added quickly, squeezing his neck affectionately with her hand. "I'm saying that because I'm afraid you're going to get yourself into trouble. I don't want you to do that."

Hunt almost smiled. Her face glowed with concern. Her eyes were tense, her brow was wrinkled, and she was sucking her upper lip in again. He put his arms around her waist and held her close, resting his head on her shoulder. She felt warm against him, and he felt warm inside for her.

"I don't feel insulted," he assured her. "I'm glad you care enough to say what you think." He leaned back and looked her in the eyes. "But whether or not you understand, and whether or not the shit hits the fan, I *need* to pursue this. If I don't find out what I saw in there, what cut my hand ..."—he shrugged—"... it's gonna eat my insides out. The idea of that thing running loose in a building full of sick people makes me very nervous. So I'm going to call Tom. Maybe he's rested and can remember something about what we saw. I don't know. I'm just going to give it a shot."

Julie smiled, put a hand on each side of his face, and kissed him fully. "I love you," she whispered. She leaned forward again and rubbed the tip of his nose with hers. "Very. Much."

"Yeah, I guess I'm pretty great, huh?"

She stood up, got the bag of food, and left the kitchen, saying, "Don't be long."

Hunt moved back over to the table, ran a finger down a page of the phonebook until he came to CONRAD, THOMAS. He punched the number out on the phone and waited.

"Hello," said a woman's voice. She sounded a little hurried.

A half-second later, Tom's groggy voice said, "Yeah?"

"Um ... hi," Hunt said a little sheepishly. He'd apparently interrupted Tom's wife in the middle of something and awakened Tom at the same time. There were few things he hated worse than calling someone and waking them up. "This is Martin Hunt. Is ... uh ... Tom there?"

"Well," said Tom's wife, "he's in—"

"I'm awake," Tom interrupted, sounding as if he was trying to convince himself as well as them. "I got it, Kim."

She hung up.

"God, Tom, I'm really sorry about waking you."

"No problem, don't worry about it." He cleared his throat and sniffed a few times.

"If you don't feel like talking now, you can call me back and—"

"No, no, I'm up. What can I do for you?"

"Well, I was wondering if you'd like to maybe get together this evening sometime—so we could talk."

"Oh, yeah, that. I haven't really had a chance to think about it much. I thought I'd talk it over with Kimberly ... uh ... see what she thinks. What did you have in mind?"

"I don't know. I thought we could meet someplace for a beer or two. Maybe you'd like to come over here this evening. What do you say?"

"Sure, that sounds good. Let me get back to you in a couple hours."

"Okay. And ... uh ... Tom"—Hunt took in a breath and

let it out slowly, thinking of what Julie had said about Tom—
"sometimes I have a tendency to sound a little ... pushy. I want
you to know that I'm not trying to push you into doing anything
you don't want to do, and if I start sounding like I am, you have
my permission to tell me to put it in a sock."

Tom's chuckle sounded a little like a bullfrog's croak, but it
was good-spirited, nonetheless. "Will do. I'll call you back."

When they hung up, Hunt felt somewhat better about the
whole thing and went to his bedroom to join Julie with a little
smile on his face.

7 - TOM

KIMBERLY WAS ON her hands and knees in the kitchen, cleaning up some mess on the floor. There were large chunks of broken glass scattered across the linoleum. Tom stepped into the doorway and looked down at her.

"Careful where you put your feet," she said. Actually, it was more of a snap. "There's glass all over the damned floor."

"What happened?"

"Oh, those *boys*," she replied, spitting the word from her mouth. "Luke tried to get a bowl of Jell-O from the refrigerator by himself and he dropped it."

Tom sat down at the kitchen table in his robe, rubbing the top of his head absently. "I'm sure it was just an accident."

"Well, of *course* it was an accident." She stopped her scrubbing motions and looked up at him over her shoulder. "But they shouldn't do things like that—they're clumsy, their hands are small, they can't carry big bowls like that around by themselves. Accidents like that shouldn't happen. Luke could've asked *me* to get the Jell-O, but, *no*, he had to do it himself."

Several things came to Tom's mind: *He's just trying to be a big boy, trying to do things for himself. We can get a new goddamned bowl, but he's only going to be six once. We were all that way then and we all made the same kind of mistake now and then. Still do, in fact. Just because he's a little guy—*

But he kept them to himself. He figured he should go as easy as possible if he was going to bring up Hunt and his creepy crawlers.

"Where's Luke now?"

"I sent him to his room."

Tom clicked his tongue softly, wincing a little. "I don't think that was the thing to do, Kimberly."

"Would you rather he stick around and get a beating from me?" Tom rubbed his forehead slowly and methodically with his hand. "How about Bobby?"

"Next door playing."

That figured. Bobby was the outgoing one, the athlete, the social animal. Three years Bobby's junior, Luke was quieter, not as playful or active. He had friends, but he didn't seem to spend as much time with them as Bobby did with his. Luke stayed in the house more, looked at books and listened to music. He asked more questions and seemed to be more thoughtful than Bobby. Tom thought how the poor guy must be feeling, exiled to his room for a simple little accident. He would go see him when he was through talking with Kimberly.

"You really shouldn't be doing that, hon," Tom said, getting up from his chair. "Let me."

"Oh, Tom, it's only a little Jell-O, for heaven's sake. Don't worry." She got up the last of it and struggled to her feet. Tom held out a hand, but she ignored it.

"I'll get these pieces up," Tom said, carefully stepping around them and bending down to pick up the larger ones. He tossed them into the trash under the sink, then got the broom out of the little utility closet next to the refrigerator and started sweeping up the tiny glistening specks.

"What did Dr. Hunt want?" Kimberly asked, washing her hands.

"He just wanted to talk."

"*Talk?* About what?"

"Well, actually, he wanted us to get together and talk. This evening."

"Why? Are you two becoming chums or something?"

Tom silently swept the tiny slivers of glass into the dustpan, then put the broom back in the closet and set the dustpan up on the counter carefully. He turned to Kimberly and, motioning to the table, said, "Have a sit, hon."

Kimberly sat down slowly, never really averting her eyes from Tom, suddenly looking very suspicious. She'd just dried her hands and they looked red against the very puffy blue dress she was wearing. "What is it?" she asked, her tone less irritated and more interested, even cautious.

Tom sat down across from her and carefully explained every

detail of his experience in ER. He told her how Hunt wanted very badly to get his, Tom's, support.

"You did see it, then?"

"Well, no, I ... well, I don't know, really. That's one of the problems. I just. Don't. Know. I think I saw ... something."

"Well, that's better than nothing. You could at least speak up for him. You've always told me how much you think of Dr. Hunt. You might be able to help him."

Tom took in a deep breath and drummed his fingers on the tabletop a few times, preparing himself for her reaction to what he was about to say. "If I do, though, I might lose my job."

"*Lose your job?*" She put her hands on top of the table and splayed her fingers, pressing her palms down hard. "For god's sake, Thomas, how can you even think of doing it, then?"

"Like you said, Kim, I like Hunt. Always have. Most of the doctors over at the hospital ... hell, most doctors *period* ... are pricks. He kind of stands out. And, like I told you, I *think* I might have seen *something.*" He stood, tossed his arms outward helplessly, then let them slap to his sides, all in one smooth motion. "I don't know what to do."

"Well, it seems to me," Kimberly said flatly,

(Here comes the smart-ass remark we've all been waiting for)

"that the fact that you might lose your job over it would decide it for you."

"That's what I thought, at first. But I've been thinking about it and—"

"And you've decided that being able to eat three times a day maybe isn't that important, huh?"

Tom sat down again and propped both elbows on the table, folding his hands under his chin. "Kimberly," he said levelly, trying to control his voice, "I'm discussing this with you. I'm trying to get your opinion. Now, whatever it is, is it necessary to give it to me in a manner befitting a bad nightclub comedian? Would you rather I just make my decision without at least talking about it with you?"

She took her eyes away from him for a moment, looking down at her lap. "You're right," she said softly. "I'm sorry, Tom. But that ... well, it scares me. The thought of losing your job ... well, *one* of us has to work, and ... well, with the kids, of course, I ... I certainly couldn't go back to work."

Tom bit down lightly on his tongue. It was easy to take that remark as a jab of some sort, but he tried to tell himself that she was trying, honestly trying.

"I know, hon. I ..."—he shook his head, reached over, and took her hand in his—"... I guess it would be best if I just kept my mouth shut."

"Is there anything you could to do help him without ... well, without getting yourself into trouble?"

"Maybe. I'll ask him. I'm supposed to go over to his place this evening and talk about it."

Kimberly lifted his hands to her lips and kissed them briefly, then smiled at him. "It's the thought that counts, Tom. At least your heart's in the right place."

"Yeah. Guess so. I'm gonna go call him." They both stood at the same time.

Something crunched softly under Kimberly's shoes. "Damn!" she hissed under her breath, searching the floor carefully for stray bits of glass. "Sometimes I could just *kill* those boys."

Quietly cringing inside at his wife's thoughtless remark, Tom left the kitchen, his hands buried in the baggy pockets of his robe, and started down the hall to the bedroom. Just as he started to turn and go through the bedroom doorway, Tom heard the soft, muffled sobs of his son farther down the hall. He continued until he came to the boys' room. Then he tapped lightly on the door with his knuckles.

"Who-zit?" Luke asked through his poorly hidden sobs.

"It's your dad, tiger. Can I come in?"

"Guess so."

Tom went in, softly closing the door behind him. Luke was curled up on his bed with his shirt off, crumpled up between his two little hands. He had his back turned to the door. Luke seemed very small on his bed, in the shadow of the upper bunk. Tom went over and sat on the edge of the bed, careful not to hit his head on Bobby's bed. He put his hand on Luke's head and caressed his blond hair. "What's doin', tiger?"

Luke just sniffed loudly in reply.

"How come you've got your shirt all balled up like that?"

He sniffed again. "Got mad, I guess."

"Because of Mom?"

He silently nodded his head clumsily against his dampened pillow.

"Well, that wasn't a good thing that happened, I guess, but she didn't really mean to hurt your feelings, Luke."

The boy suddenly turned to face his father. His nose glistened and his eyes were puffy and red. "If she didn't mean it, then why did she call me a clumsy rug rat? Huh?"

Tom found his lips puckering of their own free will, as if he had bitten into something terribly sour. "Remember, Luke, when we talked about the baby Mommy is carrying in her tummy?"

He nodded, reaching up to swipe the back of his hand across his nose.

"Well, remember how I told you it is with mommies carrying babies in their tummies, how they sometimes get really cranky, like you used to when you needed a nap? Well, sometimes they say things they don't mean. That's what your mom did today. She didn't really mean it."

Luke shifted his position until he was half sitting with his back propped against two pillows, his shirt still balled up between his hands. His face was very tight, clenched with concentration. He looked as if he were trying to make a decision.

"What are you thinking, tiger?"

The boy looked up at his father, his lower lip tucked outward just a bit. "I dunno. I was just thinking. About how Mom ..."

Tom tilted his head, waiting. "How Mom what?"

"'Member we talked about monsters this morning?"

"Uh-huh."

"Well, today, when Mom was screaming at me, I ... I thought she was a monster."

(lions and tigers and bears, oh, my)

Now, why had that silly thought suddenly popped into Tom's head? He found himself picturing the four of them—himself, Kimberly, Bobby, and Luke—on Halloween two years ago. Tom had thought it would be fun if he and Kimberly dressed up and went trick-or-treating right along with the boys. Kimberly hadn't been crazy about the idea, but the boys were so enthusiastic that she'd decided to go along with it. They'd all agreed to dress as characters from *The Wizard of Oz*. Luke wanted to be the Cowardly Lion, Bobby the Tin Woodsman. Tom decided he would make an ideal Scarecrow with his long, skinny body. And, of course, Mom was elected to be Dorothy. Kimberly spent a number of very irritable days making the costumes, and when she finally got to her own, the sewing machine broke, she couldn't find the right material, and she wasn't able to find an appropriately braided wig. So she took the easy way out: she tossed together a few pieces of black material, made herself a paper hat, slapped on a little makeup, carried a broom, and went as the Wicked Witch of the West.

Tom and the boys had skipped down the road arm in arm, chanting, "Lions and tigers and bears, oh my! Lions and tigers and bears, oh my!" Meanwhile, Kimberly, in an unusually good mood after all the fuss over the costumes, had run circles around them with her broom saying things like "I've got you now, my little pretties!" and "Give me those ruby slippers!" They'd all had fun, although it really wasn't as nice as it could have been without Dorothy along.

That seemed to Tom a strange thing to come to mind all of a sudden. It should have been a pleasant memory, it should have brought a little smile. But now it seemed … dark. It didn't feel comfortable anymore, that memory of Kimberly darting in and out of the bushes and shadows with her pointy black hat and broom.

(I've got you now, my little pretties!)

"Your mom's not a monster, Luke," Tom said, thinking he'd been silent far too long, lost in thought. "That's not a very nice thought, and you should try not to think of it. Even if there were monsters—"

He was going to say, —*your mother isn't one of them.* But, for some reason, he couldn't. His mouth stopped moving, his jaw closed, and his tongue froze. He started to frown, but forced it back.

"There are no monsters, Luke, and your mother loves you dearly. Got that?"

Reluctantly, he nodded.

"Now, I'll bet you an ice-cream cone at Swensen's that your mom is gonna be in here later on to give you a big hug and kiss, and she'll probably make you some more Jell-O. Now, until then, I want you to try to think some good thoughts, okay?"

"I'll try," he said in a broken voice.

Tom leaned forward and kissed Luke on the forehead, then stood and headed toward the door.

"Dad?"

He turned back to his son. "What, tiger?"

"I know you're trying to make me feel better, Dad. But sometimes you talk to me … well, like I'm a little kid still. I'm *six,* Dad. Okay?"

Tom held back his chuckle with tightly clenched lips and nodded. "Okay, Luke. I'll try to remember that." He went to his own room then to call Hunt. He decided that, after he hung up, he would go tell Kimberly that she was to make up with Luke. Tom didn't want to lose his bet.

8 - MEGAN

ONE OF THE things Megan hated most about working in a hospital was the windows. They were all made with tinted glass, so it always looked darker outside than it really was. Clouds had been gathering all day and now they were growing dark; it looked like night outside through those tinted windows.

Megan had nearly twenty minutes before her four hours of volunteer work were up. She put in eight hours a week, more than most were her age while school was in session. As long as she was able to keep up with her homework, she didn't mind. Those four hours usually went by pretty slowly on Thursdays, though, because she and Ross always got together on Thursdays for—

Well, that was probably over with, so why think of it now. And this was Tuesday, anyway, so Megan tried to keep her mind on her work, which, at the moment, was delivering a stray wheelchair to the geriatric ward. The chair was a temperamental one; the little wheels in front had minds of their own and were frequently veering off into the wrong direction.

Two nurses were walking rapidly down the corridor toward Megan. They hardly seemed to notice her, they were so deeply involved in their conversation.

"Anyway," said the shorter of the two, a round little lady with short graying hair, "the guy, as you know, turned out to be the killer the police have been chasing for so long. The one who's killed all those women and girls. Sliced their throats and stuff. Well, Dr. Hunt was on duty, and I guess he took care of him ..."

Her voice trailed her down the corridor, and the other nurse, a tall, gaunt woman who gave Megan the impression that she was probably younger than she looked, listened intently.

The morning's incident in ER seemed to be the talk of the hospital. Megan wondered if everyone was talking about the story Beth had told her in the bathroom, about the black-worm thing Dr. Hunt had supposedly seen crawl out of the killer. Megan hoped not. She'd been thinking about it a lot since she'd spoken with Beth, and she didn't like the idea of the hospital buzzing about Dr. Hunt again, like they had over that business with Dr. Porter. Why the hell couldn't they just let him alone? He didn't deserve the treatment all the busybodies in the hospital gave him. And Napa Valley Hospital was full of *those*, to be sure. Yes, she'd been thinking about Dr. Martin Hunt a lot today.

(Hey, how 'bout that dream, kiddo, so vivid you could not only feel his skin with your tongue, but you could taste it, nice and salty, and you could smell his musky odor, and if you think about it, kiddo, you can almost taste and smell him right now, can't you?)

She'd had the dream more than once. Not that she minded. It was very pleasant. So pleasant, in fact, that waking up was a disappointment. One time, she'd actually awakened smacking her lips.

Megan knew it was ridiculous. Like a grammar-school girl having a crush on her homeroom teacher. It was a waste of energy, but ... well, it was sort of involuntary, like breathing. He was such a nice guy. He seemed so sensitive and tender, as schmaltzy as that sounded. Those twinkling eyes and that cuddly, bearded smile made him *look* the way she wanted Ross actually to *be*: caring and honest, as if he could make her feel like she were the only girl in the world. But he was probably nothing at all like she imagined him to be.

(But, oh, wouldn't it be fun finding out!)

Megan was suddenly jarred from her thoughts by the realization that her renegade wheelchair was heading straight for the wall. She quickly steered it back on course, conjuring a vision in her mind of an orderly with a flashing red light on his head, hurrying up behind her, telling her to pull over, then asking to smell her breath. She was smiling at that thought when she pushed the chair up to the nurses' desk in Geriatrics.

"Hi," Megan said to the tall black nurse. "Somebody said you needed a chair up here?"

"Oh, yeah," the nurse replied, getting up from the desk. "Thanks a lot." She took the chair and wheeled it a little farther down the corridor, but Megan paid her no further attention. She was looking at something else: room 307.

The door was shut now. Megan wondered what Mrs. Brewster was doing, if she would be intruding if she were to drop in for a short visit before going home. The old lady had specifically asked for her to stop by. Megan stepped forward decisively, held her hand out, and pushed the door of room 307 open.

All the lights in the room were out and the shades on the two windows were pulled. One shade was not quite pulled all the way down, and a bit of dim light was able to push its way in through the smoky pane. As soon as she stuck her head in, Megan looked to the right at Mrs. Webster's bed, but the woman was not there. There was a large indentation in the mattress where the woman usually was, but the covers were pulled back, and the bed was empty.

"Mrs. Webster?" Megan whispered. She didn't know why she was being so quiet, but there seemed to be something about the room that called for hushed tones, cautious moves. Maybe it was the darkness, maybe the fact that the room was quite warm and the air very stale. Maybe—

Whump

Megan's shoulders jerked at the sound, the muffled voice. She looked over at bed B, the bed with "the Whiner" in it, as Mrs. Webster had called her. There stood the woman's massive frame; Mrs. Webster was standing beside the Whiner's bed, her back turned to Megan. She was stooped forward a bit, and she seemed to be doing something.

Megan stepped into the room and let the door swing shut behind her. "Mrs. Webster, I don't think you should be—" Megan stopped speaking and took a step forward, the skin on the back of her neck suddenly feeling too tight. *What the hell is she thing?* Megan wondered.

Mrs. Webster had her head bent forward, and it was moving, up and down. Her arms were moving, too, the great folds of flesh that hung from them jiggling with every motion. They seemed to be holding something up, lifting something, then lowering it, lifting, lowering. Then Megan saw. It was the Whiner's arm Mrs. Webster was holding. Megan could see the frail little woman's bony hand hanging limply from the arm that Mrs. Webster was suspending. And then Megan heard.

Chewing. Noisy, sloppy chewing.

The chewing stopped, Mrs. Webster's head bent down, her arms raised, lifting the Whiner's arm.

(I never get enough to eat)

Then there was a little jerking motion, and Megan heard something else. A soft tearing sound. Then more chewing. It still didn't quite make sense to her because the thing that seemed so obvious couldn't possibly be happening, could it?

(Dear God, please don't let her be doing that, please God, not that)

"Muh-Mrs... ." Megan had to stop and swallow. Her throat made a dry clicking sound and her hand automatically lifted to touch it. "Muh-Mrs. Webster?"

The big woman lowered her roommate's arm and turned to look over her fleshy shoulder at Megan. And to smile. She dropped the skinny arm and turned her whole body around

(Jesus Christ what's on her lips what's that stuff on her mouth that dark stuff what is it what is it)

and took a step toward Megan, still chewing, but not quite as noisily because now she was smiling, too, happy to have a guest. Those thick, rubbery lips worked furiously, trying to maintain the smile and keep the chewing going, too, and the tip of her tongue

(dear God in heaven what's in her mouth what is she chewing on that could be sooo red)

peeked out from between those glistening lips to catch a tiny speck of something that she'd missed as she said, "Did you bring me anything to eat, honey? Did you?"

Megan's hand clapped loudly over her mouth and her shoulder jerked as she fought to hold down her gorge because she'd gotten a glance—just a tiny glance, but it was enough—of the Whiner, lying in bed behind Mrs. Webster.

The poor woman's glassy eyes were wide and her mouth was opening and closing, opening and closing, with even more of a collapsed look to it now than it had before because *now* the woman was in a great deal of pain, Megan was sure, because Megan had gotten just a glimpse of the Whiner's left arm, the arm that Mrs. Webster had been holding, the arm that really wasn't much of an arm anymore ...

"I get so hungry in here," Mrs. Webster continued, taking a step forward. She had no slippers on and her feet were very broad and calloused, her toes were very fat and lumpy. "They never feed me enough in here, so I hope you brought me something to eat." She chewed a little more as she continued toward Megan, then smiled again. "You bring me anything, honey?"

"Nuh-nuh-noooo," Megan said into her palm, but it was only a whisper. No matter how hard she tried, she could only whisper, because everything was starting to move and turn and spin, and she staggered back several steps until she could feel the door at her back. "Geh-back, away, get away, away—" She put one hand behind her and began to feel for the handle of the door, but it was very difficult because it seemed her hands had no more feeling in them, just a whole lot of sweat that was making them very slick and sticky.

An ever so tiny whine came from the frail old Whiner in bed B as her collapsed-in mouth worked and worked like the mouth of a desperate fish.

And Mrs. Webster just kept coming, always looking as if her great body was about to topple over because she just wasn't very good on her feet. Her lips kept wiggling, smiling, chewing, licking, speaking: "Didn't you bring me *anything*, honey, anything at *all*, like a nice little *treat?*"

Megan's hand wrapped its numb fingers around the metal handle on the door, and then she realized that she would have to step forward in order to pull the door open, and that would bring her a step closer to Mrs. Webster and the little snack she was just finishing up so loudly and so sloppily, but she really had no choice because she *had* to get out of there, so she stepped forward, just one step, one safe and necessary step, keeping one hand firmly on her mouth, the other tightly wrapped around that door handle, because wouldn't it be awful if her hand slipped and the door closed again just as big old Mrs. Webster got close enough to reach out and—

The door was open and the light from the corridor was flooding into the horrible, dark, deadly room and Megan could no longer stand on her feet because her legs were no longer under her control. They were shaking, convulsing, and she fell to the mercifully cold floor and then things *really* began to spin and rock and dim, but just before the blackness came and just before all the sounds were silenced, Megan heard one final thing: the sound of glass shattering inside room 307 and the ragged, fading scream of the pasty-skinned, fat Mrs. Webster.

Then Megan passed out, before she was able to utter even a whimper.

9 - HUNT

AFTER TOM'S RETURN phone call, Hunt and Julie ate some of the Chinese food she'd brought, made love, ate some more, made love again, and read their fortunes. Then Hunt showered and dressed. Julie, however, stayed in bed and slept.

Awhile later, Hunt turned on the television in the living room and watched the news long enough to see brief interviews with Officer Birney, Carl, Julie, and a glimpse of Tom. The reporters asked some rather silly questions.

"What were the killer's last words?"

"Did Collinson say anything regarding his victims or the murders he committed?"

None of them asked any real newsy questions. It was all *National Enquirer* stuff. Oh, well, if that's what people wanted to read, it was okay with Hunt.

Tom said he would come over around seven for a couple of drinks. Hunt tidied up the living room, which he'd allowed to get rather messy. Usually, Julie cleaned things up for him—she insisted on it—but she'd been pretty tired these days. Julie never seemed to get sick, and she was about the only employee of the medical center who hadn't come down with the flu that was going around, so she'd been filling in for others, doing double shifts, and generally working her ass off. After cleaning up, Hunt sat down with a beer and a copy of the new Asimov and read until the doorbell rang.

When he let Tom in, he saw that the reporters, for the most part, had gone. The few remaining had retreated to cars parked beside the road in front of the house. He gave Tom a beer. Then they sat down in the living room, Tom on the sofa and Hunt in his favorite old rocker. Tom wasted no words.

"Look, Dr. Hunt," he said slowly, "I realize that you need someone to back you up on that ... well, what you saw. I've given it a lot of thought, and I did see something. I don't know what, though. But I—"

"That's okay," Hunt interrupted excitedly, leaning forward and pointing at Tom with the hand that held his beer. "Just the fact that you saw something is good. I just need—"

"Wait. I'm not finished."

Hunt stopped speaking and wrapped his fingers around his beer can a little tighter, anticipating Tom's next words. His heart sank; he'd thought, for a moment, that Tom was going to help him.

"I'm afraid, Dr. Hunt, that I'm just not in a position to speak out right now. My wife is pregnant with our third child and ... well, I can't afford to put my job on the line, which, I think you know, is what I'd be doing. Pazulo is pretty upset by the whole thing. I don't need to tell you that."

Hunt bowed his head and stared at his lap for a few moments. He was on his own. He realized that he probably looked very disappointed, so he tried to compensate for it by looking back at Tom and smiling. "I understand, Tom. No problem."

"Wait a minute I'm not backing out altogether. I'd like to help somehow. I mean, if I can stay anonymous, I'd like to do whatever I can. Whatever you saw ..." —Tom closed his eyes for a second, as if regretting his words—"... whatever *we* saw, I mean, should be identified."

Hunt nodded, sipping his beer. "That's what I've been saying all along, but nobody will listen. Even Julie thinks I should keep my mouth shut and my nose clean."

"Well, maybe you can do it without getting into any trouble, without being public about it. Know what I mean?"

Hunt stared at his beer can, feeling the beginning of a headache. How could it be done? Where would he begin? He didn't even know what he was looking for. "I know what you mean. But I don't know what to do."

Tom leaned back on the sofa, relaxing a little, as if a weight had been lifted. He drank some beer, then scratched the back of his neck with his hand. "Well, let's see. You say the thing came out of Collinson's nose?"

"Right out of his left nostril. He was just lying there, rattling on a bunch of nonsense when this—"

(It's gonna come now)

The words were clear to Hunt, as if they'd been spoken rather than simply thought, and he stopped, mid-sentence. His head tilted to one side and his brow furrowed.

(It's gonna come and dying won't matter, won't make a difference)

Hunt put the beer between his legs, leaned forward with his elbows on his thighs, and put his palms on his cheeks, rubbing his face thoughtfully.

"What?" Tom asked, "What is it?"

"I don't know. I was just thinking of something Collinson said. He was going on about being the Dark Christ, chanting some stuff I couldn't make out. Then he said, 'It's coming and dying won't matter, won't make a difference.' Like he knew he was going to die, like he *expected* it."

"Do you think he meant anything by it? He sounded pretty crazy, from what I heard."

"I don't know. It just seems odd that that thing came out of him at about the same time he died. I mean, it kind of goes along with what he said, you know?"

Tom finished the beer and crushed the can in his hand loudly. "You said he was chanting something. You couldn't make it out?"

"Sounded like some kind of foreign language."

"Was it familiar to you at all?"

"Uh-uh. But he said something about the Second Key. Something about, uh ..." Hunt tapped his bearded chin with an index finger, trying to remember. "Something about the 'great spawn of the worms of the Earth,' I think. I don't know. He said something about Satan, too: 'The All-Powerful manifestation of Satan'—that was it."

Tom said something about its all sounding very strange, but Hunt didn't really hear him because his mind was suddenly racing. What had Collinson been talking about? Did it have anything to do with the creature that had slithered out of his nose?

Why should it? he thought, annoyed at his sudden excitement. *But, then, why shouldn't it? It's all pretty crazy, but just why the hell shouldn't it fit together?*

Tom was speaking again.

"Pardon me?" Hunt said.

"I said that if there's anything I can do to help you, as long as I can do it, well, you know, quietly, please let me know."

"Oh, sure thing, Tom. Appreciate your offer."

Hunt was very tempted to say, *Fine, buddy, tippy-toe around and don't make waves, but if one of those suckers comes up and bites your ass, don't come running to me.* He realized that was harsh, though, and chided himself for the thought. Tom had been nice enough at least to offer his help. Hunt decided to accept the offer and stay off the guy's back.

"Give my regards to your wife, Tom," Hunt said with a smile, taking his beer in hand and standing up in front of his guest.

Tom stood, too, looking a bit flustered and confused.

"I'd like to meet her sometime. Your kids, too." Hunt started toward the front door and Tom followed uncertainly. "Maybe we can all get together sometime. If the weather gets a little better, maybe you could come over here for a barbecue. Julie loves barbecues." He opened the front door, reached out, and shook Tom's hand. "I think we could have a lot of fun together. Thanks for dropping by, Tom. I really do appreciate it. Take care."

"Sure. You, too." Tom stepped out the door and Hunt shut it behind him.

Hunt turned his back to the door and leaned against it, scratching his beard absently. *That was rude,* he thought. But he didn't really care because his mind was suddenly spinning like a top. Things that Collinson had said were repeating themselves over and over again in Hunt's mind. He was looking for something— one little thing—that would link Collinson's words and actions to the thing that Hunt had seen. Something that would confirm his vague suspicion that they were connected. Part of him wanted badly to find that link so there might be some explanation for what he had seen.

Another part of him, however, didn't. Because, for some reason he couldn't put his finger on, he was afraid of what he would find.

10 - KIMBERLY

"GODDAMMIT, BOBBY! HOW many times have I told you to wipe your feet before you come into the house?"

Kimberly had been stacking the dishes in the dishwasher when she heard the front door open and the sound of young voices, Bobby and his friend Keith. They had rumbled through the living room and into the kitchen. When she looked down, she saw the muddy footprints they were tracking in behind them and she became furious. She leaned against the dishwasher and put one hand on her forehead, closing her eyes with dread when she imagined the living room carpet. When she snapped at Bobby, both boys froze in place, looking at her with mouths open.

"Look at this," she continued. "Just *look* at this! Mud all over the ..." She smelled something rank and sniffed a couple of times just to be sure. "Dog shit! That's dog shit, Bobby!" She pointed a finger at the prints on the floor and looked at Bobby, waiting for him to speak. Finally, she said, "Clean it up. Right now."

Keith said, "I can help if—"

"You'll have to go home now, Keith," Kimberly said. "You boys shouldn't be out this late, anyway. It's nearly eight o'clock."

"See you later," Bobby said.

Keith turned and left with his head bowed.

"You didn't have to yell at us, Mom," Bobby said softly, getting a rag from under the sink.

"Bobby," she said, her voice still trembling, "I have told you and told you to wipe your feet before you come in. If you got this shit all over the carpet ... I'm just sick of cleaning up after you kids, that's all. Do you understand me?" Her voice was beginning to raise and she finally spat, "*Sick* of it! You're old enough to clean up your own messes. In fact, you're old enough not to make them in the *first* place!" She looked down at Bobby; he was on his hands and knees, trying to clean up the mess, but he was only making it worse. "Go to your room," she demanded quietly.

Bobby looked up at her with wide eyes and said, "But I'm not fin—

"You obviously can't *clean up* messes as well as you can *make* them. Just go to your room, Robert." After Bobby left, sniffing quietly, trying to hold back his tears, which Kimberly strongly ignored, she put the last dish in the dishwasher, then carefully bent down to get the cleaner from under the sink, when she felt it coming. The bulge began in the pit of her stomach and quickly rose as it got bigger, making it almost like a cramp, but it really wasn't a pain, it was a *feeling*, a feeling she couldn't control once it started. Anticipating the tears that would come very shortly, she backed herself toward the kitchen table and sat down. She buried her face in her hands with her elbows on the tabletop and began to sob, quietly, though, so she wouldn't attract the attention of the boys.

Those poor boys, she thought. *Having to put up with me for a mother.*

This always happened after an outburst, the uncontrollable sobbing. But her temper was uncontrollable most of the time, too. She hated herself after blowing up like she had to Bobby. And in front of his friend, no less. She wondered if Keith went home and told his mother that Mrs. Conrad threw temper tantrums. That's all they were, she realized. At the moment they hit her, they always felt justified; triggered by some mess made by the boys or something they'd broken, they always seemed necessary at the time. She felt that she was going to teach the boys a lesson this time. But all she accomplished was a lot of yelling. Then, afterward, she always realized that her outburst was ridiculous. Bobby and Luke were actually good kids. When she thought about it, she realized that they never really did anything to warrant her shouting spells.

And, god, the looks in their eyes. That's what always got her, the way they looked up at her while she was yelling at them, saying the horrible things that always seemed to roll out of her mouth like gumballs out of a jammed penny gum machine, the names she called them, the way she made them sound worthless. Afterward, she would play it back in her mind and sometimes she would even see it from their side, and she would realize how she must make them feel: like their mother didn't have an ounce of love for them. But that wasn't true! She loved them dearly. At least, as dearly as she could. Somehow, though, she just didn't seem able to love them as much as she always thought she would. Kimberly had gotten pregnant before she and Tom were married. They had planned on getting married, anyway, so they just did it a little sooner. The baby had been stillborn. They were both heartbroken, but Tom had been even more crushed than Kimberly. For some reason, she'd found it rather easy simply to take the loss in stride. Tom wanted to try again. Kimberly was very reluctant, though; Tom had thought it was because of the loss of the first baby, and she'd allowed him to think that because it had been an easy explanation. She only hinted at the real reason she was afraid to have a baby: Kimberly didn't think she would ever make a proper mother. When they had approached the matter one evening, Tom had said, "Honey, I've seen you with kids and you're a natural! Don't be silly! I want a boy, how 'bout you?" His smile had been so warm, so hopeful, and, underneath all that, so pleading.

They had Bobby and things went pretty well at first. He was such an adorable baby, as all babies seemed to be in the eyes of their parents. He was quite an addition to the house. But after a while, the novelty

(Novelty? *For god's sake, how could you ever think of him that way? He's your son, not a Pet Rock or some rare tropical fish!*)

wore off, and she found herself knee-deep in filthy diapers and regurgitated baby food; her sleep was frequently interrupted, and as Bobby got older, what he didn't break he put into his slobbering mouth.

Of course, the addition of a son to their family required Kimberly to stay home, so she had to quit her job. She'd been working as an auditor, gathering the experience she needed to get her CPA degree. Of course, she'd been studying for the CPA exam, too, and, for a while, had hoped to keep that up, even though she was unable to work at the time. That was soon dropped, too.

She'd become a full-time mother.

"I'd like to have another baby," Tom had said one day, quite out of the blue. "I think it would be best for Bobby. He shouldn't grow up without a brother or sister. It would do him good. Us, too, I think. So I'd like to have another."

"Go ahead," she'd replied nonchalantly. "Have another I don't mind. It's your turn, anyway. I've already had one. Well, two, actually. But only one successfully."

"Aw, hon, are you still worried about that?" he asked, putting his hands on her shoulders. She remembered that, during that time, their sex life had taken a dip. Caring for the baby took from her any energy she'd ever had left over for lovemaking, so they'd been sorely lacking. She also remembered that, on that particular day, the feel of his hands on her shoulders had been very stirring, just that little bit of pressure in such an unlikely place. And she'd started to cry, just like she was crying now at the kitchen table, with great, wracking sobs that made her hiccough loudly. Tom had taken her in his arms, then, a dark look of worry suddenly clouding his face. "What is it, babe?" he asked in the lulling tone he used to do so well. He never seemed to speak in that tone much anymore.

"I don't know," she'd sobbed, "I just ... I just don't think ... I don't think I'm much of a mother to Bobby."

"Oh, god, honey, not *that* again! You know you're a good mother, as well as I do. Bobby's crazy about you. Sure, you have bad days; everyone does. I bet even Mr. Rogers yells once in a while. He just does it off camera."

Sure, she'd thought, *you think that because you know only what you see, you don't know what goes on in my head, you don't know about the times when I can see myself beating the shit out of that baby because he won't stop screaming, the times I want to press a pillow over his face to stop the noise, the times I want to make him sit forever in his own shit and piss because I get so sick and tired of changing him, and you aren't around when I scream at him so you never hear the things I say, the awful things I say to my own son, my own goddamned son!*

But Tom had talked to her, talked and talked, and, in the end, convinced her that another child would be a good idea. So, when Bobby was three, they'd had Luke, a quiet baby, compared to Bobby, but a very curious baby who began crawling at an early age and poking his clumsy fingers into everything, breaking things, rearranging things. It was then, when she had two children to watch over, that Kimberly began having uncontrollable outbursts, when she finally began letting all of that anger out. She'd tried boxing it in at first, but she couldn't, and the more she let out, the easier it became to do. Soon, she didn't care if Tom was around or not. Hell, *he* didn't have to take care of them, so he had no right to complain about her anger. First, he worked all day at the lab, then was switched over to nights, and he slept all day. Either way, she was left with the boys, so he had *no right* to complain. And he didn't, really. He would tell her, now and then, that he didn't think she was handling certain situations in the best way possible, but he would always do it quietly. One time, she'd blown up at his soft-spoken little protest.

"Maybe I'm not handling it right!" she'd shouted. "But I was never *meant* to handle children! I'm an *accountant,* for Christ's sake! Give me a balance sheet and tax returns and I can handle *that!* But I'm *not* a goddamned baby-sitter!"

This had set off a fight that lasted for several days, days of icy silence at the table and nights of Tom's sleeping on the hide-a-bed in the living room.

And now she was pregnant once again. The pregnancy had been a surprise, the result of one solitary forgotten birth-control pill. It was a rather rare occurrence, her doctor had told her, but one that had to happen to, of all people, Kimberly Conrad.

Tom had suggested an abortion when he saw how strongly she felt against having another child, but that was out of the question. She'd felt badly enough when her first baby was stillborn (although she'd gotten over it relatively easily); she didn't even want to think of how she'd feel knowing that she killed the baby herself. And putting the baby up for adoption would simply keep her awake nights, wondering where he or she was, if he or she were happy.

(Wouldn't it be happier with anyone else besides you? You're actually going to keep it and make it live under the same cloud those two boys have had to live under when you could turn it over to someone who will give it the love it deserves?)

No. Adoption was out of the question, too.

That left her no option but to keep the child, and the thought of that depressed her horribly. And that made her even more hostile toward the boys. And that made the sobbing spells come even more frequently.

What a vicious, ugly circle.

She was still sobbing uncontrollably when Tom came in the back door. He saw her sitting there, red-faced and trembling, and immediately stepped over to her side and put an arm around her shoulders. She covered his hands with hers and clenched them tightly.

"Kim, honey, what's the matter?" he asked.

His words made her cry even harder because that was the closest he'd come in years to speaking to her in that lullaby tone of voice that had always had an almost druglike effect on her. Hearing it again made her realize how very much she'd missed it, as well as how very much things had changed. Not in any identifiable way, really. They'd just ... *changed.*

"Huh?" he asked again. "What is it, Kimberly?"

"Everything," she said just before gasping deeply for air. "I don't know, Tuh-Tom, it's juh-just ... *everything.*"

Tom got down on one knee and a look of panic flashed through his eyes as he put one hand on her large belly. "Are you sick? Is it the baby?"

"No, no, I'm not suh-sick." She swiped a knuckle under one eye, then under the other, wiping away tears. "I'm just ... scared."

"Scared of what?"

She looked him in the eyes and took a long time to answer. "Tom, I really don't want this baby."

"Well, I know you've been apprehensive about it, but I think once you've—"

"No, Tom, I do not want this baby."

He stopped talking and she could see that, up until now, he'd really thought she'd change her mind, or that perhaps she really wasn't as against another baby as he'd thought.

"But, even if it weren't too late for an abortion," she said, "I couldn't do that, because I just couldn't live with it. And I couldn't live with myself if I gave it away, either, I just *couldn't.*"

"But ... why, honey? Why don't you want it?"

The tears began gushing again before she could answer and her words were once again mixed with sobs. "God, Thomas, are you *blind?* Can't you *see?* I'm horrible with the boys. I'm a horrible mother. Can't you see that? I scream at them, I call them names. When they make mistakes or do things wrong"—she gestured to the footprints on the floor and Tom glanced down at them—"I jump all over them."

"That's natural, Kimberly. They know you love them, they know—"

"Oh, Tom, of course I *love* them, but not enough. I don't love them the way I should." Her crying had subsided a bit, but she knew very well that it had not stopped for good yet. "Buh-before I had Bobby, I thought, 'It'll be okay, after he's born you'll love him because that's the way mothers are, they love their kids.' But I was wrong. It's not that way at all. Maybe with other women, but not with me. I'm just not a mother." She looked at him for a while, moving her mouth, but unable to get her words out. "Tom, I ... I nuh-never ... Tom, I ..." She gulped and sniffed and shook her head.

"What, honey?"

Her face screwed up again and she began to sob mid the words tumbled out like great stones down a mountain: "Don't you see, Tom? *I never wanted them!*" She took in a rasping breath, her eyes clenched tightly, her nose wrinkled and running, and one hand on her head, lightly clutching her blond hair in a fist. "I never wanted our children," she hissed, "and I hate myself for it, I *despise* myself for it, because they're good boys, they really are, they're dear boys, but I never wanted them and, God help me, Thomas, I don't now, I really don't care. Can't you get it through your head that I *just don't care!*" She leaned forward into his arms and collapsed into sobs, holding him tighter than she had in a long time.

Tom muttered reassuring words to her over and over again, telling her that she was just upset, that she needed some sleep, that of *course* she cared and of *course* she wanted their children; she loved them with all her heart, he was sure, and she was a wonderful mother, she'd just had a bad day, and he would call in sick so he could stay the night with her because he didn't want her to be alone in such a state and maybe they could do something with the boys tonight, or maybe tomorrow night if she didn't feel like it now, because he had tomorrow off, too. He told her not to worry because everything would be fine and she would feel much better soon. He loved her, and everything would be all right.

But Kimberly knew better. Things wouldn't be all right because now she'd said it all, she'd bared her feelings, and now that they were out in the open they were more real than they'd ever been before. Tom couldn't see that, though. Tom, ever the optimist, was sure that things would be fine simply because he *said* they would be fine.

He led her to the bedroom and told her to take a shower.

"I think you'd feel a lot better after a hot shower," he said, still holding her in his arms. "Or maybe a bath. Then you can go to bed. I'll take care of the boys tonight."

"I need to talk to them," she said thickly. "I haven't even talked to them this evening. Just *yelled*." She shook her head pitifully and said, "I've been a monster."

Kimberly thought she saw Tom blink several times with what looked like surprise when she said that, but she hardly paid any attention to it.

He swallowed and licked his lips. "Take a bath first, hon. I think you'll feel a lot better. Then you can talk to the boys. Okay?"

She nodded slowly. "Okay. Thanks, Tom."

He held her tightly and said, "That's why I'm here, love."

Kimberly took a bath and tried to feel better, but it wasn't easy.

11 - TOM

IT HAD BEEN a little while since Tom had slept a night through and awakened in the morning like a normal person. Even the buzzing of the alarm clock was a rather welcome sound. He heard Kimberly's hand slap down on the clock to silence the obnoxious noise. Then she took in a sleepy breath and said, "I'll wake the kids and make some coffee."

He'd seldom heard Kimberly say that since he'd started working nights, and he realized that he'd sort of missed it. It wasn't a particularly happy statement; it was spoken with a cranky tone and sounded rather annoyed. But it felt good to be waking up with Kimberly.

Tom lay in bed and let himself wake up very slowly. In his foggy state, he replayed bits and pieces of the previous evening. He'd never seen Kimberly in such a condition before. She was a pretty solid woman, and crying was just not her way. And he'd never heard her say anything like what she'd said the night before, the things she'd said about the boys and about herself. He'd heard her speak badly of her abilities as a mother before, quite tearfully once, but never like that. She'd been near hysteria for a few moments and Tom had been frightened.

He had to admit that Kimberly was impatient at times. But the boys loved her.

(I thought she was a monster)

Tom cleared his throat loudly, at the same time clearing his head, and reached over to turn on the clock-radio that was on his side. It was tuned to an all-news station in San Francisco. The announcer's words caught his attention immediately.

"——fery Collinson, but Dr. Hunt has been unavailable for

comment. To make matters worse for the Napa Valley Hospital, later that afternoon, approximately twelve hours after the arrival and death of Collinson, Rosella Webster, an elderly patient, was found eating her roommate, Cora Ebberson, *alive*. The discovery was made by seventeen-year-old Megan Crawford, one of the hospital's volunteers. Immediately after being found, Mrs. Webster threw herself from the window of her third-floor room and died instantly on the pavement below. The medical center has yet to comment on the incident, but one official was said to have—"

Tom suddenly found himself wide awake, and his skin seemed to be creeping over his bones, He sat up in bed, his jaw hanging open, and reached over with one hand, clumsily turning the volume down on the radio.

"My god!" he whispered softly to himself as he swung his long legs over the side of the bed. His right hand reached over and began absently scratching his moderately hairy chest.

Tom knew Rosella Webster. He'd drawn her blood several times. He'd even had a number of conversations with her. She was a little batty, quite a character. Always complaining about never getting enough to eat at the—

"Oh, *Jesus!*" he hissed when the thought registered, covering his face with one large hand. She was always saying she never got enough to eat! *Well,* he thought darkly, *she found something to munch on yesterday.*

He knew Megan, too. Poor kid was probably scarred for life.

Tom wondered if Dr. Hunt knew yet. Mostly, he wondered what his reaction would be, if maybe he would make something out of *this* the way he'd made such an issue of the night Collinson came in. That probably wasn't fair, Thomas realized. Hunt really thought he'd seen that thing.

Thinking of Hunt brought back Tom's visit with him the night before. The doctor had suddenly acted so strange, so preoccupied. He'd rushed Tom out of his house as if he were expecting a whole troupe of dancing girls to drop in and he wanted to have them all to himself. Tom wondered what he'd had on his mind all of a sudden. He wondered if it had anything to do with his recollection of what Collinson had said just before dying. Perhaps he'd gotten some sort of hunch and had wanted to be alone to follow up on it. Oh, well ...

Tom got out of bed and headed for the shower. He decided that maybe he would skip breakfast this morning.

12 - JULIE

JULIE ENDED UP doing another double shift, just as she'd suspected she would. She'd really doubted that Shirley Hogan would be recovered from her bout with the flu. No one was getting over it very quickly.

Her first shift went quite well, but by the end of it she was feeling very tired. She'd not slept as well as she'd hoped the day before, nor as long. Before leaving for work, though, she'd been alert enough to remember Randy Sheckley's address for Tracy, hoping that, after getting it, she would leave Julie alone.

At the end of her first shift, Julie went to the cafeteria, as usual, for a cup of coffee. She missed not meeting Hunt there, as was their custom. He wouldn't be there for some time, she knew. Well, he was due a rest. So was *she,* she realized, and she was seriously thinking about dipping into some of her sick leave to get it, if necessary.

At the coffee machine, she overheard two nearby orderlies buzzing about yesterday afternoon's incident with old Rosella Webster. The whole hospital was talking about it today, just as they'd been talking about Jeffery Collinson yesterday. They always seemed to be talking about something at the hospital, some sort of scandal or controversy, but they'd gotten almost more than they knew what to do with in the last thirty-six hours.

Julie supposed Rudy Pazulo was fit to, be tied what with all the black publicity the medical center had gotten in just short of a two-day period. He was probably trembling in his shorts, wondering what was going to happen next.

Good Lord—a patient eating her roommate! It was like something out of one of those awful "true" detective magazines with all those sensational articles about the boyfriend who screwed his girl friend's corpse after blowing her brains out, or the young boy who skinned his parents alive. It made her shiver.

She assumed Hunt had heard of it by now and thought she could probably guess his reaction to it all. One of the things Julie so admired about him was his awareness of patients, whether they were his or someone else's. Hunt's mother had spent the last year of her life in a hospital, and, as a boy, he had spent a great deal of time with her. He therefore sympathized with anyone confined to a hospital bed and felt that the person's stay there should be made as comfortable and as tolerable as possible. He'd often gone into a rage upon learning that a patient had been neglected in some way. Upon hearing of Rosella Webster and her roommate, he'd probably automatically felt that the hospital was, in some way, at fault. He was also probably disturbed by Megan Crawford's involvement. Megan had come into ER a number of times to transport a patient or to deliver or pick up something, and she had developed quite a friendly, flirtatious rapport with Hunt. Perhaps Megan didn't realize she was flirting—Julie knew that, at Megan's age, that was possible, although unlikely—but she flirted, nonetheless. Hunt was flattered by the attention and was rather fond of the girl. Julie thought that he was probably worried about the possible effect the incident could have on the girl.

With her Styrofoam cup of coffee in hand, Julie went up the stairs to the third floor and down the corridor toward OR and Tracy Parker. Julie had always doubted Tracy's abilities as a nurse; the girl was simply too self-centered, she thought, realizing that she was being rather judgmental, but also realizing that she knew Tracy well enough to know the opinion was justified. When she'd learned Tracy wanted to be a surgical nurse, she'd become even more concerned. Working in surgery required a certain alertness, a sharp edge that she did not think Tracy possessed. But, then, she'd never seen Tracy in action, so perhaps her evaluation was unfair.

Julie was nearing the double doors—each of which sported a NO ADMITTANCE sign—that led into the operating room, fishing around in the pocket of her uniform for the address as she walked, when she heard a high, piercing scream. She stopped in her tracks and looked around for the scream's origin. It came again, followed by a cracked, chillingly giddy laugh. There was

a crashing sound, as if someone had slammed his way through
a door, and it was then that Julie realized that the sounds were
coming from beyond those double doors. Others were stopping
in the corridor and listening to the sounds. Suddenly there were
voices, several voices, all speaking at once, chaotically.

"No, stop!"

"What are you—"

"Oh, dear God, dear *Gaaawwd!*"

"Dr. Hollister, don't, don't!"

"God, Roily, aw, god, *noooo!*"

"Just because I *can*, goddammit! *I can!*"

"For Christ's *sake*, somebody *stop* him! *Grab him!*"

Among all the muddled, fearful voices, Julie recognized one.
Tracy Parker.

Julie's blood ran cold through her veins as she stood in the
corridor. The others around her exchanged quick, shocked
glances, but, for what seemed like years, no one moved. Then,
all at once, everyone started toward the double doors. Julie
moved with them, not knowing what she was going to do, staring
absently at the NO ADMITTANCE signs. She was able to take
only three steps, but they seemed like very long, slow steps
because her mind had begun to race, registering everything she
had just heard

(Dr. Hollister)

(Rolly)

(Just because I can)

and comparing it with things she'd heard before.

("You know, Tracy, sometimes you get so fed up," he says,
"that you just want to reach inside your patient and)

"Oh, my god!" she breathed.

(scrape the sucker out. Just because you can.")

As she took her last step, she heard movement just on the other
side of the doors before her, footsteps, heavy and plodding, and
a voice in her head screamed at her, pleaded with her to turn and
run because she didn't want to see this, she didn't want to be
around for this, she really didn't, but she *couldn't* because she
was a *nurse* and she *worked* here and she *was obligated* to help
when she was needed and it sounded as if she was needed, so it
didn't matter what was on the other side of those doors because—

But it suddenly was no longer on the other side, because the
doors exploded open and framed the tall, grinning figure of

Dr. Roland Hollister, clad in surgical greens, his mask now a crumpled little cloth hanging around his neck, that obscene grin splitting his sharply angled face wide open and his usually tired-looking, bleary eyes now round and crazed, seeming to look not *through* her, but *into* her like razor-thin beams of hot light, but that wasn't the worst of it, nor were the big splotches of darkening blood on the front of his surgical greens and the little black-red lumps that were clinging to the material, because the worst of it all was what Dr. Roland Hollister held before him in his hands, dangling between his bloody, gloved fingers and over the edges of his palms like a snake, like one long, glistening, black-red-gray snake, slippery and quivering.

Julie had seen them before, pictured in the color pages of textbooks all through high school and college, and she'd seen them once in ER when the victim of a stabbing had rushed in holding them desperately in his hands so they wouldn't slip out of the wound that had been slashed in his stomach, except none of those had been like this, like what Dr. Hollister held in his hands how, grinning, even laughing softly deep in his throat, just two feet in front of her, and she jerked her hand from the pocket of her uniform as she took in a breath to scream, just like the nurse behind her was doing now, but before a sound came from Julie's mouth, Dr. Hollister took a step toward her and spoke in a voice that was so dry and chapped that it seemed to be filled with dirt: "Here, girlie! *Catch!*"

His arms made a sudden jerking motion and the visceral mass that was heaped in both his hands slowly crossed the two-foot gap that lay between him and Julie, as if in a dream or in a slow-motion sequence in a movie, and, after an eternity, it slapped onto her breasts and wrapped over her shoulders and around her neck and the scream tore itself from her lungs as she threw her body backward, hitting one of the nurses with a flailing arm, and hit the floor of the corridor with a wind-gushing *clump*, then immediately began crawling frantically on her back, pulling herself with one arm while using the other to slap at the obscenity that clung to her like a hungry child as she screamed, *"Get it off me! Get it off! Please, take it off, somebody, ple-heeeze!"* All the while she really didn't-know what she was saying because her mind was reeling now and nothing seemed to make any sense at all except the fact that she needed to get it off—she *had* to get it off before it stained her uniform, because she couldn't wear a uniform that had such a dreadful stain on it, could she?

There was suddenly a face hovering over her and she began wailing because she thought, at first, that it was Dr. Hollister about to drop some other horror onto her, but it was only an orderly, a young, attractive, blond-haired orderly who looked at once intensely concerned and about to be sick, which, just a second later, he was, kneeling beside Julie and leaning away from her, retching onto the floor, and then *no one* was helping her and she felt alone and deserted and she did the only thing she possibly could at the moment.

Julie clenched her eyes tightly shut, opened her mouth, and screamed endlessly.

13 - HUNT

DURING THE NIGHT, Hunt had dreamed, once again, of Jeffery Collinson. The killer told him in a smirking, conversational tone that it was all going to come now, just as he'd said before.

"You just wait and see, Doc," he'd said. "Just 'cause I'm dead don't make no difference." He chuckled. "They killed Jesus, didn't they?"

Hunt had awakened unrested, showered, and fixed himself some breakfast and watched the "Today" show on the little ten-inch television he kept in the kitchen. Gene Shalit was panning the newest Neil Simon film when Hunt turned the set on, and by the time his eggs and bacon were sizzling in the frying pan, Jane Pauley was introducing a break for local news.

When he heard what had happened at the hospital the day before, Hunt simply stared at the little black-and-white set with his mouth open. He turned the stove off and called Julie at work. An unfamiliar voice answered and told him that she was very busy at the moment and was unable to come to the phone. Hunt left a message for her to call him back, but apparently she never got it; by noon, she still hadn't returned his call. By that time, though, there were other things on his mind.

When he'd heard about Rosella Webster, something clicked in his mind that automatically linked the horrible event with Collinson. He was disturbed, however, by the fact that he did not know *why*. Of course, two bizarre incidents occurring so close together in the same place did make them look suspicious. But *he* was the only one who thought Collinson's death bizarre because *he* was the only one to see that damned crawler thing come out of him! Perhaps if he hadn't seen that, he wouldn't be feeling the nibbling of—what was it? fear? dread?—concern at the back of his mind like a tiny, invisible piranha.

He sat down on his sofa with a large mug of coffee and basked in the silence of the house. A wind was picking up outside and beginning to whisper around the corners. Sometimes it brought with it raindrops that slapped against the windowpanes. Hunt sat on the sofa, sipping the coffee, thinking very slowly about Jeffery Collinson, and Rosella Webster's afternoon snack.

(It's gonna come now)

What's going to come? That crawler? It may bite a few people, but surely one little creature that size couldn't do *too* much damage, could it?

Why had Rosella Webster thrown herself out the window of her room after being found? Surely the old woman had blown a fuse. Why would being found make any difference to her?

Hunt heard the sound of the paper lady's little Toyota pickup slow to a brief stop out front, then drive on, and, without even donning a coat, he went out and retrieved the paper.

The *San Francisco Chronicle* ran a full one-page story on Collinson with a bold headline that read: 32-MONTH REIGN OF TERROR ENDS HUMBLY. There was a picture of a younger Collinson with his hair combed and his face shaven. But there was something about him that came through his clean-cut look. Part of it was in his restrained smile, part of it in his slightly tensed brown eyes. Hunt studied the picture for several seconds and soon realized that it wasn't as if something were looking out through Collinson, but rather like Hunt was looking *into* something *through* Collinson, something infinitely deep and very, very dark. A bottomless pit.

He dragged his eyes from the picture and read the article from beginning to end. It told vaguely of Collinson's past. He'd grown up in the Napa Valley, mostly in the area of Calistoga and Pope Creek. His mother, now confined to a mental hospital, and father, a traveling Evangelist, had been divorced since he was seventeen. Reverend Collinson had been unavailable for comment, although Mrs. Collinson had talked to the reporter.

The article quoted the letter that had been found with the body of Collinson's last victim. The letter had been put in a plastic bag and tucked neatly into the gaping space that had once been the dead woman's throat.

To the Worms,

We'r one step closer now, closer then you think.
When it comes, you'l all thank me.

I am of Him that liveth forrever.

Worms. He'd said something about worms in ER. Something about the worms of the Earth. And what are we closer to now?

The article went on to say that Collinson had ended each letter with the line "I am of Him that liveth forever" (with "forever" usually misspelled). It was a line that appeared frequently in the Satanic Bible, but it had been useless to the authorities in tracking down Collinson. The reasoning behind his letters would remain a mystery now that he could not explain them. The newspaper concluded that that was just as well, because one was hard pressed to explain the writings of a madman.

But just how mad was he? Hunt wondered, allowing his arms to relax and making the paper crumple loudly in his lap.

It suddenly occurred to Hunt that when Collinson had said his death would not make any difference, perhaps he meant it would actually *initiate* whatever was to come.

Maybe, he thought, setting the paper aside, *that crawler can do more damage than I'd thought.*

Hunt quickly stood, grabbed his coat and keys, and drove to the hospital.

"This is not a good time, Martin," Pazulo said when Hunt entered his office. "I'm very busy, as you probably know."

"Don't worry, Rudy. This shouldn't take too much of your time. I'd just like to ask you a couple of questions." Hunt walked over to the man's desk and leaned forward with his hands on the desktop. "Don't you think it a bit odd, Rudy, that what happened here yesterday took place soon after the release of that thing I saw come out of Jeffery Collinson?"

"Oh, come on, Martin. I don't have time for this."

"Just answer me. Don't you?"

"Actually, it doesn't surprise me in the least, the way *my* luck has been running."

"I *told* you something would come of that—"

"Martin, for crying out loud, even if you *did* see some black..."—he waved his hand in front of him, searching for a word—"... *pancake* run out of ER, what could it possibly have to do with some crazy woman chewing on her roommate? *Huh?*"

Martin was silent for a moment. He hadn't even asked *himself* that question. It was a good question, too. What could the crawler have to do with Rosella Webster's mind snapping? He fumbled in his coat pocket, removed a cigarette, and lit it, puffing intently. As if inspired by the smoke, he suddenly had a reply.

"It came out of Collinson's nose, right?" he asked.

"So you say," Pazulo replied.

"Which means it had been stuck up around here, right?" Hunt touched his fingertips to his forehead. "And what's up here, Rudy?"

"To tell you the truth, Martin," Pazulo said drolly, "I'm beginning to think it varies from person to person."

Hunt plopped down in the vinyl-covered chair facing the desk and sighed, "There's just no way to get through to you, is there, Rudy?"

Before the man could answer, his phone rang. He picked it up and said, "Yes," grabbing a pencil with the other hand and poising it over a pad, preparing to write. After a few seconds of listening, however, the pencil slipped from his fingers and his face clouded over. "Oh, my god," he whispered. "But, was Dr. Hollister—" He stopped abruptly and listened some more. "*Julie* Calahan, you say?"

Hunt leaned forward sharply, his heart skipping a beat. "What's wrong?" he hissed. "What's happened?"

Pazulo held up a quieting hand and said, "I'll be right there." He hung up the phone and stood in one motion. When he looked at Hunt, he made no attempt to hide his disgust and anger as he said flatly, "Come with me." He took long, quick steps toward the door.

"Rudy, what's going on?" Hunt asked as they hurried down the corridor, Pazulo staying slightly ahead of him, his fists clenching and unclenching at his sides.

"Something happened in OR," Pazulo said, trying to keep his voice even. "Roland Hollister was performing an exploratory and he ... he apparently went berserk."

"What do you mean, he—"

"He opened the patient from sternum to pelvis and gutted him."

"Christ!"

"That was Dick Severson on the phone. He says OR is a madhouse, a bloody mess. Hollister ran out of the hospital."

"But what does Julie have to do with this?"

"She was standing outside OR when Hollister came out," Pazulo replied, taking the stairs two at a time, keeping his voice low. "He stepped out and threw ... he threw something on her. She's in a mild state of shock." As they stepped out into the corridor of the third floor and headed toward OR, Pazulo turned to Hunt and said, with a brief, humorless smile, "Never thought I'd say this, Martin, but I'm glad you were here when this happened. It'll make it easier on Julie."

Julie was lying on a sofa in the faculty lounge next to OR. She was wearing one of the thin, mint-green patient gowns and her uniform was on the floor in a lumpy, bloodstained heap. A young, dark-complexioned nurse who smelled strongly of perfume was standing next to the sofa. Before Hunt could approach Julie, an orderly hurried to her side with a blanket and covered her shivering frame.

"If that's not enough, just speak up," the orderly said.

Hunt recognized Tracy Parker in the far corner of the lounge, her white uniform blotted with blood. She was sobbing quietly, being comforted by another nurse. Hunt remembered Tracy had been having an affair with Hollister.

Hunt got down on his knees by the sofa while Pazulo asked the orderly what had been done with Hollister and where he was.

"Julie," Hunt said softly.

"What are you doing here?" she gasped, opening her eyes.

Hunt put one hand on her shoulder, the other on the lump beneath the blanket that he knew was her hands. His cigarette continued to burn, held between two fingers, and the smoke rose past his face like a floating spider web. "I was having it out with Hopalong Asshole," he replied with a smirk, jerking his head in Pazulo's direction. "How are you?"

Her face started to curdle, and for a moment Hunt thought she was about to cry. Her eyes were red and puffy and he could tell by the way she spoke that she'd already shed a lot of tears. Julie fought it back, though, and her face relaxed again.

"I'm better," she whispered.

"You weren't hurt, were you? I mean, he didn't hit you or anything?"

She shook her head. "No, but he ... he threw ..."

"That's okay, hon, you don't have to talk about it if—"

"*Intestines,* Martin—he scraped his patient out, just like he said he wanted to. Then he threw them on me." She wasn't strong enough to fight the tears this time, and they came. Her shoulders came forward, and she began to make that tiny coughing sound in her throat that always made Hunt know that she was considerably more than just a little upset. He lifted her toward him and held her, crushing his cigarette out nervously in a little ashtray on the end table.

"Julie," he said quietly, almost a whisper, because he didn't want to upset her more with his question, "what do you mean, he *wanted* to?"

She just kept crying for a while, but the sobs gradually became further apart. "Tuh-Tracy told me he was guh-getting kind of weird lately," she said into his ear. "Shuh-she said he was doing strange things and ... saying things. He told her once that he was getting so fed up with everything that sometimes he just wanted to reach inside his patients and clean them out. Just because he could. And"—she pushed away from Hunt a little so she could look him in the eyes—"he said that when he did it, when he did that to that poor man in OR. He said, 'Just because I *can,* goddammit, I *can!*' And then he ran into the corridor and you should have seen his eyes, Martin, his eyes were round and bulging and ... they were an animal's eyes, Martin."

Hunt's memory conjured up a bright, vivid image of Jeffery Collinson's eyes: round and bulging. He blinked to erase the picture, and he realized that Julie's eyelids were looking very heavy. She leaned her head forward, pressing her forehead to his, and she chuckled thickly.

"Dr. Greeley gave me a sedative just before you came," she said, "and I'm starting to feel it. Martin, I'm scared to sleep. I don't want that to happen again, and I'm afraid I'll dream of it."

"Don't worry about it. Sleep's the best thing for you. Would you like me to take you home with me?"

She leaned her head back a bit and a look of intense relief crossed her face. "Oh, yes. Please take me home."

At home, Hunt put Julie to bed, then went into the living room and lit a cigarette. He stood at the sliding-glass door that led out to the patio. Below that was a gently sloping embankment that ended in a small stream. A light rain was falling and all the greenery below was wet and dripping.

Hunt had never known Roland Hollister very well, but he knew that many of Hollister's fellow workers thought him to be a bit flaky, perhaps too flaky to be wielding a knife over trusting patients. This, however, went far beyond the realms of flaky. What had happened in OR was a nightmare.

Hunt was not only disturbed by what had happened, though. He couldn't stop thinking of what Julie had told him. What Hollister had said to Tracy sounded like something one would say while in a bad mood, while feeling down. As dippy as the doctor was, he'd always been a very jolly sort. Hunt couldn't imagine him saying such a thing with the intention of actually *doing* it. But it had apparently been on Hollister's mind. Something he'd thought of once and then filed away, not for future use but because it was in his way, it was a useless thought that served no purpose, something he would never do. So the thought had been neatly tucked away somewhere in the back of Hollister's mind, perhaps, where such thoughts are secretly stored.

But he *had* done it! Why? What would make a doctor, no matter how flaky, do such an unspeakable thing?

Maybe the same thing that would make a fat old woman eat her hospital roommate alive?

The thought came automatically and unbidden.

Might Mrs. Webster have made a facetious remark in passing about eating the lady in the next bed? To whom might she have made it? A nurse? Her doctor? The person who came in to clean her room?

Megan Crawford?

The hand holding his cigarette stopped midway to his lips and Hunt stood that way, staring out through the glass, for a long time. Then he turned, crossed the living room, and went into the kitchen and opened the telephone directory.

14 - MEGAN

"I'M SORRY, BUT Megan is resting right now and she's not taking any calls."

Megan came out of the hallway and into the living room just in time to hear her mother speak so condescendingly into the phone. Megan held an empty glass from which she'd just drunk some milk, and she was returning it to the kitchen. Her mother's words made her stop, though, and she looked at the woman with annoyance.

"I can take a message, if you'd like. Who's calling, please?"

"Mother, I can take my own calls!" Megan hissed, now wanting the caller to hear and know that her mother was treating her like some sort of invalid. She'd been ridiculously protective since the incident at the hospital yesterday.

"Dr. Hunt? Well, I'll tell her you—"

Setting her jaw, Megan stepped forward and wrenched the phone from her mother's hand. "Hello?" She cast an icy glance at her mother, who walked away, mumbling something about how she was only doing what was best for Megan, trying to help her recover from the horrible ordeal, so on and so forth. "Hello, Dr. Hunt. I'm sorry, but my mother thought I was sleeping."

"How are you, Megan?" he asked. There was some sort of fluttering activity in Megan's stomach when she realized that he was actually concerned.

"Oh, I'm okay, really. Better than everyone *thinks* I should be."

"What do you mean?"

"Well," she said, lowering her voice a little so her mother wouldn't hear and bitch about it later, "everyone seems to think I should be walking around like some zombie, an empty shell of a person. Like I was raped, or something. I'm okay. I saw an awful thing, I fainted, I went home, and now I feel better about it. 'Course ..."—she chuckled quietly—"... I won't be doing any more volunteer work."

"I can understand that."

There was a crackling silence on the line and Megan wondered why he was suddenly quiet. Finally, he spoke again.

"Do you mind talking about it, Megan?" he asked. "About what you saw?"

"Well, no." She shrugged absently. "Not really. Why?"

"Because I wanted to ask you a couple of questions. Before you went in to find ... Mrs. Webster, did you talk with her at all? Earlier in the day, maybe?"

"Yeah. I took her to X ray when I first got there."

"Okay, did she say anything about ... about what she did? About ... eating ... the lady in the other bed? Maybe in passing?"

Megan had never heard Dr. Hunt so uncomfortable and inarticulate, and it was suddenly rubbing off; she swallowed loudly and began to tap the empty glass nervously in her hand against her blue-jeaned thigh. "Yes, as a matter of fact, she did. Why do you ask? How did you know?"

"Do you remember what she said?" he asked, sounding a little excited now. "Can you remember *exactly* what she said, Megan?"

"Well, she complained about her roommate whimpering all the time, and about never getting enough to eat. She was always saying how hungry she was." Megan closed her eyes, remembering, and with the memory came a familiar hand that ran its cold fingers down her spine, then held her stomach in its icy clutch. She was annoyed by her reaction to the memory because it was all *over*, dammit! She went on, her voice trembling imperceptibly. "And, at one point, she told me she got so hungry sometimes that she could eat the Whiner—she called her roommate the Whiner. She said it would shut the old woman up. That's what she said."

"Anything else? Did she mention anything else that was maybe a little ... crazy?"

Megan sniffed and realized that her eyes were becoming misty. "Um, let's see. She was saying the hospital wasn't kept clean, that's right. She said there were black, ugly diseases crawling all over the place and no one kept the place—"

Dr. Hunt gasped. It was just a little gasp that sounded as if he'd tried to hide it from her, but it was obviously one of surprise, with perhaps even a thread of fear woven into it.

"Dr. Hunt?" Megan asked. "Are you all right?"

"Yes. Yes, I'm fine. Did uh ... did Mrs. Webster say she'd *seen* any of these ... these diseases?"

"No, not really. I just, you know, kind of figured she was a little crazy. I didn't take it seriously then. Do you think ... I *should* have, Dr. Hunt?"

"No, no, of course not. But, thank you very much, Megan, for answering my questions." He was talking faster now, as if he were rushed. And his voice had raised in pitch, as if his throat had closed just a tiny bit.

"Dr. Hunt, what's going on? What's wrong?"

"Oh, it's nothing, really, Megan." He chuckled, but it was dry and forced. "Just curiosity. Maybe, if you'd like, you could come by the house someday and have lunch with Julie and me, okay? Thanks again, Megan."

He'd hung up before she could speak. She replaced the receiver, wondering what was wrong.

15 - HUNT

AS JULIE SLEPT, Hunt sat in the dark living room, sipped a martini, and smoked one cigarette after another. One thought repeated itself over and over again in his mind: *What has Jeffery Collinson done?*

Something was very wrong at the Napa Valley Hospital, and Hunt knew—deep in the center of his bones, he *knew*—that it was what Collinson had been cackling about before he died.

(It's gonna come now)

What it was and why, Hunt could not even begin to guess. But he suspected that perhaps it wouldn't be too hard to find out. A lot would be written about Jeffery Collinson in the next two weeks or so. Maybe some reporter would inadvertently pull something out of the killer's past that would give Hunt a clue. Maybe Hunt could gather information of his own. He was, after all, on vacation. But where should he start? Exactly what should he do? He wasn't sure.

Whatever it was, though, it had to be soon. Immediately. Because, as melodramatic as it sounded, Hunt realized something that shot a chill all the way up his spine until he could feel it in the back of his throat: *It may already be too late.*

16 - KIMBERLY AND TOM

IT HAD BEEN a good day. Better than she'd expected. After her outburst the night before, she was sure she'd be uncomfortable with Tom and the boys. But she hadn't been, not at all. She'd talked with Bobby and Luke briefly the night before and kissed them goodnight, trying to assure them she was no longer angry. After they went to school that morning, she and Tom had a big breakfast together, which he had cooked. Then he watched Kimberly's morning soap, "Loving," with her. Mrs. Tillay, their neighbor, had come by and asked if Tom knew anything about heaters because here had stopped working. Mrs. Tillay was a divorcee with two children, a boy and a girl. She always seemed to be on the edge of collapse. She was always breaking things, losing things, running out of things. Tom and Kimberly felt sorry for her, although they were often a bit irritated by her. Their pity came from the fact that one evening her husband, a plumber, had gone out to see a movie and had never come back. Their irritation came from the fact that she was constantly turning to them for help. After Tom had gone over and fixed her heater for her, he and Kimberly went window-shopping and came across a sale at a children's clothing shop where Kimberly bought a couple of items for the baby. She'd done that numbly, with no real feeling toward it at all, which was rather unusual. After eating lunch out, they picked up the kids at school.

Having that time alone with Tom made her feel like she hadn't felt in years. Maybe … just maybe … things would be okay.

The boys had been put to bed feeling content after a day of playing video games with Tom, going out to dinner at Chuck E. Cheese's, then seeing a double feature. They hadn't had so much activity in one day in a long time.

Kimberly was quite tired, too. She stood in the bathroom looking at her reflection in the mirror over the sink as she brushed her hair for the last time. She could hear Tom lying in bed taking long drags on a joint he'd been saving for the right time. He'd felt badly that Kimberly couldn't join him, but she'd told him that she probably wouldn't even if she weren't pregnant. It just wasn't for her anymore, she thought.

"I think the boys really enjoyed themselves, don't you?" Tom asked with a soft little cough.

"I know they did. It was nice to see them having so much fun." She put her hairbrush down, then opened the medicine cabinet and removed the toothpaste. She was putting some on her toothbrush when she heard something. She stopped, tilted her head to listen, and heard it again. Something in the wall, scraping and crunching. "Tom," she said, "we've got mice again, dammit!"

"How do you know?"

"I can hear them right now. In the wall. God, how I hate them. We'll have to do something right away."

"Yeah, I'll get 'em tomorrow. Little buggers."

She began brushing her teeth vigorously. When she was finished, she rinsed her mouth out, replaced the toothpaste and brush, then turned out the bathroom light. Something caught her eye. The light from Tom's bedside lamp shined softly into the bathroom, holding back total darkness. That dim light glimmered on something. She looked down into the sink. It was something in the ... no, it was just shining on the sides of the drain, that was all. But when she leaned forward and looked carefully ... well, it looked as if there was something black and thick in the drain. And when she turned her head just a little this way and that, it even seemed to ... move. She clicked her tongue and shook her head, chiding herself. The thought of mice in the house again had given her the creeps. The drain just needed cleaning out. She went into the bedroom and crawled into bed with Tom.

"Enjoying yourself?" she asked him.

He was just finishing the joint when he turned his head to her and smiled. "Yep. I feel great. Have all day, in fact." He put it aside and wrapped his arm around Kimberly, turning off the bedside lamp.

"Tom," she whispered. "I really had fun today. Being with you and the kids ... it was just what I needed, I think."

"That's why we did it, honey."

"Thank you," she said, kissing him softly and warmly.

* * *

Marijuana always made Tom sleep the sleep of the dead, and waking up the morning after was like coming up from the bottom of a deep quarry. It wasn't entirely unpleasant, though, especially when he didn't *have* to get up. When the alarm clock went off, it sounded as though it were at the far end of a long tunnel. He heard Kimberly's hand slap down on it, then vaguely heard her voice.

"... kill the kids ... make some coffee."

Tom managed to mumble something, but turned over and allowed himself to remain in the murky waters of semi-sleep for a while.

When he started to wake up again, it seemed as if a great deal of time had passed. He turned on his back, reached up and rubbed his eyes slowly, but hard, groaning leisurely. Something was ringing. It wasn't the alarm clock. He blinked his eyes open with effort and lifted his head. Kimberly was gone. The alarm clock was silent. The *doorbell* was ringing! Tom squinted at the clock, but the numbers on it were blurry. He shook his head, mumbling to himself, and struggled out of bed, putting on his robe.

"... ringing somebody's doorbell at such a godless hour of the morning, sheez! Honey? Kimberly?" He staggered out of the bedroom and down the hall to the front door, calling Kimberly's name a few more times, wondering why she hadn't answered the door herself. He looked out the little peek hole and saw Mrs. Tillay standing on the doorstep, shifting her weight from one foot to the other. He opened the door and she smiled nervously at him, her short, round frame covered by a long, heavy brown coat that she'd put on over her robe. Her light brown hair was flat on one side and wiry on the other; she'd just gotten out of bed herself.

"Oh, Tom," she said in her airy voice. "I'm sorry I woke you. I didn't know you were off last night."

"Oh, that's ... that's okay," he muttered. "What can I do for you?"

"Oh, um, I just discovered that I'm all out of eggs, Tom, and I've got to have *something* to feed the kids for breakfast this morning, so I was wondering if I could borrow a few eggs, if you've got any to spare, of course."

As she talked, Tom stepped aside and gestured for her to come in. "Yeah," he said, "no problem. C'mon into the kitchen." He shuffled ahead of her, scratching the back of his neck wearily.

"I just don't know how I could've forgotten to get eggs last night, because I had a long list of things to get when I went down to Safeway, but they just managed to slip by me somehow. You know how that goes?"

"Sure." He led her into the kitchen and opened the refrigerator. "Help yourself," he told her, waving a hand to the egg tray in the door.

"Oh, thank you so much. Where's Kimberly?"

"Probably with the boys. Kim!" he called weakly. He turned around and froze, staring at the counter across from the refrigerator.

The cutlery block that held all the knives in the kitchen in individual slots had fallen over. It had been leaning against the wall at the far end of the counter. Now it was lying flat and most of the knives had slid out of their slots. Two had fallen into the otherwise empty sink. But one knife was missing. The biggest of all, with an eight-inch blade and a dark wooden handle.

"Kimberly?" Tom said again, but with a hollow voice. He lifted his head and looked through the doorway that led to the hall. He heard her speaking, very softly, and mixed in with her voice was a sound. A steady, rhythmic thumping.

"... finally ... your messes ... bickering ..."

"How are your boys doing, Tom?" Mrs. Tillay asked. "You know, they really should get together with my children more. I'm sure they'd have a lot of fun to—"

Before she finished, Tom left the kitchen and went down the hallway, past his own bedroom, past the hall bathroom, and as he neared the boys' room, the thumping became louder and he could hear that it was sort of cushioned, it had a sort of wet sound to it, and Kimberly's words became clearer.

"... because I'm fed *up* with it ... don't understand me or even *care* ... could've *been* somebody ..." A small grunt broke through her voice with each thump, and Tom suddenly felt very badly about what was going on down the hall and he took the last few steps very quickly and nearly dove through the doorway of his sons' bedroom, his hands gripping the doorjamb.

Kimberly was on her knees beside Luke's bed, her back to the door, and her hands were joined in front of her, her fingers wrapped tightly around the handle of that missing knife, lifting it up, then plunging it down, up and down, up and down, muttering to herself all the while, grunting, little puffs of air coming from her now and then. Her hands were red, Luke's bed was covered with red, and there was even red on the Star Wars sheets hanging down from the upper bunk, where Bobby lay, still, one arm hanging over the bed's edge, the sleeve of his pajamas red, so red and wet ...

"*Kimberly!*" Tom screamed, throwing himself forward into the room, toward his wife and sons. "*Kimberly, for god's sake, what are you—*"

In the blink of an eye, Kimberly turned her body around and faced him, lifting the knife high above her head and opening her mouth to release a shrill, threatening shriek. Her light blue nightgown was blood-splattered and her eyes—dear God—were like disks, so wide, so glistening, and so filled with hate, pure, fiery hate.

Tom felt his chest begin to heave and he found himself gasping for air because it was so hard to breathe and he felt his face become so tense, as if it would break soon, and his eyes filled with tears, tears that were simply there, coming from nowhere, and he took another step forward, reaching out a hand to her, wanting to stop her, make her tell him why, make her undo all of this—

"Staaaaay *back*, Thomas," she growled—it was actually a growl that might come from an animal, a wild animal—as her lips curled upward slowly into an ice-water smile.

"God, Kimberly, what've ... aaaww, Kuh-Kimberly, what have you done?"

She struggled to her feet, her round, protruding belly, covered with the blood of her sons, holding her down, holding the knife before her as she moved carefully, so steady, so sure, not a hint of trembling in her hands.

"Guh-give me the, the knife, Kimberly, give it to muh-me ... oh, Christ, are they dead, Kimberly? Have you killed them? Oh, Jesus Holy Christ!" He couldn't stay back anymore; he had to get to his boys and he walked forward, taking his attention from her completely, his arms outstretched, his hands quaking, tears flooding down his cheeks. "Oh, dear Christ, Kimberly, look what you've *dooooooone!*" When he looked at Luke, Tom felt the threads of his mind rapidly unraveling and tangling together, tying themselves into knots, because his boy was lying under blood-soaked covers, arid the covers had holes in them, so many holes, some of them so close together that they formed larger, gaping holes, and Tom knew that they went right through those blankets and into his son's body, and he turned to his wife, the woman who had suddenly become a stranger, an intruder in his house, a monster,

(I thought she was a monster)

and he screamed, "*Look what you've—*"

But before the last word was out, Kimberly's hand moved like lightning and light flashed on the long blade of the blood-streaked knife as it came and sank into the patch of flesh between his neck and shoulder and Tom fell back screaming, moving very slowly, as if he were on the moon, feeling the blade slide back out of him, held tightly in Kimberly's grip, and he hit the floor hard, partially on his side facing the doorway where Mrs. Tillay had suddenly appeared, dropping the eggs she held to the floor so her hands could cover her mouth, which opened and released a horrified scream, her little head jerking back and forth spastically. Tom pressed a hand to his bleeding wound and screamed at Mrs. Tillay, "Call for help! *Get help, now!*" She disappeared down the hall, still screaming, and Tom turned back to Kimberly, who still faced him with the knife held out threateningly before her, and she began to speak, the words flowing from her mouth like gushing water, running together rapidly.

"I tried to tell you I tried to tell you I never wanted them but you wouldn't listen you had to be so fucking sweet so fucking happy and optimistic so fucking sweet but you know now don't you know now that I was telling the fucking *truth!*" She began to back up slowly as she spoke, her eyes full of fire, her breasts rising and falling with each gasp of air she took. "I never wanted *them* and I never wanted *you* and I don't want this fucking *animal* that's growing and breathing inside me now, do you under*stand* me, do you un——" There was a *bump* as Kimberly tripped over one of Bobby's shoes that was left on the floor at the foot of the bed and she fell back against the small space of wall left over by the bed and then into a corner of the room, where she slid down until she landed in a sitting position, her legs stretched out before her, spread wide, her belly sticking up like a large pillow, but she hardly noticed the fall; she just kept talking and talking. "—understand me, I don't want it, I just want to *kill* it, I want to *kill* the fucking thing—" Her hands shot upward, lifting the knife above her, and Tom realized what she was going to do and he threw himself forward on the floor, reaching one hand toward her, using his other bloody hand to lift himself up from the floor, but he was too late, he was just too late, because Kimberly brought the knife down in a blur of silver and red and plunged it into her large, round belly and into the lump of life inside as she continued to babble. "—*kill it, kill it, kill it*—" Her fists were wrapped tightly around the knife's handle, and once it was inside her, she twisted it, first to the right, then to the left, and her voice became hard and gravelly and twisted itself into something Tom couldn't recognize at first because it was so alien to all the blood and death that filled the room, but when he realized what that sound was,

(Sweet holy Christ, she's trying to laugh, she's trying to laugh!)

he thought he was going to vomit, but he couldn't, he couldn't do that now because maybe it wasn't too late for her, maybe there was something he could do, even now, but that thought was shattered when he saw the blood appear at the corners of her still-smiling mouth, and the look in her eyes changed when she saw the expression of hopelessness on his face; her eyes filled up with a filthy kind of *glee* as her legs began to make a slow, final pedaling motion; in and out they went, as if she were on an invisible bicycle, and her harsh, attempted laugh curled itself into words, her last words: "*Kiiilll ... the ... fffucking ... ani ... mal.*"

Kimberly became silent. Her legs stopped moving and her head slumped forward and Tom could see tiny flecks of blood spattered through her blond hair.

He lay there forever before finding the strength to pull himself toward Kimberly, white-hot pain shooting from the stab wound in his shoulder with each movement. But it could not compare to the pain he felt at what had just happened. He reached his hand out and grasped Kimberly's bare ankle; her skin was soft, it was soft and smooth, just like always, but nothing else was just like always, not now, not anymore. He pulled, trying to pull her toward him, but he didn't know why. Maybe it was because he could feel nothing in his arms and legs and he was scared to get up for fear of discovering them useless. He pulled her toward him a ways, away from the wall, and she was soon in a prone position on her back, her head tilted to her right, facing him.

"Je-hee-zus, Kimberly, what have you duh-duh-done?" Tom

sobbed, his tears stirring everything before him into a liquid blend of colors and distorted shapes. He got up to a squatting position and wiped his tears away with one hand, smearing some blood across his forehead. He could smell it. He smelled it every day, he worked with blood, it was his profession. But never like this, never his family's blood, splashed around a room like paint in an artist's studio. His shoulders jerked with his sobs and he could feel blood trickling down his back and chest beneath his robe. "Kimberly ..." The name came out of him as a squeak, an almost comical sound. He looked down at her face, her eyes still open but with only the whites showing, her chin hanging down loosely, and then he saw it moving out of first one nostril, and then the other, pushing itself out effortlessly, black and wet-looking, long and gelatinous. A short, staccato scream shot from him as he leaned away from the two black strands that were crawling from his wife's nose and joining together on the floor to form a flat, round puddle until they at last dropped from her face and began to move away from her as one. Then it stopped, seemed to tense, seemed to scrunch up like a muscle, and suddenly it was shooting from the floor straight into Tom's face, and clinging to his cheek, covering part of his nose, pushing itself into his right nostril, until Tom slapped his hand over it, hit it, clutched at it, threw it off and brought himself rapidly to his feet, the feeling in his legs suddenly restored. The thing hit the floor with a thick *plop* and immediately started to move away when Tom kicked his foot out and tried to step on it. He got a glimpse of something long and snakelike shooting from the middle of the creature and wrapping itself around his ankle, burning, cutting into his skin, and at the same time pulling his foot out from under him until he was once again on the floor, face up. He scrambled on his side, then on his knees, and he looked around the room.

It was gone.

The sobs came then, shaking him as hard as any person could, making his whole body convulse and his head throb, and, through the sobs, between the short, spurting breaths he took, he groaned, "Duh-dear ... Guh-God, what's ... happening?"

BOOK TWO

The monsters are all over. You just can't see them,
because they're just people, like you and me.
—Mrs. Collinson

1 - AFTERMATH

ON THAT BLOODY morning that was to leave a ragged-edged black hole in his life, Tom was taken, babbling, to the hospital, leaving behind policemen to investigate his home, look over the heaps that were once his family, and to question the hysterical Mrs. Tillay. Tom had lost consciousness before any of them arrived but never actually realized it because he dreamed while he was out, dreams that were so vivid that their reality exhausted him. He saw his sons, his wife, and his unborn child die a hundred times in his unconsciousness, and he felt the blade of the knife more sharply each time his blackened mind relived the event.

In his hospital room, his mother and stepfather sat at his bedside, his mother silently wringing her hands, her lips taut, her eyes red and tear-streaked. His stepfather, Ridley Jessum, a tall, stately man with silver hair and a mustache, sat by the window, looking through the glass, occasionally standing to pace back and forth at the foot of the bed. When he kept it up too long, Hannah Jessum would glance at him and say quietly, "Rid, please *stop* that. Go down to the cafeteria, or something."

"No," he'd say, sitting down. "I'd rather stay."

When Tom awoke, it was with a sudden jerk of his whole body. His eyes snapped open and he gasped raggedly. Hannah stood immediately and put her hand on his forearm.

"No! Kimberly, no, for Christ's sake, no, you've—"

"Tom, it's okay, you're in the hospital now, it's—" A sob caught in her throat. "It's your mom, honey, you're in the hospital and it's … it's over."

He stared up at her, his face a taut mask of fear, then suddenly clutched her arms in his hands. His breath came in frightened gulps as he glanced from his mother to his stepfather, who was reaching for the CALL button to summon the nurse. As his eyes darted back and forth between them, Tom's face began to relax and his breathing began to slow, his grip weakened on his mother's arm, but she did not pull back. Instead, she stepped closer to the bed and, placing her hand on his good shoulder, she began to massage it gently with her fingers and thumb. Tom leaned his head back on the pillow and started to close his eyes, but they popped open again and he stared up at his mother.

"Are ... are the kids okay?" he asked with a muddy voice. "How are the boys?"

Hannah twisted her rosy lips to one side, a gesture Tom had recognized since childhood as a sign that she was choosing her words very carefully.

"No, Tom, the boys aren't okay," she said, her voice on the edge of breaking.

His head lifted from the pillow again. "They're dead, aren't they? She killed them. Didn't she?" He watched a tear roll down Hannah's sticky cheek. "*Tell* me!"

"Tom, boy, maybe you should try to relax," Ridley said, his usually level voice quivering a bit.

Tom turned his pleading gaze to the man. "Why did she do it? Why?" His voice rose and fell in pitch, like a little roller coaster.

The door swung open silently and a young nurse walked in, smiling plastically, her white uniform making hushed, crisp sounds of motion. She looked Tom over, asked him if he felt any pain or nausea.

"I think he needs something to relax him," Ridley said with the tone of authority that came so naturally to him.

The nurse—her name badge read MONA SPIROS—muttered a reply, then turned and left, saying she'd be right back.

"Is she going to get the boys?" Tom asked in a whimper.

"No, hon," his mother replied softly. "I think she's going to get something to relax you. Just lie still now. She'll be back in a minute." She looked across the bed at her husband, worry creasing his craggy face, and, amid her pain, she felt a rush of love for him, because she knew he truly was worried. After the death of her first husband eleven years ago, Hannah had vowed never to marry again. Her relationship with Dave, her first husband, had not been a terribly successful one, and if he had not stopped by a bar on the way home from the end of a big construction job, and if he had not drunkenly plunged his car into the river and drowned afterward, it probably would have ended in divorce, anyway. She'd grown tired of his coarse manners, his rough attitude toward everyone and everything. Ridley, on the other hand, was gentle and yet stern, polite but opinionated: a welcome blend of contrasts in one kind, loving man.

At first, Hannah had wondered how well Ridley and Tom would get along. Tom was on his own, of course, and he wanted her to be happy, but she wanted there to be peace in their family. She wanted her husband and son to be at home in one another's presence. She was pleasantly surprised when Rid had taken Tom to his side almost as if they were old buddies. At the wedding, he'd said to his stepson, "Thomas, I have a great deal of money, and I'm always making more with my two wineries. If you ever, for any reason, need it, it's at your disposal. If you don't want to take it, I won't force it upon you or be offended. I just wanted you to know." Being like his father in that respect, Tom had never asked. But he was grateful.

Now Hannah watched her husband look down at Tom as if he were his own son, his silver hair catching the dull, clouded sunlight that shined through the window, and she once again thanked the good Lord in heaven for the day she'd met him at a wine-tasting ceremony. He was one of the best things that ever happened to her.

The nurse returned, silently gave Tom a shot, told him to relax, then left again.

After a while, Tom began to quiet down; his head seemed to clear and he seemed to grasp the situation, finally, without reacting to it strongly. He asked his mother in a calm, flat voice, "Is Kimberly dead, Mom?"

Hannah nodded, trying to hide the stab of pain she felt for her son.

"Mom?"

"Yes, Tom."

"I'd ... I'd like to have them cremated. Kim and the boys. I want them cremated."

Ridley leaned forward and said, "Look, son, you don't have to think about that now. We can—"

Tom turned to him and the man stopped speaking. Before, when Tom had been unconscious, Ridley had not fully noticed how the younger man looked. Now that he was awake and moving, the change in Tom's face was more than noticeable; it was shocking. His otherwise olive-tinted complexion was drained of color. His cheeks were hollow and dark wrinkles had appeared around his eyes.

"Did you see them?" Tom asked him. "They can't be buried like that. They can't. I want them cremated."

Hannah imagined for a moment her two little grandsons, those two loving and playful boys, reduced to a pile of ashes kept in small urns. Her chest began to tense and her throat became hot with unborn tears, but she held them back, telling herself she'd done enough crying already for a while and needed to remain strong for Tom.

Dear God, she thought, *help him to hold up under all of this.*

Tom's eyes were looking heavy and the lids were lowering.

Hannah went back to her book when he was out once again, and Ridley returned to the chair, where he sat and stared out the window.

Outside, March continued toward April, but winter said no to spring for a while. Chilly breezes continued to blow and dark, barrel-chested clouds remained huddled together above. It was almost as if nature had sided with Tom Conrad and knew that to warm the air and uncover the blue of the sky would be to mock his tragedy. So she patiently held spring at bay for a while longer, quietly reflecting the dark, cold, seemingly endless dusk that his life had suddenly become.

With the agreement of Kimberly's parents, who had flown in from Colorado, Kimberly, Bobby, and Luke were cremated as Tom had requested, and they agreed there would be a small, brief service the next day. They wanted it over with as soon as possible. It was held in the local Presbyterian church, the denomination in which Kimberly had been raised. Tom did not attend the service. He stayed in his hospital room, his mother and stepfather in the room with him, saying much in their silence. Tom remembered how well his mother had taken the death of his father. She was a strong woman. When he was a little boy and would hurt himself and go to his mother, she would always say, "Go ahead and cry, honey, but you can take it. You're tough, just like your mom." She wasn't very big, but she had the best posture of anyone Tom had ever seen. And her face was angular, always held upward. She glanced at him and smiled, and Tom realized he'd been staring at her. He'd been staring at her, filling his mind with fluffy thoughts so he wouldn't have to think about anything else.

Everything else.

There was no more "everything else." They'd been burned this very afternoon and put into jars. He was no longer a father. He was no longer a husband. He was just a man who felt as if he had nothing left inside him. A man with a big hole in his shoulder, given to him by his wife. Crazy wife. Dead wife. Just a man. A lab tech. Tom the Tech. He almost laughed at that.

Hannah told Tom about the stories being run by the local papers about the ... tragedy. They'd all strongly emphasized Tom's innocence. His obvious innocence, she'd added. Tom did not read them.

Tom received flowers from well-wishers. He received cards of sympathy from some of the boys' teachers and learned that the students at the school were given half a day off yesterday, Friday, to remember their fellow students, and the flags had flown at half-mast.

They were fine boys, one of the teachers, a Mrs. Helm, wrote. *I'm sure you were proud.*

Not proud enough, said a voice in Tom's head, and it left a bitter feeling in its wake, like medicine leaving a bad aftertaste in the mouth.

Cards and flowers were brought in from his coworkers. The one he liked most came from Julie Calahan. It was a single yellow rose and a small, plain card that read:

I'm here if you need me. Love you, Julie.

Thinking of Julie made Tom think of Hunt. And when Hunt came to mind, so did something else. He'd been pushing it out of his memory ever since he'd come to the hospital, but now his blood ran cold and his insides turned to shattered glass when he thought of that thing crawling out of his wife's head and the tentacle that had sprouted from it, cutting his flesh with a stinging swipe.

He would have to tell Hunt. It had to be stopped, and Hunt would be the only one who would listen to him. Just as Hunt had thought that he, Tom, would listen. Now he was not only ready to listen; he wanted to *do* something. But ... not yet.

On Sunday, the day Tom was to be discharged, Hannah and

Ridley went down to the cafeteria for lunch while he dressed and gathered his things. While they were gone, the door to Tom's room opened cautiously with three quiet knocks. In walked a man wearing a police uniform. He was of average build, except for his belly, which stuck out over his belt somewhat. He was dark-skinned, Hispanic, somewhere in his late forties, with a bushy mustache and streaks of gray in the black above his ears.

He held a hand out and shook with Tom, introducing himself with a flash of his I.D. "Mike Garza," he said with a smile, his voice very deep. "I ... uh ... have to ask you a few questions, and I thought this would be as good a time as any. Mind?"

Tom shrugged noncommittally and sat down on the side of his bed, gesturing toward a chair. "Have a seat."

Garza sat down, taking out a little leather-bound notepad. "Um, we got most of our information from Mrs... . uh"—he glanced at the book—"Mrs. Tillay, so we've got it pretty straight, I think. She woke you when she came to the door, you invited her in, went to get your wife, and found her ..." His sentence hung in the air like a man slowly spinning in the breeze at the end of a rope. "Is there anything you'd like added to that?"

Tom thought a moment. "No. Nothing that would really make any difference."

Garza's mouth worked beneath the mustache, and it looked as if he were chewing on the hair. "Do you know why she did it, Mr. Conrad?"

Yes! Tom's mind screamed. *She did it because something made her do it! Something crawled in her head and did something to her, made her kill our sons, used her, possessed her! Whatever it was, it's still out there! And there may be more ...*

"No," he heard himself say over the wailing of his mind's voice echoing in his head. "I don't. She ... she had no reason and she ... she was a good woman and a good mother, and she loved our little boys." He stared down at his lap for a long time, then looked back at Garza. "Is there anything you know that I don't? That you can tell me, I mean? About my wife?"

His mouth worked some more as he thought. "Autopsy didn't show anything. We don't know any more than you do."

Tom nodded and sighed.

Garza asked him some more questions—tedious questions about the details of that morning—then put his notepad away and stood. He did not smile, but his face was warm.

"Mr. Conrad," he said softly, "I'm very sorry. Thank you for your cooperation." He shook his hand again, then left.

Tom sat still on the bed for a while, staring at his feet, seeing flashes of that bloodied blade rising and falling now and then in his mind.

Autopsy didn't show anything.

Whatever it was, whatever it did, it left no traces. It had simply passed over his wife like the shadow of a cloud.

Tom picked up the phone, dialed 9 to clear the line for an outside call, then called Martin Hunt and asked him to come see him. Hunt sounded reluctant, wondering in a mumble if Tom was up to it.

"I'm *asking* you to come, aren't I?" Tom insisted.

A few moments after Tom hung up the phone, Hannah and Ridley returned.

"Are you ready, honey?" Hannah asked.

"Um, I was wondering if you two would mind driving to the house ahead of me," Tom said. "See, I've got this friend coming to see me. Then he's going to drive me home. Is that okay with the two of you?"

"Is anything wrong?" Ridley asked him, concern softening his bass voice.

"Oh, no. I just want to be alone with my friend for a while."

They agreed and went ahead of him, taking his things. Tom sat in a chair staring out the window while he waited for Hunt, hoping absently that he would soon become used to the bandage on his shoulder that was so annoying now.

When Hunt arrived, he was quite obviously uncomfortable. He didn't seem to know what to say. This surprised Tom; Hunt was always sure of himself, always knew how to handle every situation.

"Tom, I ... I won't even try to tell you how sorry I am," Hunt said quietly. "I'm not one for sending cards or flowers in situations like this. I think it can sometimes make it worse. I just sort of ... wait the bad time out, you know?"

"Thank you." Tom stood. "I don't want to waste words, Dr. Hunt, but I'd rather not talk here. I've been discharged and I was hoping you'd agree to drive me home so we could talk."

Hunt's brow furrowed. "Well, sure."

A nurse wheeled him down the corridor to the elevator, then through the lobby and out to the parking lot where Hunt's car was parked. Tom hated being made to look helpless in the wheelchair, but it was standard procedure for discharging patients.

In the car as they drove out, Hunt asked, "What's up, Tom?"

"I saw it," Tom said.

"Saw ... what?" Hunt's voice could not hide the fact that he already had a very good idea *what*.

"That thing you saw in ER a few days ago. Or at least something just like it. It was in my wife. It crawled out of her face after she killed our sons and herself." It was quite an effort for Tom to keep his voice from cracking.

Hunt swallowed audibly, pulled himself up straight behind the wheel, one hand rummaging in his coat pocket for his cigarettes. "Did it ... did it crawl out of—'"

"Her nose. Just like with Collinson. I saw it. And it grabbed my foot. Cut the skin around my ankle with this ... this tentacle that grew out of the top of it. It cut me and pulled me down so I couldn't stop it."

Hunt lit a cigarette, took a drag, then blew the smoke out rather than simply exhaling as he usually did. He tried to ignore the slight trembling of his fingers. "What do you want to do, Tom?"

"What do you think? I want to help you. It killed my family. I'm not sure *how*, but I'm sure it *did*. And maybe there's more out there. I want to find it, Doc. And kill it."

Hunt nodded slowly, moving the cigarette up and down gently with his lips, his knuckles a creamy color because he was gripping the steering wheel so tightly. "Good," he said. "We will."

Tom returned to his empty house, which now seemed like a huge, stony cavern in which memories fluttered back and forth in the dark corners like tiny bats. He talked a lot to Hannah and Ridley, never really saying anything, trying hard not to think.

He immediately began making arrangements to move.

2 - THE SEARCH BEGINS

BEFORE TOM LEFT the hospital, Dr. Roland Hollister was found on the narrow, twisting road that led from Calistoga to Santa Rosa, splayed on the trunk of his mangled car, which had gone off the road, hit a tree, then rolled into a creek. Hollister had been thrown through the windshield. It was determined that he had died instantly.

"And I bet," Hunt said to Julie immediately after hearing the news on the television, "that as soon as he was dead, one of those goddamned things crawled out of his nose."

"You think there's more than one?" Julie asked.

Hunt shrugged. He hadn't realized he was speaking of "those things" until he stopped to think about it. "Yes. I suppose so."

Once he was back home, Tom gathered up all the belongings he wanted to keep and left the rest for Kimberly's parents to sort through. He put the house up for sale and immediately found himself a small, reasonably priced apartment in St. Helena. Everyone thought it would be a while before he came back to work, but Tom felt differently. He wanted to work, *needed* it. His shoulder was healing up nicely, and rather quickly, too. He wanted to return to the lab and work as many hours as he could. Unlike his shoulder, his other wounds would not close so fast, and he wanted to be busy so he would perhaps be able to ignore the aches that would come with the slow, laborious healing.

He'd packed, notified the real-estate agent, and found an apartment within two days of leaving the hospital. On the third day, in the middle of the afternoon, Tom dropped in, unannounced, on Dr. Hunt. Hunt was fixing a late lunch for Julie, who had just gotten out of bed. They were both surprised to see him.

What didn't surprise them, however, was Tom's appearance. His tall, thin frame seemed even thinner, his face gaunt and pale.

"Sorry I didn't call," Tom said to Hunt at the door, "but I ... well, I don't have my phone in yet—in the apartment, I mean."

"Come in, come in," Hunt said, a little too rapidly. He held a celery stalk in one hand and a knife in the other, and, as he shut the door behind Tom, he realized the significance of the knife he held and tried to keep it out of Tom's sight. "Don't worry about not calling. I've been half expecting you to come over soon. Would you like some lunch? I'm just making a salad and we're having some sandwiches."

"Ah, no, thanks. But, I'd like a cup of coffee, if you've got it."

"Sure. Come on in the kitchen."

He followed Hunt in, said hello to Julie, and sat down across from her at the table.

"God, I look like a bag lady," Julie said. She was in her robe and her hair stuck out wildly in all directions. "I just got up."

"Yeah," Tom said, looking down at the tabletop, "I haven't been up long myself. I've been sleeping too much the last couple days. I need to get back to work."

Hunt stopped chopping celery at the counter and turned to Tom. "Sleep is good for you, Tom. You don't need to go back to work so ... well, so soon." He turned to Julie briefly and said, "Could you put some coffee on, hon?" Then he turned back to Tom.

"Oh, I'm okay. I think working would be good for me right now. Working and finding that ..." He glanced at Julie, whose back was to him as she filled the Mr. Coffee, then turned back to Hunt. "Uh ... can we ..."

Hunt nodded.

"Finding that thing. That's why I'm here, really."

Hunt quickly put the last of the salad together and dished it out next to the sandwiches. He put both the meals on the table and then Julie joined him over their lunch. "Sure you don't want anything to eat?" Hunt asked Tom.

He nodded in reply. "I was wondering what you had in mind. I mean, how do you think we should go about this?"

Hunt chewed slowly and thoughtfully on his sandwich. "Well, I've been reading everything I can get my hands on about Collinson. He's in all the papers now, of course. I honestly feel that whatever these crawlers are—and I think there are several, there *have* to be—Collinson is to blame for them."

"But he's dead."

"Yes, but *they* aren't. Maybe if we can learn something about his past—something he did, maybe, I don't know—we can learn something about these things. It's a shot in the dark, I guess, but it's all we've got."

"Where do we start?" Tom asked immediately, leaning forward a bit, anxiousness shining through the pasty color of his drawn face. Hunt could tell he was more than serious about getting to the bottom of whatever it was they were after.

"Collinson's mother is in the state hospital in Hana. I think we should talk to her first."

Hana State Hospital was a combination of concrete sterility and dark, rusty antiquity. Its well-kept lawns were shaded by tall, darkly green trees that gave a feeling of warmth to its otherwise staunch professionalism. Hunt turned his BMW off the highway that led into and out of Napa and onto the quaint-looking little road that went to several parking lots around the hospital.

When he suggested talking with Mrs. Collinson the day before at his kitchen table, Tom had insisted they do so as soon as possible. Hunt had gently questioned Tom's jumping in so quickly after going through such a horrible experience, but Tom had countered with the fact that jumping into it was his only balm at the moment. So Hunt had called a friend of his who worked at the hospital and learned that Mrs. Collinson was allowed visitors and could even leave the hospital if she wished. He was told that she was staying there mostly by choice. They had agreed that Hunt would do most of the talking and, if anything that seemed important was mentioned by Mrs. Collinson, Tom would jot down any notes he felt were necessary.

They were led to the visiting room, which was equipped with a stereo, shelves of books, stacks of magazines, and a television. There was also a pot of coffee in the corner. They sat down at a round table that had issues of *Time* and *People* on it, and they waited for about five silent minutes before Mrs. Collinson was escorted in.

She was a very small woman with thin silver hair and an equally thin face. It was not an unpleasant face, however; the cheekbones were high and she seemed to be on the verge of a smile. Her eyes were not as easy to look at, though; they had a hurt quality to them, a look that might be found in the eyes of a small dog that had been beaten and cowed. They darted a lot here and there in motions of sparkling gray caution. And her slight shoulders were gathered forward a bit, as if constantly prepared for punishment or unexpected attack. She wore a plain powder-blue dress over her frail frame and seemed to hurry to her chair, as if she weren't comfortable standing. The first thing she said to them was, "Are you reporters?"

"Uh ... no, Mrs. Collinson, I'm—"

"Good. I've talked to a lot of reporters lately, and I'm fairly tired of it."

"I'm Dr. Martin Hunt."

Her nearly nonexistent eyebrows ducked downward toward her deeply set eyes. "That sounds familiar."

"Yes. I was the doctor who tended to your son when ... after his accident."

"Ah," she said, tilting her head back, looking down her razorlike nose at him with an air of examination. "That's right. Hunt." She placed one bony, blue-veined hand on top of the other on the table and absently fingered a corner of one of the magazines. "So you're the one he was with when he died."

"Uh ... yes."

"My son didn't spend much time with others these last few years, far as I know. I'd wondered who was with him when he breathed his last. Did you try to save him?"

"Yes, we did, ma'am, but he had severe internal injuries, according to the autopsy report, and by the time we got him, there was really little we could—"

"You shouldn't've tried so hard," she said quietly, looking away from Hunt's eyes at the space over his shoulder.

"Pardon?"

She did not reply.

Hunt fidgeted just slightly and said, "Well, this is Tom Conrad. He's ... uh ... a writer, and we're exploring the possibility of perhaps doing a book on your son. Would you have any objection to talking about him?"

"That's all I'm doing these days—talking about him to reporters and news folks. Ain't you seen me on TV?" she asked with a papery chuckle. "Everyone wants to know about the killer. My son the killer. "She continued to stare over Hunt's shoulder.

Hunt glanced at Tom, who was looking at the woman, intensity shading his face. He looked as though he were about to speak, but he remained silent. Hunt had practiced what he would say to Mrs. Collinson the night before; he wanted to be tactful in case she was touchy about it, but he'd promised himself he would get to the point quickly. He leaned to the side a bit, catching the woman's eyes and tilted his head as he said, "You told the reporters that you hadn't known of the killings. At least, you hadn't known your son was the killer."

"Yes, and if you read enough of them, you'll know I also said that it didn't surprise me in the least."

"Why is that?"

"Because my son ... was a monster. He was a monster, Dr. Hunt."

Hunt and Tom exchanged quick glances as if to remind one another that they were speaking with a mental patient.

"Was he ... say, violent as a child?"

"My son was never really a child. I sometimes think he had the mind of an adult from the time he came out of my womb. 'Course"—she smiled a bitter smile, revealing teeth that were getting longer than they should be—"I'm a crazy woman, so what do I know?"

"Well"—Hunt cleared his throat softly—"what makes you think that? About your son, I mean? You must have a reason."

"'Course there's a reason, Dr. Hunt, and I don't mind talkin' about it, so you can stop actin' like you're handlin' a fragile china doll. I believe that children are not evil from birth. I believe they learn to be evil from us; we *give* them that." She emphasized her words by tapping a thin index finger on the tabletop. "My son was evil from the time he was a little babe." They waited for her to go on, but she did not.

"Whatever gave you that idea?" Hunt asked.

She looked from one to the other, smiling rather defiantly. "You're writin' a book, you say? You gonna tell your readers you got some of your information from a crazy woman? A woman in a mental home? I can see how you're lookin' at me, you know. Like you wanna hear what I have to say, but you plan to take it all with a grain of salt. Isn't that right, Dr. Hunt?"

"Well," Hunt replied slowly, "we *do* want to hear what you have to say, Mrs. Collinson. And, well, quite frankly, you don't strike me as a crazy woman."

She chuckled her brittle chuckle again. "Thank you." She turned to Tom. "You're the writer? Don't you want to write things down? You're not very convincin', you know."

Tom started and fumbled in the pocket of his sport coat, removing a small notebook and pen. "Yes, I, I'm going to write it down." His voice was a bit hoarse and sleepy.

"You want to know why I think my baby was evil? Well, I don't *think* it, I *know* it. When I held him in my arms to my breast to feed him, sometimes he would look up at me with them big, watery brown eyes, them warm eyes, and then they would narrow, get thin, get a sort of testin' look in them, as if he was examining me, maybe, and then—this was after he'd just started gettin' teeth—then, while he was lookin' up at me, lookin' me right in the eyes, he would bite down on my nipple as hard as his little baby jaws could. And that was harder than you prob'ly think. Then, when he got a little older, he would pick things up, like a vase, say, from a table or somethin', and he would look at his father or me, and he would wait. He'd just wait until one of us, or both, turned and had our eyes on him, and then he'd drop it—no, he'd *throw* it—onto the floor. Then, usually, he'd … he'd smile." She shifted in her seat, reached up with her liver-spotted hands, and fingered the small collar of her dress.

Hunt wondered absently just how old she was, and decided that she was probably younger than she looked.

She placed her hands back on the table and went on, her pause short. "I remember a time when he was just a tiny babe and his father was given a little kitten by one of the members of his congregation. I was showin' the kitten to little Jeffery and he got the queerest look on his face. It was a frown. But it looked so out of place because it was such an *adult* frown. Almost as if he weren't satisfied with the kitten! He stroked its fur, gentle-like, touched its ears, then, so quickly that I couldn't stop him, he plunged his finger into the kitten's eye. Gouged the poor little thing's eye out."

Mrs. Collinson was staring over Hunt's shoulder again, as if she were seeing the event take place behind him and describing it to them as it happened.

"Well, Mrs. Collinson, a little baby that young would have no understanding of—" Hunt began.

"But then, Dr. Hunt," she said, looking at him again, "my baby smiled. Once the kitten was yowlin', swipin' at its bloody face with its paws, Jeffery smiled and cooed."

Hunt sniffed and Tom scribbled briefly on his pad, his eyes glancing up regularly at Mrs. Collinson. Before Hunt could speak again, she continued.

"Jeffery's father always hated him, he did. He always seemed to sense somethin' about him. But, while I knew he was different, I loved him. He was my son and I loved him. And Jeremiah, my husband, he held that against me. So it became like a little war, a quiet little battle that was constantly goin' on between my husband and the two of us. I tried to protect him— Jeffery, that is. I tried to protect him from his father and then, as the boy got older ... from himself." She paused once again to reach up and adjust her collar nervously, but in a relaxed sort of way. "He hated school, my Jeffery did. But he liked the companionship it brought. He liked bein' with the other children, and he liked animals, too. Like that little kitten we kept after tendin' to its eye. It wandered around the little trailer we lived in, real cautious, its eye a dark, scarred mess, and it wouldn't get near Jeffery. He tried playin' with it ... well, *he* called it play ... but it wouldn't let him."

Hunt swallowed, even though there was little moisture in his mouth. He was becoming increasingly uncomfortable. The woman across the table from him was talking, in a remarkably casual way, about someone who was obviously—obvious to Hunt, anyway—very disturbed and in need of treatment, and yet she had treated him as a perfectly normal child.

"Mrs. Collinson, didn't other people notice that your son was ... different?"

"I tried not to give 'em the chance. I didn't let him go over to his classmates' houses like most kids; I didn't allow him to attend little birthday parties or Halloween parties. The thought of him bein' with other children without me there frightened me. As it was ... well, there were several things that we had to ... work hard to cover up."

"What things?"

"Oh ... things he did to his pets. Others' pets. Things he did to ... to other children."

Hunt fidgeted in his chair and noticed that his palms were sweating. He yearned for a cigarette, but there was a bright NO SMOKING sign on the wall above the television. He opened his mouth to speak but, again, she continued.

"And he always turned to me to help him. We buried his sins together. In a dark cave that only we knew about. His father never knew about that place, but he eventually learned of the things Jeffery had done. Some of them, anyway. That's when he had me put in here. And he kicked Jeffery out. Told him he never wanted to see his wicked face again. Told him to go to the devil, where he should have gone in the first place. Jeffery was seventeen then. He hardly knew his father. The only time they spoke or were really together at all was when Jeremiah put him to bed at night. He thought it was important that the boy learn to worship, so he saw to it that Jeffery had a little worship every night before goin' to bed. But they were never close." She smiled at Hunt, looking down her nose again. "Now this. Jeffery's punishment was death. Mine's bein' here. To sit and remember that I could've stopped all of it long ago. I took him to a psychiatrist once, without Jeremiah knowin' about it, 'course. The doctor told me the boy should be committed at once, but I wouldn't have it. I could've prevented the deaths of all those young women. All those ... people."

"I understand that you don't have to stay here, though, Mrs. Collinson," Hunt said softly.

"Oh, but I want to. It's safer. In here, nothing is unexpected. Everyone in here is *supposed* to be crazy, so there are no surprises. Now, if you'd seen my son when he was a little boy, you would have thought he was nothin' more than a little boy. You wouldn't have known what he *really* was. A little monster who delighted in evil. That's the way it is out there." She nodded her head toward the window across the room. "The monsters are all over. You just can't see them, because they're just people, like you and me. They're supposed to be normal. Safe. They can hide their evil, whether it's the smallest of lies or the complete destruction of another human being. No, thank you, Dr. Hunt. I'm much happier in here."

Hunt began wringing his hands in his lap. There was something about Mrs. Collinson's words that sounded very familiar. They were not unlike the way he had been thinking lately. She seemed to feel the same way about *everyone* as Hunt felt about the little crawlers that had brought Tom and himself to see this woman. He wondered if he dared tell her about what he'd seen, or perhaps just drop a hint and see if she picked it up.

"Mrs. Collinson," he said, "I get the idea from the way you talk about your son that perhaps you feel he was ... well, that his evil, as you say, was more than just a part of his personality. Is that true?"

"Are you askin' me if I think my son had some sort of supernatural power?" That defiant smile again. "Dr. Hunt, nothin' I could ever learn about my son would surprise me. In fact, now that I've had time to think about raisin' him, about the horrible mistakes I made, about things he did, the ways he acted—just the way he would *look* at me sometimes—I think that they shouldn't've buried his dead body. They should've burned it. Then they should've burned the ashes. Because sometimes, at night, when I'm in my bed tryin' to get to sleep, I can hear footsteps outside my door. I hear him stop, then knock. Then I can hear him whisper for me. 'Mother,' he says, 'Mother, come out now. It's time to go bury my sins, Mother.' When he comes," Mrs. Collinson said, "he stays outside my door all night long."

Julie was waiting for them at Hunt's when they returned. "How'd it go, guys?" she asked when they walked in. She was sitting on the sofa with the day's newspaper spread out beside her.

"Well," Tom said tiredly, plopping down on the other end of the sofa without removing his coat, "she's a pretty strange lady. 'Course, I guess it would be safe to say the whole family is strange, even though we haven't met the father yet."

"But we got his address from Mrs. Collinson," Hunt said, taking his coat off and hanging it on the old-fashioned coatrack by the door, removing a cigarette from one of the coat's pockets. He walked over to them and sat down in his rocker, lighting up. "We got the name of the psychiatrist she took Jeffery too, also."

They gave Julie the whole story, telling her everything they'd learned from Mrs. Collinson. Hunt did most of the talking and Tom simply nodded or voiced occasional agreement, scratching the back of his neck slowly, almost groggily.

"She really loved him," Julie said quietly when Hunt was finished.

"And feared him," Hunt added. "I think we learned something. Mrs. Collinson believes that her son was ... well, that he had certain abilities. Supernatural talents, maybe. Didn't you get that idea, Tom?"

Tom nodded slowly. "She never really came out and said so, but I think she believed that, yes."

"She never came out and said a lot of things. Like that cave. I wish she would've told us where that damned thing is. We might be able to learn something from that."

"Then, again," Julie said, "maybe it's better that you *don't* know where it is."

A band of smoke slithered from between Hunt's slightly parted lips. "Maybe."

"So," Tom said, sitting up a little straighter, but still looking slumped, weary, "what do we do next? Go see Reverend Collinson?"

"Wait a minute," Julie interjected, holding up a hand. "Just before you got back, I saw this. Another article about Collinson." She tapped a fingertip on the opened paper beside her. "It mentions a girl in here, an old girl friend of Collinson's. It doesn't say much about her, really. She's got a record: shoplifting and drugs, that sort of thing. She says that Collinson's death is 'a real loss.' " She looked up at Tom, then Hunt. "Think she'd be any help?"

"Sure," Tom said before Hunt could answer. "Where is she?"

"That's the problem. It just says she's working as a waitress in Yountville. Doesn't say where, or anything." Her eyes were scanning the article.

"What's her name?" Hunt asked.

"Becky Haber."

"We could look her up in—"

"I already tried that," Julie interrupted Tom. "She's not listed."

"Well, there aren't *that* many restaurants in Yountville, are there?"

"There are enough," Hunt replied. "Look, I think the best thing to do now would be to give it a break. Why don't you get some food and a good night's sleep, Tom? Then we can do some more tomorrow."

"I feel fine, Doc. I'm not even hungry." That was a lie. His stomach was growling. "I'd really like to—"

"Doctor's orders, Tom," Hunt said with a smile, but also with a serious shade in his voice. "If we start early tomorrow, we could probably cover a lot of ground. Tell you what. Why don't I fix supper for you here? I'm really a good cook. Ask her."

"Sure is," Julie added,

"Thanks, but, no. I can stop and get something. I'd like to eat out tonight, in fact. But, thank you. I mean, for everything. For your help and ... everything."

"It's nothing. Just take care of yourself, Tom," Hunt said.

3 - A BELIEVER

TOM DID INDEED want to eat out, but not at just any restaurant. He drove down the St. Helena Highway toward Yountville after leaving Hunt's. The sunset glowed in his rearview mirror like a sore in the sky bleeding through swollen, dark clouds. As he drove past vineyards and hills tinted an eerie orange by the sinking sun, he thought of Becky Haber and wondered what kind of girl could go with someone like Jeffery Collinson? If he could find her, what might she be able to tell him about her ex-boyfriend? Tom didn't even know what he was going to ask her. He regretted that he was not as eloquent as Hunt.

When he arrived in Yountville, he parked his car, stepped out into the newly born evening, and, starting at the south end of town, he went into the first restaurant he came to, a little Italian place. There was sawdust on the floor and the air was rich with spicy aromas.

"Just one this evening, sir?" asked a broadly smiling waitress whom Tom had not seen approach. She was short and plump and held a menu before her in both hands.

"Uh ... well ..." Tom shifted his weight from one foot to the other, slipped his hands into his coat pockets, then out again. "Um ... actually, I was just wondering if ... uh ... a girl by the name of Becky Haber works here."

The little waitress lowered the menu and tilted her head, looking at once disappointed and suspicious. "Haber? No, there's nobody works here by that name."

He shrugged. "Oh. Well, thanks." He took one step back, then turned and walked out.

Hunt had been right. There *were* more than enough restaurants

in Yountville. Although small, it was the kind of town in which
no one really seemed to live; people just seemed to pass through.
It appeared to have been erected with tourists in mind and,
because of that fact, there were more restaurants than one would
expect to find in a town so small. Tom came to a little one called
The Crepe Vine. Kimberly used to love going there. So did the
kids, in fact.

(But we won't think about that now, will we)

He went inside, numbing himself to the familiar surroundings,
the memory-laden smells, and asked, once again, if Becky Haber
was around. She was not. He thanked the waitress, his words
sounding very fuzzy to him, and left.

As he walked down the sidewalk, he passed two restaurants—a
deli and a coffee shop—that were already closed. He realized that
Becky could be employed by one of them, in which case his little
search would be a waste of time. But he continued. He walked
on past quaint little gift shops, a candy store, a stationery store,
their windows all dark and sleeping. Only the restaurants and a
small grocery store remained open. At the fourth restaurant he
came to, a small Mexican place, he was greeted by an attractive,
young Hispanic girl who said, between smacks of her chewing
gum, "Table for one?"

He stammered again, then asked her if Becky Haber worked
there.

The girl blinked. "No, she don't work here, but she's my
roommate."

Tom's hands jerked from his coat pockets in surprise. "What?"

The girl giggled. "We got an apartment down on Vineyard
View, by the horse ranch." The girl nodded her head in a vague
direction. "You been going to all the restaurants looking for her,
or something?"

"Yeah, as a matter of fact, I have."

"You came to the wrong town for that," she replied, shaking
her head and giggling again. "Becky works at a little bar-and-
grill down the block called Willy's."

"Ah," Tom said. It was a sigh that seemed to burst from his
lungs quietly. "Thank you. Thanks a lot."

"What are you, a friend of hers, or something?"

"Uh ... not really. Well ... no."

"Oh. Well, if you're somebody she don't wanna see, don't tell her I sent you." She smiled, lifted her hand, and gave a little wave with her fingers, then turned and disappeared around the corner.

Tom picked up his pace as he hurried toward Willy's, his arms swinging at his sides. He tried to formulate a few questions to ask her, but he couldn't. He was too worried that she wouldn't want to talk to him at all. Maybe he should have left it to Hunt. Hunt knew how to handle people. Tom didn't. Tom knew how to handle blood, urine, graduated cylinders, serum skimmers, and the like. Strangers were out of his league. But he was going to give it a shot, anyway.

Willy's was loud and dark. Milky strands of smoke hung in the air just below the heavily shaded lights like the patiently waiting webs of a dark spider. There was a long bar, and a few tables. The walls sported the logos of various brands of beer, some of them sparkling with little lights, and there were two tapestries that Tom could barely make out in the dim light: one pictured dogs sitting around a table playing cards and smoking cigars and cigarettes, and the other pictured the same group of dogs seated around a boxing ring, excitedly watching a fight. A jukebox was playing loud, twangy country and western music and three couples were dancing. It occurred to Tom briefly that they were dancing quite poorly, but the thought was unimportant and his mind rejected it quickly as his eyes narrowed to slits, trying to cut through the murky atmosphere to find someone who looked as if she might be Becky Haber.

He walked over to the bar and found an empty stool, his movements slow, his head turning back and forth, scanning the group of people. He caught bits and pieces of conversation.

"... goddamned thing snapped right off ..."

"... *never* go out, then you bring me *here*, of all the ..."

"... with tits the size of mothballs ..."

"Whatta you need?"

Tom turned on the stool to face the voice behind the bar and immediately knew, somehow, that he was looking at Becky Haber.

She was not tall, but she did not appear short because she was so painfully thin. She wore a plain, tight shirt with blue and white stripes and a somewhat ratty V-neck collar. Her collarbones pressed against the shirt's thin material. Her breasts were tiny with a wide, flat space between them, their small size accentuating the small lumps that were her nipples. Her ribs formed a track down the front of her body, and her neck and throat were no more than a skinny bundle of cords and tendons. Her face was so taut that, for a moment, Tom had the impression that her skin had been pulled tightly over her face and gathered in a little bun at the back of her skull. Her brown hair looked dry and coarse; it looked like straight strands of very dry dirt that were clinging together magically. Her hands were on the oak bar, and Tom saw that her wrists were like sticks that might break at the slightest touch. She smiled at him, waiting for him to answer, flashing clean but crooked teeth.

"Um ... well ... what do you have?" Tom asked finally. "I'm pretty hungry."

"I can get you something from the grill," she replied. "We got great burgers. Steak sandwiches. What sounds good?"

"How about a cheeseburger?"

"You got it. Anything to drink?"

"Give me a Henry's."

Her eyes, set back in the sockets in the way an old woman's eyes might be, blinked at him, an intentional blink, as if to say, *Comin' up.*

Tom watched her walk over to the little window that looked in on the kitchen and give his order, then saw her go to the tap to get his beer. She came over and thunked the mug of beer down on the bar before him and smiled again.

"Excuse me," he said quietly. "Are you Becky Haber?"

Her smile teetered for just a second, then regained its balance. "Yeah. I am. Why?"

"Well, I was wondering if I could ... uh ... well, have a word with you."

She shifted her weight behind the bar and her smile did fade this time. "You a reporter?"

"No, no," he assured her, wagging his upheld palm back and forth between them. "I'm not a reporter." His mind raced suddenly; he wondered if he should use the writer story he and Hunt had used with Mrs. Collinson. Maybe not. It might not go over too well with Becky.

"You a cop, then?" she asked before he could go on.

"No, not that, either."

"Then what do you want with me?"

"Well, I ..." He sighed and reached his hand around to scratch the back of his neck as he wondered what to say, what might get the best results. He could make up something else, maybe say that he was an old friend of Collinson's. But she might be able to catch him in that lie. It would probably be best, he decided, if he told the truth. "I'd like to talk with you about Jeffery Collinson."

"What about him?" She sounded very defensive and suspicious.

"Um ... I work at the Napa Valley Hospital. I was there when he came in."

The tightness around her lips relaxed and her shoulders slumped a little. "You saw Jeffery? You were there, I mean, when he died?"

"Uh ... yeah. I was there."

She chewed on her lower lip a moment, sucking it in between her teeth. "You're not a reporter?"

Tom raised both palms reassuringly for just a second. "Swear it," he said.

She glanced over her shoulder. "Well, I can't talk for long," she said, turning to him again.

"That's okay. Just a few minutes is all I ask."

"Okay." Becky turned and stepped over to the window, sticking her head in pensively. "Connie?" she called, sounding apologetic.

"Huh?" snapped a harsh voice.

"Urn ... do you think you could cover for me?"

"*Now?*"

"Just a couple minutes, Con? Please?" Becky pressed her palms down on the narrow deck and glanced at Tom with a dark look that seemed to be worry. Maybe desperation. "It's this old friend of mine. Haven't seen him in like six, seven years, and he can't stay long. I'd really appreciate it, Con. Please?"

The two-way door to the right of the little rectangular window swung open and a stocky woman in her forties with bright red hair came out. "Oh, all right, Becky, but no more tonight, 'kay?"

"Promise. Thanks, Con." Just then, someone put a plate through the window: Tom's order. Becky picked it up and came over to him, more of a bounce in her walk now. "Here," she said, putting the burger down before him. "Why don't we go to a back table to talk." She came out from behind the bar and Tom followed her through the smoke and the noise, past the dancers, the jukebox, and the canine tapestries to a small table in a dark corner of Willy's.

She was wearing a pair of faded blue jeans on her pencil-like legs, and a pair of sneakers with no socks were on her feet.

"How did you know I was here?" Becky asked as they seated themselves at the table.

"Well, I didn't. I just knew you were a waitress in town. From the paper. So I just looked around till I found you."

"Hmph!" she grunted lightly. "Great place, isn't it? Willy's, I mean. Goin' on twenty-six and I'm workin' in this dump," She shook her head slowly. She watched Tom bite into one of the fries that came with the burger and said, "If those aren't done yet, let me know. I'll take 'em back to Willy. He's really lousy with fries."

"They're fine."

There were a few moments of silence as Tom took a bite of his burger, realizing just how hungry he was. Becky watched him, sizing him up, seeming to decide whether or not she could trust him.

"What did he say?" she asked suddenly. "I mean, before he died. Did he say anything?"

"I just got there a couple seconds before he died. I didn't really hear him say anything."

"What ..." She put an elbow on the table and placed a fingertip between her lips. Tom noticed that her nails were bitten down to their limit. "What did he look like?"

Tom swallowed and looked across at her; her eyes were buried in shadow. "Not good. He was in pretty bad shape. And he was ... well, I guess he was out of his head when they brought him in."

She smiled slightly and shook her head, a look of girlish admiration brightening her gaunt features. "No. Maybe they *thought* he was, but that was only 'cause they didn't understand anything he was sayin', probably."

"What do you mean?"

"Nobody ever understood Jeffery. 'Cept me. It was like we'd known each other for years when we met. We were ... well, we were sort of lookin' for each other. Know what I mean?"

"When did you meet?"

"'Bout six years ago. I was workin' in a newsstand place in Napa. Y'know, a little hole in the wall with magazines, newspapers, paperbacks. Jeffery came in there for the latest *Heavy Metal*—that was the only magazine Jeffery ever read— and he kept lookin' at me. Glancin' at first, then starin'. And I kept lookin' at him, too. He was kind of dirty, dumpy, y'know, but that didn't make any difference to me, 'cause I don't think appearance makes a person any less of a person, y'know? I try to keep my eyes open to what's, like, on the inside, not just outside. Anyways"—she smiled then, remembering—"Jeffery asked me out then. Well, not really *out,* I guess. He asked me over to his place to listen to some records. I know, I know, dumb line, old as God, but I figured it was okay because there was somethin' to him. I could tell then. Somethin' in his eyes that ... well, that really got to me. So I went. We were together for three years after that."

"I hope you won't take offense," Tom said cautiously, "but Jeffery Collinson was a dangerous guy. He always was, since he was a kid. You're lucky to be alive today."

She giggled and shook her head. "No. I was never in any danger. 'Cause I understood him. We related, we ... we were together up *here.*" She tapped her temple with a bony finger. "I understood what he was doin' and why he was here. I was never in danger."

"Well, *I'd* like to understand him *too,* Becky, I'd like you to help me if you would. Tell me what he was thinking, what made him tick. Why did he kill all those people? Why was he the way he was? Do you know? Can you explain it to me?"

She looked bitter for a moment; she frowned and waved a hopeless hand at him. "It can't be explained. Jeffery was what he was. Just 'cause what he did—what he *needed* to do—went against all the stupid man-made laws everybody lives by, they all thought he was some kind of maniac, like a Jack the Ripper, or somebody. Even though I never saw him while he was doin' that, I knew he was doin' it, and I knew why. And it made me happy, it made me proud. Nobody but me understands that he was doin' it all for *us.*" She pressed her palms to her meager breasts to include herself. "So that we could live the way we're meant to, do the things that are in all of us. *Deep* in all of us. Things we've buried and decided to call wrong and evil. He was here to save us from all those ... those labels. He was like Christ, only he was savin' us from all those chains Christ locked us up with, y'know?"

The Dark Christ, Tom thought, remembering what Hunt had told him about Collinson's rantings. He could tell this girl had believed in Collinson then, when she was with him, and she still believed in him just as fervently. She looked normal, although unhealthy. Collinson must have had quite a philosophy to have sold someone on it so well, even one single person.

"No, Becky, I *don't* know," he said. "I don't understand any of what you're saying. What exactly was he trying to do for all of us? And how did he plan to do it?"

She shook her head again and sighed. She seemed to be feeling pity for Tom. "'Course you don't understand. You couldn't, really, and you won't. Until it all happens. And it will. Even though he's dead. Everything he's done will bring in the time of darkness, just like he wanted. Can't be stopped now. But I guess it can't be understood, either. Like I said, I was the only one who understood him. He told me everything, shared everything with me, even his special secret place. The place he went to think, to write in his diary, to hide his deep thoughts and his ..." She seemed distant now, speaking as though the words were not originally hers. "... his darkest sins."

Tom's heart skipped a beat and he reached across the table to put a hand on her arm. *"The cave?"* he hissed.

Becky Haber pulled her arm gently from Tom's hand and her head tilted with sudden suspicion. "How do you know?" she asked. Her voice sounded hurt, betrayed. "How the hell do *you* know?" She leaned far forward over the table and lowered her voice to a rasp. "I don't even know who you are. Here I'm tellin' you all this stuff and I don't even know who you are or why you're here."

"I just want to understand, Becky. I want to know what you know." Tom tried hard to sound sincere, but he was too excited now. He remembered her mention of a diary. "Do you still have his diary, Becky? Did he leave that with you?"

"That's nunna your goddamned business!" she snapped, but quietly so no one else would hear her. Her voice was nearly lost in all the music and laughter around them. "Who the hell ya think you are, a total stranger, comin' in here and askin' me all these questions? Are you a cop? Still houndin' him even though he's dead? Can't you let him—"

"No, Becky, I am *not* a cop."

"Then whatta you wanna know all this stuff for?" She leaned forward just a bit more and dim light pushed away the shadows of her eyes. He could see the smoky blue color of her eyes through the angry slits they had become.

Tom's mouth worked silently. He didn't know what to say. It had all been so easy up till now. She'd been talking so freely, so smoothly, even though he hadn't known what she was saying.

Now he was expected to explain himself, and he didn't know what to say.

"Get away from me," she ordered. "I don't wanna see you again, whoever you are, *whatever you* are. Just keep away from me. Someday you'll see, you'll know what he was doin'. And you'll be sorry. I can promise you. Now, get outta here. Go pay Connie for the burger and get the hell outta here before I have ya thrown out."

"Please, Becky, I just want to—"

"Get out." She slapped her palms down on the tabletop, stood, and walked away without looking back at him.

After a few moments of staring at his food, Tom stood then, too, and left.

4 - THE LENGTHENING SHADOW

SOMETHING WAS WRONG.

Although she couldn't pin it down, Megan Crawford knew that something was out of place and, now that she was really thinking about it, had been for the last week. She'd recovered perfectly from the nightmare in room 307. Megan had known she would, although everyone around her had been worried; she prided herself in her ability to bounce back from bad experiences. But now, when she looked around her, it looked as if—as silly as it sounded—everyone *else* had been horribly affected by something and as if, unlike Megan, they *weren't* bouncing back.

She lay on her bed, gently stroking her black-and-white cat, Boston; he purred loudly, stretched out beside her, and occasionally made the sound that had earned him his name: a meow with a sort of Eastern twang to it, as if he'd been born and raised in Boston—*meeeaaah*. Toto was playing on her small but adequate stereo and her mind was wandering back and forth over the past week.

Mrs. Skerritt was an old woman who had lived four houses down from the Crawfords ever since Megan had been a little girl. Her husband had died many years ago and the story went that Mrs. Skerritt had promised him, on his deathbed, to continue tending his garden after he was gone. He had taken great pride in his flower garden in front of the little yellow house. She kept her promise; for as long as Megan could remember, the woman could be seen daily, even during the winter, caring for the small patch of land that had once made her husband so happy. When others commented on how pretty the garden looked, Mrs. Skerritt usually replied with something like, "Yeah, but someday I'm just gonna have enough of it and pull them all out by their roots." It was always said in a good-natured way, so no one took it very seriously. A few days ago, Mrs. Skerritt had gotten out of bed in the middle of the night and apparently taken an old hoe to the entire garden, destroying it all, even those flowers that had not yet bloomed. She was found curled up in the middle of the mess in her long flannel nightgown the following morning, dead of a heart attack.

Mr. Rand, the school librarian, was in the hospital in a coma. He'd just freaked out in the library a couple of days ago, throwing books and screaming at students. Megan had heard that he ran around the library with bulging, crazed eyes, yelling about "all the quiet" and taking swings at people. He'd pulled a whole bookcase down on top of his own head. Nobody knew why.

Of course, there were those weird things at the hospital: Mrs. Webster and Dr. Hollister. And Tom Conrad's wife going crazy with a knife.

Just a few minutes ago, Megan had gotten a phone call from Winny Albertson. A pretty strange one. Winny hadn't been to school all week, and Megan had neither seen nor heard from her during the weekend. She'd called Winny a couple of times, but her mother had answered and told her that Winny was asleep, and, the second time, in the shower. On the phone earlier, Winny's voice had sounded thick, as though she'd been crying.

"Jeez, girl! Where you been?" Megan had asked.

"Here at home," she'd replied slowly.

"Are you sick? You've missed school."

"Well, sort of. I guess."

"Are you coming back tomorrow?"

"I ... I don't know."

"Your mother must be shitting bricks, huh? With you missing all this school?"

"Well, she ... she doesn't know. Please don't tell her—you won't will you?" Her last words had been spoken suddenly, as if to get them all out at once.

Megan hadn't replied for a few moments. She'd heard Winny's quiet sobs on the other end of the line.

"Win, what's the matter? You want me to come over?"

"No-no-no, don't come over. I'd ... I'd like to talk, though, so would it be okay if I came over there?"

"Sure. Can you drive? Want me to come get you?"

"Uh-uh. I'll be okay. Be right there."

When the doorbell rang, Megan rushed out of her bedroom to get it before either of her parents did. She didn't know what kind of shape Winny would be in, and she didn't want to have to explain anything to her parents. She *never* wanted to explain anything to her parents. She opened the door and, immediately, Winny said, "Can we go to your room?"

The girl was a shambles. Her black hair, once quite long, had been cut severely short, and it had been done poorly, unevenly, making Winny's head look a little lopsided. She was wearing her heavily rimmed glasses instead of her contacts, something she seldom did anymore. Her rather thin lips looked swollen, and the absence of makeup on her face, along with everything else, made her look as if she'd just crawled out of bed and reluctantly thrown herself together. She held schoolbooks to her breasts, her shoulders were hunched, and her head was slightly bowed. She wore a baggy sweatshirt and jeans, but no coat despite the chilling breeze that had arisen that afternoon.

"Who's at the door?" Megan's mother called from the kitchen.

"It's just Winny. We're gonna go to my room and study together."

"Oh, good," her mother replied, always happy to hear of her daughter's studiousness.

Megan pulled Winny inside, closed the door, and quickly led the teary-eyed girl by the hand to her room.

"What's going on, Winny?" Megan asked, closing and locking her bedroom door, her voice a mixture of concern and annoyance that Winny hadn't come to her sooner about whatever it was that had holed her up the last few days.

Winny sat down on the side of Megan's bed, letting her books fall from her arms onto the floor, and began crying quietly. She took her glasses off and clamped a hand over her red, puffy eyes. Boston jumped up on the bed beside her with a welcoming "meeeaaah," but it only made Winny gasp and twitch. Megan sat down beside her and put her arm around Winny's shoulders.

"What is it?" she asked again, this time in a whisper.

"My brother," Winny gulped.

"Oh, god, is he all right? Is he hurt, or sick?" Megan felt a pang of dread. Other than herself, she knew that Winny's brother, Chuck, was just about the only friend the girl had. Considered too whiney and immature by most of her classmates, Winny was usually ignored by the others at school. And, what really enraged Megan, Winny just wasn't attractive enough for any of the guys around to single her out and at least get to know her. If something had happened to her older brother ... well, then Megan could understand Winny's condition.

"Nuh-no, he's not hurt. He came over Friday night. Mom and Dad were guh-gone." She waved a hand rapidly back and forth, signifying that she couldn't talk yet. She swallowed and breathed deeply a few times, until her sobs had passed. "I ... I guess I should tell you everything first. See, when Chuck and I were growing up ... well, you know we've always been close, Chuck and me. We're the closest two people in our whole family. Sometimes, at family get-togethers and stuff, people kinda think we're weird, I guess, because we prefer each other's company to everyone else's, so we usually go off by ourselves and talk, or something. We've just. Always. Been very. Close." She punctuated her words by patting her palms on her thighs, "Once, a couple years ago, I was really depressed, so he had me over to his apartment. He wanted to cheer me up with some grass because he knew I'd never tried it before, so we sat around and, you know, toked up. He'd even called off a date so he could have me over. Well, we were stoned, listening to music, and he told me he loved me. I said I loved him, too, and then we started talking about how close we've always been and how five years' difference in our ages was hardly noticeable and then ... and then he suh-said, he said that he would like to take me to bed and make love to me. 'I wanna make love to you like you deserve to be loved,' he suh-said, and I said—well, I was shocked and couldn't speak for a while—but then I said, 'We can't do that, you know we can't do that, Chuck, we *can't!*' I ... I guess, down inside, it didn't sound too bad, 'cause ... well, I guess I needed that then. But ... my *brother* ...'"

She coughed and slapped her chest, wiped her eyes, her lips, then went on.

"Then he comes over Friday night and ... and ... and Mom and Dad are gone and ... my god, Megan, you should've seen him. It wasn't Chuck, it wasn't my brother. He looked crazy. I mean, his eyes were, like, bulging and wet and he was smiling so ... well, like an animal, or something. I was just laying around the house trying to write that paper for Loveless's history class and I was just wearing this T-shirt and these shorts I've got—you know, those ugly yellow ones—and I was laying in front of the

fire trying to write and he just sort of bursts in and says, 'Ah, you
look like you're waiting for me, sis. Time to take a break from
those studies. We're finally gonna do it,' he says, 'we're finally
gonna do it to it,' and he hurries over to me, unbuckling his belt
and taking his pants off—"

Winny's face began to twist up with the memory and more
tears began to flow as she continued to speak. Megan, a knot
tightening in her chest as her mind automatically jumped ahead
of what Winny was saying, held her friend closer to her.

"—and I don't know what the hell to think or do, and before I
know it, he's on me and lifting my shirt and ... and ... Chuck"—
she paused, turning to face Megan—"raped me. He raped
me, Megan. My buh-brother *raped* me!" She buried her face
in Megan's shoulder and clutched at her arms until they hurt,
sobbing uncontrollably.

Megan held her for a while, even rocked her, until the crying
subsided some. Winny leaned away from her, wiped her eyes
again, and said, "Mom and Dad don't know anything about it,
and I wanna keep it that way. The last two mornings I've left the
house at the right time, pretending to go to school. I go sit in the
park or in a coffee shop, or I go to Santa Rosa and see a movie,
only I never really *see* it, I just sit in the theater like a zombie. I ...
I take a lot of showers and I eat out and say I'm with friends so
they won't see my face ... my lips. I told them I got my hair cut
because I was tired of fighting with it."

"But why? Why did you cut it?"

She stared at Megan for a few moments and chewed on her
lips. "He ... he ... well, my lips got cut on my braces 'cause he
was so rough and they swelled—"

"But your hair."

"He ..." Her face started to screw up again. Then her words
came out in a rush. "He jerked himself off and he came on me—
he came on my face and in my hair and then he rubbed it all in
and I just couldn't stand it, Megan! I had to cut it all off, I had to
because I just couldn't stand it. I had to come tell you, I had to tell
someone because I just couldn't hold it in anymore. And it had
to be you because ... you're the only friend I've got now, Megan.
Chuck just isn't my brother anymore. He's gone crazy. He's a
maniac. If you could've seen him, seen his eyes ..."

Megan was gritting her teeth and her scalp was beginning

to tingle with anger toward Chuck. "Where is he?" she asked. "Where did he go? What is he doing?"

Winny shrugged and rubbed the back of her hand under her nose vigorously. "I don't know. He just left. I guess he's not home 'cause Mom said she's been trying to call him to invite him over for dinner and he's never there." Her head jerked around toward Megan and her eyes filled with dread. "What am I gonna do, Megan, if he comes over? I can't handle that. Not after this. What'm I gonna do?"

"Winny, did he say anything that might tell you what brought it all on?"

She shook her head, another sob catching wetly in her throat. "No. He hadn't been drinking; there was no liquor smell on his breath. And he hasn't been able to afford grass lately, not for months, what with changing jobs like he did, and you know Chuck doesn't do any hard stuff. He just ... he just kept laughing and saying how much he'd always wanted to ... to do it to me." She put a hand over her face and whimpered.

Megan blinked. Frowned. Why did that ring a bell? The fact that Chuck had said he'd always wanted to "do it" with Winny— why did that seem to sound familiar? Dr. Hunt ... calling her on the phone ... asking her those questions about Mrs. Webster ...

(did she say anything about ... about what she did about ... eating ... the lady in the other bed maybe in passing maybe in passing)

It was as if he'd suspected something, suspected that the old lady had mentioned eating the Whiner, suspected that she'd been wanting to do it for some time, perhaps.

First of all, that weird stuff in the hospital, then Tom Conrad's family, then Mrs. Skerritt, then Mr. Rand, and now Chuck. All of it passing smoothly over people around her—some she knew and some she didn't—like a big long shadow that just kept getting longer and darker. *Probably more stuff I know nothing about, too,* she thought. And all of it within the last week. Since that killer had been brought into ER and had died.

(Dr. Hunt—you know, in ER?—everybody's saying he thinks he saw something crawl out of the guy's face. Out of his mouth or nose or something. It was a worm, long and black. Crazy, huh?)

The memory of Beth's words at the hospital last week made Megan feel chilly.

Boston rubbed up against Megan's elbow, purring, then crawled into her lap and curled up comfortably. Megan stroked his fur absently as Winny sniffled.

What does Dr. Hunt know?

5 - MAN OF GOD

WHEN TOM DID not call Hunt the following morning, Hunt assumed he was still in bed getting some much needed sleep, and decided to leave him there. He and Julie could go talk with Reverend Collinson and report back to Tom later. He told Julie he thought it might be wise to use the this-is-my-friend-the-writer approach he and Tom had used with Mrs. Collinson, so Julie said she'd dress for the part. They stopped by her apartment and she changed into black pants, a soft pink shirt, a gray angora vest-sweater and a darker gray corduroy blazer.

"All you need now is a pipe," Hunt chuckled as they left her apartment, and she slapped him on the shoulder.

Mrs. Collinson had given them her husband's address and phone number, but Hunt decided it would be best if they not call ahead, taking the risk of finding him gone, rather than taking the risk of being turned away on the phone. At least they would have a foot in the door.

"What if he doesn't want to talk about his son?" Julie asked as they drove down Silverado Trail toward Calistoga, where the reverend lived.

"Judging from what his ex-wife said, he might not even acknowledge the fact that he's ever *had* a son," Hunt replied, not without a little dread in his voice. "We might not learn anything from him."

"What do you expect to learn, if anything? I mean, just so I'll know what he's looking for. I don't know. Maybe I can charm something out of him."

"I'm sure you could, but we don't want to make him too suspicious. I really don't *know* what we're looking for, but I'm sure we'll know it when we find it." He shrugged uncertainly. "Something will hopefully ring a bell soon. Something that will explain the things he said in ER that night. Something we can connect to those ... things."

They rode in silence for a while after that and Julie began to wonder what this reverend might be like, if he might be like either of her grandparents: fanatical, strict in every way. If so, she was afraid she might find it difficult to hide the discomfort that she would no doubt feel in his presence. She hoped she wouldn't make things difficult for Hunt.

Reverend Jeremiah Collinson lived in a medium-sized silver-and-white mobile home in a mobile-home park that looked bigger than it really was because it was nearly half-empty. There was a cream-colored Volkswagen bus parked in front of the trailer, looking as if it had seen a lot of traveling over the years. A faded bumper sticker read THE LORD IS MY SHEPHERD. Hunt parked behind the bus and they got out of the car. They were approaching the trailer when the door opened up and Reverend Collinson stepped out on the small wooden porch that had been built—apparently rather carelessly—and placed beneath the door.

Reverend Collinson was a portly man with rosy cheeks and a smile worthy of a department store Santa Claus. He had a head of thick red hair, peppered with gray and carefully combed, and below his slightly cleft chin there was a pouch of jiggly flesh. He wore a long-sleeved white shirt, a black-and-gray-striped tie, and black pants. Putting one hand on his round belly and the other on the porch railing, he said, "Hello, there. How are you this morning?"

"Just fine, thank you," replied Hunt, returning the man's smile.

"Reverend Jeremiah Collinson," he said, coming down the porch steps, his shiny black shoes thumping on the wood. He held his hand out and Hunt shook it.

"I'm Dr. Martin Hunt. This is Julie Calahan."

"And what can I do for you people?" His smile never faded.

"Well, Reverend, I'm a doctor of emergency medicine. I work at the Napa Valley Hospital. In the emergency room."

Collinson's cheeks moved; the corners of his mouth trembled. "Yes," he said, his tone a bit lower.

"I worked on your son when he came in last week. Jeffery."

The rosy cheeks relaxed and the smile fell away. His head tilted back a little.

"Jeffery Collinson *was* your son, wasn't he?" Hunt asked when it was obvious the reverend was not going to reply.

Collinson's mouth smacked open and the flesh beneath his chin quaked. He took in a breath and said, "Yes, he was."

"Well, Julie, here, is a writer. She's interested in—"

"Excuse me," Collinson interrupted politely, "but are you sure you're not reporters?"

Hunt started to answer the question, but Julie beat him to it.

"I have a background in journalism," she said with a smile, stepping forward, "but I'm not working as a reporter currently. In fact, I'm hoping that the book I want to write now will establish me as a writer and I won't have to go back to reporting."

Collinson joined his hands in front of him, just below his belly, and smiled again. "And what is this book to be about? My ... son?"

"As a matter of fact, yes. Your son is very much in the news right now, and ... well, at the risk of being indelicate, the public is very interested in him. They would like to know more about him."

"Well, it seems that the newspapers have been doing more than enough to satisfy them lately."

"That's true, but ... well, I don't mean to talk down my own profession, but newspapers have a habit of giving the public what they would *like* to hear rather than what they *should* hear. The truth. I'd like to get that from you and from others who knew Jeffery."

"The truth," he muttered, glancing down at the dirt around his feet. "I'm afraid, Miss—Calahan, is it?—Miss Calahan, that the truth in this case is rather dull, not dramatic in the least."

"Then so be it," Julie replied smilingly. "I'll leave the hyperbole to the papers. The truth is what I want, however mundane it may be."

Reverend Collinson stuck the tip of his tongue behind his upper lip and moved it back and forth over his teeth thoughtfully. "If I were to answer your questions for your book, would I be able to see what you write before it is printed? And would I have any say over it? Would it be subject to my approval?"

"Certainly."

"Well." He checked his wristwatch, then joined his hands in front of himself again. "I have an appointment in about forty-five minutes, so my time is limited. But if you'd like to come inside for a cup of coffee, I'll see if I can help you at all." He smiled and turned, leading them up the porch steps and into his trailer.

Once his back was turned, Hunt glanced at Julie and she winked conspiratorially. He wanted to commend her on a job well done, but that would, of course, have to wait. He was surprised by her assertiveness; she was so convincing, so professional. He was glad she'd come with him.

Julie, on the other hand, was feeling increasingly nervous as she entered the mobile home. Hunt looked pleased, but would he stay that way? She wasn't sure what to ask Reverend Collinson, and she thought he might become suspicious if Hunt were to ask all the questions. She would play it by ear and hope that Hunt could find a way of stepping in and giving her a hand without looking too obvious.

Collinson's home was small and cramped. The first thing they saw when they walked in was a large, framed sheet of gold-tinted paperboard hanging on the wall directly across from the doorway with the Twenty-third Psalm penned in large but delicate and fragile-looking letters. Stacks of books had been pushed up against the wall and piled on a small chair that faced a tiny, dusty organ. There was a small sofa—almost a loveseat, actually—and a rocking chair, on all of which were scattered books and papers; there was a little television set and an end table with a reading lamp on it next to the sofa. To the immediate right was the kitchen, and Julie could hear the coffee maker that was gurgling on the counter; to the left was a narrow hallway that led, apparently, to the bathroom and bedroom. To the right of the hallway, standing alone in the corner was what seemed to be a sort of lectern. On top of it rested an enormous Bible. The cover was of thick, brown leather, slightly worn around the corners, and etched in gold in the very center of the book's cover were the words HOLY BIBLE. It had not a speck of dust on it. Hunt noticed something hanging on the wall above it. It was a crucifix, over a foot long, intricately carved in wood. The figure of Christ, naked except for a spare cloth hanging loosely before the crotch, was gaunt and obviously near death. His head hung forward and the features of the face had been done in sharp detail. The eyes stared pleadingly, and yet defiantly, ahead, straight at Hunt. The air was splayed wildly around the crown of thorns that was piercing the scalp, and carefully painted streaks of blood streamed down the face. It was so realistic that Hunt thought he could almost see the blood running. The figure made him think of Jeffery Collinson looking up at him with those bulging eyes,

(It's gonna come now)

but he turned the memory off immediately.

"That was made for me by a young man who has recently accepted Christ as his Savior," Reverend Collinson said proudly when he noticed Hunt looking at the figure. "I think it's very impressive, don't you?"

Hunt nodded. "Yes. Very talented young man."

"Please excuse the mess here," Collinson muttered, clearing away the books and papers on the sofa and chair. "Just step around these things here. See, I'm preparing for another series of meetings and it involves a lot of reading—sorting through songbooks for the appropriate hymns, that sort of thing. It's a lot of work, really, but I enjoy it." He smiled and Hunt glimpsed a silver cap over one of his molars. "Take a seat, please. Would you like some coffee? I'm making some."

"I'd like some, please," Julie said.

"Sure." Hunt nodded.

Collinson went into the kitchen behind the sofa, where Hunt and Julie settled down, and they heard a cupboard open, mugs clinking together thickly.

"Perhaps you folks would like to drop in on the meeting," Collinson said happily. "I'd love to have you come. It's going to be held in Torrance Auditorium. Would you be interested in coming?"

Hunt and Julie looked at one another and Julie gave an almost invisible shrug, as if to say, *I'm game if you are.*

"We just might do that," Hunt replied. "Thanks for the invitation."

"Oh, no invitation necessary. Everyone's welcome. Uh ... are you church folks? Do you have a denomination, if I may ask?"

"Uh ... I have no religious background," Hunt said rather quietly.

"I was raised a Seventh-day Adventist," Julie replied.

"Ah, yes. I know many of the Adventist people. Fine people, too. But I am of the belief that all denominations are one in the eyes of our Lord, Cream? Sugar?"

Julie asked for cream, and Hunt said he wanted his coffee black.

"Yes," Collinson went on, "I believe all churches have their hearts set on pretty much the same place: heaven. We all have different ways of getting there, of course, but God knows what's in our hearts." He walked back into the little living room and handed them each a cup and saucer, then returned to the kitchen for his own. He came in and sat down in the rocking chair. "Now, Miss Calahan, it is Miss, isn't it? Yes, now, how can I help you?"

"Well ... um ..." Julie glanced at Hunt as she retrieved her glasses from the inside breast pocket of her blazer and put them on, then took a pad and pen from a side pocket. "I'd like you to tell me a little about Jeffery as a child. What was he like? Was he ... different? An average little boy?"

Hunt watched her as she adjusted her glasses and opened the pad. She'd come prepared.

Collinson sipped his coffee, then smacked his lips gently, making the flesh around his face jiggle some more. "Well, Jeffery was definitely not average. He was a ... an unstable boy. He ... he had quite a temper and would become rather violent at times if he didn't get what he wanted. We tried to make him happy. We tried pets, but he ... well, he just didn't know how to handle animals. Jeffery had no respect for ... others. For life. Human or otherwise. He was very selfish. He always turned to his mother for answers, for comfort. She was a far different parent than I and was inclined to give Jeffery his way."

"We chatted with your wife yesterday," Hunt said quietly.

"Did you?" Collinson's face was suddenly without expression. "Was she ... coherent?" A smile flashed across his lips, then disappeared.

"Oh, yes. She told us of your son's temperamental nature. His cruelty toward animals."

"Yes." He sipped again. "Of course, you have to remember she's not a well woman. You must realize that since she's in that place. She's *never* been well, and I'm sure that a good deal of Jeffery's ... sickness was due to his exposure to his mother. I, on the other hand, tried to employ some discipline in raising the boy. I tried to instill in him some respect for others. And God, of course. Most importantly, God. I tried to teach him the importance of keeping God uppermost in his life. But every spiritual flame I managed to ignite was always doused by his mother. It was a very unfortunate situation all the way around. Looking back on it now, I think it might have been good for the boy to have seen a counselor, a therapist of some sort. But ..."

"Your wife seemed to think you would've disapproved of therapy," Hunt said when he realized Collinson was not going to go on. He didn't want to antagonize the man.

Collinson cocked a brow. "Did she? Well, there were so few Christian therapists around then. The mind is something that should not be toyed with without the Lord's guidance, I believe. Jeffery was already ... well, confused."

"Reverend Collinson," Julie said, after taking a drink of her coffee and replacing the cup on the saucer, which rested on the end table, "your wife said that you asked Jeffery to leave your home when he was ... I believe seventeen?"

Collinson leaned forward, holding his coffee out before him, and sucked his lips between his teeth for a moment. "Miss Calahan, please remember that my wife—my *ex*-wife—is not a clear-minded woman. I did not ... well, I didn't *ask* him to leave."

"Did you tell him?" she asked.

Don't push him, Julie, Hunt thought, wishing she could read his mind.

The reverend's face clouded over a bit. His lips pulled together and he did not take his moistly glistening eyes away from Julie. "Nor did I *tell* him to leave. I was experiencing a tremendous struggle at that time, Miss Calahan. I could see my family falling apart. My wife was quite obviously losing her mind. My son was ... he was very bitter toward me. He resented all that I'd tried to teach him about God, about good and evil and the respect one must have for them, in different ways. He had ... his own ideas. He wasn't interested in mine, and the tension was making our family life unbearable. I did everything I could. I prayed my heart out, I consulted other ministers and asked for their guidance. In the end, the only solution seemed for us to go our separate ways. I believe it was *God's* will."

Julie frowned and tilted her head, somehow puzzled by the reverend's words. "What kind of religious background did you give Jeffery?" she asked.

Collinson leaned back in the chair and shrugged with one shoulder and put a hand on his large belly. "As I said, love and respect for ... for God. The importance of daily worship. Prayer."

"You mentioned good and evil."

He shifted his position again, crossed his legs, and took in a deep breath. "We've got to make sure we're on the right side, don't you think?" He smiled again, that warm minister's smile, usually reserved for his congregation, Hunt was sure.

"You said Jeffery had his own ideas," Hunt said. "What were they?"

Collinson fidgeted in his chair some more, making it rock slightly, and shifted his coffee from one hand to the other. "Oh"—he shook his head with an air of dismissal—"they were the ideas of a confused young boy torn between two completely different ways of thinking, Dr. Hunt. He was a bright boy, but his intelligence was ... well, clouded. Wasted."

"Reverend Collinson," Julie said, "you mentioned that—"

"Uh ... I'm very sorry, Miss Calahan, Dr. Hunt, but I'm afraid I'm going to have to be going soon. I have a very busy day ahead of me. As I said, a lot of work goes into these meetings."

"Yeah." Hunt smiled and nodded. "I'm sure it does. Well, thank you for your time. Could we get together again, maybe?"

Collinson stood. "Well, I don't see how I can be of any further help to you."

"Oh, there are several questions I'd still like to ask," Julie replied as she and Hunt stood with the reverend.

"Well ..."

"Please?"

Hunt realized Julie *meant* it. She seemed very anxious to continue the interview.

"I'll make you a deal," Collinson said after a moment of thought. "I'll agree to meet with you again if you give me your promise that you'll come to my meeting next week. Okay?" He smiled and the silver cap glittered.

"Deal." Julie held out her hand and the reverend shook it gently. "Thank you for your time, Reverend, I really appreciate it."

Collinson turned to Hunt and shook his hand, too. "Dr. Hunt, may I ask what your interest is in this?"

"Oh, well"—Hunt put his hands smoothly into his pockets—"I'm a friend of Julie's and I know how much this means to her, and I was there in ER, of course. I thought it might help if she had someone along who had actually been involved in it."

"I see. I notice you've managed to shy away from the press through all of this."

"Yeah, I don't particularly care to draw much attention."

Turning to the door and opening it, Collinson said, "I have a question that you may not want to answer, since the reporters have seemed to have difficulty getting it answered. What, if anything, did Jeffery say in the emergency room before he died?"

"Mmm ... well, it was mostly incoherent."

"Did any of it make sense?" The tone of Collinson's voice was persistent. He seemed to be saying, without words, that he had answered their questions; now he would like Hunt to answer his.

"He said he was the Dark Christ. And that ... well, he said, 'It's gonna come now.' I don't know what 'it' was, but he said that his death would make no difference. He was in pretty bad shape, and I guess he knew he was dying."

Collinson's head tilted back as Hunt spoke, very slowly, and his jaw slackened. The small watery eyes widened slightly and his fleshy cheeks lost some of their color.

"You wouldn't happen to have any idea what he was talking about, would you?" Hunt asked.

Collinson was still for a few seconds; his gaze had seemed to turn inward to examine his thoughts. Then he shook his head—it was almost a jerk, really—and said, "No idea at all. He was ... a very sick young man."

"Yes, he was."

They went down the creaky wooden steps toward Hunt's car and Collinson stood on the porch watching them. "I'll look forward to seeing you again," he said, but the anticipation in his voice did not sound positive.

As they drove away from the trailer and out of the mobile-home park, Julie was silent.

"You're good at that," Hunt praised smilingly. "You almost had *me* convinced you were a writer. What, did you study acting as a kid, or something?"

Julie's arms were folded across her breasts; she looked chilled. She didn't reply to Hunt's compliments for a few moments and he stared at her, his smile melting.

"I don't like him, Martin," she finally said. "I don't like anything he said in there."

"Collinson? What? What don't you like?"

"I'm not sure, really. Just ... did you hear the way he talked? It was like everything he said had been carefully planned and rehearsed."

"Well, he's a minister. Eloquence is part of his profession."

"Maybe, but ... did you find anything funny about what he said?"

"I don't take religion seriously, Julie, so I can find something funny about almost *anything* a minister says. What didn't you like?"

Her upper lip rose and her forehead wrinkled in a look of frustration; her nose screwed up, pushing her glasses back a little. "I'm just not sure. Something about what he taught his son. About God, I guess. That business about good and evil. I don't know, it just sounded ... not right."

Hunt was beginning to pay less attention to his driving and more to what Julie was saying. Not only had she conducted the interview professionally and smoothly, but she had picked up things that Hunt had not. "Well, what is it, Julie? It may be what we're looking for!"

Her hands fell to her lap and her fingers began twitching with one another. "Well, when I was a little girl, my grandparents were *constantly* telling me about God and religion, the doctrines of their church, the Ten Commandments, that sort of thing. And, of course, they always told me about evil. Satan. The fallen angels. The wages of sin, et cetera, et cetera. One thing they *never* told me, and that I've never heard from anyone in any other religion, is to have respect for any kind of evil. Good, yes. But never evil. Collinson said something about teaching his son to have respect for both good *and* evil." She turned to Hunt, her eyes squinting a little and her nose still screwed up. "What the hell kind of philosophy is *that?*"

Hunt had been looking from the road to Julie and back again as she spoke. "Maybe he meant it should be respected in the same way one respects, say, a rattlesnake—cautiously avoiding it. Know what I mean?"

"I thought of that, but ... well, it just doesn't seem to fit. Then when he was talking about his family falling apart. He said, 'I believe it was *Gods* will.' Did that sound funny to you?"

"No. People like him are always saying that."

"But it was his inflection. It was the way he said 'God.' It was as if he'd thought about it for a long time and decided it was God's will rather than someone else's, as if it *might* have been the will of another, but he'd come to the conclusion that it was God's. You follow me? Now, that's pretty strange because people like him say that *everything* is God's will. There is no other will to them. And he got so uncomfortable when we were asking him about the way he raised Jeffery."

"I noticed. But he did hate the kid, from what the mother says."

Julie held out her hand, palm up, and looked down at it. "When I shook his hand, his palm was slimy with perspiration. He was nervous. Maybe even scared. But what really caught my eye was—"

"The expression on his face when I told him what his son had said in ER," Hunt finished for her, knowing what she was going to say.

"You got it. He looked like somebody just told him he's got six weeks to live."

"So what do you think?"

"I think it's pretty obvious that he knows something. Don't you?"

Hunt nodded slowly. "Yes," he said. "I do."

Reverend Jeremiah Collinson watched his two visitors drive away in the shiny silver BMW, his hands fussing nervously in front of his belly. As the car drove out of the mobile-home park, Collinson turned and went back inside. He returned to the kitchen, raised his arms, opened a cupboard door, and reached behind the Quaker Oats and the box of Wheat Thins, his fingers searching for the bottle that contained his most shameful vice. Clumping the whiskey bottle down on the counter, he got a glass from another cupboard and sloshed some of the liquor into it, lifting it to his lips. He noticed his hand was trembling rapidly. The whiskey burned its way down his throat and into his stomach, then coursed through his body rapidly with a welcome, relaxing warmth. He took another drink and the shaking in his hands began to recede.

The boy was in tremendous pain, he thought, leaning against the kitchen counter. *Probably on drugs, too. He was probably just babbling a bunch of hysterical gibberish. Didn't mean a thing. Maybe Dr. Hunt misunderstood what he said. Sure, maybe there was a lot of excitement in the emergency room; he doesn't have time to listen to a lot of nonsense being spouted by some young ... punk. Didn't mean a thing.*

Collinson stepped over to a small window in his kitchen that looked out over the south end of the park. But he did not see the two bare concrete platforms that marked the empty spaces beside his trailer. Neither did he see the huge brown-and-white trailer three spaces down from him, the flaps of its brown-and-white awning trembling in the light, chilly breeze. He did not notice how the sunlight, shining through the spotty holes in the clouds, made speckled designs on the ground, designs that danced and swirled as the clouds moved slowly across the sky. What he did see, in the eye of his mind, was his son backing down the front porch steps of the larger trailer in which they'd lived over in Pope Valley. He saw the blood-red anger that had darkened the skin of his son's face, his forehead wrinkled so severely that he looked older than seventeen, his squinting eyes, his head craning forward, and his smile, oozing hate and disgust, the smile that never went away as he kept backing away from the front door, even as his lips worked rapidly, spitting words at his father like lumps of slimy, bitter phlegm.

You're wrong, you're so fuckin' wrong, and someday you'll see just how wrong you are, only then it'll be too late for you and for everybody like you, still clinging to your stubborn ideas and beliefs that won't do you any good when it all finally comes, no good at all! You keep tryin' to teach me that bullshit and you won't shut up long enough to see that I can teach you, *because I've found the truth, the real truth, so when the Darkness comes, I'll be ready. But you … ha! When it all finally comes, you're gonna be screamin' to your fuckin' god and you're gonna see that all these years, you been talkin' to yourself!*

Reverend Collinson had tried to make the boy stop, tried to shut him up. He'd shouted at him to leave silently and keep his perverted thoughts to himself, but the boy had ignored him. He'd tried to stop him with physical force, but Jeffery had not let him get close. He was a wiry boy and he darted back and forth with the speed of a white-hot laser beam, a mocking smirk on his face, his eyes sparkling with the Devil's laughter. Jeffery had been very wary of his father ever since that night a couple of years before when the reverend had awakened to a pathetic moaning sound coming from somewhere in the trailer. He'd gotten up and followed the sound to the laundry room, where he'd found Jeffery hunched, naked, over the trembling figure of a small dog. The brutal movements his son was making there on the floor, surrounded by towels and shirts and underwear and skirts all awaiting the wash, had made the reverend ill. He'd reached down with a growl and grabbed the boy's shoulder, jerking him around violently, glimpsing the blood that spotted his son's belly. Without a thought, he began beating the boy back and forth across the face, around his neck and shoulders, shouting at him, telling him he was an undeserved curse, a monster that didn't have an ounce of the humanity God had intended him to have. The dog crawled on its belly to a corner of the small room and cowed in a pile of dirty sheets, quivering like gelatin. The boy's mother had come, finally, and shouted at the reverend to stop. The relationship between the boy and his father had never been good, but from that night on, it was nearly unbearable.

Jeffery had finally left, walking away from their mobile home, shouting things over his shoulder now and then, until his words were indistinguishable, until he was finally out of sight. The reverend had gone into the trailer after his son left, and he'd poured himself a drink.

"And you a man of God," his wife had said quietly, flatly, standing in the living room, her face tear-stained.

Collinson's teeth had clenched together in anger. He'd gulped the last of the whiskey down and said, "A man of God, Grace, but only a man. Only a man, who's had to live under the weight of a barbaric son and a sick wife, neither of whom has any concept of reality whatsoever, neither of whom has one iota of respect for our Lord, or for life, neither of whom has any standards or morals or prin—"

"If I'm so sick," she'd said, her voice still soft, barely audible over his bellowed words, "then why don't you put me away, Jeremiah?"

And he had. Within the week he had her institutionalized. She'd gone along with it surprisingly well. She'd been silent, passive. It almost seemed to be what she wanted.

It wasn't long after that that Jeremiah and Grace Collinson had divorced. An ugly thing, Collinson realized, but unavoidable.

He emptied the glass of whiskey, walked over to the counter, and poured himself just a bit more. His hands were no longer shaking, but he was shaking on the inside.

It's gonna come now.

At first, when Jeffery had begun to form his own ideas from the books he was constantly reading, their covers wrapped in paper so the titles could not be seen, the reverend thought them to be the muddled thoughts of a confused boy. They weren't things he was trying to teach his son! They were perversions! But as his

son's ideas began to develop, as Jeffery began using them to form
questions that the reverend could not answer—not only because
he did not know how, but also because the questions chilled his
blood and he didn't *want* to answer them—a tiny alarm began
to go off deep within the man, at his very core. He was able to
ignore it for a while, but it got louder and louder and went off
more and more often, set by his son's level, carefully calculated
words. Collinson often thought that if Jeffery had not left when
he did, the boy might have driven him mad. But then he left, and
the alarm finally went away. And now he was dead. Collinson
had thought the alarm had died with him. But he was wrong.
It had been set off again by what Dr. Hunt had told him. And
he poured more whiskey into the yet unfinished glass, trying to
quiet the nerve-wracking klaxon that was sounding inside him.

He swallowed, then held up the glass and stared at it before
him. God would understand. Other people might not, but God
would. Collinson's nerves got worse as he got older, and he could
not afford to let them ruin his whole day. He had a good deal of
work to do for the Lord today. Yes, he was a man of God. But he
was only a man.

Only a man.

6 - MEGAN'S FANTASY

JULIE HAD NOT intended to become involved. Not that she didn't believe Hunt or Tom; *something* was wrong, she was sure. But the whole thing gave her a bad feeling. Although she'd not voiced her concern, she was made a bit uncomfortable by Hunt's involvement. She'd told him once already that she thought it would be best to keep quiet about it all. Once was enough.

Now she was helping.

After visiting the reverend, Hunt had dropped her at her place and then had gone to see Tom, agreeing to pick her up and take her to work that night, since her car was at his house. She found her thoughts returning to the reverend: his nervousness, his strange inflection when he'd said the breakup of his family had been God's will, that nonsense about respecting both good and evil.

She switched on the small radio on the kitchen counter and began making a peanut-butter-and-jelly sandwich as her attention drifted back and forth from the afternoon newscast to her own puzzling thoughts.

When fanatically religious people tried to raise children, she thought, the results were usually not good. She was surprised she'd turned out as stable as she had after growing up under the influence of her grandparents and their friends. A girl friend of hers had not been quite so fortunate. Her father, like Jeffery Collinson's, had been a minister. The girl, Terri Pettis, with whom Julie had gone to high school, had been a nice girl, intelligent. She'd always gotten good grades, was attractive, reasonably popular. Her major flaw, in the eyes of her parents—especially her father—was that she liked to have fun. Julie remembered the first time Terri had gone to a movie. She'd gone with Julie and a few others girls, all of them students at the same church school. They'd given their parents some story about going to a friend's house for an evening worship but, instead, had gone to the theater in Santa Rosa. Somehow, word had gotten out, and Terri's father had actually come down to the theater to get her. Julie had been the first one to see him storming down the aisle toward them, his face a mask of anger and shame. He'd sidled into the row behind them, put his hands on Terri's shoulders, and forced her to her feet, ignoring the annoyed remarks of the other moviegoers: *Sit down! Shh! Hey, this ain't the lobby, you know!* Julie remembered the words he had hissed into his daughter's ears as he nearly dragged her out of the theater. "You can lie to *me,* but you can't lie to *God!* What if *Christ* had come while you were in this theater!" What he'd said was almost laughable now, but Julie and the other girls had not enjoyed the rest of the movie. And, of course, Terri's father had told all their parents and they'd each been punished. Julie's grandparents had grounded her.

After that, Terri had begun doing anything she could to rebel against her father's strict rules and smothering beliefs. Her rebellion had ended in pregnancy by an out-of-town bum whom she'd never seen again, a shameful abortion, and a nervous breakdown.

Other friends of Julie's had gone through similar situations. She wondered what things had really been like for Jeffery Collinson as a young man, buried beneath his father's rules and standards. Had he tried to rebel like Terri? Had he perhaps gone off the deep end as a result of his father's treatment and teachings?

As Julie plunged her butter knife into the jar of dark grape jam, something the newscaster on the radio was saying caught her ear.

"——musement park in the south bay," the voice was saying. "The incident began when the operator of the Gondo-round ride, Leonard Ahem, sent the ride spinning at full speed for no apparent reason. One witness claims to have seen Ahern leaning on the control lever, watching the ride go out of control, laughing at the screaming passengers. Seconds later, one of the gondolas snapped loose and two teenagers were thrown to their deaths. When spectators and park officials rushed Ahern, the large man pushed and hit his way through the small crowd. Mabel Turner, a woman who frequents the park with her grandchildren, gives this account ..."

The solid silence that had backed up the newscaster's voice was replaced with muffled amusement park sounds: clanking rides, calliope music, laughter, and shouting. Then a trembling voice spoke above the background noise.

"—but it all happened so fast! That little cart flying away from the ride—and I can only thank God my two little grandchildren weren't in it—then that horrible man, smelling like a bear, pushing through the crowd, knocking me over like that—he was a monster! A maniac! His eyes were all big and his teeth were snapping! I'm *sure* he was on drugs!"

All the clatter was cut off immediately and the calm, level voice of the broadcaster continued.

"Ahern fled the crowd and climbed up the platform of the Rat Trap Roller Coaster, reached the track, and was hit by a string of cars carrying schoolchildren on a field trip. Seven of the children were injured, none critically. Ahern was killed instantly. The result of this morning's autopsy showed no sign of drugs or alcohol, and Ahern's actions remain unexplained."

Julie lowered the butter knife onto the kitchen counter.

His eyes were all big and his teeth were snapping!

A thought uncurled itself in the back of her head, like a snake that had been waiting silently and patiently in the dark for just the right moment.

Whatever it is, it's spreading.

She finished making her sandwich, ate it too quickly with a glass of milk, brushed her teeth, then went to bed. But she did not sleep very well.

Late that afternoon, the sun had come out and the weather had warmed up somewhat. But with evening, the cold had returned, and later that night a fine mist rolled in that floated gently over everything and seemed to keep watch.

"Where are you going?" Megan's mother asked the girl as she opened the front door.

Megan turned and saw her mother standing at the top of the stairs in her robe. "I've got to run over to Winny's. I left a book with her that I need tonight."

"At *this* hour?"

"I *need* it, Mom."

"Did you ask your father?"

Megan's shoulders slumped. "No."

The woman turned her head and looked down the upstairs hallway. "*James.* Do you want Megan going out this late?"

"If she needs the book, honey," came the muffled reply, "she needs the book."

Megan watched her mother shake her head and disappear down the hallway, muttering disasters to herself, something about her daughter being mugged in the middle of the night by someone wearing L'eggs over his head. Megan sighed as she walked out the front door, closing it behind her, remembering that she'd always been told her teenage years were the best years of her life. *Not if my mother can help it,* she thought, getting into the car.

Megan was not going over to Winny's, of course. Winny was probably in bed by now, but not sleeping. She was probably lying on her back, staring up into the darkness, watching reruns of her own rape.

Last night, Megan had tried to talk Winny into returning to school. "I'll stick with you, Win," she'd promised. "I'll walk all over campus with you if you want, so you don't have to be alone. I think it would do you good to get back. And you know how hard it's going to be to catch up the longer you stay away."

"*I can't,* Megan," Winny had replied tearfully. "I just can't. I can't think about studying, I don't want to be around anyone—anyone at school, anyway—because I feel so ... I don't know, so *bad.*"

Megan had not pushed it. But, after Winny had left that night, Megan had not been able to return to her homework. She couldn't stop thinking about Winny, about Mrs. Skerritt, Mr. Rand, Tom Conrad and Dr. Hollister, Mrs. Webster. And Dr. Hunt's phone call, his questions, the quiet certainty that she'd heard in his voice, as if he'd already known the answers.

Her classes had seemed to stretch on forever today. Mrs. Schmidt had reprimanded her in algebra for not paying attention to the lecture, and she'd completely blown a quiz in Loveless's history class.

During her lunch break, she'd gone to a phone booth and looked up Martin Hunt in the directory. His home number was unlisted. She couldn't remember Julie's last name, or she would have looked her up, too. Julie was probably the only way she could get in touch with Hunt, now that he wouldn't be at the hospital for a while. She would be risking looking like an idiot taking her thoughts to him, but maybe he knew something. Dr. Hunt was very open-minded and willing to listen to anything. If anyone would lend an ear, he would. So she'd decided to find him.

She pulled the car into the medical center's parking lot, turned off the ignition, got out, and walked into the emergency room entrance. The waiting room was empty, but a salt-and-pepper-haired woman with no chin sat at the receptionist's window.

"May I help you?" she asked.

"I'm looking for Julie."

"Julie's not in yet," she replied, checking her wrist-watch. "I expect her any minute. Do you need a doctor?"

"No, no. I'm fine. I just need to speak with Julie. I'll wait."

"Fine."

Megan sat down on one of the vinyl sofas, folded her hands neatly in her lap, and waited.

"And the woman who was there, who saw it, said that the guy's eyes were great big and he was snapping his teeth," Julie said, turned in the car seat to face Hunt. "And then it hit me. That's the way Hollister looked. Crazy. Like a lunatic. His eyes so big they were about to pop, all glisteny and wet. And that's the way Collinson looked, too." She tucked one corner of her lower lip under her teeth lightly. "Do you think ... I'm paranoid, maybe? Looking for it?"

"Christ, *no!*" Hunt replied quickly. "Why do you think we're doing what we're doing? I think it's important to notice anything in the news or around us that's a little ... strange. And I think we'll be seeing more of it as time goes on."

Hunt had spoken with Tom for a while that morning, after seeing Reverend Collinson. He'd shared with him everything Collinson had said. Then Tom told Hunt of the conversation he'd had with Becky Haber.

"We would've gotten to her, Tom," Hunt said. "You should've gone home to bed."

"I wanted to see her then. I got plenty of sleep, anyway. I woke up at eleven this morning in a sweat. Those nightmares I keep having ..."

"Well, from what she told you, it sounds like Collinson had the ingredients for some sort of cult."

"Yeah, it sounded that way. But I don't think that's what he had in mind. Seems that whatever his ... I don't know, *beliefs* were, they were very private. He tried to keep them pretty much to himself, it seems—until he found Becky, someone who was maybe confused and looking for something to believe in, and let her in on his little secret."

"That's all you could get from her?"

"Yeah, something about a time of darkness that was coming. Maybe that's what Collinson meant when he said, 'It's gonna come now.' The Christians speak of the Time of the End; maybe Collinson believed in the Time of Darkness. Except Becky spoke of it like it was going to be something good, something that would make the world a better place. Pretty crazy."

Crazy, maybe, but also unsettling. To Hunt, anyway. Now Julie had told him about this incident at some amusement park that sounded very familiar. He wondered how many other people had been affected by these things.

Or if, perhaps, they were just chasing shadows.

He pulled the car into a parking slot and he and Julie got out. "You don't have to walk me in," she said.

"I'd rather." His shoes clacked on the pavement as they walked hand in hand to the entrance to ER, then went inside.

"You're a bit late, Julie," said Beverly Hendricks, the tall, skinny, chinless wonder who had the shift before Julie, and whom Hunt considered one of the prime bitches of the universe. He'd worked with her for a short time once, but when he'd had enough of her condescension toward both her patients and her coworkers, he told her that he hoped when *she* had to be rushed into ER sometime, *she* would be cared for by someone as incompetent and inconsiderate as *herself*. She looked at him briefly and, with her nose slightly upturned, nodded and said, "Dr. Hunt."

He simply nodded to her in reply, then turned to Julie and put his arms on her shoulders.

"I wish you would've let me get my car and drive myself," she said quietly, "so you wouldn't have to get up so early in the morning."

"Won't kill me."

"Julie," Beverly said, "you have a visitor in the waiting room. Some girl."

Julie tilted her head curiously and stepped up to the receptionist's window. "Yes?" She saw Megan Crawford sitting with her hands in her lap looking a bit nervous.

Megan nearly jumped to her feet, her arms at her sides, and stepped forward. "Um, hi, Julie. Remember me?"

"Sure." She smiled and leaned forward toward the window. "What are you doing here so late?"

"Well, waiting for you."

Hunt stepped forward into the girl's view and they saw her eyes widen.

"Dr. Hunt!"

"Hi, Megan. How are you?"

The girl stepped forward again and put her hands on the small ledge, the fingers of her right hand wrapped lightly around the pen holder attached to the desk. "Dr. Hunt, I need to speak with you if it's okay."

"Sure, but … uh … did you want to see Julie about something?"

Megan laughed with embarrassment. "Well, I wanted to see Julie about getting in touch with you."

There was silence, until Hunt said, "Oh," and then there was more silence.

"It's pretty important, I think," Megan said quietly.

"Well, the kitchen is closed, but there's a coffee machine in the caf," Hunt said, coming out into the waiting room with Megan. "Would you like to go down there?"

"Sure."

Hunt told Julie he'd stop by before he left, then went downstairs with Megan. They exchanged small talk as they spoke about school, about what Hunt was doing with his time these days. When they finally sat down with their coffee, Hunt asked, "So what's going on?"

"Remember when you called me a while back and you asked me questions about Mrs. Webster?"

Hunt nodded.

"Well, I've been thinking a lot about that. And I'll tell you why." She told Hunt about Winny, going through the story just as she'd heard it. Then she told him about Mr. Rand, and Mrs. Skerritt and her flower garden.

As her stories unfolded, Hunt felt his grip tightening on the little Styrofoam cup before him and had to relax it to avoid crushing it between his fingers and spilling the hot coffee everywhere.

"Maybe it's just my imagination," Megan went on, "but

it seems like there's a lot of weird stuff going on. And those questions you asked me on the phone ... well, it just seemed like there was some sort of connection. You know, when you asked if Mrs. Webster had mentioned anything about eating her roommate before she did it? Well, she did. And it was sort of the same way with Winny's brother, and with Mrs. Skerritt, like I said. They'd all ... I don't know, it's like they all *wanted* to do the crazy things they did, like they all thought about it for a while. Know what I mean?"

Hunt was nervously scraping the bottom of his cup back and forth on the tabletop and it made a sharp, squeaky Styrofoam sound. "Megan, I'm going to ask you a question, but I want you to keep it to yourself. Please, promise me it'll just stay between us."

"Sure," she replied, leaning forward as if she'd been waiting for this.

"Did your friend say anything about ... about an *animal*, maybe? Something small and black crawling around her brother when he raped her?"

Megan's face darkened a bit; one eye squinted a little more than the other and her lips became taut. She shook her head and said, "No, she didn't. Why? What do you mean?"

"A bug, maybe? A worm? Did she get a glance of anything like that?"

"A *worm*? Then you really *did* see something in ER?"

Hunt said nothing, and his silence made Megan blush. She looked away from him, embarrassed.

"Some people were ... talking about what you said you saw in ER that night the killer came in."

"And you didn't believe it?"

"Of *course* not!" she said, quietly but emphatically. "You know how people talk in this place. I don't believe anything I hear. But now ... well, I guess if you really say you saw something, then ... you did."

Hunt broke into a smile and a breathy chuckle. "Thank you for your vote of confidence. I wish everyone had that much faith in me."

"What ... *did* you see?"

Reaching up and scratching his beard slowly, Hunt once again swore her to secrecy, then told her the story of what he'd seen in ER on that very early Tuesday morning.

"God," Megan whispered when he was done, her chin hanging loose and her eyes glued to his. "And you think it might have something to do with what happened to Winny?"

"I'm not sure, but I think there's a chance. Do you think I could talk with her?"

"Oh, no, she'd never talk with you about it. I mean, nothing personal, of course," she added quickly. "But it was really hand for her to tell *me,* and *I'm* her best friend. I don't think she'd ever talk about it with someone she doesn't know. But I can talk to her some more. I can ask her anything you want to know."

Hunt inhaled thoughtfully to keep from smiling at the young girl's eagerness to help him. *That girl has such a crush on you,* Julie once had told him, *I bet she'd forfeit her entire college education in exchange for a pair of your undershorts.*

"I don't know, Megan. Maybe we should wait. Hell, I really don't know what I'm waiting for. Tell you what," he said, taking a napkin from the holder in the center of the table and removing a pen from his coat pocket. He began writing. "This is my phone number. If you learn anything, or if something happens that scares you—anything at all—call me." He handed her the napkin with his phone number scrawled on it. "And for god's sake, if you see something small and black, kind of wet-looking, get the hell away from it!"

Megan smiled all the way home. Sitting across from Dr. Hunt and listening to him, talking with him, being given his *phone number* for crying out loud, had been the most fun she'd had in weeks. She'd half expected him to be a little put off by her coming to him, but he'd been very receptive. Even concerned for her safety.

The image of Dr. Hunt chuckling, giving her that sparkling half-smile, and saying *Thank you for your vote of confidence* remained in her mind, frozen, as if a Polaroid had snapped and the picture had developed immediately for her to keep in her memory.

In the time she'd known Ross, while they were going together, they'd never once had a conversation as comfortable and as relaxing

(Or as weird, either, but what difference does that make?)

as the one she'd had with Dr. Hunt, however brief it might have been. Ross just never talked that much. He let his *hands* talk *for* him. All he ever seemed to be interested in, now that she thought about it, was sex. And blow jobs. He always wanted her to suck him off, *always*. She didn't mind that; in fact, she rather liked it, but he insisted that she let him come in her mouth, and she hated that. He'd even forced it upon her twice.

She wondered what kind of relationship Hunt and Julie had. She was *sure* they were nothing like she and Ross had been. They were probably much more mature about everything. Dr. Hunt was probably very sensitive toward Julie in every way. He probably gave her little gifts and kissed her a lot. If she didn't want him to come in her mouth, Megan was sure he wouldn't. She imagined that sometimes they just held each other, maybe in front of a fire or something. Being physical and romantic didn't necessarily mean *having sex*.

When Megan got home, she could see through the front window the glow of the television set; she hoped her mother wasn't up.

It was her father. He was sitting in front of the television watching Letterman and eating Oreos.

"Hi, hon," he said quietly.

"Hi, Dad."

"Get your book?"

"Um ... no. Winny didn't have it. Guess I left it with someone else. I'm going to bed. Is Boston around?"

"Somewhere. Damned cat's acting weird tonight. I think he's horny or something."

Megan went upstairs, undressed, brushed her teeth, and went to bed. She didn't sleep for a long time, but when she did, it was with thoughts of Dr. Martin Hunt and his sparkling face.

Megan's eyes snapped open in the dark and she was awake instantly, aware of the movement of her tongue back and forth over her lips and the faint but distinct taste of salty skin left over from her dream. She could feel the insistent pounding of her heart against her ribs, like the knock of an impatient caller. When she finally moved beneath the tangled covers, she realized that the long T-shirt she wore to bed over a tiny pair of panties had bunched up just beneath her breasts. Suspiciously, with a smirk, she reached down and touched herself; the crotch of her pants was sticky and warm. She giggled, threw back the covers, and slid her legs over the edge of the bed, sitting up.

A band of soft, cloudy moonlight cut through the slit between the curtains over her window and ended in a small puddle on the floor. Megan reached for the lamp on her bedside stand and switched it on. With the sudden flare of light, subdued by the little shade over the lamp, Megan gasped. The large figure of her black-and-white eat, Boston, sat primly beside the lamp, staring at her.

"Jeez, Boston," she whispered, "you scared me." She pulled her shirt down, then reached over to pet the cat.

A low, throaty rumble came from deep inside the animal and erupted into a sharp, spitting hiss as one paw, sharp claws extended, swept out before him at Megan's hand, barely scraping her skin.

"*Ouch!*" Megan gasped, jerking her hand back and holding it tightly with the other, more startled than hurt. "Damn you, Bos! *Stop* that!" Scowling, she stood and stepped toward the cat, holding both her hands out cautiously to pick him up. "C'mere, Bos, and knock that shit off."

The cat craned its head forward, its upper lips pulled back over its small pointed teeth, and its rough pink tongue rose and fell as it hissed again. Its ears were flat against its head as it stood up on all fours and arched its back like a cardboard cutout tacked to someone's door at Halloween.

Megan slowly lowered her arm and squinted at the animal as it moved back on the small nightstand, pulling its head down until it was beneath the lampshade, its face bathed in the light. Megan saw that something was wrong with her cat. Its face was somehow misshapen. Its eyes were ... they seemed lopsided, or something; they seemed to be bulging from the head. And around the eyes, caught like teardrops in the soft black fur, was a clear, thick-looking substance that reflected the light from the lamp.

"Kitty cat," she mumbled to her pet absently, taking one minute step forward. "Here, puss. What's wrong, boy." He was growling again, but he seemed to look frightened at the same time.

(Leave go away get someone get away from it)

Something was wrong here. Suddenly, the safe, familiar darkness of her bedroom had become stale and ominous and she knew she should get out, get away from the cat, go down the hall to her father, or just downstairs to let her damned imagination calm itself, but she couldn't move because, deep inside of her where nightmares formed, she was too certain that if she were to turn around she would see behind her the hulking, smelly form of old Mrs. Webster, her face a greenish-blue, spotted with crusty mold, even more bloated than she was in life, smiling at her with rotting teeth, holding out one puffy and decaying hand,

(Anything at all, *like a nice little* treat?)

and so she couldn't turn around, she *couldn't,* because if Mrs. Webster wasn't standing there, then it would probably be something *else,* perhaps something *worse.*

(Black, ugly diseases)

A whimper uncurled from deep within Megan, a whimper that might have been a scream had her energy not been sapped by what she was seeing: Boston tensing his whole body, crouching down slightly, just before he *pounced!*

The cat knocked the lamp off the bedside stand and it tumbled onto Megan's pillow, then rolled down onto the mattress. The lamp's light danced madly over the walls and ceiling as it shifted back and forth over the bed.

The animal clamped itself onto Megan, its front claws sinking into the flesh just below her neck, its bloated face pressing to her cheek, its fetid breath brushing over her skin as it bit and bit again.

Megan stumbled backward, almost fell, little "ah-ah-ah" sounds trembling from her throat as she reached up and dug her fingers into the animal's body, tearing it off of her and holding it out. The cat growled and hissed, spat and snapped at her, its front claws swiping again and again before her face, its body writhing in her tightly clenched hands.

"Buh-Boston, Bos, Jesus—"

She almost dropped the animal but held on, suddenly finding her fingers around its throat as tears began to sting her eyes. She squeezed and the cat made gurgled choking sounds and began to thrash more violently as Megan sobbed. The cat's eyes began to flow with the thick substance, began to bulge farther and farther, and the skull began to

(my god what's happening)

shift and pulse almost fluidly until one glistening orb popped quietly from its socket and hung loosely and Megan could hear a soft tearing sound and then a muffled cracking and at the same instant the cat's body stopped moving its skull opened like a large egg and Megan's stomach began to churn as one slender black tentacle slithered out of the opening of the cat's head and found leverage and lifted itself out and then for a brief moment *(scream for Christ's sake scream scream scream)* nothing. There was an instant of total blackness and suffocation and a rushing feeling, like blood racing through her body at an incredible speed. And then. Nothing.

She opened her eyes and found herself seated once again on the side of her bed next to the overturned lamp. Absently, without even thinking about it, she lifted the lamp, adjusted the cord, and returned it to the stand. Then she put her elbows on her knees and her palms over her face. Her eyes were stinging and tearing badly. She felt dizzy, a little nauseated, and she could feel ... it was distinct, and yet unfocused. It was inside her head ... the smooth feeling of ... *movement.*

Oh, dear Christ, she thought, a gasp catching with a click inside her throat, *it's inside me. It's insi—*

"Megan? You okay?"

Her hands tore away from her face and she looked up to see the shadowy figure of her father standing at her bedroom door, which was cracked open a few inches. And then she suddenly relaxed. Her arms rested heavily in her lap. Her shoulders slumped somewhat. She almost sighed heavily.

"Yeah, Dad, I'm fine. Just a nightmare." She smiled.

"Oh." His voice was heavy with sleep. "Well, call if you need anything, okay?"

"Sure."

She could hear him shuffle down the hall. She waited for a long time. The toilet flushed. More shuffling. Then silence. She looked around the room. Boston lay in an indefinable heap in the black shadow at the foot of the bed.

She lay back on her bed, suddenly feeling weak, and rested her hands on her stomach. She smiled again and the smile did not go away. She felt different, but ... *so good.* There was still a strange sort of movement in her head, but now it was gentle, a seductive caress. When she closed her eyes, she saw Dr. Hunt.

What a dreeeaaam, she thought. *Licking him from head to foot, tasting his whole body, letting him touch me, feel me ... nothing like Ross, that asshole, that self-centered, insensitive asshole, always wanting me to suck his stubby cock so he can shoot his stuff down my throat, never caring that maybe I don't like to do it that way ... but Dr. Hunt would never be that way, he would never be so cold and so harsh ... why couldn't I have been with him instead of Julie, why couldn't he fall in love with me and forget her?*

Her eyes opened. Her smile widened. Megan stood, quickly dressed, put on a coat, got her car keys, and went downstairs to the telephone. She punched out the number of Ross's bedroom phone.

"'Lo?" his voice grunted after several rings.

"Ross, this is Megan," she whispered.

"M'gan? What? What time is it?" There was the rustle of groggy movement on his end of the line.

"I need to see you."

"See me? Now? Juh-Jesus, Megan, it's nearly four o'clock. Are you all right?"

"Ross, I *have* to see you! I ... Ross, I've been ... wrong."

"Well ... well, you, you can't come over here. You'll wake everyone up. Can't it wait?"

"No, it can't. I want to meet you at the parte. Vineyard Park. At the entrance. In ten minutes."

"Goddammit, Megan! I've got school tomorrow!"

"So do I. This is important. Please, Ross."

"Sheez, Megan ... okay. Okay."

Quietly, Megan left the house after hanging up the phone, got into her car, and drove to the park.

Vineyard Park was very small, located just outside St. Helena. Its grass was choked with weeds, the picnic tables were falling apart, and the park was usually empty during the day. At four in the morning it looked virtually dead.

Megan parked her car at the small, cramped-looking entrance and waited for Ross. He drove up behind her and she immediately got out of the car and walked back to him, getting in on the passenger's side.

"I really hope this is good, Meg, because I'm—" Before Ross could finish, Megan fell on him, burying the fingers of one hand in his thick blond hair, tucking the fingers of the other under his belt, and kissed him deeply and long. When she finally backed away, he gasped, "Jesus, what was *that* for?"

"I've been wrong, Ross. I've handled our relationship so immaturely, just like you told me that time, remember? You told me I had to grow up some more before I could ever have a real relationship with a guy. You were right. I've missed you.

And tonight ... tonight, I dreamed about you. I'm so hot for you, Ross! And I'm gonna do it." She began to unbuckle his belt, her fingers shuffling rapidly and her breath coming in heavy bursts.

"What?" Ross asked, a bit nervously. "*What* are you gonna do?"

She tilted her head up and smiled at him, tugging his pants down to his knees and pulling him out of his undershorts, holding him in her hand, stroking, pumping purposefully. "I want you in my mouth, Ross. I want you to come in my mouth, just like you always wanted."

"Have ... have you been crying, Megan? Your eyes ... have you been smoking some grass?"

Her only reply was a deep, throaty laugh that was soon garbled as she bent her head down and plunged her mouth over him. Her head bobbed and twisted frantically, and she chuckled and grunted as she moved.

"Megan ..." Ross began, but never finished. His eyes slowly fell shut and he leaned his head back against the window, the pattern of his breathing changing. He groaned.

And then Ross screamed.

A few minutes later, Megan was standing in a phone booth in front of a dark Chevron station, fishing a wrinkled napkin out of her coat pocket. She was giggling, almost drunkenly, flicking her tongue back and forth over her bloody lips. She'd left Ross unconscious and bleeding badly in his car. *He'll probably bleed to death,* she thought, giggling again. *Serves him right.*

She dialed Hunt's number, then tried to calm her giggles before he answered.

"Dr. Hunt, this is Megan," she hissed into the receiver.

"Megan?" He seemed to awaken instantly, immediately alert. "Are you okay?"

"I need to see you. Now."

"Now? You're all right, though?"

"I need to see you, Dr. Hunt."

"Okay, okay." He gave her his address and told her he'd be waiting.

Megan hung up and left the booth giggling, leaving a dark smear of Ross's blood on the phone's mouthpiece to dry and harden.

* * *

Hunt got out of bed, put on his robe, and went into the kitchen to put on some coffee. His adrenaline was flowing and he noticed how quick and jerky his movements were.

Something had to be wrong, or he was sure Megan wouldn't have insisted upon coming to see him. The question was, *what?*

Only a few minutes had passed when he heard a knock on his door. He opened it to find Megan standing on the porch clutching her coat tightly in front of her.

"Come in," he said. She smiled and walked into the light of his living room. "What's going on, Megan?" he asked, closing the door and turning around.

She laughed and opened her coat, letting it drop to the floor around her feet. She was naked underneath.

Hunt's mouth dropped open and he said dumb-foundedly, "Your clothes ..." knowing it sounded stupid.

"Left them in the car," she whispered, stepping forward. "I won't be needing them in here. Not for what we're going to do." She held her arms out for him as she walked toward him.

Then Hunt took a quick step back, the color draining from his face. "Jesus Christ, your eyes!" They were bulging like Ping-Pong balls from her head and fluid rolled thickly from them down her cheeks.

"I only have eyes for you," she sang, giggling, putting her hands on his shoulders. "I've wanted you for *soooo loooong,* Doctor. Martin. *Hunt.* That rhymes with *cunt,* and I've got one of *thoooose.* All for you."

Hunt could feel her breath hot on his face and he could smell it: *blood.* Then he saw dark streaks of it between her teeth and drops of it, like drying paint, on her throat and chest. "My god!" he whispered, because he could not muster a voice. "What have you done?"

"I want to lick you aaalll over," she said through her wet, suggestive smile.

Hunt put his hands firmly on her shoulders and held her back. "Megan," he said loudly, *"think* now, *think* what you're saying, what you're doing!"

"I know what I'm doing. I'm getting *wet!* For you. Wanna feel me?"

"Megan, it *has* you! It's inside you now, Megan, making you do this! Stop and think what you're doing!" He moved his hands from her shoulders and put one on each side of her head over her eyes and held her head back, looking into her nose, examining her eyes, trying to ignore his own frightened reflection in her swollen, seemingly dead eyes. A useless thought sprang to his attention: *They used to be such playful eyes.* "Megan, come lie down on the sofa, just lie down and keep still." His hands were on her shoulders again and he was trying to turn her around and move her toward the sofa. She wouldn't let him.

"You wanna do it on the sofa? It's so small!" She giggled again and reached between his legs, gently squeezing his genitals.

"I'm trying to help you, Megan, please—"

"If you wanna help me, then why don't you take off that robe?"

He pushed her roughly to the sofa and got her down on her back. He reached up and flicked the light on, lifting the shade so the light shined on her face.

"That hurts!" Megan snapped, putting a hand before her face to shade her eyes. "Dammit! Turn that off!"

"I just need to look at—"

"What the hell are you doing?" she shrieked, pushing him back violently, trying to sit up. "I wanna *fuck* you, that's all! What's this shit you're trying to do here?"

"Megan, you're sick, you're—"

Before Hunt was even sure what he was going to say next, Megan moved with lightning speed, leaping up from the sofa and pushing him back, her hand snaking under his robe, her fingers clutching, holding.

"Goddammit!" she hissed. "Don't you understand how badly I want you, how long I've wanted to fuck you, to ... to do *everything?*" Her grip tightened on his genitals and Hunt's body tensed.

"Megan, I don't want to hurt you, but I will if you don't get off me."

"Nail," she breathed, bending down to run her tongue up his neck. Hunt could smell the sharp odor of blood. "Just stay here and let me take care of you."

The front door opened. Megan was on her feet in an instant, rage flaring in her face like a bonfire.

Julie stood in the doorway, her face registering both fatigue and shock. "Martin ..." she said quietly.

"*Bitch!*" Megan screamed. "Can't you leave him alone for one fucking second? He wants *me!*" Her voice lowered to a raspy hiss. "And I want him!"

Hunt was quickly behind her; he wrapped his arms around her and held her tightly. "Help me!" he shouted to Julie. Julie hurried forward, but Megan's hand—the only one free—lashed out and sliced four neat, bloody streaks into Julie's cheek. Julie screamed and fell backward. Then Megan's hand doubled into a fist and swept downward, hard, hitting Hunt between the legs. His grip on the girl immediately fell away and he leaned forward, his face screwed up, his stomach suddenly churning as tendrils of pain curled hotly upward into his abdomen.

Megan stepped forward and kicked Julie in the back with one sneakered foot; she kicked her a second time. "Selfish *cunt!* Want him all to yourself!"

Julie grunted in pain and crawled away from the crazed girl.

Megan turned back to Hunt, swept the lamp up in one hand, the light blacking out when the cord came out of the wall socket, and she smashed it down on his upper back. He fell forward with a sudden release of breath and she kicked him, too. "Too fucking *good* for me, Mr. Hotshot Doctor? Well, I'll have you if I have to kill you first, and I'll have you when you least expect it!" She grabbed her coat and stormed out.

Julie crawled over to Hunt and put a hand on the back of his head. "Are you all right?" she asked, her voice quavering.

He nodded without looking up from his curled, kneeling position. "I will be. God ... I wish I could've ... stopped her."

They remained hunkered on the floor together for long, silent minutes, waiting for their pain to subside.

Megan Crawford did not live to see the light of day. She returned to her house, not as careful to be quiet as when she'd left, went up to her room, and stared at her reflection in the mirror over her dresser. Dr. Hunt had complained about her eyes, hadn't he? So had Ross. They were ugly eyes. If she wanted Dr. Hunt, her eyes would have to be different. She would have to change them. Giggling, Megan picked up a letter opener from her dresser and plunged it into her right eye. She was dead before she could do it to the left.

7 - CAVE OF SINS

THE COLD COBALT of dawn was bleeding into the sky by the time Julie composed herself enough to cry. They remained silently on the floor for a very long time, then moved to the sofa, where Julie suddenly leaned heavily on Hunt's shoulder and began to cry.

"'S'okay, hon," Hunt murmured, still trying to recover from the ever-so-slowly waning pain in his groin and lower abdomen. "I ... there was nothing we could do."

"How did it happen?" she asked.

"I don't know. She just called me a while ago and said she had to see me, that it was very important."

"She had ... blood on her face."

"Yes, and I don't even like to think how that might have come about."

"I wonder where she went." Julie sniffed sharply, then coughed.

"I'm sure we'll learn in the morning. Well, it *is* morning ... you know what I mean."

Julie lifted a hand to her temple and rubbed slowly. "I have a terrible headache. A bodyache, in fact."

"Is that why you're home early? You're sick? And ... how did you get here?"

"I got really sick, started chilling, so Carl called Gloria to come in early and replace me. Gloria's husband drove her in and offered to drive me home. I had him bring me here because ... I didn't want to be both sick *and* alone. Hope you don't mind," she said, but her tone of voice revealed her certainty that he didn't.

"Bite your tongue," Hunt replied, holding her close and kissing her, "if you haven't already during all the fun and excitement.

Let's get you to bed and I'll take a look to make sure you're okay. We can put something on those scratches, too."

She went into the bathroom, washed her face, and Hunt dabbed some alcohol on the scratches. Then she undressed and got in bed.

"You're gonna have some bruises," Hunt told her, looking her back over, "but I think you'll live."

"Not if I don't get some sleep." She curled up under the covers and smiled at him tiredly. "You coming?"

"No. I'm gonna stay up for a while. Have a cigarette or two." He bent down and kissed her softly. "Sleep. I love you." He went to the bedroom door and switched the light out, whispering, "If you need anything, just call me." Then he shut the door quietly, feeling, smilingly, like a father.

Later that morning, as Julie slept on, Tom came over, looking tired and worn, although he claimed he did little but sleep and think. He said the main reason for his sleeping was to avoid thinking, but the sleep always brought with it nightmares. He sat down in the kitchen with Hunt, who was still in his robe, and asked for a cigarette.

"I didn't know you smoked," Hunt said, handing one over to him.

"I don't," Tom replied, lighting it clumsily. He puffed, squinted, held back a cough, then let the smoke flow from his mouth and nostrils. "I *have* smoked, but I don't regularly." He took another drag, then looked over at Hunt, who was lighting one of his own. "I thought you said you were quitting."

Hunt held the cigarette up between two fingers and said flatly, "This is my last."

They talked casually for a while, smoking quietly sometimes. Then Hunt told him about Megan's visit earlier that morning. Tom's face remained disturbingly blank as Hunt spoke, as if the story was not affecting him at all, but Hunt knew it was. When he was finished, they stared silently at one another over the table.

"You didn't see it?" Tom asked finally.

"No, but I know it was there."

Tom nervously stubbed out what little was left of his cigarette and asked for another.

"You know," Hunt said, handing one over, "Megan has always flirted with me. Playfully. Julie's always told me she has a big crush on me. That was flattering, but I really didn't think much of it. But when she was here, doing all that, she told me she'd wanted me for a long time. And I think maybe she had. But she was too bright and had too much self-respect to throw herself on me like some ... some hard-up hooker. Until that thing got to her. Then her inhibitions dropped. That's what it seems to do to everyone. The old lady at the center, she'd said something about eating her roommate once before, she'd said it to Megan. But it was just in passing, almost like a joke, maybe. Still. The thought was there. And she did it. Hollister had said that he sometimes felt like ... like gutting his patients. He did."

Tom's lips opened dryly and, in a deadly monotone that was so without emotion it seemed to be coming from a machine, he said, "Kimberly said that sometimes she felt like she could kill the kids. And ... she said she didn't want the baby. Now I know she didn't, because she was ... she was spilling everything, everything she hadn't told me. Everything she'd kept inside. And there at the end, she said ... she said that ... that she never wanted me, really. Never." The plastic expression on his face never changed, but his eyes filled with tears and they spilled down his flat cheekbones and into the valleys of his sunken cheeks. "If she never really wanted me or ... or the kids," he continued, his voice thick and wet now, "she ... she must have been miserable all those years we were together. Miser-miserable." He lifted the cigarette to his lips with slightly trembling fingers and left it there, hanging from his mouth so he could puff on it with every other breath.

"Would you like to lie down, Tom?" Hunt asked.

"No. No, dammit, I don't want to lie down!" he snapped. "I want to *do* something! I want to do something before it's too late. What are we waiting for? For the damned things to creep up on *us,* for Christ's sake? I've seen enough, thank you. I don't care to deal with them firsthand, if you don't mind." He got up and began pacing around the table then stopped and leaned against the counter, facing Hunt. "I'm sorry, Doc," he said quietly. "I know you're just concerned about me."

"Don't apologize, Tom. You're keeping yourself a little too bottled up, if you ask me."

Tom shrugged noncommittally and took another drag on the cigarette. "If you ask *me*" he said, his tone just a shade brighter, "I think we should go find Jeffery Collinson's old psychiatrist. Today. Now, in fact."

* * *

The last Jeffery Collinson's mother had heard of Dr. Avery Lippincott, he was retired and living on a hill just above Rutherford, where he occasionally wrote articles for small psychology magazines. They found that he was still there. Hunt called ahead, told him about his friend the writer, and with a gentle, smiling voice, the doctor welcomed them to his home with unexpected enthusiasm.

Dr. Lippincott's house was rather large, located at the end of a long private drive with a gate that was already open for them when they arrived. Hunt parked his car in front of the closed garage and they went around the immaculately tended yard to the front door, where they were greeted by the doctor.

"Did you have any trouble finding the place?" Lippincott asked, smiling, as they came up the walk.

Hunt said they had not, although they actually had passed the gated drive once without noticing it.

"Most people do. Unless they want to find it bad enough." He led them inside and took their coats. "A reporter came by last week to ask me a lot of sensational, gossipy questions about Mr. Collinson, most of which I couldn't answer for ethical reasons. But I'm afraid I talked the young man's ear off, anyway. I'm sure he was glad to leave, answers or no."

They introduced themselves and shook hands, Lippincott hung their coats on a coat tree by the door, then beckoned them into the house. He was a small man, but gave the impression that he might have once been bigger. His complexion was very fair, and, except for a tiny bald spot on top of his head, he had thick, wavy hair that was near the end of a transformation from red to gray. His wiry eyebrows were set high above his green eyes, and the left side of his small mouth seemed always to remain curled upward slightly.

He led them into his spacious and spotless living room. It had a showroom feel to it; nothing was out of place, there wasn't a trace of dust to be seen anywhere, and the air was fresh. He offered them seats.

"So, you're writing a book," he said, looking from one to the other.

"Actually, Tom is writing the book," Hunt replied. "I'm just sort of following along because of a personal interest." He explained to Lippincott that he'd treated Collinson in ER and wanted to learn more about the young man.

"Well, as I said," Lippincott sighed, rubbing his palms up and down over his thighs, his hands swishing over the material of his brown pants, "there are some questions I simply cannot answer because of ethics. I'm sure you understand—being a doctor, I mean." He turned to Tom with a look of interest. "Have you written anything before? Perhaps I've read you. I read a great deal."

"No. This is my first, really." Tom's speech was a bit strained. "What is it you'd like to know?"

"Mostly, your overall opinion of Collinson," Tom replied. "His mother told us she'd taken him to you."

"You spoke with Mrs. Collinson?"

"Yes."

"Hmm." Lippincott looked down at the floor for a moment, his eyebrows lowering some, his fingers drumming on his thighs. "Interesting people. Mrs. Collinson was very sincere. She wanted her son to be helped, I really believe that. But there was a limit to what she was willing to do. I told her he had to be institutionalized immediately. She refused and that was that. I never saw them again."

"Could you tell us briefly why you thought he should be institutionalized, Doctor?" Hunt asked.

"Well, I can't go into any of the personal details, of course. That wouldn't be right."

Hunt noticed the firmness in the doctor's voice when he mentioned ethics for the third time. The man was probably in his seventies, living alone, widowed or divorced. He had nothing to do but write now and then, read, and tend his house and yard. His career was over. But he seemed still unwilling to let go of it. So he hung on to his integrity.

"Jeffrey Collinson was unlike anyone I've ever met," the old man said, standing and pacing slowly back and forth in front of his visitors. "He seemed an introverted child at first, a sort of angry look on his face all the time. But I found that he was much more than that." He stopped his pacing and looked at them, folding his arms in front of him. "Are you familiar with the id, ego, and superego, gentlemen?"

Tom shrugged.

Hunt said, "Not so much that I couldn't have it explained to me and not learn anything new."

"I'll start with the super ego," he said, pacing again, now gently stroking his smooth chin with a thumb and forefinger. He looked and sounded very professional. "Our super ego is our conscience, basically. It's our morality. It strives for perfection. It tells us to avoid conflict. 'Don't make waves,' it says.

"Our ego deals with reality. Head on. It sees things as they are and helps us keep a good handle on things, you might say." He walked over to the fireplace, his back to them for a few seconds, then turned and faced them, his pleasant face looking truly serious for the first time.

"The id, however," he went on, "is the little monster in each of us. And it is forever banging on the bars of its cage, wanting out. It's the selfish part; it wants immediate gratification: sex, food, money, whatever. And it fights to avoid pain. We ... most of us ... keep the id neatly tucked away. Our ego keeps it in check for us. It postpones the id's satisfaction until the time is right." He propped his elbow up on the mantel of the fireplace, which was just a bit too tall for him to do so comfortably, but he seemed not to notice. "Jeffery Collinson did not do that." He stared silently between their chairs for a few moments, his brow wrinkled with thought.

"Could you ... explain?" Tom asked.

Lippincott sniffed. "Jeffery seemed to do an adequate job of keeping it in the basement, if you will. But sometimes he would take it out. Like many people take their dogs out for walks in the evenings. Jeffery ... nurtured it. Placated it. *Fed* it." More silence. Then: "It ruled him. Owned him. And he seemed to not just *let* it rule him. He *wanted* it to rule him." He began pacing again, his hands joined behind him, twitching absently. "I begged his mother to let me help him, but she wouldn't let him out of her sight. I let it go at that, but to this day I've felt ... I've felt ..." He stopped pacing and turned to them as if he'd forgotten they were in the room. His little eyes widened a bit. Then a burst of breath escaped his lips and he smiled, sitting down again. "Perhaps I've told you too much already, but ... well, I must admit I've thought about him a lot over the years, that boy. Even ... dreamed about him. Not pleasant dreams, either, I'm telling you. I ..." The burst of breath again. "Perhaps it sounds silly, but I've often thought that, if someone were to cut him, he would not shed blood. I've often thought that ... that his veins flowed not with blood, but ... but with blackness. Pure. Thick. Blackness." His breath puffed from him again and Hunt recognized the sound finally as a nervous chuckle. The doctor rubbed his hands over his thighs. "But we all know that's ridiculous. Don't we?"

Hunt began pacing. As if he'd picked it up from the old doctor. Tom sat on Hunt's sofa, slumped, looking straight ahead, and looking very weary. And yet his eyes held an energy that pierced his weariness, that shined like sunlight through dirty windowpanes. Julie was curled up in the recliner.

"Stop pacing," she said. "You're making me nervous, and I'm too sick to be nervous." Her voice was heavy from sleep and from the throbbing in her head.

"But ... but it makes ... *sense,*" Hunt said, gesturing with his hands, a cigarette planted between two fingers. "It makes a crazy, scary sort of sense."

Neither Julie nor Tom spoke. Hunt continued to pace.

"What if," he said flatly, "just what *if* Collinson's id, his ... his dark side, whatever, had become so strong, so, so *dominant*, that it actually became a ... a *thing?* A ... an *animal.*" Hunt stopped and looked at Tom. Then Julie. He drew on his cigarette, waiting for them to speak, to argue the logic of his statement. But they'd already done that. They'd argued, although weakly. Their arguments had seemed to be mere exercises in reality. They'd not even been real arguments, just statements refuting what they knew *could not* be, what they knew *had* to be *impossible.*

What they *hoped* was impossible.

But now they remained silent.

Hunt stood in front of Tom. "Tom," he said quietly, but his voice was still charged. "Tom, it's an idea. Crazy, but, then, what *hasn't* been so far?"

"She knows," Tom said, almost whispered, as if he were speaking to himself.

"What?"

"She knows. Becky Haber. She knows, but she wouldn't tell me."

"You think I should try talking to her?"

Tom shook his head. "No. I'm going to. Again."

"She's liable to have the bouncer bounce you out of the place."

"Not at work. I'll find her at home."

"You know where she lives?"

"I can find her."

"Want me to come?"

He shook his head again, but did not speak.

"Why, Martin?" Julie asked suddenly.

Hunt turned and faced her. "Huh?"

"There are tons of evil, rotten people in the world. Why did Jeffery Collinson's *id,* or whatever the hell, suddenly sprout up like ... like crabgrass? Why not somebody else's? Why not *everybody's?*"

Hunt walked some more, but slowly, shrugging. "I don't know. Maybe that's what we're looking for. The *why.* Maybe it *can* happen to others. In which case we need to find out why pretty fucking *quick.*"

Hunt pressed the telephone receiver to his ear and heard the solid, thrumming sound of the phone at the other end ringing.

"Hello?" said a tinny voice, pinched through miles of wires.

"Reverend Collinson?"

"Speaking."

"Hello, this is Dr. Hunt. Martin Hunt. Remember me?"

"Oh, yes. Hello, Dr. Hunt. How are you?"

"I'm just fine, thank you. I was wondering if we could talk again."

"You and me?"

"Yes." Hunt caught his mistake. "Well, Julie is down with the flu right now."

"Oh, I'm sorry. I'm afraid I can't, Dr. Hunt. I'm very busy right now."

"I'm sure you are, but this would only take a few minutes. I'd ... uh ... Julie wanted to get a couple questions answered."

"Such as?"

"Well, if we could get together—"

"Not today ... as I've said. But perhaps if you told me what she wants to know, I could get back to you." He did not sound as cooperative as he had before.

"Well, it was ... uh ... concerning your son's religious background. You mentioned teaching him about good and evil, Reverend, about respecting the—"

"Yes, Dr. Hunt, I did mention that, and I see no reason for me to mention it again since you seem to recall it quite well."

"Well, what she wanted was perhaps a little more detail. Maybe if you could sort of outline for us what it was you taught Jeffery. What it was, exactly."

Silence. Then: "I don't see the relevance of that to your friend's book, Doctor. And, quite frankly, I'm not sure this is your *friend's* book—if, in fact, there *is* a book."

Hunt clenched his fingers around the receiver. "Reverend, are you familiar with the id?"

"The what?"

"The id. It's a psychological term, sort of. It's—"

"Dr. Hunt, I really do have to cut this short. I'm on my way out the door. Perhaps we can talk about this later."

Trying to hold in his sigh, Hunt said, "Yes, okay. Sorry to bother you."

After Hunt had hung up the phone, he turned to Julie, who was now seated at the kitchen table.

"Well?" she said.

"As my father often says," Hunt replied heavily, "it's beginning to smell like someone shat upwind."

The night was cold. Tom lifted his wrist and pushed the light button on his watch: two-seventeen A.M. He waited in the dark, out of the light cast by the bare bulb glowing just above and to the right of the door of apartment 12. From the location Becky's roommate had mentioned to him earlier.

(We got an apartment down on Vineyard View, by the horse ranch)

He'd found the apartment building, then read the mailboxes out front to get the apartment number. The curtains were pulled over the window and there was no light inside that he could see. Apparently, her roommate was not home, either.

He didn't care what he had to do. He was going to get the location of that cave out of Becky. If possible—and he knew inside that he was determined enough to *make* it possible—he would get her to *take* him there.

He waited.

The sound of a car around the corner of the building. Slowing. Stopping. The ignition being cut off. The door opening. Closing. Footsteps scraping along the cement. Keys clinking together. A soft, muffled voice. At first he thought she was not alone. Then he realized she was simply mumbling to herself.

He waited.

She came to the door, put the key in the knob, turned it. Tom stepped quietly out of the darkness, put his hand firmly on the back of her neck, praying that it wasn't her roommate or someone else, and pushed her into the apartment. She squealed with shock, sounding as if she was pretty sure it was a friend pulling a joke. Tom shut the door behind him, then pulled her closer to him.

"Turn on a light," he said quietly.

"Who the *fuck*—"

"Turn on the light."

He heard a click and the room was awash with light.

"*You!*" she spat. "I *knew* there was something wrong about you. Whatta you want?"

"I don't want to rob you or hurt you. I don't want to do anything illegal. I just—"

"You've already forced yourself into my—"

"*Listen to me!*"

Becky's head snapped back on her skinny neck and her eyes flared. Her lips pursed together angrily.

"I want you to take me to the cave," he said.

"That cave is none of your god—"

"I said I don't *want* to hurt you, but I *will* unless you do as I ask."

"Why?" she almost whispered. "Why's it so important to you? Do you just wanna try to destroy what Jeffery did? To—"

"Whatever Jeffery *did,* it destroyed my whole family!" he roared, the power behind his voice surprising even him. "I want to find it and stop it before it does that again. Now, I am, by nature, *not* a violent man, but either you tell me where that cave is, or I'll *beat* it out of you." He realized that every muscle in his body was taut and he was tightening his grip on her neck. For a moment, he actually thought her neck might snap and her head might suddenly plop to one side at a sickening angle.

The anger in Becky's face was rapidly giving way to fear; her lips relaxed and began to tremble. "You're ... you're hurting my neck."

"I'm thinking of *breaking* it," he threatened. When he heard those words come from his mouth, his flesh crawled like some sort of reptilian creature over his bones. He was scaring himself.

Becky swallowed and her mouth made a dry, parched sound

when it opened again; she licked her lips with the tip of her tongue. "It's ... it's just north of—"

"You're coming with me," he said, pushing her around and toward the door.

"But, it-it-it's late and dark and—"

"I've got a light in the car." She opened the door and he pushed her out, switching off the light himself. Just outside the door, he leaned forward and whispered in her ear, "And if you scream, you're a—"

(dead woman dead woman dead woman)

The words echoed in Tom's head before he spoke them and his lips clamped shut, pulling his head back and taking in a deep breath. Becky turned cautiously to look at him, waiting for him to continue. He did not. He could not.

But she understood.

The moon was hiding and the woods were black. They were black and damp and Tom was genuinely afraid that they would become lost in the night. He held his long flashlight tightly in his right hand, making wide, searching arcs with the bar of solid light that shined ahead of them, while holding Becky's elbow perhaps tighter than was necessary with his left hand. They'd been walking for what felt to him like a very long time, but it had actually been under five minutes.

"You're sure you know where we're going?" he asked her, his voice a little hoarse from the brisk walking and the cold. And his fear.

"Positive. I wish you'd quit squeezing my elbow like it's a goddamned grapefruit or something."

He held back on his grip for a few seconds, but was holding her arm tightly again. His mind chidingly told him he was hanging on to this stick of a girl because he was afraid, but he quickly (and somewhat weakly) countered that with the fact that he didn't want her to run off into the dark. *She* knew these woods better than *he* did; it would be very easy for her to lose him. He *already* felt lost.

"It's just up ahead a ways," she said.

Tom could hear the sound of a stream giggling at him in the dark. Something moved in the bushes and he froze, madly swinging the light in the direction of the sound. He spotted the tail end of a raccoon waddling into the shadows. He turned to Becky. With the shadows cast by his light creasing her face, making her look old far beyond her years, he could see that she was staring at him. Smirking.

"Someday you won't have to be afraid," she said softly, almost soothingly. "That's why Jeffery did what he did. So you wouldn't have to be afraid."

His eyes blinked several times when he realized how badly he wanted to slap her. Hard. Instead, he continued on, holding her next to him. "I'm afraid be-*cause* of what Jeffery did," he snapped, picking up his pace. Then, quietly: "Whatever the hell that was."

Becky Haber snickered. And it was a cold sound. Empty.

After a few more minutes of silent walking, she stopped beside him. "There it is," she said, pointing ahead.

He shined the light in the direction of her finger and he saw it.

The stream was louder now, very close. The ground at his feet was getting spongy. Up ahead was an embankment, no taller than he, and in the embankment was a hole. Vines hung down over it like long, bony fingers with bulbous, arthritic joints. It was black. Blacker than the darkness that surrounded them.

"C'mon," Tom croaked, walking toward it cautiously. He kept the flashlight's beam pinned on the small cave as they neared it; half expecting to see someone

(something? *that's crazy stop it stop it*)

step out to greet them. To greet *him.* Perhaps Jeffery Collinson, his bones shattered and crooked. Or. Worse yet.

Perhaps. Kimberly. Bloody. Cut. Smiling. Holding something in her arms. A lump. A messy, tattered *lump.*

It's a girl, Tom! Just like you wanted!

He clenched his eyes shut and jerked his head rapidly from side to side a couple of times, erasing the images.

They stopped at the entrance. Tom could not move. Could hardly breathe. He did not want to go in. It could hold just what he'd been looking for

(*you don't know what the fuck you're looking for it could be anything anything aaany* thing!)

But he did not. Want. To go *in.*

"Afraid?" Becky asked, smiling. Her crooked teeth looked like fangs in the dark. "Afraid to go in, Mr. Hot Shit?"

He glanced at her, then back at the cave, unable to reply.

"Look. I'm not afraid." She took her arm away from him, and

he could not hold on to it. Then she stepped forward, still smiling. "This is the safest place in the world. The *holiest*." She went in and the darkness swallowed her whole.

Pulling one foot up from the soft, sucking ground, Tom ducked his head to keep from hitting it on the upper part of the cave's short opening, and he followed her in.

The darkness held a smell. It was a moist and yellow smell that made Tom think of flaking flesh and muscle that was rotting away from old, brittle bones. It licked teasingly at his nostrils at first. Then he inhaled. The smell hit him with such force that he tossed his head back lightly, bumping it on a low-hanging rock.

"*Ouch*, dammit!" Tom snapped. He looked over at Becky, rubbing his head gently with a palm.

She stood in the light. She was still smiling. Comfortably.

Stooping forward again, Tom advanced a few more steps, then stopped and looked cautiously around him.

The cave's darkness seemed to push hard at the beam from the flashlight, trying desperately to smother it. Things hung from the cave's ceiling: webs, vines, a lethargic lizard on a rock, its head turning slowly to look at the newcomers. There were places in the cave that Tom's light seemed unable to illuminate; they were spots of such blackness that it looked to Tom as if perhaps the world simply ended there, falling away in spots. He turned a bit, moving the light around, dancing it across rocks and lumps of earth, small spiders that scurried for cover, large elaborate webs that looked almost like Halloween decorations. The circle of light flashed over something and Tom sucked in a breath of the stale, sticky air, sweeping the beam backward.

Becky stepped into the light and looked down at the thing, still smiling. "Jeffery's sins," she said. "Remember I told you? He brought them here. They were necessary. For what he was doing, I mean."

Tom stepped forward, feeling an uncomfortable pressure on his chest. "*Them?*" he asked, his nose wrinkling and his eyes narrowing, almost completely closing as he looked down at the small child's skeleton curled up behind a rock, its knees tucked up under its collapsed jaw; its arms—no longer attached to the shoulders, but simply lying in place—had once been wrapped around the knees, hugging them closer to its chest. The skull had been crushed; one entire side was bashed in. "Are there more?" Tom whispered.

"Everywhere. Back there. Some are buried, I think." She casually gestured over her shoulder with one thumb.

"Dear God, they were ... they were children."

She smiled up at him. "So was he when he did it."

Tom swallowed hard and rubbed his dry throat with one hand, then turned, swinging the light around, starting to speak: "Let's get the—" But he was silenced by an explosion of movement coming from the darkness ahead of him, a thousand sounds, the sputtery, leathery sound of little wings flapping frantically and a black cloud coming forward, as if the darkness had come alive and detached itself from the sides and floor of the cave to pounce upon him like a wildcat leaping from the bushes. Tom could not hold in the scream that pressed its way from his lungs as he lifted his arms and took two stumbling steps backward, dropping the flashlight and falling back on his ass, landing on something that collapsed beneath him with a soft, almost strangely relieved, crunching sound. He moved off it, but he kept his head down as the bats flew madly around overhead like a living tornado, aiming themselves at the opening and finally fluttering out into the night.

Tom swept the light up in his hand and shot to his feet, his mouth open wide, sucking air into his lungs as he spun around and looked down where he had fallen. It was now just a crushed pile of bones, but, just like the other one, it had once been a child.

"They're just little animals," Becky said softly, staring after the bats.

Tom turned to her viciously, his lip pulling back over his teeth as he growled, "Get that fucking diary, *now!*"

She giggled, a girlish sound. "Still afraid." She turned and walked toward the back of the cave, into the darkest part of it, and Tom fixed the light on her, watching her carefully. "It's been a while. It might not be here anymore."

"Find it."

She walked over to a small group of rocks that formed a U with the opening facing the wall. She stepped over one of them, then squatted down, passing her hands over the rocks as a blind person might slide his hands over the face of a stranger. She slid one hand down between two of the rocks and Tom cringed inside, knowing he would not do that, not without a lot of light. She wedged her hand under one of the rocks and pulled up hard, grunting. It budged only slightly. She relaxed, then pulled again, moving the rock, but not turning it over as she seemed to want. Tom was considering stepping forward to help her, but he tensed when something skittered out from under the rock and disappeared into the dark.

"*What was that?*" he rasped.

"Just some little animal," she replied, annoyed at his fear. She struggled with the rock a bit more and, with a loud, almost masculine, grunt, she overturned it. She put both palms down on the ground where the rock had been, caressing it, groping. She found nothing. She moved to the next rock, put her hands on it, reached down its sides, feeling; she nudged it.

Again, something shot across the ground through the blackness. Another. Still another.

"What the hell *are* those things?" Tom croaked.

"Just ... I don't know." She didn't sound so confident now.

"Goddammit! Where's that diary?"

"It's ... it used to be between two of these rocks over here. Like I said, it might not—"

"Get out of the way," he snapped, storming over and getting down on one knee. He shined the beam down between two of the rocks, made sure nothing was there, then ran his hand through the space to make sure he wasn't missing the book. He moved to the next rock. Shined the beam down. Blackness. Impenetrable. A ... a hole of some sort?

It moved.

Scurried off in the dark.

"Oh, Jesus ..." he whined, hardly recognizing his own voice. "They're in here!"

"What?" Becky asked. She was standing beside him now.

"Did you see it?"

"What was it?" She stepped over the rocks and walked in the direction taken by the small black thing.

"*Don't!*" he hissed. "Let's just get the diary and get the hell out of here!" He stood and began kicking at the rock until it finally rolled over with a thud. Then he turned and kicked at the next one. "You're sure it was here? In these rocks?" He looked over at her. "Becky!"

She was across the cave from him, leaning forward, looking at something on the wall. It was one of those black areas; she seemed to be leaning over a hole and looked as though she might, at any moment, fall in. She reached out her hand. Touched the blackness.

And they were on her in the blink of an eye, crawling up her arm, over her shoulders, her neck, in her hair, over her breasts, and, before he screamed, Tom heard her take in a breath and say, in a happy voice, a voice filled with victory and with the knowledge, the *certainty*, that comes with being irrefutably *right,* "It's here! It's finally come! *It's here!*" And then, her further mutterings covered by Tom's scream, she dropped to her knees, then fell forward, face down, and began to writhe in the darkness, barely visible now because the darkness was covering her.

Tom's scream stopped and his mind began to race.

There's nothing you can do for her now, nothing, nothing, just get the diary and get out, get out, get out, because they're here and there's a lot of them and they'll take you faster than you can blink.

His whole body quaking, Tom looked down at the rocks, kicked another, and something was suddenly clamped to his foot and shooting up his leg until he swung the flashlight downward, hitting his own shin hard but not feeling the pain because it knocked the thing flying into the darkness so he could keep looking and he did as Becky kept shuffling around on the ground and he started to look up but he couldn't because of the things he was hearing the wet noises and the sound of Becky trying to speak but failing because something was in her mouth and probably in her throat too and even deeper than that after all this time they were probably *inside* her for Chrissakes doing God knows what and he *had* to find that diary because they would be doing it to *him* soon and—

—something scraped against one of the rocks. Tom shot the light down at it. It was a box. A book-shaped box. He bent down and reached for it, but his hand pulled back. He stared at the thing, his heart exploding again and again inside him, his lungs sucking in breath desperately. He finally forced his hand downward and felt the cold, now-flimsy box against his skin, making sure it was a box, then lifted it, only to get a glimpse of the black thing beneath it before it sprang itself upward and latched onto his neck.

"*Nooo!*" he screamed as he dropped the box and slapped his hand over the slimy thing on his neck, sinking his fingers into it, ripping it off, screaming again, with pain this time, as he felt it suddenly begin to eat at his hand, slice through the skin like razor blades, and he swung his arm hard through the air. The thing released and sailed into the darkness. Tom reached down with his bloody hand, got the box, and turned, bounding for the opening. But. Not without one look.

He saw the black heap on the ground, moving over her body, which he could not see. Except. For her arm. Which was no longer an arm. It reached up from the writhing lump. White and red. Only spots of flesh remained. Most of it was gone. Fingers of bone twitched. Clawed. Then the arm dropped. And she was gone.

He turned, a terrified whimper passing between his lips, and, in a matter of seconds, he was gone, too, the diary in its box clenched tightly beneath one arm.

BOOK THREE

There are a lot of wolves
lurking on the edge of the pasture.
—Reverend Jeremiah Collinson.

1 - THE DIARY

HUNT WAS AWAKENED from a deep sleep for the second night in a row by a frantic knocking at his front door. He got out of bed without waking Julie and hurried, in his robe, to the door, a tight pang of fear shooting through his chest. He'd heard all about Megan's suicide the night before; it couldn't be she.

(Could it could it?)

After all that had happened, would it be terribly surprising to open his door and find Megan standing on his front porch with a letter opener sticking from her right eye? No. But it wasn't. It was Tom.

"Jesus Christ!" Hunt muttered sleepily, pulling Tom inside and sitting him down on the sofa.

Tom's chest was heaving up and down with raspy, gulping sounds and there was blood spattered on his light green shirt and thin brown jacket, streaked on his cream-white face, and covering his left hand, which had obviously been badly cut. Under his right arm he carried a dirty, tattered box tied with an old yellowed string. His head moved forward and back with each gasp, his mouth closing, then opening wide to suck in air, like a fish out of water.

"They tuh-took her duh-down!" he wheezed. "They skuh-skinned her alive!"

It was several minutes before Hunt could get anything out of Tom that made a bit of sense. First, he had to calm him down. Then he tended to his hand, for which, he insisted, he should be taken to the hospital, but Tom refused for the moment. Julie was awakened by all the commotion and helped in calming Tom.

A while later, he was on the sofa, almost finished with his second brandy, still shaking, when their attention finally turned to the box he'd brought with him. It was on the table in front of the sofa next to an ashtray that held the growing pile of cigarette butts that Hunt had been smoking since Tom's arrival. They all found themselves staring silently at it.

"It's the diary," Tom said hoarsely. "She took me to it." Quietly, Tom told them of his experience, having given them only small hysterical fragments over the last twenty minutes or so. "There was nothing I could have done," he whispered, shaking his head, staring with wide eyes at the box, which no one had touched yet. "Nothing. They just ... *had* her and ... and she was *gone.*"

Hunt glanced over at Tom, wanting, for a moment, to say something, to tell him it was okay, he'd done his best, he had to save himself. But, suddenly, nothing was important—*nothing*—except opening that diary. But he was afraid. Just as Tom had said *he'd* been afraid to go into that cave. It could be filled with a bunch of lunatic gibberish. That was most likely, in fact. Then, again ... it could contain something just sane enough to be ... *dangerous.*

Tom sipped his brandy.

Julie made a thick sniffing sound and rubbed her eyes.

Hunt took a long drag on his cigarette.

Their eyes were all staring somewhere in the area of that box.

Hunt leaned forward and reached slowly for the box. He touched it. It was cold and damp. He placed it in his lap. The only light was a lamp by the front door and some light coming down the hall from the bathroom. He reached up and switched on the reading light by his chair. Tom and Julie leaned toward him. Hunt fumbled with the string; it was tied awkwardly, tightly. The string fell away from the box and gathered limply in the lap of his robe. There were two snaps on each end of the rectangular box and Hunt unfastened them; it was difficult because they had apparently gone unopened for some time. He lifted the lid off the box and Tom and Julie scooted to the very edge of the sofa. The diary was in a thick plastic bag, which Hunt opened. He removed the book.

It was very simple. A dark green cover with a yellow border and yellow letters in the center that read MY DIARY. A small lock held the book closed. Hunt ran his hands over the diary, front, back, and sides, but found no key with which to unlock it. So he hooked his fingers under the edges of the small strap lock and pulled until it tore loose. He lifted his cigarette to his lips, puffed, then put it out in the ashtray, glancing at Tom and Julie. Then he opened Jeffery Collinson's diary, turned to the first page, and began to read.

> *Everyone is wrong. The only way this world can be a good one, the only way human beings can ever be truly happy, is through evil. When everyone realizes that, we can set our souls free. We can finally be the people we were meant to be. I have been sent into this world with this message. The message of Evil.*

Hunt read slowly, clumsily, because the words were scrawled and misspelled, the pages were stiff and warped. He paused for a moment, reading a few lines ahead of himself, then continued aloud.

> *Evil is only a word. What it really is is good. It's pure and perfect. It's inside of us all. It's what makes us up. We don't learn to be evil. We learn to be good. Because good don't come naturally. Evil does. We're all prisoners unless we throw away all the lies we been living and let the evil come out. Humans all want the same things—power, sex, money, anything that feels good and makes us strong. Good don't get those things. Evil does. That's why we got to be evil.*
>
> *Christianity and all other God-religions that ask for good works and self-sacrifice must end. Evil must win. Must rule. I am going to make evil rule. I'm going to do it with my life. I am going to live a life of evil. I am going to be exampling to those around me. I am going to bring in the evil wave. I am the Dark Christ.*

Hunt stopped and looked up. "That's what he said. In ER. He kept saying he was the Dark Christ. He was—"

"Keep reading," Tom whispered. Hunt quickly lit another cigarette and went on with the diary.

They went through the entire book that early morning. None of the entries was dated, and the handwriting never improved or matured, so they really had no idea when each entry had been written. Sometimes Collinson wrote about his thoughts and ideas. He wrote about Adolf Hitler, saying he thought that the Holocaust was a heroic gesture by Hitler, but that the man's reasons for doing it were wrong, his priorities were misplaced (all of this poorly written, of course, with childish grammar), and that Hitler had not gotten the result he could have—the result that Collinson knew *he* would achieve: the triumph of evil. He said that Hitler's main mistake was having others do all the work for him. He maintained that the evil would have had to be Hitler's, not anyone else's, for the desired result to have been achieved.

Sometimes Collinson wrote about his experiences, things that he had done. One entry began:

> *Today I fucked Melissa Kintry to death. She*
> *had blond hair, blue eyes, and was seven years*
> *old.*

He wrote of torturing animals and verbally abusing and tormenting retarded children in front of a school of special education that had just opened nearby. He wrote of his mother's feelings toward his actions and told of how she had found a cave in which to bury his sins. He let her try to cover up his actions because, to him, that wasn't important. It didn't matter who knew or didn't know about what he was doing. All that mattered was that it was being done. "Someday," he wrote, "it'll all come. And my work will be over."

Several times throughout the diary, Collinson made reference to a quote from the Satanic Bible, although he never identified it and never made quite clear why he seemed to think it was so important:

> *Can the wings of the winds hear your voices*
> *of wonder?; O you!, the great spawn of the*
> *worms of the Earth!, whom Hell fire frames in*
> *the depth of my jaws!, whom I have prepared*
> *as cups for a wedding or as flowers regaling*
> *the chambers of lust!*
>
> *Stronger are your feet than the barren stone!*
> *Mightier are your voices than the manifold*
> *winds! For you are become as a building such*

*as is not, save in the mind of the All-Powerful
manifestation of Satan!*

*Arise!, saith the first! Move therefore unto
his servants! Show yourselves in power, and
make me a strong seer of things, for I am of
Him that liveth forever!*

At one point, as Hunt read, Julie made a stifled sound of
disgust in her throat, stood, and left the room. She came back
a few moments later with a brandy and sat down. Hunt had not
stopped reading.

The sun was just beginning to rise when Hunt read the last
page, then slowly, softly, closed the book. He raised his head and
looked at his companions. No one spoke for a long time.

"It's all so preachy," Julie said.

"He grew up with a preacher father," Hunt replied simply.
"His father had a message to preach. So did Jeffery. He wrote it
down the best way he knew how: like his father might."

"Everything makes sense now," Tom said, "all that stuff that
Becky said. She actually believed that what Collinson had tried
to do—or ... or what he *did*—was *good*. She believed in him.
And ... and when those things attacked her, she said that it had
all come, finally. She ... I think she was right."

"But what *are* they?" Julie asked.

"I think we know." Hunt lit yet another cigarette and stood,
beginning to weave nervously amid the sofa, the chairs, the
coffee table. "They're ... *him,* Collinson *made* them. I think we
hit it on the head after we talked with Lippincott. Collinson lived
a life of ... of such *unspeakable* evil that he created a *thing*—or
things, rather—that were actual physical manifestations of ... of
wickedness ... of evil."

"That's ... that's impossible," Julie insisted quietly.

"I think it's high time we stopped worrying about what is
and isn't possible," Hunt replied somewhat sternly. "I honestly
believe that is what has happened."

"But why did they kill Becky?" Tom asked. "She was ... she was
for the damned things. Christ, she was actually glad to see them!"

"If I'm right," Hunt said, "and I think I am, then these things
have no loyalty. Collinson himself died. Maybe it was because of
his injuries. Maybe not."

"Where are they all *coming* from?" Julie asked emphatically.

Hunt stopped pacing for a moment and shrugged. "Maybe they multiply, I don't know. They're ..." His face tightened and became thoughtful. "They're almost like a disease. They strike randomly. Just as someone in perfect health can get rabies if they're bitten by a rabid dog, the most moral and pure-hearted person can perhaps become evil if ... if entered by one of these things. They affect the brain, maybe, since they enter the skull. Then things the victims only *thought* of doing in the past, they do. Like Hollister ripping out his patient." Hunt began pacing again, gesturing with his hand, his cigarette trailing a string of smoke. "*Also* like a disease, the creatures can harm their victims physically, as they did Becky Haber. Or me." He glanced at the faint remains of the cut on the back of his hand. "Or they can be carried by someone, like a disease can be carried, and spread to others, as they were carried by Megan. And Kimberly." He walked over to the ashtray and stubbed out his cigarette. "So far," he said quietly, pressing the butt into the ashes, "we don't know exactly why he went to all this trouble to make them, what put the idea into his head. And. There's no cure." He went to the front door, opened it, and stepped outside to stare at the slowly bluing sky. A few small clouds hung lifeless in little groups.

It's going to be sunny today, he thought absently.

Inside, Tom and Julie remained silent on the sofa, Julie leaning her head back, her eyes closed, still holding her glass, the brandy gone now. Tom stared at the diary, leaning forward now, his elbows on his knees, his chin resting on the knuckles of his fists. There was something in the book that had triggered off a faint but distinct mental bell in his head while Hunt was reading it, but Tom had kept quiet about it and allowed Hunt to continue. Now he couldn't remember what it was. He stared. And thought. Finally, he reached forward, picked up the diary, and opened it. The binding snapped and crackled when it was opened, and Tom was very careful not to damage the book. He scanned the pages, not wanting to read through very carefully again, looking for that sentence, or perhaps that word, that had perked his attention earlier.

"... from the grave."

Tom's eyes stopped, moved back, and read again. His lips moved slightly, hitting his *s*'s and *t*'s audibly.

"What I'm doing may kill me, but dying won't matter, because what I'm doing will go on from the grave."

Tom's eyebrows gathered together and his mouth hung open slightly, the tip of his tongue running back and forth over the edge of his upper teeth.

From the grave.

He thought back to the time of Collinson's death. There was something he should be remembering, he was sure. He put the book down and walked out to the porch where Hunt stood, his hands stuffed into the baggy pockets of his robe. Hunt glanced at him, then turned his gaze back to the sky.

"Do you know the coroner?" Tom asked.

"The new one?"

"The ... the *new* one?" Tom turned to him, puzzled.

"Uh-huh. Healy retired about a week or so ago. Suddenly."

A trap in Tom's mind snapped shut on that fact and held tightly. That was it. He'd read about it in the paper and completely forgotten, almost instantly. There were too many other things going on. Things that, unfortunately, ruled his thoughts, and would probably continue to do so for a very long time. Tom had known Walter Healy's son years ago. They'd nearly grown up together. Then Jim had left for L.A. to pursue a career in cinematography. They'd lost touch too quickly. But Tom had occasionally visited Walter and his wife, Jan, until just a few years ago, when the kids started taking up so much of his time that he'd lost touch with *them,* too.

Now Walter Healy had retired. Suddenly. And right around the time of Jeffery Collinson's death. Was Healy ill? Perhaps Jan had gotten sick. Healy was too devoted to his work, though. And he was always as healthy as could be. Jan was too supportive ever to hear of him giving up his work just to care for her if she were sick. No. There was something in all of it that made Tom uncomfortable.

But what did it all have to do with "... what I'm doing will go on from the grave?"

"Why do you ask?" Hunt muttered.

"Oh, I don't know. I used to be close to Healy's son. Whole family, really. I just thought of them. Maybe I'll go to see them today." Tom's words were casual, but the more he thought about it, the more he couldn't wait for the day to get under way so he could visit Walter Healy.

2 - THE BIBLE

"GET SOME SLEEP," Hunt said, kissing Julie lightly. "I'm gonna shower, dress, and get some breakfast. Then as soon as the bookstores open, I'm gonna try to get my hands on a copy of the Satanic Bible."

"Let me come with you," she said, standing from the sofa and wrapping her arms around him, leaning her head on his shoulder.

"No way. Go to bed."

"But I'm not sleepy."

"So read a book or something. Drink lots of fluids. Eat soup."

"You got a little Jewish blood in you or something, Mom?"

He led her to the bedroom, put her to bed, then shed his robe and showered. In the shower, standing still for a few moments, just letting the hot water hit his chest and run down his body, he thought again of the diary.

Collinson had not explained the significance of that quote from the Satanic Bible. Perhaps it had just caught his fancy and meant nothing. Then, again, it might have had a part in the creation of those crawlers. Maybe even an inadvertent part.

The quote had included the line "I am of Him that liveth forever." That was how Collinson had signed all the letters he'd left with the corpses of his victims. It had to mean *something*.

When Hunt got out of the shower, Julie was no longer in bed. He could smell pancakes cooking. He dried and dressed, then went into the kitchen to find breakfast ready.

"Some nurse you are," he said with a smile, sitting down at the table.

"I know how to take care of sick people," she said, pouring

him some coffee. "I don't know how to *be* one. So. What do you hope to find out with that bible?"

"As usual, I'm not sure." He spooned some sugar into the coffee. "I want to find out the meaning of that quote, that thing about the worms of the Earth. It meant something to him. He referred to it a lot in the diary, and he was screaming bits and pieces of it in ER. As well as something that sounded like it was in another language. Maybe the bible will explain it. If not, maybe I can find someone who can."

Julie watched him butter his pancakes, then pour on some syrup.

"You gonna eat?" he asked her.

She shook her head. "My stomach's a little upset."

He gave her an I-told-you-so look and said, "You should be resting."

"Cut it out. It's not from the flu. I'm ... I'm nervous. My stomach always gets upset when I'm nervous."

"Nervous?"

She looked down at her slippered feet. "Scared's more like it. About what's going on."

Fork in hand, he stopped chewing and looked at her for a few seconds, silent. His lips smacked when he opened his mouth. "Yeah. It *is* scary. I feel the same way. A little." He took another bite.

Julie walked over to him and put an arm around his shoulders, smiling crookedly, but not comfortably. It was a dark smile. "Liar," she said.

He turned his head toward her. "Okay. More than a little."

They were both terrified. But they were hiding it well.

Hunt covered St. Helena, Calistoga, and Napa. None of the bookstores had a copy of the Satanic Bible on hand. They all offered to order it for Hunt; it would take a week or so. He smilingly thanked them, but, no. He couldn't wait that long.

He went to Vallejo. Same story. But a young man dressed in leather with bleached blond hair and a small green ponytail was able to give him some help.

"We don't have it," he said. "It's pretty hard to find. We could order it, or you could go to a specialty bookstore. The occult, Satanism, that sort of thing."

"Is there one around?" Hunt asked hopefully.

"Not in town. There are a couple I know of in San Francisco, if you don't mind the drive."

Hunt said he didn't mind the drive at all and got the names and addresses of two occult bookstores. He stopped at a phone booth to call Julie and tell her where he was going, then drove to the city. It took a little more than thirty minutes to get there and about fifteen to find the first place.

It was called The Wolfsbane and was so small he passed it twice before spotting the little black-and-white sign above the door.

When he walked in, he smelled incense, dark and sweet. For a bookstore, The Wolfsbane was rather poorly lit. Shelves of books lined the walls, and tables with books stacked on them were arranged in an orderly fashion. The aisles between the tables and bookshelves were very narrow. In the far corner of the bookstore, a light shining above it to draw attention, was a tall, black, delicately constructed birdcage. Inside, on a thick branch that had been perched in the center of the large cage from one side to the other, was an enormous owl. At first Hunt thought it was stuffed. He stared at it for several moments upon entering, and it stared back. Then its huge eyes blinked and Hunt almost gasped.

"Can I help you?" a deep voice asked.

Hunt turned to his right. There was an L-shaped counter in a front corner of the store. Behind it sat a burly man leaning back in a squeaky chair smoking what looked like a thin cigar. He wore a black short-sleeved shirt; what there was of his neck was very thick, and his upper arms were huge, although not all muscle. He had a head of thick black hair that was not combed, and a bushy mustache. The counter itself was actually a glass showcase and inside were a number of bottled and packaged herbs, a skull-shaped ashtray, and several books that looked like antiques.

"Uh ... yes," Hunt said a bit uncertainly; he was very uncomfortable. "I'm looking for a copy of the Satanic Bible."

"Paperback or hardcover?"

"Uh ... paperback, preferably."

The man fitted the cigar between his lips, stood, and came out from behind the counter. He was well over six feet tall, and as he walked, he watched Hunt suspiciously. Hunt knew he probably did not resemble the typical patron of The Wolfsbane. The man went to the back of the store, near the owl's cage, and stopped in front of one of the shelves, ran his fingers along the book spines, then removed a black paperback with white letters on the front. He came back and handed the book over. Hunt got a whiff of the cigar, and it wasn't a cigar. It had a sweet smell, not marijuana, really—not unlike incense.

"This what you're looking for?" the man asked, sitting down again.

"Yeah." Hunt stood before the counter, opened the book, and began thumbing through the pages. He turned to the table of contents and ran a finger down the list. At the very end, it gave the page number for the Enochian Keys. He flipped through it, but none of it was familiar. He went on to the Second Key, breathing the words silently to himself.

"'Can the wings of the winds hear your voices of wonder?; O you!, the great spawn of the—'"

"Excuse me, but are you gonna read that, or buy it?"

Hunt's gaze snapped up at the big man behind the counter and he smiled nervously. "Yeah, I'm sorry." He stepped forward, put the book down by the cash register, and got out his wallet. "This is kind of important to me," he said as he handed the man a five. While he waited for his change, he said, "Uh ... do you know anything about this stuff?" He gestured to the black book.

The man shrugged. "A little." He looked up at Hunt slyly. "Some of my best friends are Satanists," he said with a throaty chuckle.

Hunt chuckled with him.

"Why? What do you need to know?"

"Well"—Hunt picked up the book and found the Second Enochian Key—"I need someone to explain this to me. This ... Key." He held it out to the man and showed it to him.

Handing over the change, the man took the book and looked over the page. His thick eyebrows bunched together as he read. "Hmm," he grunted. "Enochian Keys. Yeah, they're like ... uh ... well, they're sort of like spells, or ... um ... hymns. Yeah, like the Christians have hymns, you know? Well, that's sort of what these are to the Satanic Church. Only they're supposed to have some sort of magical power. I don't know. It's all in here." He waved the book a little, but kept looking through it. "Why do you ask?"

"Well, I'm ..." Hunt laughed, realizing he was about to tell this man his story. That wouldn't do at all, would it? "Just ... wondering." Then a thought struck him: *This guy* works *here! Surely he's heard lots of weird shit already, he's probably used to it. Maybe he even* believes *some of it!* "Um ... actually, I was just wondering if it's possible to use those ... those Keys to ... to, say, *create* things?"

The man cocked his head. "You mean, like people, or something?"

"Not ... really. Like—" *This is such a crazy thing to be telling a total goddamned stranger!* "—like evil."

"How d'you mean?"

"Well, let's say someone wants to ... um ... create a physical manifestation of evil. See what I mean?"

The man thought for a moment, staring down at the book. "You thinking of doing this?"

"*No!*" Hunt replied a bit too quickly and too enthusiastically. "I'm just ... wondering."

He eyed Hunt suspiciously again. "Well, like I say, I only know a little about this stuff. But I really doubt it. I mean, I don't *think* so."

"Do you know anyone who *might* be able to tell me?"

"You mean, do I know any Satanists?" The guy chuckled again, shaking his head. "A couple. But you ask them a question like that and I know right now they're gonna tell you no. See, they got people coming to them right and left asking questions like that, just waiting for them to admit to something like that. Creating evil." He snorted. "What are you, a reporter or something? Doing a story on the Satanists for *Rolling Stone*, maybe? You think they're stupid? Even if they *did* do stuff like that, they'd deny it." He held up one beefy palm. "I'm not saying they *do,* you know. Like I say, some of my best friends are Satanists." The throaty chuckle again.

Hunt pocketed his change and took the book, a feeling of hopelessness beginning to flower in his chest. "Thanks." He left the shop thinking that he'd perhaps made the trip for nothing. He had the book, but no explanation. Of course, maybe if he sat down and *read* the damned thing ...

Feeling a little better with that thought, he got into his car and headed for home.

* * *

Julie was beginning to get hungry. The rumblings in her stomach shed their anxious feeling and took on an emptiness that made her think of peanut butter and jelly.

Peanut butter and jelly was a childhood favorite of just about everyone Julie knew. But they had outgrown it somewhere along the line. Not Julie. It had stayed with her all along. Hunt was frequently poking fun at her love for the childish sandwich, and she always went along with it laughingly, but if it were possible for a person to be deeply devoted to a food, Julie Calahan was deeply devoted to peanut-butter-and-jelly sandwiches.

For the last forty-five minutes, she'd been lying in bed reading the latest William Goldman. She put the book down on the bed beside her, threw the covers back, and went into the kitchen in her nightshirt. She hummed. She'd been humming to herself ever since Hunt had left. And she felt her hands trembling, too. She couldn't *see* them tremble if she held them up before her. But she could *feel* it. She knew why she was doing these things, but she refused to allow herself to think about it. Instead, she read, or listened to music. She'd even baked a chocolate cake right after Hunt had left, just a quickie, one of those Betty Crocker jobs, not because she wanted to eat it, she just wanted to do it, and the warm smell of chocolate cake baking still lingered in the kitchen. The cake sat on Hunt's cake dish on the counter, the big transparent bell-shaped lid encasing it like royal jewels.

She opened the refrigerator and took out the grape jam, set it on the counter, unscrewed the lid of the jar, and set it down, then reached above the fridge for the bread. The loaf slipped from her fingers and fell with a thump to the floor, the wrapping making a crinkling sound. She bent down to pick it up—

—and heard a sound.

Her fingers clutched the bread automatically and she shot up and spun around, her eyes searching the kitchen.

The refrigerator hummed.

The cuckoo clock ticked.

The faucet dripped.

An empty coffee cup sat on the kitchen table.

The cake sat under its clear covering.

A pile of dishes lay in the sink.

A dish shifting, maybe?

Her grip on the bread began to relax and she put it on the

counter. Her fingers had pressed deep marks into the loaf. She stepped over to the sink and looked at the dishes.

"Jesus, Martin," she muttered tremulously, "don't you ever wash your damned dishes?"

They formed a little hill in the sink with spaces and gaps between the dishes and pans. Old food clung to the plates. The gaps between them were dark.

Silence.

Julie sucked in on her lips, trying to laugh inside. She started humming again: *New York, New York*. It was the first thing that came to her mind. She passed the sink, reached up to one of the cupboards, opened it, and got out the peanut butter. She tripped on the plastic mat again and almost fell.

"Go*dammit* Martin! Get *rid* of that thing!" she hissed, clumping the jar of peanut butter down on the counter and looking over her shoulder to glare down at the rectangular, piece of plastic. She unscrewed the lid of the peanut-butter jar, fished out a butter knife from the silverware drawer, and plunged it into the Jif, scooping out a gob and spreading it onto the first piece of bread she'd taken from the loaf. She scooped out some more. Spread it. Then she put the knife down on the peanut-butter lid, took another slice of bread out, lifted the knife—

—and the little door on the cuckoo clock flew open and the tiny wooden bird popped out and cuckooed with what seemed to be, at the moment, a thunderous voice, and Julie spun around with a yelp, the knife slipping from her hand and clanging to the floor, sliding, leaving little peanut butter skid marks behind it. Julie slapped both her hands over her breasts and let out a long, relieved breath, her chest heaving beneath her palms. She could feel her heart hammering against her ribs. She leaned her hips against the edge of the counter and breathed, "Jesus. H. *Christ!*" She stood there a moment, her eyes closed, her hands still pressing to her chest. Then she stepped forward, bent down, picked up the knife, and muttered "A mess" to herself, her voice unsteady. Then she turned around and reached her hand out, her fingers wrapped around the hard handle of the butter knife, and slid the dull blade down into the jar of grape jam and screamed the scream of her life when the jam slid up the knife and latched itself to her wrist and scurried up her bare arm, tingling, scratching, cutting her skin in tiny places as it moved, catching the light and glistening like a clump of black phlegm, past her elbow to her upper arm and under the sleeve of her nightshirt.

The scream came from deep inside her as she threw herself back, away from the counter, her arms flailing, the butter knife sailing through the air like a little missile and clattering into the pile of dishes. Julie's back slammed into the edge of the kitchen table. Then she rolled to the left, falling to the floor on her side, her right hand, by this time, slapping her shoulder where the creature had slid under her shirt, trying desperately to dislodge it from her skin, which it continued to cut as it moved upward toward her neck and head. With a garbled cry of fear and pain, she curled the fingers of her right hand underneath the neckline of her nightshirt and pulled down with all the might her flooding adrenaline could afford her; the shirt tore at a slant down the front and she slapped her hand onto the small black creature and closed her fingers into a fist, tearing it from her skin with a scream, throwing it blindly, drops of blood from her now-bleeding hand following it through the air. As soon as she was free of the thing, she was on her feet despite the pain that standing caused her, and her hands were clattering in the cutlery drawer until her fingers closed on a large carving knife. She spun around, her lower jaw jutting out, strands of hair hanging over her eyes, her shirt torn down the middle, blood trickling from her shoulder and over her mostly bared breasts.

She couldn't see it. Until she turned to her right. It was clinging to the door of the refrigerator like an obscene, overgrown magnet waiting for a note or a recipe to hold up. Little staccato chirps, hoarse and dry, came from her throat each time she exhaled as she began to back away from the refrigerator, holding the knife with both hands until she could take the pain no more and released it with her bloody hand so she could hold the hand close to her and try to ease the pain until a ropelike tentacle slid from the black thing, which, despite the absence of eyes, seemed to watch her as she moved away, and the tentacle wrapped around the wrist of her injured hand and began pulling her toward it, hard, the tentacle feeling thick and tough, although it didn't look thick at all, and she lifted the knife and swung it down, expecting the blade to slice through on the first strike, but it only gave the thing a shallow, harmless cut, which was just enough to make the tentacle release her and pull back, covering the four feet or so between them with as much speed and ease as it had when it shot out at her, disappearing into the little black glob. Without wasting a second, it dropped to the floor and was on her foot in an instant and she was kicking, but it was holding on and cutting her some more, making its way up her leg to her knee and—

—she lifted the knife and, screaming in anticipation of the pain, brought the blade straight down onto the creature and onto her leg just above the kneecap and her scream continued and intensified, her eyes clenched so tightly shut they felt as though they might push back into her skull, which was pounding furiously now with pain and fear and pain and—

—the thing slid its way up the blade of the knife unharmed despite the fact that the blade had impaled the creature in its center and made its way again to her hand, but not before she pulled the knife from her leg, rolled onto her side, swept her bloody hand upward, groped for the round knob on top of the cake dish lid, pulled it downward, overturning the dish and knocking the cake to the floor with a spattering of chocolate icing. She swatted the creature on the knife down onto the plastic mat, releasing it from the blade, then slammed the cake lid over it tightly, pressing down on the lid, her teeth grinding together, her shoulders bouncing with the sobs that were now pouring from her fluidly, sometimes coming out as hysterical words—

"My *cake*, my *cake*, goddammit!"

—other times as wet coughs and gagging sounds, moans, even laughter.

The creature scurried from one side of the lid to the other, pressing itself against the hard plastic, extending tentacles that pushed upward against Julie's hold, until it finally gave up. And stopped. And situated itself in the center of its little circular prison. And remained perfectly still. With no eyes. And yet. Watching her.

Trying to hold back her sobs, Julie turned her head away, unable to look at the thing any longer, her blood dripping down on the lid, running down its sides in little ribbons. She fixed her gaze on the kitchen doorway and prayed as she had never prayed before that someone would fill it.

"Martin," she sobbed, "pleeeaaase, come home. Come *hooommme!*"

3 - THE CORONER'S REPORT

TOM'S BANDAGED LEFT hand throbbed—Hunt had stitched up the cuts that needed stitching, using materials he kept in a satchel in his bedroom—but the throbbing was okay because it sliced through his weariness and crystallized his thoughts as he talked with Walter Healy.

Tom had not seen Healy in some time—six years, to be exact. The man had aged considerably in that time. Tom figured him to be somewhere around sixty, but he looked as if he was pushing seventy. His face was longer, thinner, and he had jowls that hung loosely over his jaws like a basset hound's. His silver hair was receding on the right and left above his temples, almost forming a widow's peak in the middle over his forehead. There was a great deal of space between his nose and upper lip, as if his mouth had dropped since Tom had seen him last. But the most disturbing thing was that his speech slurred ever so slightly and Tom could smell liquor on his breath; perhaps he was mistaken, but Tom could not remember Walter Healy *ever* touching alcohol, and, after all, it *was* just past noon.

Tom had arrived unannounced and was greeted at the door by Healy, who slapped him on the shoulder with a grin, shook his hand, and went on about how long it had been, asking him about what the hell he'd done to his hand. Then Jan had come out of the kitchen, wiping her hands on a small towel, wearing an apron that said GOD BLESS THIS MESS; when she saw who it was, she'd stopped for a moment, her mouth open, not sure what to say, and Tom realized that, of course, they'd both heard about Kimberly and the kids

(goddammit, don't even think *about that, don't let it even*

cross your mind *or you'll sit here like a zombie just let it pass let
it pass)*

and didn't quite know how to act, although Healy was
handling himself very well. Jan decided not to mention it and
gave him a hug and a light kiss on the cheek, telling him to stay
for lunch, that she would be having company soon, but not to
pay attention to them and to stick around.

Healy led him into his study and seated him in his very own
favorite "fat chair," which was so comfortable Tom thought he
might fall asleep in it.

And there he sat, his hands pounding with pain, watching
Healy stand over a small table with bottles of liquor arranged on
it in no particular order, fixing himself a martini.

"You sure you don't want a drink?" Healy asked.

"No. It's a little early for me."

"Yes, a common misconception. If God had intended us to
drink only at night, He never would have created the sun." Drink
in hand, Healy walked over and sat down in an old wooden chair
that creaked under his weight, which had changed a great deal
since they'd last seen one another, too: there was much less of
it. "Thomas," Healy said, his eyes suddenly looking strained,
"although you may not want to hear this, I'm going to say it
anyway to make myself feel better. I am terribly, terribly sorry
about ... your family. Jan and I, when we heard about it, were
going to get in touch, but ... well, we thought it best not to."

Tom swallowed hard, his mind screaming at him

(ignore it pass over it pass over it)

as he stammered, "That's all ... I'm ... thank you, Walter. But
I'd ... I'd rather not talk about it."

"Don't intend to. Just wanted you to know you were in our
prayers."

Tom nodded. Clearing his throat, he asked, "How's Jim?"

"Wonderful. He's still working on those dreadful low-budget
horror films, but he's sure he won't be there long. He'd love to
hear from you."

"I'd love to hear from *him.*"

"My son wouldn't know a postage stamp if one came up and
tweaked his nose." Healy sipped his drink and smacked his lips.
"What brings you by after all this time?" he asked with a warm
smile.

Smiling back, Tom said, "I heard you retired. Suddenly."

The corners of Healy's mouth twitched and he raised his drink to his lips again, Tom assumed to cover it.

Tom shrugged lightly as he continued. "I thought maybe you or Jan were ill. I thought I'd check up on you."

Healy shook his head, smiling again, although it seemed to Tom to be a bit forced. "No, we're in perfect physical health."

There was an edge to the man's voice, a strange, almost imperceptible emphasis on the word "physical," and then it hit Tom: *They never said a word to each other at the door, never even glanced at one another, not for an instant.*

Why that was strange, he didn't know. They'd been married for how many years? The honeymoon was over, nobody was affectionate all the time, except the Healys had always been the most affectionate people in the world, and Tom had always wished they were *his* parents because they were always so friendly and warm to each other and therefore friendly and warm to everyone around them and *some*thing was wrong, *some*thing didn't feel right here.

"I'm glad," Tom said after what felt, to him, like an eternity of thought. "But, then, why did you retire?"

The smile stayed there as if it had been carved in granite. His eyebrows popped up, wrinkling his forehead. "Enough was enough, I guess. My work just wasn't—" a short intake of breath, as if to steady his voice—"interesting anymore. I'm at the right age. Probably should have retired sooner."

Casually and suddenly, watching Healy's face slowly, Tom said, "Did it have anything to do with Jeffery Collinson?"

Healy's face collapsed. The wrinkles fell from his brow, his jowls dropped like lead weights, his eyes sagged, and his lips parted slightly. His throat moved up and down, but he did not speak.

Tom knew he'd hit on something. He leaned forward and looked intently at the old man.

"Walter, you've known me since I was a kid," he said softly. "You and Jan raised me every bit as much as my own parents did. You know me and trust me, even though we haven't seen each other in a long time, and you know that I'm a very rational, logical person. Well, Walter, something is wrong, something very bad is happening, I can't really explain it because I don't know what it is yet, but I *do* know that it all goes back to Jeffery Collinson. Dr. Hunt—you know Martin Hunt? At the medical center?—he's on to it, too, and we're trying like hell to get to the bottom of it, because, Walter, Jesus, people are dying, a lot of people. Like Kimberly and ... and my sons." His voice almost cracked, but he beat it. "Now, I can see something's wrong here because the air's got a chill to it and you're tipping 'em back pretty damned early in the day for someone who's never taken a sip in all the years I've known you. I think you know something. And I think you should tell me. Because just maybe I can do something about it."

They stared silently at one another for a long time, Healy looking scared. He gulped the rest of his drink down, stood, made another, then came back. His free hand hung loosely over the edge of the chair's armrest and his fingers twitched irregularly. He took a swallow of his new drink, took in a deep breath, and said, "My report was false." His words slid together some, but they were very clear. He fell silent again for a few seconds, then went on. "I don't know what killed him, but I'm willing to bet it wasn't the car that hit him. I'm willing to bet my life. It was that thing inside him."

"Thing?" Tom asked after a long pause. "What *thing?*"

Healy opened his mouth, jutted his jaw, and continued, without looking Tom in the eye. "I opened him up for the autopsy and there was this smell. I've been doing that for thirty years plus, and I know every conceivable smell that can come out of a corpse, no matter how fresh or how old. And I've never in my years smelled a smell like that. Anywhere. It was ... *black.* If the color black had a smell, it would be *that.* Actually, it was more of a thickening of the air than an actual odor. And inside." He stopped abruptly and took another drink. "Inside. He was black. At first, I thought his insides had been burned. Then I looked closer. It was ... there was nothing inside that corpse but a ... black. Gelatinous. *Mass.* It didn't move at first, but when it did ... when it did—" He reached his hand up, pressed his palm over his mouth and rubbed downward twice, then chuckled. Giggled, really. Humorlessly. "—I pissed my pants. Like a baby. Then I moved away because this, thuh-thuh ... this *tentacle* slithered up—" He curled his hand into a claw and raised it slowly, all the while staring at Tom's chest with distant eyes, "—and then another. And another. And ... and they, they tugged at the flesh, at the edges of the incision. And my assistant—some young guy, a rookie, scared the living shit out of him; he's probably,

as we speak, bussing tables at a Sizzler Steakhouse and having
nightmares about this every night, because I know *I* do—this
guy opens his mouth and takes in a long breath and I knew, I just
knew, he was going to scream, and I held up my hand and told
him to shush, because I realized what it was trying to do. What
... whatever the hell it was, it was trying to close up the incision,
trying to seal itself back in." He gulped and opened his mouth
again with a loud, dry smack. He took a few more swallows of
his drink. "Didn't make a sound except for a ... a sort of ... of
squishing noise when it moved."

Healy shifted in his chair and the wood creaked; as if on cue,
Tom fidgeted, too, his eyes riveted to Healy.

"I was," Healy went on, "terrified. Scared out of my mind. I kept
watching it, didn't want to get near it, and the kid with me kept
glancing over at me as if to ask what to do next. Finally. Finally,
I moved forward. Cautiously. It ... the thing didn't have any eyes
or any ... hell, it didn't have *anything,* but I could tell it was ... it
was watching me. Moving like a snail, I ... I sewed the guy back
up. All the while, it watched me. The tentacles pulled back in like
... like a radio antenna on a car, only with that squishy sound. And
it watched me. It knew what I was doing, I'm *sure* it did, because
it ... *let* me. Otherwise, I'm sure it would've killed me. I don't
know what it would've done to me, but I know it would've killed
me dead." He cleared his throat and, for the first time since he'd
begun telling the story, he looked Tom in the eye. "We stood there
for what seemed an hour, just catching our breath and staring at
each other. Then I told the kid I was sure he'd be a much happier
young man and not lose any friends if he just kept his mouth shut
about it, because I knew that if either of us breathed a word of it
to anyone, they'd lock us up and feed the key to an elephant." He
finished his drink and set it aside, then rubbed his palms together
noisily. They were moist with perspiration.

"I falsified the report," he concluded, "and the guy was buried,
thank the good Lord, without being embalmed. Then. I retired.
And I hope to God that, for as long as I live, I never *ever* see another
dead body. I don't think I could take it, Thomas. I really don't."

Tom drove too fast on the way home. His thoughts were still
with Walter Healy, whose nights no longer held rest, but, rather,
nightmares with long black tentacles and invisible eyes. He'd
not told Jan. Until Tom had come, he'd kept it all inside, started

drinking, stopped talking, had become cold and unfriendly. Everyone noticed the change. No one knew why. He wanted to keep it that way.

Tom told him to try to forget it and put it out of his mind because whatever it was it would soon be gone. And, much to his surprise, Tom actually felt confidence in his words.

On the way to his apartment Tom decided at the last minute to go to Hunt's. But when he thought about telling Hunt and Julie of what he'd learned, the alarm bell went off in his head again. He couldn't. Not yet. He knew what he had to do now, he just didn't know *how* yet, but when he did, he knew that *he* would have to do it. Not Hunt. Not Julie. *Him.* Tom Conrad. Because it was going to be deadly.

And then he realized what he was thinking.

Dying won't matter.

When he got to Hunt's, he saw Julie lying on the sofa under a blood-spotted blanket and he almost began to cry because he realized that his days were filled with too much blood now. Far too much.

"My god!" he whispered. "What happened?"

"She's okay," Hunt said, rushing toward him, "she's gonna be okay. C'mere." He took Tom's elbow firmly and led him into the kitchen.

Tom entered the kitchen with his gaze downward and the first thing he saw was the blood and chocolate on the floor, then the plastic floormat with a circle cut out of it. A bloody knife lay on the floor. He felt a sickening rush of déjà vu and almost threw up.

Then he saw the transparent bell-shaped object on the table with gray electrician's tape running tightly around the bottom of it, attaching it to the circular, sloppily cut piece of plastic from the floormat, and he knew what was beneath the plastic even before he got close enough to see.

He stepped over to it and saw inside the small black creature.

Watching them.

4 - THE CREATURE AND THE PREACHER

"ARE YOU OUT of your fucking *mind?*" Hunt snapped frantically. "You try to get this thing under a microscope and you run the risk of *losing* it. We've got to find out how to *kill* it! We may never catch another one of these things before it catches *us!*"

"But if we know how they work, we'll know better how to kill them!" Tom returned, waving a hand toward the thing on the table.

"You'll never get that thing out of there and under a microscope, Tom, be serious, it'll have you like *that.*" Hunt snapped his fingers sharply.

Tom pulled a chair away from the table—a good distance away—and plopped down into it. He knew Hunt was right.

After Tom arrived, Hunt had explained to him what had happened. He'd gotten back from San Francisco to find Julie on the kitchen floor, bloody and screaming, holding the thing under the cake dish lid. Thinking fast, Hunt had cut away the plastic with a knife, sealed it with electrician's tape, then cared for Julie, who was, by that time, quite hysterical.

"She's got a bad gash on her leg," Hunt had told him quietly, "and she's lost some blood. But, otherwise, she's okay." He also told Tom what he'd learned from the man in The Wolfsbane. "I don't know if that Key had anything to do with these buggers or not. It was obviously important to Collinson, but he could've done it without really knowing *how* he'd done it. That's not important now, though. What's important is doing something with *this*. I'm gonna leave that up to you for now. Think you could come up with something? Maybe you could get something from the lab that would kill it."

Tom shrugged absently, staring at the creature. "If I could just get a little piece of it, maybe ..." he said weakly.

"Look, Tom, no 'devoted scientist' shit, okay? This is not *The Thing* here, you understand me? Don't fuck around."

Tom looked up at Hunt and laughed hollowly, shaking his head slowly. "You know, of the three of us, you're the only one here who's really on top of things."

The sadness and pain in Tom's eyes made Hunt ache. He reached down and squeezed his shoulder. "We're in this together, Tom. Nobody's a hero. Yet."

Tom nodded and said with an empty tone, "Yeah. Not likely any of us *will* be, either."

Hunt left Tom in the kitchen; he went into the living room, sat down, and began reading the book he'd bought again, turning first to the Second Enochian Key. He read in silence for a while.

Then Julie said, "Is that book any help?"

Her words startled Hunt. "How are you?" he asked, squatting down beside her.

"I'll live. Is it dead? Did you kill it?"

"No, we've trapped it."

"In *here?* Oh, Jesus—"

"No, no, it's okay. Tom's gonna try to figure out a way to kill it. We don't know how yet."

"I stabbed it, Martin, I stabbed it right through its middle and it just sucked the blade in and crawled up the knife! It wouldn't die!"

"I know, but we're doing our best."

She relaxed some, winced when she adjusted the position of her shoulders. "Is that book any help?" she asked again.

"Well, I've found a couple interesting things. You know all that stuff Collinson was babbling in ER? I found what it is." He explained to her what the Enochian Keys were. "They're written here in English and Enochian, that strange language Collinson was speaking in. Before each Key—there's nineteen of them—there's a little explanation, a paragraph sort of defining each Key. The one before the Second Key says that it's simply paying due respect to the lusts that are the sustenance of our lives. Doesn't say anything about conjuring up evil."

"Then ... you don't think anything in that book did it?"

After a moment's thought, he said, "I'm beginning to think not. I think we were much closer to the 'why' than we thought." He looked at Julie, putting the book aside. "Reverend Jeremiah Collinson. Whatever it is that he's not telling us is the reason Jeffery turned to this book in the first place." He put his palm flat on the book. "Maybe Jeffery thought this book was going to help him conjure up his wave of evil, his Time of Darkness, or whatever. But I don't think it did. I think Jeffery did it all by himself, inspired somehow by his father." Hunt stood, disappeared for a moment down the hall, then returned wearing his windbreaker.

"Where are you going?" Julie snapped.

"I'm gonna go see the reverend."

She started to sit up. "Then I'm coming with you."

"Oh, no, don't move, hon, just lie down," he said, coming to her side.

"Pardon my French," she said, "but there is no goddamned fucking way in this *world* you're gonna leave me alone again."

"Julie, you can't, you're—"

"Shut up, Martin, and help me get dressed."

He blinked. He'd never heard her talk like this before.

"I'll lie down in the backseat, if you want, but I'm *not* staying here."

"But, Tom's here and—"

"So's that *thing!*" She was sitting up now, the blanket pushed aside. "Wanna give me a hand?"

With a sigh of resignation, he helped her to her feet and led her into the bedroom.

Tom stared at it.

In its own way, it stared back.

His arms were folded on the edge of the table as he thought. Fire might do it. Hell, he didn't have the slightest idea what these things were made of—*water* might do it, for all he knew! He fingered the bandage on his hand as he thought.

He would have a much better chance of getting it right the first time, he realized, if he could get a little piece of the damned thing under a microscope, look it over, figure it out. Maybe if

he could cut the top out of the lid and reach in with something
... cut a piece out quick-like, then replace the cover again ... Of
course, he would have to take it down to the lab and, because he
hadn't been there in a while, and because of what had happened,
he would attract a lot of attention and everyone would want to
talk to him and extend their condolences and, of course, they'd
want to know what the hell he was carrying around under the
cake dish lid—his pet jellyfish, maybe?

Hunt and Julie were going to see the reverend. They'd be gone
awhile.

Tom stood, got his coat from the living room, slipped it on,
then returned to the kitchen, where he rummaged through the
drawers until he found what he wanted. He took out a dish
towel, unfolded it, and draped it over the makeshift cage. Then,
carefully, his heart picking up its pace just a bit, he picked it up
and carried it in his arm as he walked out to the car ...

The reverend was looking over the outline of his sermon for
the night, but he wasn't really seeing it. First of all, because he
was hot. He knew that made no sense; despite the sunshine, it
was a rather chilly day. But tiny beads of sweat had broken out
on his face like a rash and he could feel it running down his
back and sides under his soft, white shirt. Second of all, because
he'd had a bit too much of the firewater. He knew it was idiotic
to drink any liquor when he was supposed to be preaching that
night, but the reason he drank was ... the *noise*. He kept hearing
things in the trailer. But it wasn't the usual sound of the trailer
settling. Not even the ice falling into its box in the door of the
fridge. No, these noises were softer than all the ones that usually
surrounded him. And yet they were ... more noticeable.

He sat in his chair, the broom leaning at his side against the
armrest. On the lamp table was a glass half filled with whiskey.
He fumbled with the papers in his lap, reached over for his drink,
sipped it, and almost spilled it down his shirt when he heard
it again, when he heard that soft, whispery squishing sound of
something wet and soft moving somewhere, somewhere near—

—under the sofa!

He clopped the drink back down, picked up the broom, and
dropped to his knees in front of the sofa, sticking the broom into
the darkness beneath it, swinging it back and forth, clenching

his teeth together as he did, feeling the sweat tumbling down his temples.

There were two short knocks on his door and it startled him; he snapped his head around to look at the door.

"Who is it?" he called, a little too loudly, he realized immediately.

"It's Dr. Hunt," came the calm reply.

"Hunt," Collinson grunted to himself. "Come in."

The door opened and Hunt walked in, his hand on Julie's elbow. She was limping.

"Hello," Collinson said, not sounding overly friendly, as he crawled away from the sofa, laid the broom down, and stood. He slapped his palms together a couple of times in an up-and-down motion.

"Anything wrong?" Hunt asked.

Collinson smiled at them and shook his head, wiping sweat from his forehead with one palm. "No, no. Just crickets, I think. They're thick around here." He turned to Julie. "You're limping, young lady. Hurt yourself?"

She nodded sheepishly, uncomfortably. "Stairs," she said.

"Well, Dr. Hunt," Collinson said, joining his hands in front of him, "I believe I said everything I have to say to you the last time we spoke. What brings you here this afternoon?"

"Your son's diary," Hunt replied, holding up the old book.

Neither of them could miss the flinch that darted across Collinson's face as he glanced down at the book. Returning his gaze to Hunt, he said, "What about it?"

"Everything. What he wrote, what he believed. We think you can explain all of it to us."

"Why should I? You have no authority. If it were important, I would have heard more from the police by now. I haven't. Even if you're writing a book—more likely an article for the *National Enquirer,* why ..."—he glanced at Julie coldly—"... why the devil should I explain *anything?* I owe you nothing. I'm a busy man."

"Busy getting drunk?" Hunt asked quickly. He'd smelled the whiskey the moment he'd come in. Then he'd seen the glass on the lamp table.

Collinson's beefy fists clenched at his sides, his shoulders straightened, and he shouted, *"Get out of my house!"*

"Not before I've read something to you, Reverend Collinson." Hunt quickly lifted the book, opened it, and read through some of the passages. He read of Jeffery Collinson's goal of ushering in a wave of evil, a Time of Darkness that would release the wickedness in all human beings; he read of God being a weakling, a joker; he read of Jeffery's self-proclaimed position as the Dark Christ. And as he read, Reverend Collinson slowly backed away from them, one hand wandering behind his back to feel for the chair, where he finally plopped down, his face ashen. Ending with a line about the insignificance of Jeffery's likely death, Hunt slapped the book shut carelessly and looked hard at Collinson.

"Your son is dead, Reverend Collinson, but he's done something. He's done something horrible that has stayed behind him. It's got something to do with what he's written in this diary, and I think *this*"—he pointed at Collinson with the diary—"has something to do with the way *you* raised him! When Jeffery died, something crawled out of—" Hunt stopped for a second, ran what he was about to say through his mind. Was it that important that he tell Collinson about it? Mightn't it sound awfully ... drug-induced, perhaps? Fuck it. "Something crawled out of his nose, something long and black and mushy, and it cut the back of my hand. Not long ago, something very similar to it crawled out of the wife of a friend of mine. *After she'd killed her sons and herself!* Right now, we've got one of those things, we've got it under plastic, and we're trying to figure out how to kill it. There seem to be a lot of them, Reverend, and they seem to be all the hell over the place, and just maybe something you can tell us will help!"

From the chair, Collinson stared at the diary in Hunt's hand. "Where did you get that?" he asked weakly.

"Doesn't matter. What matters is *this*" Hunt said, carefully taking Julie's bandaged hand in his and holding it up. "She got this from one of those things that crawled out of your son. A young girl was eaten alive by them; her skin was peeled right off her bones." Hunt's voice was darkening with anger and impatience as he continued; he let go of Julie's hand and stepped toward Collinson threateningly. "Who knows, Reverend ... maybe you're *next.*"

Collinson began to tremble. His puffy cheeks and the flesh beneath his chin quaked and his eyes slowly grew. He licked his lips dryly, grabbed his drink, finished it, then returned the glass, but hit it on the edge of the table and it fell to the floor.

"This is insane," Collinson said, standing. "How could my son have ... have ... done this?"

"That's what *we* want you to tell *us*," Julie answered. "If not *how*, then at least *why*. What did you teach him, Reverend? What sick things did you teach him about good and evil?"

"Have you come here to blame this insanity on *me?* I raised that boy the best way I knew how." He waddled around behind the sofa, as if for protection. "I ... I taught him everything that I ... that I thought was ..." His chin jutted out and his breathing suddenly became rapid and shallow, as if he were about to cry, which, they soon realized, he was. He tried to smile. "I didn't teach him anything *bad*. Really! It was all ... all carefully thought out and ... and I still think I'm right. He just ... "He returned to his chair and dropped into it heavily. "He just took it all wrong, I guess. All ... wrong."

Julie limped over to the sofa, directly in front of the reverend, and asked, in a gentle voice, "And what was that, Reverend Collinson?"

He looked at her, his eyes misty and pleading, silently begging her to believe him, to realize that he meant well. "I ... I taught him that we must all love God. Worship and respect Him. But I also ... I also taught him to ... to fear ... evil. I taught him of the *power* of evil." His voice was beginning to sound moist and weak and he swallowed once, hard, then once again. "Look, I love God. I've devoted my whole life to Him. I've won countless souls for the Lord at my meetings and with my pamphlets and even my little flyers that I circulate. Sometimes just a few words are all a person needs. But, but ..." He looked up at Hunt, whose face was hard and cold. His anger was showing. Collinson jerked his eyes back to Julie, who was more receptive, softer, safer. "But, just look around you. Look at what's become of the world. Doesn't it make you see the strength of the dark powers? Doesn't it make you scared? Even just a *little*? I ... I've always felt that it's ... safer to fear *them*, too, to try to appease *them* once in a while. I ... I did a little exploring in the black arts. Not much, you understand. Just enough. I've always had a comfortable life, and I've attributed it to that. And so I passed it on to my son. I ... I just had no idea he would take it so far."

Still holding the diary tightly in one hand, Hunt put his hands on his hips and began fidgeting, his jaw tight with anger. He couldn't believe what he was hearing.

"Why do you think he took it so far?" Julie asked.

"I don't know, I don't know. He ... when he was a little boy he was fine about it. He was fascinated, wanted to know everything I could tell him. Then. As he got older. He would ... he would tell me I was very wrong. He would tell me I was living a great big hoax ... a ... a cosmic practical joke, in trying to live both ways, please both sides. He ... he told me that someday his ideas would overcome mine and all currently established religions and sects because ... because his ideas were far stronger. I didn't know what he was talking about at first. But I began to piece it together after a while. The boy had become obsessed with ... with evil. With ... with *wrong*. He soon had no regard for goodness. For God. And once, he told me that I was working for a weakling. God, I mean. Just like he wrote in that diary. He told me that God's way, the Christian way, has to be adopted, has to be *learned*. Evil, he said, just has to be *released*."

Hunt took three rapid steps toward the reverend, who blinked fearfully at his approach, looking like a puppy about to be kicked. "And after all of this, you still go around preaching to people? Preaching the Word of God?" His last three words dripped with sarcasm.

The reverend looked down at his lap and did not reply.

"You've got a bumper sticker on your van outside," Hunt continued, pointing toward the front door, "that says 'The Lord Is My Shepherd.'"

Before he could go on, the reverend said, "Oh, but He is, Doctor, He *is*. It's just that He has a lot of sheep to watch over. And there are a lot of wolves lurking on the edge of the pasture. Don't you think it makes sense for one to do what one can? To try—"

"I don't want to hear any more," Hunt said, turning to Julie. "Let's go."

Julie stood slowly and went to Hunt's side. He took her arm and they turned silently for the door.

"Wait!" Collinson rasped, a note of secrecy to his voice.

Hunt turned impatiently.

"What ... *are* they?" the reverend asked, leaning forward in his chair, his head tilted slightly, his face pleading. "I mean, what are they, exactly? These things. I ... I think I've heard them. Crawling around underneath things, in dark corners. It's almost like ... they're waiting. Waiting for something."

"Maybe," Hunt said simply before he and Julie walked out, "they're just waiting for you to understand."

After the door shut behind them, Collinson put his elbows on his broad thighs and tented his palms over his mouth, whispering, "Oh, dear God, dear God," over and over again, his eyes closed, until he finally dropped to his knees hard in front of the chair, locked his hands together, turned his face upward, and began to mutter, "Dear God in heaven, forgive me my ignorance, my selfishness, my lack of faith. Forgive me my shortcomings as a father, dear Lord, I never meant it to happen the way it did, You *know* that was never my intention, never, Lord, never," and he went on and on, his words picking up their pace, but his voice remained a harsh whisper, the taste of whiskey still sharp in his mouth, his fleshy eyes closed tightly so he could not see the small black creature that was suddenly scurrying across the floor and it clamped onto one thigh, then up his leg and over his round belly and full chest and up his throat in lightning seconds until it was on his face and he felt the rushing feeling as if stale air was blowing hard up his nose and then the smothering feeling and then the mercifully brief moment of blackness and nothingness and then—

—he was once again seated in his chair, his hands trembling slightly, his head a bit dizzy, and then—

—everything suddenly felt fine and comfortable and good because he had work to do and there was a meeting coming up, and then—

—he smiled.

Outside, Hunt opened the car door for Julie and she got in. She'd been talking quietly every since they'd left the reverend's trailer.

"He said he *hears* them, Martin," she said tensely. "There could be some in there with him."

"I really don't care," Hunt said flatly, closing her door and going around to his side to get in. "He's sick. As sick as his son ever was, except *he's* got his goddamned pulpit to hide behind." He started up the car and was ready to drive away when they heard the reverend's voice. They both looked up at the trailer's door.

Reverend Collinson was standing on his porch, holding the trailer door open with one hand, using the other to loosen his collar around his thick neck. He was smiling. Sort of. His upper lip pulled back a little too far over his teeth and his lips looked

as tight as a tautly stretched rubber band. He slipped his fingers
out from under his collar and waved at them to wait a moment.

Julie rolled down her window and said, "Yes?"

He swept his hand across his forehead and Julie saw little
particles of sweat fly from his fingertips. His eyes were teary.

"You *are* coming, aren't you?" Collinson asked. "To my
meetings, I mean. At least one, please, I would feel ..."—his
smile widened—"... honored. The first one is tonight."

Hunt muttered, "Fat fucking chance you misera—"

Julie put a hand on his thigh. "No, wait. Maybe we should.
It couldn't hurt. The whole thing ... I mean, his strange theories
and everything ... it intrigues me. I've never heard anything like
it, and I want to see how he handles it while he preaches. If at all."
Without waiting for Martin to reply, she stuck her head out the
window and asked, "What time?"

"Eight o'clock. Torrance Auditorium. We're really going to set
some souls on fire tonight, I can assure you. I'd like you to come
and see that I'm not ... not so bad, after all. Will you?"

"Yes, we'll come," she assured him, trying to smile.

"Good. *Good.*" He rubbed his palms together gleefully, letting
the door swing slowly shut behind him. Then his smile faltered
and he frowned, his eyes dropping away from Julie. "Oh, dear,"
he said. "I've got to go. I've got to go ... go build something." He
looked at her again. "Build something for the meeting tonight."

"What's that?" Julie asked.

He grinned. "A cross."

Tom entered the lab through the back door, which had a sign
on it that said STAFF ONLY. The cake dish lid was held carefully
under his arm, the dish towel still draped over it. The thing
inside had not moved once. The drive over had been a nervous
one for Tom. Every few seconds he would glance at the thing in
the seat next to him, feeling somehow that, under that towel, it
was patiently waiting for the right moment. He did not want to
provide that moment, but it was a risk he needed to take.

Once inside the door, Tom stopped and looked around. He
could hear voices, activity. To his immediate left was the glass-
cleaning room. The door was open, but it was dark inside. He
stepped in, flicking on the light, and closed the door behind him.
There was a window that looked out of the room and into the

laboratory, and Tom was plainly visible, but no one had noticed him yet.

The room was a mess. Empty boxes were stacked sloppily against a wall and the cupboards. What looked like a cross between a bank vault and a prop from the set of a science fiction movie filled a corner of the little room. It was used to clean the vials and jars and bottles, but it wasn't being used now.

Tom carefully set the covered lid on the counter amid the clutter of boxes and jars, beside three corked bottles filled with a bluish liquid. Hands on his hips, he looked around the room, chewing his lips. Then he turned and went out the door, turning the light off.

His first idea had been to cut a hole carefully in the top of the lid and reach in with something, something sharp, to cut a piece out of the creature, but he knew that wouldn't work because those things were damned fast and it would be on him before he could blink, so he ditched that idea.

But he had another one. And he was sure it would work. He *prayed* it would work. And Tom Conrad *never* prayed.

Steeling himself, he walked into the lab. It was a large room filled with long narrow tables; on the tables were shelves of bottles and vials. There were a couple of typewriters, rows of machines covered with dials and gauges, switches and knobs, and there were numerous microscopes. They were all in a day's work to Tom and he paid them no attention. But his eyes quickly scanned over the people in the room. An Oriental lady was hunched over a microscope; a guy was working with the coulter counter; two women were standing in front of the schedule board, one agreeing to sub for the other; Hank Milland sat on a stool at one of the tables, writing something on a clipboard and talking at the same time with the young man sweeping the floor. All the faces were familiar, but Hank was the only one in the group Tom knew at all because, a couple of years ago, they had worked a shift together.

"Hi, Hank," Tom said, approaching the older man.

Hank was somewhere in his fifties, with dust-colored hair, rosy cheeks, and a little paunch. He looked up from the clipboard and stopped speaking, his mouth open in mid-sentence. He snapped from the surprise in a couple of seconds and grinned, standing, and putting down his pen. He held a hand out to Tom and said, "Tom, m'boy, good to see you, kid."

"Yeah, likewise, Hank," Tom replied, shaking the enthusiastic hand.

Then, stuffing his hands in the pockets of his lab coat, Hank said, sheepishly, his gaze dropping to the floor, then shooting back to Tom, up and down, "Hey, Tom, you know ... um ... I ... uh—

"'S'okay, Hank. I know what you're going to say, and I'd rather you not, if it's okay by you."

Hank pressed his lips together and nodded. "Yeah. I understand. What're you doing in here today?"

"Well, I'm not working, or anything, I'm just sort of ... uh ... doing a little project. Just on my own. Kinda personal. I thought I'd borrow a little space here for a couple minutes. Anybody gonna be using the cleaning room?"

Hank's lower lip stuck out and he shrugged. "Not that I know of."

"Good. Um ..." Tom turned around, looking across the room. "Is anybody gonna need that dissecting microscope in the next few minutes?" he asked, pointing.

Hank shook his head. "What're you doing?"

Tom smiled, hoped it looked casual, maybe even jovial, and said, "Just some little thing." With a little wave, Tom walked away, darting around the lab, gathering up what he needed: a twenty-cc Monoject syringe, a few eighteen-gauge, one-and-a-half-inch needles just in case one broke, and the American Optical dissecting microscope on the far table. He smiled and said hello to those around him as he went here and there, from table to drawer. Then he carried the things back into the glass-cleaning room, noticing before he got there that Hank was watching him carefully.

He shut the door, turned on the light, and arranged the things on the counter, pushing back the three bottles of bluish liquid. He toyed with the microscope until it was ready, then snapped off the bottom of the needle case, stuck the needle on the syringe, and twisted the case off smoothly, revealing the thin, vicious-looking piece of metal. He looked out the room's window to see if anyone was watching; they weren't. But, just in case, he turned his back to the glass so no one could see what he was doing, then removed the towel from the plastic lid.

The creature remained in the exact same spot—the exact same *position*—as when Tom had first covered it.

Checking the window again over his shoulder, Tom got down on one knee, the syringe in one hand, the other hand on top of the lid. His eye suddenly began to sting and he flinched, shook his head, rubbed it with his free hand, realizing that he was sweating and some of his perspiration had dropped into his eye. He sniffed. Licked his lips. Put his palm back down on the top of the lid and scooted the patchwork cage toward him until half of it was hanging over the edge of the counter. He bent down a bit and looked up at the bottom of it, the piece of floormat that had been cut out and taped to the lid. He could see the thing through the blurry plastic: a stone-still, black spot. He adjusted the syringe in his hand until the needle was sticking upward. Then he gently touched the sharp tip to the plastic. And waited.

The creature did not move.

But would it move as soon as it felt the needle? Would it move before he could get a bit—just a tiny bit—into the syringe for the microscope?

He pushed up. Just a little. The tip began to cut into the plastic.

Tom felt more sweat on his forehead and he prayed it wouldn't get into his eyes, not now, it just couldn't, he couldn't fuck this up because it was such a good idea.

Tom had to press harder—the plastic was very firm—and the needle began to bend just a little and he clenched his teeth together with anticipation, but it straightened out as it broke through the plastic, just broke through with a clean little *phutt* and went right into it, right into the underbelly of the creature, and Tom was so relieved that he let a long breath explode through his tight lips and he realized that he'd been holding his breath and now he breathed heavily to make up for it but he had to be careful, he had to remain steady because he wasn't finished yet, not until he had some of that thing in the syringe, so he started to tug on the plunger, tug just a little bit to sort of test it, sort of see how strong the thing was, what kind of consistency it had, because maybe he wouldn't be able to suck any of it out, maybe it was a lot tougher than he thought and he would end up trying another method, after all, but, no, he pulled on the plunger and sure enough some of the black thickness began to ooze down through the needle and into the plastic tube he held in his hand, and when he had enough—he didn't need much at all, just a little bit, just a little— he stopped pulling, but the plunger didn't stop coming and the syringe continued to fill up with the thing and Tom pressed his palm to the flat round end of the plunger to make it stop but it wouldn't and he thought he heard himself whimper because even when he pushed *against* it and tried to force the thing back out it did no good and he knew that soon there would be no more room in the syringe and now he really *was* whimpering because—

—there was a sudden rush of movement and the plunger shot from the syringe like a bullet and Tom's hand flew backward and the plastic plunger hit the floor with a click and right next to it, landing with a wet sound, was the black creature, which had found its moment and, with its patience finally rewarded, slapped itself onto Tom's foot.

Tom shot upward, his shoulder knocking the cake lid over and to the floor, and kicked his foot out against a cupboard and the thing dropped loose. Tom's hand grabbed the first thing it felt— the microscope—and he flung it at the creature. It hit the floor noisily, shattering, clanging, but missing the target. Hank's face was immediately in the window, his brow wrinkled, his mouth working—

"—Jesus Christ, Tom, what are you—"

—and he threw the door open, but Tom ignored him, because that thing was still loose and he reached for something else, and his hand landed on something hard and cold and he screamed to Hank, "Shut that goddamned door before this thing gets out!"

But Hank didn't hear him because he was, at the same moment, screaming at Tom, "Tom, put that down, don't spill that, don't drop it!"

But Tom's full attention was on the creature, which was huddling between two cardboard Vacutainer boxes preparing to pounce—Tom knew that was what it was doing because he'd seen it before—when Tom raised his hand, raised the hard cold heavy object high so that when he brought it down it sailed from his hand straight at the creature, landing with a shattering of glass and a splashing of blue—and Hank was throwing himself backward and out the door trying to avoid being splashed, grabbing Tom's arm and pulling him with him, screaming, "Goddammit, Tom! I told you not to—"

But Tom didn't hear because he was screaming then, too, he was screaming, "Look! Jesus, look what it's doing! My god, *look!*" And they did look and they saw the fumes that were rising from what was quickly metamorphosing from a small black blob into nothing more than a wet puddle and Tom was smiling, smiling like a kid at Christmas because it had all happened so fast and so unexpectedly.

Tom's hand was hurting because he was still clutching with all his might the empty syringe that was to hold his specimen. And his face began to hurt, too, because he was smiling so. And tears were rolling down his eyes. Or maybe it was perspiration trickling down his face. Or maybe both. He didn't care.

"Tom," Hank said sternly, leaning toward Tom and away from the people who had gathered outside the glass-cleaning room, "what the hell do you think you're doing! You just ruined a very expensive scope—do you know that?—and you could've killed yourself with that—"

Tom whirled on him, still grinning. *"With what?"* he hissed, his eyes sparkling. "What was that stuff?"

"You know what that stuff is, Tom, the cleaning stuff, the aqua regia, and that shit's not Kool-Aid, Tom, you could've killed yourself with it, that's nitrohydrochloric acid, goddammit! What do you think—"

Tom looked in the room, and through the misty fumes he saw the two other bottles on the counter. If what he suspected was right, if what he thought was out there really *was* out there, those two bottles were not enough. He would need more.

"I need more, Hank," he said suddenly, ignoring the quiet mumbling around them. "Where can I get it? Is there more in the hospital?"

"Well, of course there's more in the hospital, but you can't just go—"

"Hank, someday I'm gonna make this up to you, I swear to God on my mother's grave."

"Make *what* up?"

"The big favor you're gonna do me," Tom replied, still grinning.

5 - THE MEETING AND THE GRAVE

HUNT AND JULIE had lunch at The Spaghetti Factory. They ate slowly, talking in spurts about the weather and about movies they'd seen and books they'd read. Only once did either of them bring up the thing they were both thinking about: Collinson's meeting that night.

"Look," Julie said, holding her glass of white wine in her hand, twirling it just a bit so the wine swirled and caught the light, "we don't have to go if you don't think we should. I was just ... interested."

"No, no, we'll go. It's just that I don't think there's anything more we can learn about him. About Jeffery."

"Who knows? Maybe the reverend will say one little thing, something'll slip out that'll maybe tip you off. We'll just have to keep our eyes and ears open."

He nodded.

Afterward, they went shopping—Julie needed a new sweater, and Hunt needed to look for a pair of shoes—neither of them mentioning Tom. Although they did not speak their thoughts, they were both wondering furiously if Tom had had any success in dealing with the creature.

Julie limped, wincing as she got in and out of the car. When they walked, Hunt held her elbow in a very gentlemanly way.

"I'll have to get cut up more often," she said once as they walked away from the car and into a store. "It brings out the manners in you." She smiled and he kissed her.

Not long after they ate, their stomachs began to ache, but neither mentioned it.

They finished shopping; neither of them found what they wanted. They went home and Hunt turned on the television, plopping down in front of it and staring blindly at "Entertainment Tonight," only half listening to Ron Hendren talk about Burt Reynolds's new chain of fast-food restaurants.

Julie walked toward the kitchen to make some coffee, but she froze in the kitchen doorway. Earlier, Hunt had not even tried to clean up the mess that had been made by Julie's struggle and injuries. The corners of her mouth curled downward and she raised a bandaged hand, gently pressing her palm between her breasts.

"Oh, god," she breathed, "oh, god ... Martin?" She leaned against the doorjamb, closing her eyes. "Martin?"

Hunt was at her side by the time she called him again. He looked into the kitchen for just an instant and grimaced. "Oh, Christ, sweetie, I'm sorry, just ... just come out here and sit down, hon, c'mon." He took her by the arm and led her back into the living room, sat her down in front of the television, where a douche commercial was rattling on, but by the time she was seated, she was trembling and her eyes were clouding with tears and her lips were twitching and her shoulders were jerking up and down and she leaned into Hunt as he asked, "Is there anything I can get you, hon? Anything you want?"

She moaned into his shoulder softly for a while as she cried, and then she snapped, "*Yes! Yes*, goddammit, there *is* something I want, I want *out* of all this, this whatever-it-is that's happening. I was, just two weeks ago I was a nurse and you were a doctor and we did our jobs and we spent time together and everything was okay, and then some goddamned punk comes into ER and all of a sudden everything's weird and dangerous and I keep expecting Rod Serling to step out of the goddamned shower or somewhere and tell me at the next signpost up ahead we're entering the fucking *Twilight Zone,* for Christ's sake, and I think I'm about to go *crazy!*" And then, after her voice had reached a crescendo, she collapsed against him, putting even more weight on his shoulder, and she sobbed until she had no more tears to shed.

Tom waited in his car, smoking a cigarette from the pack he'd gotten out of the cigarette machine in the hospital lobby. The car's engine was running and Tom had parked just outside the lab's back entrance. The radio was on and Tom's fingers drummed nervously to the beat of a Huey Lewis song as he drew in the smoke and exhaled it slowly. He glanced at his watch once, then continued drumming his fingers. It was getting late, but he still had plenty of time. He wondered if Hunt and Julie were back yet, if they had missed him, if they were looking for him to see what he'd done with that crawler.

Looking out his window and up at the sky, he saw the clouds were returning, promising, perhaps, a few drops of rain later on. The sun was making its slow way down toward the mountains in the west and shadows were growing in length and darkness.

Tom's fingers stopped moving. The cigarette sagged between his lips. He suddenly realized, with a bit of a chill, that the sun would be down by the time he got around to doing it. It would be dark.

But he couldn't let that stop him.

He heard the lab door open and he jerked his head around to see Hank walking toward him, carrying the gas can he'd given him to fill, his free arm swinging in a wide arc back and forth as he walked with the heavy load. Tom threw his door open and hopped out of the car, going around to unlock the trunk.

"Hank," he said, a little short of breath suddenly, "I can't tell you how much I appreciate this."

"Yeah, yeah, but it's *still* not enough," Hank said, hefting the can into the trunk, then stepping back as Tom slammed it shut. "You owe me an explanation, boyo. I want to know what the hell I've just contributed to."

"I'll tell you, I'll tell you, but not now. I don't have time. Was the money I gave you enough?"

"Not quite. I also had to use up half a dozen favors and break a few rules, too."

"You're a lifesaver, Hank. You don't realize."

"Damned right I don't realize." He followed Tom back to his door, which remained open. Tom got in, slammed the door, and Hank leaned his head into the window. "Look, Tom, I don't know what the hell is going on, but if it's illegal, or if it's dangerous, goddammit, son, take care of yourself. You've been through more than enough already."

"Thanks, Hank. Thank you so much. Gotta go."

Hank leaned away from the car and Tom drove away, heading for the hardware store.

* * *

Hunt replaced the telephone receiver. Tom was not at his apartment. He'd called the lab earlier and talked to Vicki. She'd said she hadn't seen him all day, but she'd just come on, the shifts had just changed, and maybe she'd missed him.

"Not home?" Julie asked, coming out of the bathroom. She'd just washed her face, combed her hair, and brushed her teeth, and she looked as if she felt better.

"No." Hunt leaned his hips against the table beneath the phone and folded his arms before him, frowning.

"Worried?"

"Yes." He turned around and searched the table for some cigarettes, then some matches. He lit one, drew in on it. "I don't know what I was thinking when I just *left* him with that damned thing. He's under a lot of pressure, not thinking straight. God knows what he did with it." He puffed on the cigarette; smoke flowed liquidly from his nostrils. "Or what it did with him." He set the cigarette on the edge of an ashtray and stepped over to Julie. "Feeling better?"

"So-so."

"It's getting kind of late. Still wanna go?"

"On one condition."

"What's that?"

"When we get back, you screw my brains out. I'll sleep a lot better."

He tipped his head back and laughed a happy, surprisingly relaxed laugh, then kissed her softly for a long time. "Let me change my clothes," he said, pulling away gently. "Then we'll take off."

"It's seven o'clock. We're closing." The fat woman was shuffling her way toward the door with a ring of keys in her puffy hand as Tom walked in, making the little bell over the doorway ring.

"I know, I know," Tom said quickly, "but this is very important, *very* important. If you'll just give me five minutes, I can get the stuff I need and get out of here, really. Five minutes."

"I got a husband at home waiting for his dinner," the fat woman said, her bulbous hips bobbing up and down beside her as she walked toward him. When she was standing right in front of him, Tom saw that she had a soft shade of hair on her upper lip, the same dark color as the thick and apparently not-well-cared-for hair on her head.

I'm sure he won't mind if you're a little late, Tom thought

with clenched teeth, *or if you never show your fat, hairy face at home again, you giant fucking sweat gland, now just give me—*
"Three minutes, really, that's all I need, three minutes."
"Oh, all right," she said.

Tom was past her and in the store before she finished her words, and he was looking through the gardening tools, where he found a pick and a shovel, and then he went to a rack of gloves of all kinds and picked out a pair of heavy protective ones to keep his hands from blistering while he dug, and then his eyes darted around the store because it seemed he was forgetting something, something small, maybe, something, something—

—a *pen,* because since he'd moved into his apartment, he hadn't been able to find a single goddamned pen whenever he needed one, and he needed one tonight.

He needed it to write a note.

A note to Martin Hunt and Julie Calahan.

Saying goodbye.

"I just can't get over it," Hunt said as they drove through the cool evening. A cigarette was planted between two of his fingers. "I mean, he must've gone through *some* kind of ministerial school, he must've been taught *some*thing by somebody. Where the hell did he get all these ideas about the dark powers, about ... about giving the devil a pat on the head once in a while? It's crazy. I'm not a religious man, as you know, but even *I* can see that it's crazy. I mean, if you're gonna believe in something, *believe* in it. I think ..." He stopped to take a drag on his cigarette and the smoke he exhaled immediately swept out the crack Hunt had left in his window. "I think that even those who say they don't believe in God really do. If only just a little. I mean, think about it. When an atheist gets the shit scared out of him, or hears his wife just got hit by a bus, what does he say? 'Oh, my god,' or 'Jesus Christ' —something like that. It's like we all just naturally say the names, as if we call on Them when we really need Them. All of us." He sniffed a few times, then glanced over at Julie. "What do you think?"

"Interesting thought."

Then they were silent.

There was a strange feeling of activity to their silence because their minds were racing frantically; they were thinking how very stupid they were being to feel afraid because they were only going to this old-fashioned evangelical meeting being given by a very confused and disturbed man who had somehow managed to become a reverend. There was no reason at all to feel fear because there would be a lot of people there, most likely, and what could possibly happen, even though Reverend Collinson *had* looked a bit strange standing there on his front porch with all that sweat pouring down his face and that strange pulled-back smile on his mouth, that strange look in his eye when, just moments before, he'd shed genuine tears as he told them about his son and the way he'd raised the boy—no, no, none of that was reason to feel fear now when they were doing nothing more than going to an old-fashioned revival meeting.

But they were both scared. Silently.

Hunt turned on the radio and they listened to some classical music for a while. Then he turned the dial until he found a Mathis song, and they listened to that.

Until they got to Torrance Auditorium just outside Calistoga. Cars were parked in great bunches around the auditorium and still more were trying to find parking places. Several people—a lot of families, Hunt noticed, parents with their kids—were hurrying from their cars to the building because the meeting had apparently begun already.

They got out of the car once Hunt had parked it and stared up at the building. It was big and old and painted a barn-red. Big lights had been set up outside and they flooded the night's darkness, making the parking a lot easier.

"Doesn't look like the kind of place Al Stewart would perform in, does it?" Hunt muttered.

"Huh?"

"I was here once a few years ago. An Al Stewart concert."

They headed toward the building, passing the huge sign, obviously homemade, which read:

THE REVEREND JEREMIAH COLLINSON
SPEAKS ON
THE WAY TO HAPPINESS

Something about the words painted on the sign in big, straight black letters made Hunt cringe a bit inside.

They neared the steps that led up to the two sets of double doors in front of the auditorium, their feet crunching over the gravel below them. Clouds gathered above, dark and fat, and a breeze began to dance around them, darting between their legs, whispering over their shoulders and through their hair.

And then. They stopped.

And they listened.

And Hunt's lips pressed together tightly while Julie's hung open loosely.

And they both became pale.

From inside the crowded auditorium came screams.

And the sounds of hammering.

Redwood Hill Cemetery lay somewhere between St. Helena and Calistoga, a little more than a mile off the St. Helena Highway at the end of a bumpy dirt road plagued with potholes. It wasn't on a hill and there were no redwoods in sight. It was just a small, dark field spread out under a cloudy night sky, a garden of little identifying grave markers in not-so-straight rows.

This was where people like Jeffery Collinson were buried, people who had no money and no family or friends who would claim them. Several graves in the field looked rather new, so it was impossible to tell when Tom first arrived which one belonged to Collinson. He pulled his car into the narrow, bumpy drive that went around the edge of the field, parked, then got out and opened the trunk to remove his equipment.

The shovel. The pick. A huge, incredibly bright portable light he'd had in his trunk for the last two years. And the gas can; the liquid inside sloshed around when Tom moved it.

Leaving the equipment by the car, Tom took the light and walked over to the nearest grave, reading the name on the marker. It wasn't Jeffery Collinson's. Neither was the next. Nor the next.

But he knew it was there somewhere.

"Martin ..." Julie said cautiously, clutching his arm with her fingers.

"You wanna stay in the car?"

"Are you outta your fucking *mind?*"

They continued toward the old auditorium.

Up the steps.

Across the front deck.

At the doors.

They were open, and warm, slightly stale, air wafted out at

Hunt and Julie. It was very loud inside. Loud and frightening. They heard the noise before they even entered the building—the screaming and the calling, the thunderous noise of countless hurried footsteps pounding over the wooden floor, metal folding chairs clanging together, crying, laughing, cheering, and cutting through it all somehow was the unmistakable sound of Jeremiah Collinson's voice roaring words into the chaos. And the hammering.

That's what bothered Hunt the most. The hammering.

"Want a program?"

Hunt felt Julie's fingers tighten on his arm and they both turned to the young man standing beside them in the doorway and saw his slobbering smile and his dripping eyes and his strangely shaped skull and the rectangular piece of heavy yellow paper he was holding out to them in his violently shaking hand, and Julie screamed, her bandaged hand held in front of her wide open mouth, and Hunt pulled her away from the young man, knowing immediately what was lurking behind those bulbous eyes, and he pulled her straight into the confusion, into the lake of people who were moving here and there, hurrying, tripping, kicking, all for apparently no good reason, and then his arm around Julie's shoulder holding her close to his side, Hunt stopped.

"Martin, let's get out of here, now!" Julie insisted fearfully.

"I'll take you back to the car, then—"

"Then we'll leave. *Together!*"

"No, no, I've gotta find out what's going on here." He stood on his toes, trying to scan the crowd as much as possible. "Where is that hammering coming from?"

"Then I'm staying here with you. I don't want to be alone."

They looked around.

The source of the hammering was still not evident, but the people surrounding them were taking up enough of their attention—

—an old woman lying on her back, her hands clutching at one of the folding chairs as she tried to pull herself up, her mouth working frantically—

—a middle-aged man and woman, primly dressed, pushing through the crowd, the man shouting sternly, "Let us out of here! Let us out right now!"—

—a pudgy young woman staggering through the chaos, her arms outstretched, her face screwed up in horror and streaked with tears, searching the floor as she screamed, "My baby! My baby! My little Joey, dear God, my baby!"—

—a little girl crawling on the floor with a bloodred face screaming "Maaaawww-meeeee!" over and over again until a mass of blackness latched onto her small chubby face and immediately disappeared into her ever-so-tiny nostrils, and the little girl began to convulse on the floor.

"Martin, my god, did you see that?" Julie gasped.

"They're here," Hunt said quietly, his voice completely buried in the mayhem.

And then he saw them.

Small and black. Scurrying in and out of the legs of the crowd, disappearing and reappearing in and out of the cracks in the wooden floor. They were all over. Crawling up legs. Jumping on necks and faces.

"Martin, we've got to get out of here I"

"Yeah, yeah, let's—" He started to turn with her when he saw something rise above the crowd in the front of the auditorium. Then he noticed that the hammering had silenced. And when he realized what had been done

(a cross a cross)

he thought he might become ill. Without thinking, he put an arm around Julie and held her close to him with her face buried in his shoulder because he didn't want her to see it before they got out of there.

"Goddammit, Martin!" Julie shouted, pushing herself away from him. "Let's—"

Hunt actually saw the color drain from her face; he half expected it to leave her green eyes, too, leaving them a horrible deadly white. She stared toward tire front, tried to speak, to react, but she could not.

A cross had been erected before the crowd. It was being held up by a number of burly men. It was obviously a quickly constructed cross. But that did not matter. It was serving its purpose.

The wood was soaking in the blood of a very old and very frail man whose head hung forward on his long and skinny neck. A band of barbed wire had been pressed down over his balding silvery-haired head. His mouth, toothless, was a yawning hole, and his chin hung to a point below his face. The lump in his throat worked up and down, up and down, trying to cry out for help. Except for a tattered, bloodstained white towel draped loosely around his waist, the old man was naked, and his sticklike arms, webbed with blue veins, were pulled taut as he hung from the spikes that had been driven through his wrists, and his armpits seemed to have collapsed into black cavernous holes beneath his shoulders. His ribs sliced dangerously at his graying skin, which was pulled tightly over his abdomen. His feet had been nailed together and his knobby knees were bent slightly.

"—Father in heaven and our brothers in hell," Collinson was saying, standing beside the cross, "we pray that You will accept this offering in the spirit of fellowship in which it is given, and we pray that You will have mercy on us all until our time comes to join You in the heavens or in the depths, according to Your wills. Amen."

From the never-quieting crowd came a chorus of amens and then a wave of "Praise the Lord" and "Hallelujah" and "For Jesus's sake," all at once.

Holding his mircophone in one hand, Collinson raised the other high above his head. His face was dark red; his eyes were almost insectlike in appearance, they'd grown so. His hair was mussed and his mouth seemed to be locked in a chilling, sardonic grin.

"This," he said, "this is what it's all about, brothers and sisters, this is the way to happiness. They are all the power in the universe, friends, the gods of good and evil. Not just one or the other—all of them—and they must be appeased, they must be—"

Collinson went on, but Hunt tuned him out for a moment because Julie was pulling on the collar of his coat, pleading with him, "Martin, for the love of Gaaawwwd, let's get out of here!"

A woman pushed them aside as she plowed through the group, one hand clawing at her face as she screamed, "It's in me! It's inside me!"

Hunt took Julie's elbow and turned her around toward the exit, but the exit was no longer there. Just people. A wave of people. They had been swallowed by the crowd.

"C'mon, c'mon," Hunt grunted as he started pushing his way through, shouldering people out of the way, but it seemed to do no good because they were not moving themselves across the floor, they were being moved, the crowd was moving them, had them swept up in its center, clutching them like a giant hand, and Hunt clenched his teeth and grunted, determined to kick and bite his way through if need be, and he was raising his fist to move a fat man out of the way when there was a loud pop-and-sizzle sound and the lights in the auditorium flickered and dimmed, brightened, dimmed, then flashed out, leaving them in darkness.

It was then that a hoarse, pained voice somewhere in the blackened building screamed, *"Fiiirrre!"*

Jeffery Collinson's grave was located near the back edge of Redwood Hill Cemetery, and once Tom found it he had to lug all of his equipment there from the car. But it didn't seem a chore. His veins were buzzing with energy; adrenaline flowed through his body like electricity. Clanking noisily, he carried the pick and shovel, the light, and the gas can in his gloved hands across the field to Collinson's grave and set it all down nearby.

There had been a moon earlier, but it was now hidden by the clouds that were rolling in, big and black, like giant mutations of the black crawlers that had burst into his life just a little over a week ago. The cemetery was surrounded by trees in the distance and the wind whispered through them softly, making the trees seem to talk among themselves about Tom in low tones so he couldn't quite hear.

Sometimes the wind would pick up. And it would seem to laugh at him.

Tom pushed the gnawing thoughts and images from his mind as he looked the grave over, deciding that he would need only his shovel. He picked it up, hefted it, then plunged it into the still-soft mound of earth over the grave, put his foot on the edge of the shovel and pushed it in deeper, then scooped lip some of the dirt, tossed it aside, dug the shovel in again, and—

—he froze. Something had moved. He stepped off the grave and looked around at his feet. Something had moved. He bent down and switched the light on, cursing himself for not doing so earlier, then stood and looked around some more. He could see nothing.

He realized his breath was coming in heavy spurts. He tried to slow it down, took in some deep, relaxed breaths. But they weren't really relaxed, because *he* wasn't relaxed. Swiping a hand over his sweaty face, he moved back over to the grave and continued digging.

Another scoop of dirt. Another. It began to pile up beside him.

He stopped. Took a few more deep breaths. Plunged the shovel in again.

And then the earth beneath his feet *moved*.

* * *

"Don't fret, brothers and sisters! We're all in the hands of the powers and their will shall be done tonight! *Their* will, not ours!" Reverend Collinson's voice boomed over the loudspeakers above the screams and the laughter and above the frenzied cries of "Fire! There's a *fire!*"

Hunt could smell it now, the smoke, and from somewhere in the dark he could hear the barely detectable roar that a growing fire made. And he saw the glow.

"Jesus, Martin, we've got to get out!" Julie cried. She was clutching his arms desperately.

"There's no way we can get to the exits!" he shouted to her above the noise. "It'll be easier to make our way to the front."

"The *front?* Are you crazy?"

"I've been here before. I think I know a way out!"

Not bothering to explain, Hunt tried to turn them toward the sound of Collinson's voice, toward the podium. The last time Hunt had been to Torrance Auditorium, for the Al Stewart concert, he'd gotten lost trying to find the bathroom. He'd followed the directions of someone who didn't know the building any more than he did, and he'd ended up downstairs in what seemed to be the basement. He remembered seeing a few small windows that led outside. If they could get down there, maybe they could get out the windows and go get help.

Help! Why wasn't anyone coming? Where were the police? Hadn't anyone noticed the mayhem going on in the auditorium?

Hunt concentrated on getting through the crowd and, still attached tightly to Julie, he began pushing aside the bodies that were moving blindly around him.

Suddenly there was light up front. It was shining below the cross and deepened the creases and the hollow spots on the body of the old man who now hung quietly from the wooden structure, moving only slightly, seeming now to welcome death. The light caught on the blood that was streaming down his long face and over his lips, that was pouring from his wrists and feet, and made it glisten as it ran downward in streaks.

"There's no need to scream, friends," Collinson droned on loudly. "We're in the hands of the powers now, all the powers." He stood on the podium, his arms stretched upward in a fat parody of the man hanging on the cross, the microphone now perched on a stand. "Let's sing, brothers and sisters," Collinson said. "Let's sing an old song, one that has given us comfort and strength over the years. Sing with me, friends."

Still pushing through the crowd toward the front, Hunt heard Collinson begin the song, his voice in no particular key, barely following a tune—

On a hiiiillll far awaaaayyy stood an oooold rugged craaawwwsss

—and much to his shock, he heard other voices in the crowd join in, pick up the words, all clashing with one another, some sounding happy, others in pain, others screaming the words of the song, all pouring together in a dark, nightmarish harmony—

the eeeeemblem of suffering and shaaaame

—Hunt glanced up at Collinson, who was closer now, close enough for the deep smile lines in his fat red cheeks to be well defined, close enough to see the drops of sweat that clung to his fleshy chin, and he saw that the reverend was happily conducting the song, swinging a hand back and forth, out of rhythm, spit spraying onto the microphone as he sang along—

and I loooove that old craaawwwsss where the deeeaaarest and beeest

—they were close enough to see the edge of the podium now, close enough to see the light that shined beneath the cross while the fire grew and raged behind them like an angry beast, and Hunt could not help feeling that those flames had them in mind and were burning their way through the crowd straight toward Martin Hunt and Julie Calahan—

for a woooorrld of lost siiiiinners was slaaaiiin

—he could see it off to their left, that door he had taken over a year ago in search of a bathroom, and he pulled Julie in that direction, maneuvering them through the undulating crowd, through the singers and the screamers, trying to assure Julie that they were going to be fine, they were almost there, but all the while knowing how easy it would be to trip—if one of them tripped they'd both go down—and be trampled by the terrified crowd—

so I'll cherish the oooold rugged craaaawwwsss

—Hunt felt one of the creatures on his leg, just beneath the edge of his pantleg, and he screamed a high, childlike shriek as he began to kick his leg madly, stabbing his toe into someone's shin, kicking again and again, burying his foot in the back of a man who was groping over the floor, until he could feel the little creature no more and they could press on, hearing the screams of the burning, smelling the reek of burning flesh—

till my trooophies at last I lay dooowwwn

—the door was just feet away from them when a hand reached out of the crowd and grabbed Julie by the hair, jerking her head back, pulling her away from Hunt, and Hunt became wild with anger and turned to lash out at the hand, hitting the wrist as hard as he could, hitting and kicking outward blindly, until Julie's screams stopped and he felt her holding on to him again for safety—

I will cliiing to the old rugged craaawwwss

—Hunt reached out and tried the knob, turned it, pushed on the door, but it wouldn't open, and he pushed again and again, finally letting go of Julie long enough to throw himself into the door with all his weight, breaking it open with a loud grunt, then pulling Julie in with him—

and exchaaaange it somedaaay for a crooowwwn

—and just before he could slam the door shut behind him, he heard the high-pitched death cry of the old man on the cross, gurgling and scraping its way up from a dry, closing throat.

"Where are we?" Julie asked through her gasps and sobs.

"Just off the stage. There's a basement downstairs. Windows. C'mon."

The corridor was dark, but their eyes had adjusted to the darkness. Hunt pressed a palm to the wall and followed it until he felt a doorway.

"Down here. Stairs," he said breathlessly.

They clattered down the wooden stairs until they hit the floor. Then they stopped and stared into the dark. Hunt found a wall and groped for a light switch, but found none.

"Goddammit!" he hissed, slapping his pockets until he found his cigarette lighter. He pulled it out. Flicked it. A flame stood high. A small, dancing halo of light glowed around it. He held it out before him.

The room was scattered with boxes, some made of cardboard, others of wooden slats. A table stood in the corner with more boxes on it. An empty light socket hung from the ceiling.

The windows were directly across from them. Three of them in a row. The pane in one was broken. It would be a struggle, but they could get through the small rectangular spaces, Hunt was sure.

"There," he said, moving forward.

They stopped.

Parts of the floor had moved.

A dark spot on the wall shifted.

Something scurried out from under a wooden box.

"Oooh deeeaaar *Gaaawwwd,*" Julie moaned, leaning limply on Hunt.

The dark basement was thick with small black crawlers ...

The mound of dirt beneath Tom's feet lurched a second time and he dropped the shovel and threw himself away from it, almost losing his balance and falling. The white light from the lantern washed over the grave, bathing it in a sort of lightly tinted electric blue. The dirt moved, rose, lowered, seemed to breathe, then became still again.

Tom stared at the mound for long moments, waiting for it to move again, but it didn't. He bent down, retrieved the shovel, and cautiously began to dig again, tossing the dirt aside. He was just lowering the shovel to the mound again for another scoop of dirt when a spot of the soil over the grave opened up and something shot out and disappeared into the night.

Tom was not going to let that stop him. He'd expected it. He'd been sure of it. He had to do what he'd come here for. He began digging again. After three more scoops, he was thrown to the ground and the shovel flew from his hand, landing loudly a few feet away.

The dirt rolled aside, opened up like a womb, and something rose from the grave, something long and black and writhing, and Tom knew—he immediately *knew*—that it could see him or sense him somehow because it curled around and reached directly for him and wrapped itself around his leg, making a soft slushy sound as it tightened its grip and began to pull him toward the grave and he found himself sliding over the ground helplessly because it was strong, much stronger than he, he could tell, and with a frightened sound, he reached around frantically for the gas can and his hand slapped down on the cold metal, groping for the handle, trying to pull it toward him before it was out of his reach, but his hand slid smoothly over the side of the can and his fingers missed the handle even though they continued to open and close open and close and he cried out because the thing was lifting him up, it wasn't just dragging him now, it was lifting him off the ground and in an instant he was hanging upside down, dangling like a pendant on a chain, his arms flailing, his hair swishing back and forth, he swung pendulously to the right, then the left, toward the gas can, away from it, his hands grabbing, reaching, and then he was whipped up even higher with a sudden jerk, then slapped to the ground hard and, for a moment, the lights went out, there was nothing, no sound, no feeling, and then it all came back and he was gasping for breath, trying to get his wind back after the shock, trying to move away, but the thing still held his leg tightly, pulling him back once again toward the grave and he saw the gas can getting farther and farther away and he tried to dive forward, tried to throw his arms onto the can, but his fingers merely scraped the side of it again as he was lifted up and thrown down a second time, thunder clapping sharply in his skull when he hit the ground this time, a horrible white flash exploding behind his eyes, but he held on, held on to his consciousness and swung his arms for the can, his mouth opening, his throat releasing a strangled cry of effort, but his hands missed and he twisted his head around to look over his shoulder and he saw another one, another long black tentacle, glistening wetly, rising from the grave, curling around threateningly like a cobra, reaching down and wrapping itself around his waist, and when he looked down at the grave, he saw that the dirt was being pushed up and aside by something larger, something much larger, something round and strong, and he heard the snapping and cracking of the casket as it was broken by the force of the thing inside it, and when it was pushed almost entirely out of the grave, Tom realized that it was one of them but it was bigger, it was huge because it had been growing here, growing from the time of Jeffery Collinson's burial, releasing bits of itself to spread like a disease, and now it had been found out and it was determined to protect itself and a third tentacle rose from the dirt and curled over to wrap itself around Tom's throat and it was then that Tom realized he was bleeding from the cuts the tentacles were making, they were slicing into his flesh like gelatinous razor blades and his clothes were rapidly becoming soaked with his blood as it lifted him in the air again, the third tentacle cutting off his air as it tightened around his throat, swinging him back and forth, but he did not let the lack of air deter him and he still groped for the can until his fingers suddenly and quite unexpectedly hooked underneath the handle of the gas can and it was lifted up with him and he slapped his other hand down on the lid and frantically began trying to unscrew it as he swept back and forth, as the flesh around his throat began to sting and then burn and then bleed and in seconds he could taste his own blood rising in his throat and he gagged as he was slapped to the ground again and the gas can, the lid not quite unscrewed, dropped from his grip ...

Hunt released the pressure of his thumb on the lighter and the flame disappeared.

"Martin, the light!" Julie rasped.

"Shh! Don't move. C'mere." Hunt put his arm around her and placed her hand over her face, covering her nose with his fingers. "Breathe through your mouth," he said quietly. "We're gonna try to get to those windows. Don't make any sudden moves and stay quiet. Slooowly," he breathed as they began, taking one step forward, stopping, another step, stopping ...

Something moved, skittered across the dirty cement floor, scraping over the hard surface toward them. Julie made a muffled cry into Hunt's palm, but he just held her closer and kicked his foot out at the thing, sending it rolling away.

"Shh!" The sound Hunt made was soothing, almost motherly, but he was scared to death. He could see them in great lumps covering boxes in the corner, surrounding a leg of the table, shifting now and then, waiting, readying themselves for sudden attack.

Two more shot forward, both from different directions, but not toward Hunt and Julie—instead, to the sides of them, as if to divert their attention, to put a dent in their guard.

As if to surround them.

They continued, one slow, torturous step at a time, Hunt's head constantly turning this way and that.

The singing continued above, muffled now so that the words were indefinable. The roar of the fire was just as loud as the crowd now and the screams were all screams of pain and death.

The windows were closer now, almost close enough to reach out and touch, just a few feet away. They were more closed in now, too, surrounded by the things, moving in little black clumps.

Closing in.

Slowly.

Until, all at once, in the same lightning instant, they all surged forward and they were on their feet, shooting up their legs and over their arms and Hunt could feel them cutting his skin now and he knew Julie could feel the same thing because she was screaming into his palm, her breath hot, the vibration of her voice making the bones of his hand tremble and Hunt knew it was over.

He knew ...

It was totally silent, that's what made Tom want to be sick, that the goddamned thing was totally silent as it swung him back and forth and cut his throat and made him bleed, and now the blood was gushing from his mouth and he was strangling on that as much as on the grip of the thing that cut off his air, and the other tentacle was cutting into his abdomen, slowly, toying with him, wanting him to go slowly, he was sure, but he couldn't give up, not now, because the can was still so close, still so close, on its side with the aqua regia trickling out of the loosely attached cap and he reached for it again, but missed, again, missed, and then he was slammed onto the earth for what he knew would be the last time because one more time would knock the life right out of him, it would kill him, and that would be all she wrote, so he had to get it this time, no question, no doubt, it had to be this time, and when he made that final reach, he thought perhaps his arms were jerking themselves from their sockets when he felt the can's welcome cold on his flesh and felt the liquid sloshing around inside as it was lifted with him, the life-saving liquid, although the life it saved would not be his own, because this was the end, he knew that the last thing he would ever hold was that gas can and he held it tightly, he hugged it in his arms as a lonely man might hug a lover, and his numbing fingers fumbled with the cap, unscrewing, unscrewing, unscrewing, until it finally came off and the can was open and he lifted it up as far as he could and let the liquid rain down hard, pour down like a summer cloudburst and he was suddenly lifted high, straight up, straight over the creature, and he poured the liquid out, over the black thing below him but unable to avoid pouring it on himself, too, and he knew that some of the fumes rising into the night were from his own burning flesh as well as the creature's, but he was numb now, numb and relieved, because he'd done it, he'd done it; the only thing left to do was pray that it would work, and he did, he prayed that it would work.

And that prayer was Tom Conrad's last living thought ...

* * *

Hunt began to slap at the creatures as they quickly covered his body and he lost his hold on Julie, who fell to the floor into the creatures and they covered her in an instant, and Hunt's face was suddenly covered and everything was blackened and he couldn't breathe and he knew he was about to learn what it felt like to be entered by one of them, to be filled, taken over, violated—

—but it fell to the floor with a helpless *plop*. Another fell from him. Another. And then they all fell into a heap on the floor, like leaves from a tree in fall. And when he looked down at Julie, he saw that she, too, was free of them. They had all dropped and slid from her body and were lying around her, motionless.

As they watched silently, the creatures began to sizzle and a thin blue mist rose from them as they actually began to disintegrate, to crumble, to dry up and flake into a loose, black dust.

Hunt and Julie were totally silent for several moments. Even their tremulous breathing quieted down as they stared at the remains of the small deadly creatures around them.

Julie looked up at Hunt, tilted her head, and muttered, "What just ... happened?"

Hunt was still looking at them, all over the floor, fluttering here and there like ashes. Suddenly, he reached down, took Julie's hand, and lifted her to her feet.

"Who cares?" he breathed. "Let's just get the fuck out of here."

6 - THE NOTE

AS SOON AS they'd gotten through the little windows of the basement and were on their feet again, Hunt and Julie hurried with weak knees to the car. Sirens wailed in the distance, nearing rapidly, and Hunt said it would probably be best if they weren't involved.

"Tom's done something," he said, panting, as they headed for the car. "I don't know *what*, but it worked. I wanna get to him and see if he's okay."

Once they were in the car, Hunt started it up and backed out of the parking place, speeding away from the flaming auditorium.

They headed straight for Tom's apartment first. If he wasn't there, they agreed to go to Hunt's place.

Tom's front door was unlocked. Hunt knocked twice, quickly, then barged in.

"Tom!" Hunt called, quickly looking around.

The apartment was not well furnished and Tom had never completely unpacked. Boxes still cluttered the living room. There was a chair, a television set, a stereo, a small sofa. Hunt went into the kitchen. He found Tom's note taped to the refrigerator door. Julie was not far behind him and came in just as he was taking the note down and scanning it quickly.

It had been written in haste and the sentences were crooked, the words cramped on the notepaper. Hunt read it aloud:

> *Doc and Julie,*
> *I think you were right, Doc. Those things*
> *are a result of the evil that made up Jeffery*
> *Collinson's life—maybe his physicalized id*

like Lippincott said—and that black stuff just grew and grew over the years until it was all through his body; Talked to Healy. When he cut Collinson up, he found all that was inside him was blackness. And it was alive! Sprouted tentacles. He was sewn back up and buried. Remember in his diary, Collinson said his work would go on from beyond the grave? I think that's what he's talking about. It's still there if I'm right, and I think I am. The little ones we've come across are probably just pieces of it. My guess is that it's still growing.

Took Julie's crawler to the lab. It got loose and I threw something on it. It went up in smoke. Turned out to be aqua regia— nitrohydrochloric acid. I've gone to Redwood Hill Cemetery to find Collinson's grave. Took a lot of the acid with me. If it's not enough, though, and I fail, you know what to use.

Kind of doubt I'll ever see you again. Thank you for your help and trust and most of all your friendship. Don't feel too bad about things—after what happened to Kim and the boys, I'd rather not stick around anyway. Hope this works.

> *Goodbye,*
> *Tom*

"Son of a *bitch!*" Hunt roared, throwing the note down and turning to Julie. "Let's get out there now!"

When they arrived at Redwood Hill Cemetery, they could see from the car Tom's light shining near the back of the field and they were momentarily hopeful. His car was parked in front of the cemetery, the trunk still open. They got out and hurried toward the light, Julie limping a few feet behind Hunt.

As they neared, they could see the remaining fumes still hovering over the grave, and the black heap that was left of Tom Conrad.

A lot of blood surrounded the unidentifiable heap. Hunt knew that Tom had not died an easy death.

"Oh, Jesus," Julie groaned.

Hunt turned away but did not walk for a while. They stood side by side, silently, pulling themselves together. Hunt removed a cigarette from his pocket and lit it. Then they started back slowly to the car.

Hunt pulled the cigarette from his lips and held it out before him, staring at it through his tears. "Filthy habit," he said quietly and unsteadily, just to hear something. "This is my last."

EPILOGUE

TOM'S REMAINS WERE discovered and identified. Hunt and Julie did not try to explain to the authorities the circumstances surrounding their friend's death. They knew it would only complicate things. They would never be believed. The conclusion reached was one that made Hunt and Julie ache. It was written in the papers that, after the loss of his family, Tom Conrad lost his mind and had somehow attached the blame to Jeffery Collinson. He had, according to the papers, killed himself in the act of trying to wreak some sort of revenge on Collinson's dead and buried body that only he, Tom, could have explained.

Not wanting them to live with the idea that their son had died a madman, Hunt and Julie went to Tom's mother and stepfather. Slowly, they told them the whole story. The couple listened silently, blank expressions on their faces. When the story was finished, they nodded and exchanged quiet glances.

"There's no reason not to believe you," Ridley Jessum finally said quietly. "I know a man who swears his wife was once possessed by the spirit of her dead sister." He said it as though it made Hunt and Julie's story gospel, and Hunt thought silently that if it helped make what they'd just heard more digestible, then so be it.

No one survived the fire in Torrance Auditorium. The papers said it was caused by faulty wiring. But a few disturbing stories leaked out. One fireman said that several people in the building completely ignored an opportunity to escape the fire and, instead, walked calmly into the flames. Some went so far as to call the gospel meeting a "mini Guyana." But most just called it a tragedy.

Many, many funerals took place throughout the Napa Valley in the following days.

The night of Tom's death, Julie moved into Hunt's place and the two of them never slept apart again. They slept in each other's arms and, frequently, one of them would jerk awake with a gasp and the other would awaken, too, to ease away the fear left behind by the nightmare. They always left a small light on during the night because the dark was no longer welcome in their lives.

Some nights, neither of them would sleep and it would only be a matter of time before one of them brought it up, asked a new question about the whole thing. One night, Julie asked quietly, "Do you think Collinson planned it like that—the meeting, I mean?"

After a moment of thought, Hunt said, "No, I don't. I think he probably gave regular old-fashioned evangelical meetings and kept his weird beliefs to himself, kept them private. Until that night. That night, he wasn't in control. It had him and it brought out the monster in him." He paused a moment. "Even men of God have a few monsters."

Another night, Hunt said, "I don't know how I missed it."

"Missed what?"

"The fact that that thing was buried with Collinson and had been in his grave all that time. Growing. If I'd caught it, we all could've killed it, and maybe Tom would be alive now."

"Don't, Martin. Please don't do that to yourself."

When Hunt went back to work at the hospital, they both changed to the day shift. He worked quietly, keeping out of trouble, keeping his opinions to himself. Pazulo was happy, but always a little curious about the sudden change in Hunt's personality. Hunt, however, had no more room in his life for trouble. He let other people take care of the hassles. He just wanted to live quietly and stay out of the way.

A new pressure was added to their work. Whenever a patient was rushed in from an accident, his body broken and cut, out of his mind with pain, Hunt and Julie each got a cold feeling in their stomachs, always afraid, for the first few seconds, to get near the patient. Knowing his fear was endangering the lives of his patients, Hunt left the hospital and took a job at a local university teaching emergency medicine. Julie went with him.

They were married.

They had a child.

And they lived quietly.

But always, underneath it all, there was that fear.

Every time they read about a murder in the newspaper.

Every time they heard on the radio or saw on the television of someone committing some horrible act of violence to another person.

They could not help but wonder.

If maybe.

Just maybe ...

ABOUT THE AUTHOR

Ray Garton is the author of sixty books, including horror novels such as the Bram Stoker Award–nominated *Live Girls*, *Crucifax*, *Lot Lizards*, and *The Loveliest Dead*; thrillers like *Sex and Violence in Hollywood*, *Murder Was My Alibi*, and *Trade Secrets*; and seven short story collections. He has also written several movie and TV tie-ins and a number of young adult novels under the name Joseph Locke. In 2006, he received the Grand Master of Horror Award. He lives in northern California with his wife.